The grass along the edge of the road was still wet with ... long skeins of mist lay low over the airfield but above them the sky was clear, diffused with light from an almost full moon. Steve showed her pass to the sentry at the gate and drove on, to park near the hangar. On the tarmac nearby the Whitley bomber's engines were already ticking over, the propeller blades catching the moonlight as they turned.

She held out her hand to her passenger. 'Adieu, Lucien.'

He shook his head at her. 'Au revoir, cherie. Never say goodbye . . .'

About the author

Hilary Green is a trained actress and spent many years teaching drama and running a youth theatre company. Her main claim to fame for this stage of her life is that she was the drama teacher who gave Daniel Craig, the new 007, his early experience. She has also written scripts for BBC Radio and won the Kythira prize for a short story. Hilary now lives in the Wirral and is a full-time writer.

Hilary Green

Never Say Goodbye

HODDER

A CIP catalogue record for this title
is available from the British Library

ISBN 9780340839027
ISBN 0 340 83902 3

Printed and bound by Clays Ltd, St Ives plc

Hodder Headline's policy is to use papers that are natural, renewable
and recyclable products and made from wood grown in sustainable
forests. The logging and manufacturing processes are expected to
conform to the environmental regulations of the country of origin.

Hodder and Stoughton Ltd
A division of Hodder Headline
338 Euston Road
London NW1 3BH

This book is respectfully dedicated to the late Harry Ree, the original César, and to the men and women of the Special Operations Executive who served with him in France during World War II

ACKNOWLEDGEMENTS

My thanks are due, as always, to my agent Vivien Green and my editor Alex Bonham, for their advice and encouragement. I should also like to thank Avril, Christine, Elaine, Maureen, San and especially Lynda, the members of my writers' group, for their unfailing support and their stringent but always constructive criticisms. Thanks, too, to my husband David, who is far better at proof reading than I am.

Historical Note

The principal characters in this story are, of course, fictional, but the events described are based on extensive research and many of the peripheral characters really existed. Maurice Buckmaster was the head of F Section of the Special Operations Executive, dealing with agents sent to France, and many agents actually received their final briefing in his flat at Orchard Court, complete with black marble bathroom. Vera Atkins was F Section's Intelligence Officer and after the war she spent many months trying to trace the fate of women agents who had disappeared. The training school at Garramor was under the command of Gavin Maxwell, who later wrote *Ring of Bright Water*. Leo Marks, SOE's head of coding, was the son of the bookseller who became famous through Helene Hampf's book *84, Charing Cross Road*. After the war he went on to become a film producer. The Acrobat and Stockbroker circuits really existed. The agent code-named Bob was John Starr, who was arrested as described. César's real name was Harry Ree, a Manchester-born teacher who began the war as a conscientious objector. His part in the sabotage of the Peugeot factory and his subsequent escape to Switzerland are historical fact. Pedro was Eric Cauchi, who was shot in a café brawl in February 1944, and Albert was the Comte de Brouville.

I have invented words and actions for all these people, but

I hope that none of this detracts in any way from the reality of their lives or contradicts historical fact.

Anyone wishing to learn more about the extraordinary courage of SOE's agents and their amazing stories might like to read the following:

Women Who Lived for Danger, Marcus Binney, Hodder & Stoughton, 2002

Secret War Heroes, Marcus Binney, Hodder & Stoughton, 2005

A Quiet Courage, Liane Jones, Bantam, 1990

Jacqueline, Pioneer Heroine of the Resistance, Stella King, Arms and Armour Press, 1989

Maquis, George Millar, Heinemann,1945, 2nd edn Pan, 1956

Chapter One

The grass along the edge of the road was stiff with frost and long skeins of mist lay low over the airfield, but above them the sky was clear, diffused with light from an almost full moon. Steve showed her pass to the sentry at the gate and drove on to park near the hangar. On the tarmac near by the Whitley bomber's engines were already ticking over, the propeller blades catching the moonlight as they turned.

A door opened in the hangar, allowing a gleam of light to escape, against which a figure in uniform could be seen. Then the door closed again and the officer stepped forward into the moonlight. Steve jumped out of the car and went round to open the rear door, but her passengers were already climbing out. First came a thickset man in his mid-thirties, followed by his younger, slighter companion. Both men were in civilian dress, of a cut and fabric that were subtly different from English tailoring.

Steve offered her hand to the older man. *'Au revoir, Robert. Et bonne chance!'*

He kissed her on the cheek and answered, *'Merci, ma chère Steve. Et merci pour tous tes soins.'*

'De rien, mon ami,' she replied, and turned to the younger man. He was lifting a brown leather suitcase out of the boot of the car – a suitcase that seemed, from the way he handled it, unusually heavy for its size. Steve had never seen one of

these cases open but she knew quite well what was inside. It was a two-way radio set. She held out her hand. *'Adieu, Lucien.'*

He shook his head at her. *'Au revoir, chérie. Ne dis jamais adieu!* Never say goodbye, because who knows, we may meet again, like the song says, "one sunny day".' He took her hand and she could feel that his was shaking slightly, a delicate vibration like that of a sensitive piece of electrical machinery.

'Of course,' she said. *'Au revoir, mon brave.'*

He kept her hand in his. 'You know what the French say – what we say – to wish someone luck?'

She wrinkled her nose. 'Yes, I know.'

'Say it, then.'

'Oh, all right, if I must. *Merde, alors!'*

'A toi aussi.'

He released her hand and turned to his companion. The two men moved away towards the officer who was waiting for them. Steve saw them shake hands and then they went into the hangar and the door closed behind them. She got back into the car but did not start the engine. Instead she tucked her hands into her armpits for warmth and settled down to wait. What happened inside the hangar was none of her business but she had to wait nonetheless, in case a sudden change in the weather or some other factor meant the mission had to be aborted. In that case, she had to be on hand to drive the two men back to the safe house where they had lived for the last few days.

The minutes ticked past and then the door opened again and the three men crossed towards the plane. The two she had brought were now wearing overalls over their suits and their bulky parachutes bumped against the backs of their legs as they walked. They paused at the door of the aircraft and Steve saw that each of them was handed a small package before they exchanged final handshakes with their conducting officer. Then they climbed aboard, the door was closed, the engines revved up and the plane taxied out on to the runway. Minutes later it roared low over Steve's head and turned to climb into the moonlight, heading south-west.

She started the car and drove back towards what was, for the time being, home. She was shivering and her throat felt uncomfortably tight. She forced herself to breathe deeply. This was no time to start getting sentimental. She had done this job many times over the last nine months and she ought to be used to it by now. But familiarity could not alter the fact that she hated sending these men off on missions whose purpose she was not told and whose final outcome she would never learn. It was not as if she had known these two well. They had only been with her at Gaynes Hall for three days not like Philippe . . . She reined in her thoughts sharply. Too much pain lay down that route. She told herself that she was probably overreacting because tonight was different. Tonight might be the last time. Or rather, if her plans worked out, the next time it might be her climbing into the plane.

Gaynes House was a solid, rather grim-looking country house, its square outlines made bleaker by the leafless trees in the grounds. Steve parked the car and went up to her room. There was a flask of hot cocoa on the bedside table and a hot-water bottle in the bed. It was a service she had performed countless times for other girls returning from the same job, but tonight the kindness touched her deeply and her throat ached afresh. She thought of the two men she had just seen off and wondered who they really were. 'Robert' and 'Lucien' were only their operational names and she was fairly sure that neither of them was actually French. Their accents were perfect and their manners and behaviour impeccably Gallic, and during the few days they had spent at Gaynes Hall they had lived their cover stories almost without fault. But Robert had evinced a very un-French interest in cricket and on the last evening Lucien had spoken briefly of a wife and baby son who had gone to live with his mother in Devon to be away from the bombing. From the way he spoke she guessed that he did not expect to see them again. As she sipped the cocoa she sent up a prayer that someone, somewhere was preparing a hot drink and a warm bed for both men.

In spite of the late night, Steve was up early the following morning. She packed an overnight bag and as she finished a hasty breakfast her friend Julia Bearing came into the room.

'You ready for off? Do give my love to your parents. I hope your mother is feeling better.'

Steve forced a smile. 'Thanks. I'm sure it's nothing serious. Just a touch of flu, probably.'

This time she took her own car, the neat little sports car her parents had given her for her eighteenth birthday. As she was about to start the engine one of the girls came running out of the house.

'Steve, letter for you! Post has just been sorted. You might as well take it with you.'

Steve thanked her and pocketed the letter. At the end of the drive she turned west, in the direction she would be expected to take if she were heading home to Princes Risborough. Already, she thought ironically, she was practising to deceive. She drove to Stevenage, left the car in the station car park and took the train to London.

Settled in the compartment, she remembered the letter

and took it out. A quick glance told her who it was from. '*Frankie!*' Her lips formed the name and as she slit the envelope a sense of pleasurable anticipation temporarily replaced her nervousness.

> *Dear Steve,*
>
> *Guess where I am! Well, of course, you can't and I'm not allowed to tell you – but it's lovely and warm and there is lots of sand. We've been here for three days and I can tell you we all reckon ourselves very lucky to have got this posting. Conditions are so much better than they were at Grendon. HQ have taken over a beach club and made it into the officers' club and we're allowed to use it. It's terribly glamorous and exciting, with palm trees and tennis courts and a bar with chandeliers and mirrors on the walls. I can't get over being an officer. Imagine, little Gina Franiani from Liverpool an ensign in the FANY!*

Steve smiled as she read. Dear Frankie! So clever and yet so impressionable and naive. But then, she was only eighteen.

> *But I haven't told you the best bit yet. Guess who I ran into on the very first evening? None other than the mythical Captain Nick Harper – except he isn't a captain any more, he's a major. So, you see, he does exist.*

Steve became aware that one or two of the other passengers had glanced at her and realised that she had chuckled aloud. Frankie had talked so much during their initial training about the mysterious captain, whom she had met in the middle of an air raid and who had recruited her into the First Aid Nursing Yeomanry, that they had all teased her by pretending to believe that he was a figment of her imagination. Steve composed herself and read on.

He's exactly the way I remember him, except he had a beard that first evening but he's shaved it off now. In fact, he's even better looking than I thought. And the really incredible thing, Steve, is he seems to like me. He took me to a party that first evening and we danced together all night and since then we've spent all our off-duty time together, swimming and sunbathing and talking, talking, talking. We seem to have so much in common and he's funny and kind and brave . . . well, you'll have gathered by now that I'm head over heels in love. I think he feels the same way, but it seems too good to be true. He's got to go away for a little while soon and maybe when he comes back things will be different, but I do hope not.

I mustn't go on wittering any longer. Midge and Dickie send their love. Oh, by the way, Midge and I are chums now, strange as that may seem. I won't bore you with the reason – it's a long story. She's having a great time with a rather sweet pilot called Jumbo Lampeter but heaven knows how long that will last. Midge isn't exactly famed for her constancy, is she? Dickie is OK but she's not so keen on the social whirl as the rest of us. She's not one for dancing and flirting – in fact I sometimes think she doesn't really like men at all. Still, she seems quite happy.

Please write as soon as you can and let me know what you have decided about that matter we discussed when I stayed with you at Christmas. Have you heard from Roddy? For heavens' sake, don't do anything you may regret for the rest of your life.

Take care of yourself.

Love,

Frankie

Steve folded the letter and sat gazing out of the window. Those last words had called her back to the present and to the difficult decisions facing her. She had told Frankie that she intended to break off her unofficial engagement to

Roddy, whom she had loved for as long as she could remember. Roddy was a fighter pilot, currently stationed on Malta as part of the tiny squadron fighting to keep the island free of the Nazis. They had promised that whatever happened they would be faithful to each other – but then she had met Philippe. She had not been in love with him but she had taken pity on his loneliness and his fear. Now she was haunted by guilt. Frankie had tried to persuade her that, if they both survived the war, Roddy would forgive her for that one lapse but Steve felt that she was no longer worthy of him. Now she was about to embark on a course that would inevitably mean that she was unable to keep in touch with him. He would not understand why and she would not be able to explain. She knew she must write to him but could not make up her mind what to say.

A few miles outside London the train came to a halt and rumours filtered through from compartment to compartment that there was an unexploded bomb near the line ahead of them. Steve looked anxiously at her watch. She had left herself plenty of time to get to her appointment but something like this could delay her for hours. To her relief, after a wait of twenty minutes, the train jolted into movement and they arrived in Marylebone Station only half an hour behind schedule. Steve hailed a taxi and told the driver to take her to the Northumberland Hotel.

The Northumberland had been taken over by the War Ministry and on her arrival Steve was directed to a room on the first floor. She knocked and was told to enter. The room was empty of furniture except for a trestle table covered with an army blanket and two chairs. On one of them, beneath a naked light bulb, sat a man in civilian dress. His face was clean-shaven, expressionless, almost mask-like, and he made no attempt to rise.

Instead, he nodded at the chair on the opposite side of the table. '*Asseyez-vous, mademoiselle, s'il vous plaît.*'

Steve sat.

The man went on, '*Votre nom?*'

Steve cleared her throat. She had known that her fluency in French would be an important part of her qualification for the job but she had not expected the interview to be conducted entirely in that language. However, she had been speaking nothing else for most of the last nine months so she answered automatically, '*Je m'appelle Diana Escott Stevens.*'

'*Et quel age avez-vous?*'

'*J'ai vingt-deux ans.*'

The interview proceeded, still in French.

'Where do you live?'

'My parents live at Hillfoot Farm in Princes Risborough. That's in Buckinghamshire. I grew up there and that's my home but at present I'm stationed at Gaynes Hall in Cambridgeshire.'

'Where did you go to school?'

'Heathfield House, outside Ascot.'

'A prestigious girls' school.' The pale eyes of her interrogator were lowered for a moment to a manila file on the table. 'I see from your record that you were Head Girl and also Captain of Hockey.'

'Yes.'

'You enjoy sport?'

'Yes. I've always been quite athletic.'

Again he consulted the file. 'No great academic achievements, however.' He looked up and his gaze held hers.

She answered without embarrassment. 'No, I've never been particularly good at that side of things.'

'Does that worry you?'

'Not at all. I've always found that common sense is all you need in most situations.'

'What did you do after school?'

'I spent a year at a finishing school in Switzerland, near Vevey. Then I went to Paris for six months to do a cordon bleu cookery course.'

'That accounts for your fluent French – also for your slight Swiss accent.' He glanced down at the file. 'And I see you were presented at court. Did you enjoy being a debutante?'

'Not much. I soon got bored with all the balls and parties.'

For a moment he studied her in silence. Then he went on, 'How were you recruited into the FANY?'

'A friend of mine introduced me – Lady Helena Vane. I happened to tell her one day that I should like to make myself useful and she sent me to a vicarage in West London. It turned out to be the FANY recruiting centre.'

'I see you did your initial training at Overthorpe. Your superiors there speak highly of you as a potential leader with the ability to get on with people from different backgrounds. What are you doing now?'

'At the moment I'm . . .' She stopped. This was a trap. She had signed the Official Secrets Act and was forbidden to speak about the work she was doing. This man might be working for the same organisation, but nobody had given her permission to discuss her job with him. 'I'm just a sort of glorified housekeeper,' she finished with a self-deprecating smile. Just for a second she thought she saw a flicker of expression on her interrogator's face, but whether it was approval or amusement she could not tell.

'So your cookery skills have come in useful. For whom do you cook?'

'For service personnel who are staying in the house.'

'For what purpose?'

'They are undertaking courses of various kinds. In Cambridge, usually.'

Again the faint glint of amusement.

'Do you have any hobbies?'

'I don't have much time for hobbies at the moment.'

'But before you joined up?'

'I've always been a keen horsewoman. I learned to ride very young and I have my own horse.'

'Do you ride to hounds?'

'I used to, before the war.'

'A dangerous hobby.'

'No, not really, as long as you keep your head and know your own limitations – and your horse's.'

'You talk about common sense, keeping your head . . . Would you say that that was an important part of the way you go about things?'

'I suppose it is, yes. I don't see any point in rushing into things blindfold, or taking unnecessary risks.'

'Yet hunting does require a degree of physical courage. Aren't you ever frightened?'

'Oh yes, sometimes. When you see a difficult fence ahead of you, and perhaps someone else falls, it can be quite scary. But you just have to stay calm and look for the best way over.'

'Do you have any other family, apart from your parents?'

'No, I'm an only child.'

'Are you engaged?'

'No.' Steve was not sure why she lied, but anyway it had never been official.

'You are not romantically involved with anyone?'

'Not at present, no.'

'Tell me, what is your attitude to the war?'

'It's a terrible thing, but it has to be fought. We can't just sit back and let Hitler do as he pleases.'

'How do you feel about the Germans in general?'

'Several girls at my finishing school were German. I always got on very well with them. I think it's the Nazis that are evil, not the German people as a whole.'

'Tell me about Paris.'

For some time he questioned her about her memories of the city and her knowledge of its geography. Then he asked her whether she knew other parts of France and she described holidays in Brittany and Provence. Eventually her interrogator sat back and looked at her in silence for a moment.

At length he said in English, 'Thank you, Miss Escott Stevens. Your answers have been most satisfactory. Now, I don't normally tell candidates at this stage what the job is that they are being interviewed for. That has to wait until MI5 has had a chance to check them out. However, you have already been cleared and have signed the Official Secrets Act. Besides which, it would be pointless for me to pretend that you don't know what you are volunteering for. After all, you have been dispatching agents to do it for the last nine months and I don't believe you haven't guessed where they are going.'

Steve looked at him in silence. She was still not prepared to discuss what went on at Gaynes Hall. For the first time a brief but genuine smile crossed the interviewer's face.

'Your discretion does you credit. Very well. I will tell you what they are going to do. The men and women you have dispatched will have been dropped by parachute into occupied France to work with the Resistance. You seem to me to be ideally suited for that task. It requires a cool head, a strong physique and the ability to pass as a local person without arousing suspicion. Is this something you feel you would be able to undertake?'

'Yes.' Steve's answer came immediately and she spoke almost without considering the implications.

'Now, I must warn you of the dangers. Although you are a member of the British armed forces you would not have the protection of a uniform. You would be in civilian dress and living under an assumed identity and I have to tell you that the Nazi High Command has decreed that all such people, if caught, should be treated as spies. In those circumstances you could expect to be harshly interrogated, possibly even tortured, and then either imprisoned or shot. You probably have about a fifty-fifty chance of seeing your home again.'

He stopped and Steve sat in silence, stunned by this bald statement of fact.

After a moment he went on, 'I don't want you to make a decision here and now. Go away and think about it. Today is Friday. Come back at ten o'clock on Monday morning and tell me what you have decided. There is just one thing I must impress on you. You may not discuss this with anyone. Not with your parents, or with friends or with your superior officers. If you were to do so, the consequences could be severe, both for you and for them.' He rose to his feet. 'You can go now. I can't influence your decision. All I can say is that you would be doing an important job, one that few other people are qualified to do.'

Steve walked to the door in a daze. He shook her hand and let her out into the corridor.

The mental numbness persisted all through her train journey back to Stevenage. It was not until she was sitting in her car in the car park that she seemed to recover the power of thought. The first thing that occurred to her was that she had the rest of the weekend free. She had told the others at Gaynes that she was going home to look after her sick mother, so there was no reason for her to return there. She might as well really go home.

On the drive she tried to confront the decision that she had to make but every time she brought her thoughts round to it her brain seemed to shy away, like a horse refusing a difficult fence. She wondered what her parents would be told if she decided to go ahead and what her friends would make of her sudden disappearance and what cover story she would be given. But she could not force herself to face the one crucial question.

Her mother was in the farmhouse kitchen, preparing a huge pan of stew for her husband and the Land Girls who had been sent to replace the men called up for the forces. She dropped the knife as Steve walked in and hastily wiped her hands on her apron.

'Diana, darling! What a lovely surprise! Why didn't you let us know you were coming?'

Steve kissed her and managed to smile. 'Sorry. It was a kind of last-minute thing. The opportunity came up and I had to grab it quickly.'

'Well, it's lovely to see you. How are you?' Her mother held her by the shoulders and looked into her face. 'You look a bit peaky to me.'

'Oh, I'm fine. Just a bit tired, that's all. How are you?'

'Very well, thank you.'

'And Daddy?'

'He's OK. Working too hard, of course, with the farm, and then doing his bit with the Observer Corps at night. But he's strong. He's coping.'

'You're both working too hard,' Steve said. She remembered the days before the war when they had had a couple who lived in, the wife performing the duties of cook-housekeeper and the husband those of butler and general handyman. There had been plenty of men to work the farm, too, instead of two girls who had come down from London and had never seen a cow in their lives before. They had buckled down to the job, Steve had to give them that, and worked as hard as many men, but it still left her parents with too much to do. She knew that, as well as cooking for everyone, her mother helped out with the hens and the pigs, kept bees and still managed to find time to go down to the village and lend a hand with the work of the WRVS.

'Well, that's wartime for you,' her mother responded philosophically. 'And really, you know, I don't think I could ever go back to the lazy way I used to live. I'd hate to have nothing more important to do than organise sherry parties and village fêtes.'

Steve smiled. 'You were never lazy, Mummy. You can't kid me.'

Her mother gave her a keen glance. 'If anyone's over-working, it's not me. You really do look tired. Why don't you go and have a lie-down? Your room's always ready for you, you know.'

Steve shook her head. The last thing she wanted was solitude, where she could not escape her thoughts.

'No, I'm fine, really. I'd much rather sit here and chat.'

'In that case,' her mother said, 'I'll put the kettle on. I'm sure you could do with a cup of tea. What have you been doing to get so tired? Oh, no, don't remind me. You can't talk about it. Really, this wartime security! It's coming to something when a girl can't talk to her own mother.'

'Sorry, Mummy.' Steve sat at the kitchen table and ran her

hand over her face. If she had needed to be secretive before that was nothing to her present situation. To distract her mother she said, 'Oh, I had a letter from Frankie this morning.'

'Frankie?' Her mother turned from filling the kettle. 'How is she?'

'She sounds fine.'

'Wasn't she waiting to go overseas? Where has she ended up?'

'She can't say, of course. The censor would just blank it out if she did. But she says there's sun and lots of sand, so it must be North Africa somewhere.'

'Oh well,' her mother said, 'I suppose that's safe enough now Monty's got the upper hand and the Germans are in retreat.'

'Oh, Frankie'll be all right,' Steve agreed. 'She sounds as if she's having a whale of a time. Dances and parties and swimming – and she's got a boyfriend.'

'Good. I'm glad. She deserves a bit of fun.'

Steve cocked her head to one side. 'You liked her, didn't you?'

'Yes, I did. She's a sensible, bright girl and straightforward – no airs and graces.'

'Oh, that's Frankie all right,' Steve said with a laugh. 'What you see is what you get. But she's not quite the sort of girl I used to bring home from school.'

'You mean because she's working-class and from the provinces. Well, is that important?'

'Some people find it a bit of a problem.'

Her mother set teacups and a milk jug on the table. 'I can imagine. What did the rest of your FANY friends make of her?'

Steve sighed. 'I'm afraid they gave her a bit of a rough

time to start with. Some of them just cold-shouldered her, but some of them teased the life out of her – her accent, her manners, the fact that her father owned a barber's shop. But when they realised she could beat them all into a cocked hat intellectually most of them changed their tune. You know who was the worst? Midge Granville. She made poor Frankie's life a misery.'

'That doesn't surprise me,' Mrs Escott Stevens said tartly. 'I've always felt that the Honourable Marjorie Granville was a bit too big for her boots. I know you and she were at school together and are bosom pals but I have to admit I've always had reservations about Midge.'

'Well, I saw a new side to her when we were training,' Steve agreed. 'In fact, we fell out over Frankie. But you have to make allowances, you know. Midge hasn't had much affection or kindness in her life, with that playboy father and that dreadful snob for a mother.'

'Maybe not,' her mother conceded, bringing the teapot to the table, 'but it's time she learned that she's not the only pebble on the beach. Anyway, Frankie's escaped her now.'

'That's the irony of it,' Steve said, 'she hasn't. Wherever Frankie's been posted Midge has gone too. You see, Midge may have her faults but she's really very clever. There were three of them at Overthorpe when we were doing our basic training, Frankie and Midge and Dickie Nightingale, all absolutely brilliant. So they get posted to . . . well, to wherever clever girls are needed.'

'Dickie?' her mother queried. 'What a name for a girl!'

'It's not her real name. Nightingale – bird – dickie bird. Get it?'

'You girls and your nicknames!'

'It's a tradition of the service. First names are banned. I

suppose they're considered a bit too . . . well, too girlie. That's why everyone calls me Steve.'

Her mother looked at the clock. 'Goodness, look at the time! I must get on or this stew won't be ready in time for dinner. Why don't you go and sit down and relax, darling?'

'No, I'll give you hand,' Steve said quickly. 'Do you want some potatoes peeled?'

The door banged open to admit her father, and in spite of the blast of cold air that came with him Steve had the impression that the room had grown suddenly warmer. He was a big man, blessed with apparently inexhaustible energy, and he greeted her with a shout of delight.

'Hey, here's a sight for sore eyes! Welcome home, darling.'

He held out his arms and Steve felt herself enfolded in a bear hug, her nostrils full of the familiar smells of damp tweed and dog hair. It was the smell of safety.

Later she helped with the evening milking and at dinner the conversation turned inevitably to the progress of the war.

'Thank God we seem to be making some headway, at last,' her father said. 'Now the Italians have surrendered in Tunisia Monty's really got Rommel on the run.'

At nine o'clock everything stopped, as always, for the news, but that evening the main feature was not a battle or a raid but the report prepared by Lord Beveridge proposing a unified National Health Service.

'I can't see it working, myself,' Steve's father said. 'If people don't have to pay to see a doctor they'll be trotting along to the surgery every time they have a headache. It'll be chaos.'

'Never mind,' her mother responded. 'At least the government is thinking about what needs to be done *after* the war, and that's got to be good news.'

The ensuing discussion was enough to keep Steve's mind off the decision she had to make, but once she was alone in bed she forced herself to face up to the question of why she had volunteered. Was it simply because she was running away from a possible confrontation with Roddy? She had to admit to herself that that had played a part in her decision. But it was not the whole reason. Not even the main reason. There simply came a time when it was necessary to face up to the bullies and the evil men and there was no honour in expecting others to do it for you when you were quite capable of playing a part in it yourself.

She slept very little that night and when she did drop off her dreams were full of horrors. She saw a plane crash into the field behind the farm and knew that it was Roddy's, but when she ran to it the man who climbed out of the cockpit was Philippe, who suddenly revealed himself as a Gestapo officer and dragged her off to a gloomy prison that looked strangely like the Northumberland Hotel. When she finally woke from a last, deep slumber, however, she knew that her mind was made up. Whatever the dangers and risks ahead of her, there was no going back.

At breakfast her father said teasingly, 'Guess what I've got out in the barn.'

'Some early calves?'

'No. Try again.'

'One of the cats has had kittens.'

'Wrong again. Come and see.'

She followed him out and he flung open the barn door and stood back, proudly.

'A new tractor! Gosh, isn't it smart! But what's wrong with the old one?'

'The government is so keen to get every farm producing as much food as possible that they are offering loans on very favourable terms to enable us to buy equipment like this. So I thought, why not? Two tractors means we can work twice as fast.'

'Only if you've got two drivers.'

'That's not a problem. I'm going to teach the girls.'

Steve looked at him with a grin. 'Will you teach me?'

'What, today?'

'Yes, why not? I'd love to try it.'

It was easier than she expected and she spent the next couple of hours trundling backwards and forwards hauling trailer-loads of mangel-wurzels back from the field to feed the cattle. Even on a short break like this one she liked to feel that she was making herself useful around the farm, and she knew that it pleased her father to see her tackling new skills and proving herself as able as any man.

Eventually, she relinquished the tractor to one of the Land Girls and headed for the stable, where Scheherazade, her pretty little half-Arab mare with the pale chestnut coat and the cream mane and tail, greeted her with a snicker of recognition. Steve saddled up and rode out of the farm and up on to the ridge of the Chiltern hills. It was a still, cold morning, the bare twigs of the beech trees furred with frost and a milky haze over the sky, through which the sun could be glimpsed as a pale circle. The mare was frisky, spooking at shadows and tossing her head, and Steve had not ridden for weeks, but her muscles adapted themselves automatically to the horse's movements. After a long trot up a steep incline the little horse settled down and Steve was able to relax and look around her.

This was a landscape she had known all her life, in every season. She knew every path that wound along the hillside, where the grass had been worn away to expose the chalk and flints beneath, and she could recognise every landmark in the wide Oxford plain that stretched out below her. In the beech woods that clothed the lower slopes the leaves lay thick and crisp with frost and the trunks of the trees rose straight and bare, like silver columns. As she rode she gazed around her, trying to see it all as if for the first time, trying to impress it on her memory as if she would never see it again.

Back at the stable, she unsaddled and then stood for a long time with her arm across Scheherazade's withers and her face pressed against the silky neck, blending her dark auburn hair with the chestnut and cream of the horse. The mare nudged her with her velvety nose, demanding a titbit, and Steve fed her a carrot she had taken from the store in the barn.

Back in the house she said to her mother, 'You might as well turn Sherry out to grass, you know. I hardly ever have time to ride her these days.'

That evening, in her room, Steve wrote two letters. The first was to Frankie.

'*This is just to let you know that Aunt Mary has been taken ill and I am going to stay with her for a while.*' It was a code they had agreed on when Frankie stayed with her at Christmas. '*As you know, she is quite a demanding old lady so I may not have time to write but if you send letters to my home address I'm sure I shall get a chance to pick them up sooner or later. Do keep in touch! Best love, Steve.*'

The second letter was much more difficult.

Darling Roddy,

I am afraid you may be a bit disappointed by what I am going to tell you but I think it is better for you to know in advance and not be faced with this when you come home. The fact is, I have applied for an overseas posting. I know you would probably expect to find me waiting for you but the

*chances are I won't be here. I'm sorry, darling, but I have come
to the conclusion that I can be much more useful in a different
job and, after all, that's what matters at the moment, isn't it?*

*I love you, my darling, and I shall never love anyone else, but
I want you to know one thing. If you find while I am away that
there is someone else who can make you happy, please don't
hesitate on my account. It's not fair that you should be lonely,
just because you think you have an obligation to me. I don't
know where I am going or how long I shall be gone, so I want
you to consider yourself a free man.*

*Please try to understand – and take care of yourself. All I
want is for you to be safe and happy.*

All my love, always,

Diana

The following morning she went to church with her mother
and in the afternoon she walked the farm with her father,
checking on the cows, making sure the gates and fences
were in good order, and picking up fallen branches for firewood. They spent the evening round the fire, her mother
knitting, her father doing the crossword, the wireless playing
in the background. The next day, as soon as the milking was
done, Steve kissed both her parents goodbye and drove to
High Wycombe, where she parked the car and took the train
to London.

The same man was waiting for her in the bare room at the
Northumberland Hotel but this time he rose as she entered.

'Good morning, Miss Escott Stevens. Please take a seat.'
He seated himself opposite her and looked into her face. 'So,
have you come to a decision?'

'Yes, I have. I want to go ahead with what we discussed.'

'You're quite sure about that? You have considered all the
risks?'

'Yes.' It was a lie. She had failed, whether by virtue of a conscious or a subconscious decision, she did not know, to face the potential dangers that he had outlined. She simply knew that the decision was already taken and she had to stick with it.

He gave her one of his rare smiles. 'Well done! Congratulations. You are a very brave young woman.'

She shook her head. 'I'm not brave. If you want to know the truth, I'm scared stiff.'

He nodded quietly. 'Of course you are. If you had told me that you were never scared I should have turned you down. We don't want people who don't know the meaning of fear. They are a liability to themselves and everyone else.' He looked down at the papers on the table. 'So, to business. You can return to your unit for the time being. In a day or two you will get notification that you are being sent on a training course. It will take place at an address in Surrey, near Guildford. That will be the initial assessment course. From there, if you prove to be suitable, as I am sure you will, you will be sent on for further training. Any questions?'

'What shall I say the course is for?'

'You could tell your colleagues that you are being considered as an interpreter, working for the War Office.'

'And should I tell my parents the same thing?'

'I don't see why not.'

'When I go . . . overseas, how will I keep in touch with them?'

'I'm afraid you won't be able to. Before you leave you will be provided with a cover story, posting you to somewhere well away from your real destination – North Africa, the Far East, possibly even America. You will be given a series of postcards to write, telling your parents and any friends you might want to contact that you are well and happy and including a few anodyne remarks. These will be posted from the appropriate location at suitable intervals. It is a necessary deception but I'm sure you will agree that it is better than silence.'

Steve nodded silently.

'Is there anything else?'

'No. No, I can't think of anything.'

He rose and held out his hand. 'I'll wish you good luck, then.'

'Thank you.' She shook hands with him and went to the door, feeling that she had been taken over by some automatic system that was moving her along a preordained path. 'Goodbye.'

He lifted his hand in salute. '*Au revoir – et bonne chance.*'

Chapter Two

The little train chugged along the single-track line through a landscape of spectacular beauty. Steve, peering out of the window at snow-covered mountains and deep glens clothed in black coniferous forests, where turquoise lochs glinted in the sunshine, thought she had never seen anything so lovely, or so remote. She turned back to her companions in the compartment. Some of them were dozing, others reading or, like her, gazing out of the window. They had been en route for more than twenty-four hours, snatching fitful sleep on the crowded night train from London to Glasgow and, from the look of them, they were all feeling as drained as she was.

There were six of them and, although they had met only three weeks ago at Wanborough House, the Special Operations Executive's initial assessment centre in Surrey, Steve felt she knew them all better than people she had grown up with. For those three weeks they had all been put through a relentless routine of early morning runs, assault courses, exercises in map reading and intelligence tests. They had worked together as a team to pit their combined strength and cunning and ingenuity to overcome a series of obstacles. There had also been long interviews with a man whose function had never been explained but who she guessed was a psychologist. There had been times when, exhausted and confused, she had almost convinced herself that she would be turned down and sent back to Gaynes Hall, but somehow she had come through. Now they were about to begin the real training with the words of the commandant at Wanborough still ringing in their ears.

'You think you've had it tough here? Believe me, as the Americans say, *you ain't seen nothing yet!*'

Sitting opposite her was Graham Lomax, the oldest among them and a captain in the Royal Armoured Corps. He had grown up in the French colony of the Ivory Coast, where his father had been British consul, which accounted for his fluent French. Steve had thought him rather dour at first but one evening during their time at Wanborough she had learned the reason for his sombre attitude. It was generally accepted that they did not talk about their private lives but in a rare confiding moment he had told her that his wife and young son had been killed in an air raid early in the war. He was by nature a man who kept his feelings to himself but he and Steve had developed a rapport and he had taken a protective, almost fatherly interest in her and had helped her through a number of difficult tasks.

Next to him in the carriage was Lieutenant Harry Price, the ultimate contrast to Lomax. His family was in the wine trade and he had worked before the war with one of the chief wine *négociants* in Bordeaux. He was handsome, and knew it, and obviously fancied himself as a 'ladies' man' while at the same time wanting to be seen as 'one of the chaps', which seemed to entail having a fund of dirty jokes. On the first day at Wanborough he had mistaken Steve for one of the FANY staff and had tried to flirt with her. She had disillusioned him as gently as possible but he had taken it as a personal affront. From then on he had made no attempt to disguise his hostility and took every opportunity to undermine her confidence with sarcastic asides. 'Don't let her navigate, for God's sake! It's well known women can't read maps' or 'I thought security was supposed to be the most important thing with this job. Did you ever meet a woman who could keep a secret?' Fortunately, none of the other men seemed inclined to go along with him.

Sergeant Jack, or Jacques, Baker was the son of a man who had married a French girl during the First World War and brought her home to live in Poplar, in the East End of London. As the only non-commissioned officer in the group he had been inclined to keep himself to himself at first but the initial training had soon broken down those barriers. He was fascinated by all things mechanical and never happier than when tinkering with an engine.

The last two were Daniel Jardine and the only other woman in the group, Nicole Fournier. Steve had hoped to establish a good relationship with her but the French girl had a sullen manner that repelled all overtures of friendship. Danny was an enigma – a slight, dark, deceptively youthful figure who had revealed unexpected strength and agility in the physical aspects of the training. He was the only one of them not in uniform. There was something slightly affected about his voice and manner which had some of the men muttering darkly about 'pansies', and they tended to avoid him. Steve had felt sorry for him and had made a point of drawing him into conversation, and he had responded at first guardedly but then with increasing warmth. He had an irreverent sense of humour that had lightened several of Steve's darker moments.

The train whistled and slowed, then clanked into a tiny station.

'Arisaig!' shouted a porter. 'Arisaig!'

They stirred and stretched and dragged their luggage off the racks. This was their destination, in so far as they knew it. The whole area was a restricted zone and they had had to show special passes before being allowed to board the train. Outside, a corporal waited for them with a truck and they had to endure another half-hour of bouncing and jolting before it drew up outside a rambling grey-stone building with gabled windows. It was set on the lower slopes of a mountain with, as far as Steve could make out, no other house in sight. They were ushered into a large reception hall where a good log fire burned in the open fireplace, but any illusion of cosiness was rapidly dispelled as they followed an orderly up a narrow staircase that turned at sharp angles and then along a maze of dark corridors.

The orderly paused and threw open a door. 'This is yours, ladies.'

'Both of us?' Nicole queried.

'Unless one of you wants to sleep in the stable,' he replied, then took in Steve's officer's stripes and added hastily, 'Begging your pardon, ma'am.'

It was a narrow room, with a window that looked out from one of the gables. On one side was a metal-framed bunk bed.

'Toss you for the top bunk?' Steve suggested.

'Take it, if you want it,' Nicole responded indifferently, throwing her bag on to the bottom one.

Huddled in bed at last, under inadequate blankets, Steve clasped her cold feet in her hands in an effort to warm them and felt suddenly very much alone. She got on well enough with most of the men in the group but that was no substitute for her close women friends, and she thought wistfully of Midge and Frankie out in Africa. Then, as always happened when the approach of sleep dissolved her self-imposed embargo, she thought of Roddy. At Wanborough they had been given a post office box address in London, to which friends and relations could send letters, and she had been tempted to write and tell him that but had decided against it. Best to let him go, she thought. She tortured herself with the thought that he might have been shot down but common sense told her that if so his parents would certainly have contacted hers, and they would have passed on the news. Clutching at that cold comfort, she fell asleep.

The next morning they were greeted by a short, wiry man with fair hair, wearing full Highland dress.

'Good morning, ladies and gentlemen. My name is Maxwell, and I am in command here. Welcome to Garramor. Now let me introduce the rest of the staff.'

Among these was a young woman whose dark hair and olive skin immediately made Steve think of holidays in the south of France. She greeted the two girls with a smile.

'You must be Diana and Nicole. My name is Jeanne Borrel. I have just returned from France and I shall be your Conducting Officer for the rest of your training. That means that I shall be with you, doing all the exercises and everything you are asked to do. So if you have any problems or any questions I am the first person you can turn to. Please feel free to talk to me about anything that bothers you. I've been through it all myself, so believe me, I know how it feels.'

Steve's excitement at meeting someone who had actually experienced the life of an agent behind enemy lines was cut short by a summons from Maxwell. He dismissed the men and kept her and Nicole behind.

'I'll make no bones about this. I don't approve of women being accepted for this sort of duty. I appreciate the fact that you both speak French and can pass for natives but that is not enough. The sort of work we are asking people to do out there demands courage, endurance and quite often physical strength. I'm prepared to accept that you may have the first of these but I do not believe any woman can have the same degree of strength and endurance that a man has. There will come a time when you are in a tight corner and you will not be able to cope, and then the men who are working with you will have to chose between stopping to help you or getting away themselves. I do not think any agent should put himself at risk for the sake of a girl. I know that sounds unchivalrous but it's a fact of life.'

'But I wouldn't expect him to!' Steve broke in.

'You might not, but most men would feel compelled to stick by you. That's why I'm giving you both this warning. One sign of weakness, one hint that you are not one hundred per cent up to the job, and you're out on your ear. Understood?'

It was a grim start to the course and did nothing to alleviate Steve's sense of isolation. She looked at Nicole, hoping for some flicker of fellow feeling, but the other girl turned away with an insolent shrug and a muttered '*Tant pis!*' Steve joined the others with a sinking feeling in her stomach. Now she had this to contend with as well as Harry Price's sniping.

Much of the early part of the course was an extension of what they had learned at Wanborough, but carried out in much tougher conditions. There was a strenuous regime of PT, coupled with map-reading exercises in the surrounding mountains. In spite of the cold, Steve would have enjoyed the days out on the hills, particularly when Maxwell was in charge, if it had not been for her constant fear of failing to come up to his high standards. He had a great love and knowledge of the local wildlife, and would point out the tracks of deer or badgers in the snow, telling them to learn the ways of the animals.

'It could mean the difference between life and death. You may have to live off the land – but not only that. The animals will warn you if other people are around, or if there is bad weather on the way, if you only learn to understand their habits.'

The next item on the curriculum was weapons training. Guns held no terrors for Steve. Growing up on the farm she had been used to shooting parties, and her father had taught her to use a shotgun in her early teens. At Overthorpe the FANY recruits had been taught to use a pistol and had practised shooting at targets. But this was different, as she began to realise from Maxwell's opening lecture.

'I dare say many of you have had experience of using these weapons before and may consider yourselves crack shots. Accuracy over a distance can, of course, be very useful but it is not the prime consideration in this case. Imagine that you are searching a house where you suspect Gestapo agents are lying in wait for you. You will find that you automatically adopt a slightly crouching position, with your weight on the balls of your feet. You creep along a passageway, turn a corner and come face to face with the enemy. Your life, and those of your comrades, may depend on you silencing him before he has the chance to kill you. You have no time to adopt a fancy firing position or to sight along the barrel of your gun. You are already in the correct position. You must fire instinctively and at the area of the body where you can be sure of doing most damage. That is, between the neck and the crotch. And always fire two shots. The first may be enough to kill your man but it will not stop him instantly. The nervous system does not shut down for several seconds and in that time he may have sufficient reflexes to return your fire. Two shots will stop him in his tracks. So remember, speed, instinctive aiming, and always two shots – tap, tap.'

At this point Danny raised his hand. 'Sorry, I'm never going to shoot anyone so there's no point in going through all this with me.'

Maxwell fixed him with a cold gaze. 'What makes you think you're never going to need to shoot someone?'

'I volunteered to train as a radio operator. As I see it, that involves keeping a low profile and sending and receiving messages – not playing cowboys and Indians.'

'And suppose one day you come back to wherever you are supposed to transmit from and find a Gestapo officer in the room?'

'Then if I can't talk my way out of it I'll just have to surrender.'

'And what happens next? You and your set are in the hands of the Gestapo. How long do you think you can hold out under torture? Before many days are up they will have all your codes and safety checks and then they will be able to play your set back to us, making us think you are still operational, and send all sorts of misinformation. It might interest you to know that this has happened on at least one occasion and as a result a whole succession of agents were dropped into the arms of a Gestapo reception committee.'

Danny shrugged. 'Then give me a suicide pill. Such things do exist, I believe. I'm prepared to kill myself if necessary but I won't shoot another human being in cold blood.'

For a long moment the two men held each other's gaze. Then Maxwell said, 'You realise I shall have to make a report on all of you at the end of your time here. It may be that our superiors will decide, in view of your attitude, that you are not suitable as an agent.'

Danny's face was set. 'So be it, then. I'll go back to being a hospital porter.'

'Oh no you won't, you know too much,' Maxwell said grimly, and turned away. 'Come on, the rest of you. We've got work to do.'

They began with pistols. First they were all given the standard-issue .22 Woodsman, which Steve found far too heavy for comfort. She got on better with the next weapon on offer, the .32 Colt, which was lighter and had a shorter barrel. They practised loading and unloading and then drawing their weapons and moving quickly into the crouching position. Then they were told to fire at cardboard cutouts painted in the field grey of German army uniforms. That brought home to Steve, as no lecture could, that she was being taught to kill.

At the end of the session she slipped away from the others and went for a walk in the grounds. Danny's determined stand had aroused her admiration. She understood Maxwell's arguments but at the same time she could not imagine herself firing into the living body of another human being. On the other hand, she was acutely aware of his reservations about using women as agents. She was determined to prove that she could be as courageous and reliable as a man, and she was afraid that if she refused to accept the firearms training it would be used as an excuse to fail her.

As she turned back towards the house she saw Lomax coming towards her.

'There you are!' he said. 'We were wondering where you had got to. It's lunchtime.'

'I know,' Steve said. 'I just needed time to think.'

'What's wrong?' he asked.

She looked at him. 'Graham, have you ever shot anyone?'

'Face to face? No, I haven't. I was a tank commander in

the Dunkirk debacle and we certainly fired a lot of shells at the enemy. I imagine some of those must have killed people. In fact, I know we blew up one machine-gun nest so that would have killed two or three at least. But man to man, in cold blood? No.'

'But you would do, if necessary?'

'If it was him or me, yes. Or more importantly, if it meant preserving the security of other people in the circuit. I respect Danny's conscientious objection, but if we all took that attitude the Nazis would have a free run. I suppose what it comes down to in the end is choosing the lesser of two evils.'

Steve nodded thoughtfully. 'I suppose that's it. Thanks, Graham.'

He smiled at her. 'You're welcome. Believe me, I understand your reservations and they do you credit. But this is war, Steve, and it's them or us.'

After that Steve threw herself into the training with all the determination she could muster. When Maxwell was satisfied with their performance at target practice they were taught to fire while on the move, or from a sitting or lying position. Later he took them into woodland where dummies in German uniform would appear suddenly from behind trees or swing down from the branches above. They were expected to shoot without hesitation. Any delay incurred a yell: 'Too slow! You're dead!'

The exercise brought an unexpected consolation. It quickly became apparent that she was a better shot than Harry Price.

From pistols they moved on to automatic weapons and she learned to use a Bren gun and a Sten. The Sten was the weapon favoured by SOE as it was lighter and easier to take apart in order to conceal it. They practised breaking it down and reassembling it until they could, quite literally, do it blindfold. They learned how to hide weapons on their own persons, carrying a pistol, for example, strapped to their thigh, where it could be accessed through a false pocket in trousers or a skirt, and how to transport parts of larger weapons concealed in innocent-looking packages, such as a bundle of firewood.

There was very little opportunity for relaxation and most of the time Steve was either too busy or too tired to think about her own feelings, but occasionally in the dark winter evenings she became aware once again of a sense of isolation. There was a billiard table in the big hall and the men tended to congregate round that, while Nicole made a point of monopolising Jeanne Borrel. They chattered away in French, usually about politics, the name of General de Gaulle featuring prominently, and though Steve could easily have joined in, Nicole always managed to give her the impression that she was intruding. So she often found herself sitting alone. The only other person who seemed equally at a loose end was Danny Jardine. One evening, when Steve was gazing into the fire, he sat down opposite her.

'Cheer up, it may never happen. Although,' he smiled wryly, 'in my experience it usually does.'

'Does it?' she responded. 'What makes you so pessimistic?'

He shrugged. 'Life?'

After a moment she said, 'I admired the stand you took about using a gun. But I don't understand what you're doing here if that's the way you feel.'

'It's a long story . . . ' he murmured. For a moment there was a melancholy in his eyes that touched her.

'I've often wondered why you're not in uniform,' she probed gently. 'Why didn't you join up?'

He looked at her, his gaze inscrutable again. 'I'm a conscientious objector. Do you want to give me a white feather?'

'So what on earth are you doing here?'

'I could ask you the same,' he countered.

'I just happen to speak fluent French and I thought I ought to make use of it. You didn't answer my question.'

'Where did you learn your French?'

'Finishing school in Switzerland, then six months in Paris – and holidays, of course. How about you?'

'I was born in Mauritius, so I grew up speaking French. And I've lived in France – and Germany – and Spain.'

'Goodness! You've moved about a bit.'

'Well, my parents travelled a good deal.'

'So you speak all those languages?'

'Plus a working knowledge of Turkish and a smattering of Arabic. I like to think of myself as a citizen of the world – or I used to, until the world went mad.'

'How on earth did you pick all that up?' Steve asked.

Danny pursed his lips and she thought for a moment he was not going to answer. Then he said, 'I told you my parents travelled a lot. I didn't tell you that they belonged to a travelling circus.'

Steve gazed at him, wide eyed. 'A circus? How fantastic! What did they do?'

'Oh, a bit of everything, like most circus folk, but primarily they were acrobats and high-wire artistes.'

'And you? I've noticed how athletic you are.'

'Oh yes. I performed with them from the age of five – until I ran away when I was sixteen.'

'You ran away?'

'Yes.'

Steve laughed. 'I've heard of kids running away to join the circus. Never of anyone running away *from* one.'

'Ah well,' Danny said, 'I didn't run away on my own, if you see what I mean.'

'You were with someone?'

'He came to see the show one night and . . . that was it.' Danny's eyes had grown dreamy. 'We had five wonderful years together. He was very well off. We travelled, stayed in the best hotels, met some lovely people. He educated me. I was almost illiterate when we met.'

Steve looked at him, then turned her head to gaze into the fire. She had heard men friends talking about this sort of thing – though they had usually fallen silent when they realised she was within earshot – but she had never met anyone who admitted to it so openly. She glanced back at Danny and found him watching her with ironic amusement.

'Isn't it dangerous to talk about all that?' she asked.

'Why not? To quote Christopher Marlowe, "that was in another country, and besides the wench is dead" – except it wasn't a wench and he isn't, as far as I know – dead, I mean. They can't prosecute me for something that wasn't within British jurisdiction.'

Steve paused for a moment. She felt she was on difficult ground but her curiosity was aroused. 'What happened – after the five years?'

'I suppose we grew out of each other. That was in Paris – 1937. I hung around for a while. Then I saw the way things were going in Europe so I decided to come back to England. My father was a Scot, so I have British nationality. I got a job as dresser to an actor – Selwyn Jackson, you may have heard of him. Charming man. I would have stayed with him but I hadn't reckoned on getting called up.'

'That was when you registered as a conscientious objector?'

'Yes. They sent me to work as a hospital porter in East

Grinstead. You can't imagine! Most of the patients were airmen who had suffered burns. The terrible injuries some of them had! It made me feel ashamed.'

'Is that why you volunteered for this?'

'Partly. And because of the stories that were coming out of Germany . . . about what was happening to . . . people like me. You see, my friend, the one who I spent those five years with . . .' Danny paused and Steve thought she heard tears in his voice. 'He was German. I can't bear to think what might have happened to him.' He took a breath and she saw that he was making an effort to compose himself. 'I had to do something but there was no way I was going to fight and kill people. I thought doing this I might be able to make myself useful – in a small way.'

'I'm sure you will,' Steve said warmly. 'I think it was a very brave decision.'

He glanced over his shoulder. 'I'd prefer it if we could keep this between ourselves. I don't think that lot would be so sympathetic.'

'Of course,' she agreed. 'You can trust me.'

As the days passed Steve conceived a great admiration for Gavin Maxwell. He was a remarkable man, with a combination of characteristics that never ceased to fascinate her. He could be ruthless to his students but at the same time he had a passionate love of nature and sympathy for all wild creatures. He was apparently immune to fear and would take tremendous personal risks and had little time for anyone less courageous. He was also a devotee of yoga and would hold forth on its virtues and techniques in the evenings. He introduced them all to the concept of meditation and impressed on them its potential advantages in the sort of situations they might encounter. As an illustration, he would draw deeply on the cigarette that almost invariably hung from the corner of his lips, move aside the skirt of his kilt and apply the glowing tip to his naked thigh, without showing a flicker of pain.

'There, you see? Mind over matter, it's as simple as that.'

He had other, less relaxing ways of keeping them all on their toes. Garramor was full of dark corners and passageways that turned at sudden unexpected angles. At various points around the house he had rigged up lifelike dummies in German uniform, attached to ingenious mechanisms that caused them to appear suddenly out of a cupboard or as you rounded a corner. The students all now carried a pistol at all times and it was expected that they would react instantly and shoot down the 'intruder'. As a result, even the simplest errand was fraught with nervous anticipation. Steve began to wonder after a week or so of this whether the object of the exercise was to induce a nervous breakdown in all but the toughest personalities. It also struck her as remarkable that so far none of them had shot one of their colleagues by mistake.

In the grounds of the house there was a wooden building, divided inside into rooms and passageways. One day Maxwell instructed Steve to search it for suspected enemies. She drew her Colt and crept to the main door, then changed her mind and slunk along the outer wall, raising her head only to glance through the windows. Most of them were curtained or whitewashed so that she could not see in, but at the back of the house she found one that gave her a view into one of the rooms. Seeing no one, she pushed up a sash window and climbed through. Moving as silently as possible, she crossed the room and opened the door to the corridor. Her heart was thumping. She understood that this was an important test. Maxwell still had his doubts about her and failure here could mean final rejection. She knew that she was not in any actual danger but there was no telling what unpleasant surprise might be in store for her. Coming to a closed door, she was suddenly aware of a murmur of voices from inside. Mindful of her training, she turned the door handle soundlessly, drew a deep breath and kicked the door open. Two men sat at a table, dressed in German uniform, and as she plunged into the room the door closed and a third appeared from behind it. It took her a split second to recognise that they were all dummies. She swung round and shot the one behind her in the stomach – tap, tap, two shots as she had been taught – then turned quickly and administered the same treatment to the other two. Each of them collapsed in an unsettlingly realistic manner.

'Well done,' said Maxwell's voice from behind her, and she swung round, her gun coming up into the firing position. He was standing in the passageway and recognition came only a split second before her finger tightened on the trigger. 'Three seconds,' he went on imperturbably. 'That's not bad. Any more than three and a half and you would be regarded as dead.'

'I might have shot you!' she gasped.

'Aye,' he agreed laconically, 'you might. You can go back and join the others now. But don't say a word to them about what happened. They've all to go through it, you ken, and we don't want to spoil the surprise.'

Steve staggered out of the back door and leaned against the wall. She was shaking all over and for a moment she feared that she was going to be sick. A hand was laid on her shoulder and Jeanne's voice said, 'It's OK. You did very well. It's horrible, I know, but it could happen just like that. Believe me, I know.'

Maxwell's final, enigmatic comment to Danny had weighed on Steve's mind and that evening she summoned up the courage to ask him what he had meant.

'You told Danny he wouldn't be able to go back to working in a hospital if he failed the training here. What happens to people who fail?'

Maxwell raised an eyebrow. 'Are you afraid you might fail?'

'No, I'm determined not to. I just wondered.'

'There's a workshop, up in the far northern Highlands. We call it "the cooler". Recruits who have failed the training, or agents who turn out to be unsuitable, spend six months there doing useful odd jobs. After that, it is assumed that anything they know will be out of date so they can safely be let back into the community.'

Steve shivered inwardly at the thought of being incarcerated in such a place. It would be like a prison sentence. She had another reason now to make sure that she succeeded.

One morning two strangers arrived at the house. Steve was coming downstairs and saw them passing through the hall. Both were men in late middle age, one grey haired and the other white, and she was struck by their benign, almost cherubic expressions.

'Who are the two men who arrived this morning?' she asked Maxwell at morning parade.

He smiled mischievously. 'Look like a couple of visiting bishops, don't they? We call them the Heavenly Twins. Don't be fooled by appearances.'

He refused to say any more but the warning was soon explained. The students were told to assemble in the room used for PT, where they found that a number of dummies had been strung from the ceiling. The two newcomers were introduced as Major Fairbairn and Major Sykes. Both had once served with the Shanghai police force and their speciality was unarmed combat. There followed one of the most gruelling and alarming sessions Steve had endured so far. In their introductory remarks the two men pointed out that agents might find themselves disarmed, or in a situation where it was necessary to kill silently to avoid raising the alarm. The emphasis was on the word 'kill'. A man temporarily disabled could revive and a prisoner was a hindrance. They had to learn to be quick, silent and deadly.

For the first lesson they were shown how to deliver such a blow with the edge of the hand, to the back of the neck, the bridge of the nose, the throat, or the side of the head. Once the instructors had demonstrated they were told to practise on the dummies. It was emphasised that such blows were intended to be fatal, so they must never practise on each other. When they had mastered this technique they were shown how to knock an opponent over by jabbing him under the chin with the open hand, following this up by jabbing him in the eyes with extended fingers. They learned to kick, to use their knees, heads and elbows.

'Forget all about Queensberry rules or fighting fair,' Fairbairn told them. 'These are the rules of ungentlemanly warfare.'

Alongside the fighting techniques they were being taught they continued with what was known as 'fieldwork'. They learned to navigate across open country using the sun by day and the stars by night. They learned to paddle a canoe and how to get in and out of one without creating a splash. They constructed rope bridges over rivers. They were taught how to set an ambush and how to bring down a motorcyclist by stretching a length of fishing line across a road. They even learned to drive the little steam locomotive that pulled the train that had brought them from Glasgow.

The final item on the curriculum was sabotage and demolition. The instructor for this was another Highlander, Captain Hamish Pelham Burn. For the first session they were all assembled in the lecture room. Pelham Burn held up a lump of material about the size of a cricket ball.

'This, ladies and gentlemen, is a substance known as 808. It largely consists of nitroglycerine. Here, catch!'

He threw the lump straight to Steve, who automatically caught it, to ironic applause from the rest of the group, and hastily put it down on the desk in front of her.

'Don't worry,' Pelham Burn went on. '808 is completely harmless if kept in the right conditions. If you warm it you can mould it to shape or even cut it. But if you get it too hot, so that it starts to sweat, it then becomes extremely volatile. Feel it. It's like plasticine, right?'

Steve felt the lump gingerly and then passed it to her neighbour.

Pelham Burn continued, 'The best way to warm it is in a bain-marie. Who knows what that means?'

'A water bath over gentle heat,' Steve offered.

'Right. But if you can't do that, it is possible, in an emergency, to warm it under your armpit. There is only one problem. Prolonged skin contact with this can make you very ill – headache, nausea, fever – lasting twenty-four hours or more. Also, there's another drawback. Steve, smell your hands.'

Steve raised her hands to her face and lowered them quickly. 'It smells like rancid marzipan.'

'Exactly, and the Huns recognise that bitter almond smell quite well. So don't handle the stuff any more than you can help and make sure to wash your hands afterwards. Now this,' and he held up another, slightly smaller ball of material, 'is something new. It's an explosive called RDX mixed with a plasticising medium so it can be moulded. We call it PE – plastic explosive. The French refer to it simply as *plastique*. It's much safer and easier to handle than 808. There is only one snag. Both these substances are in short supply and can only be used for the real thing. So you lot are going to have to learn your trade with good old gelignite.'

They began in the classroom, learning how to make up suitable charges for different purposes – to derail a train, or blow up a bridge or put a piece of machinery out of commission. They learned about detonators and time fuses and how they could all be put together using such common ingredients as balloons (to keep things waterproof) and sticky tape. Putting these charges together required some degree of manual dexterity and Steve had never been nimble-fingered. In sewing lessons at school her stitches had always been clumsy, and when it came to wrapping parcels for Christmas hers ended up with loose edges and creases in the wrong places. Pelham Burn was by turns amused and exasperated by her ineptitude and often held her work up to ridicule in front of the class. It was in this work that Jack Baker really came into his own. Many times he came to Steve's rescue and often ended up constructing the charge for her.

Once they had mastered this part of the course they were sent out into the surrounding countryside to put theory into practice. There was an old quarry high up in the hills that soon resounded to some very satisfying bangs. They could not, of course, use real explosives on the sort of targets they would be expected to attack in France, but they were expected to lay dummy charges without being caught. At different times they 'attacked' the electricity transformer station, various local bridges and the railway line.

It was at this point that Price saw the chance to revenge his hurt pride. Steve and Price and Danny were told that a visiting brigadier would be on a certain train and they should imagine that he was a German general and set a charge to derail it.

'Steve can set the charge,' Price ordained. 'She needs the practice. We'll act as lookouts.'

Steve duly made up and set the dummy charge, but as she lay in wait for the train Price hurried over to her and told her that she was required to report to Pelham Burn immediately. 'He's just over there, on the other side of the hill.'

Steve ran across the hillside but found no sign of Pelham Burn. She returned to her position, sweating and out of breath, just in time to hear the train whistle as it approached. She waited until it reached the chosen spot and depressed the plunger on the detonator. To her horror, instead of the gentle pop she expected there was a loud explosion and a fountain of peat rose into the air. As it subsided she expected to see the little engine lying in a tangle of wreckage, but it was chugging away into the distance, apparently undisturbed. A few yards from the line was a crater from which smoke was still rising.

Price came racing over. 'Bloody hell! You've made a real pig's ear of this! Don't you know the difference between a real charge and a dummy?'

'You bastard!' Steve gasped. 'You swapped them while I was away.'

'Prove it!' was the grinning response.

For the rest of the day Steve waited to be hauled up in front of Maxwell to account for what had happened. She was seething with the injustice of the situation, but she had a feeling that if she attempted to shift the blame to Price it would go against her. In the event, nothing happened until they were sitting by the fire after dinner, when Maxwell remarked, 'I've just had Baker Street on the line. I gather they've received a complaint from a certain brigadier. It seems he had the train window open and his dress uniform was showered with peat.'

'What are they going to do about it?' Steve asked with trepidation.

Maxwell met her eyes and winked. 'I gather they told him to send them the bill for dry cleaning and keep his mouth shut.'

The students at Garramor had soon learned that there were others in the neighbourhood who were following the same course. A few miles away was a house full of Poles and some distance in the opposite direction a group of Danes and Dutch, while up on the hillside above the loch was another house given over to the French contingent.

When Nicole heard about these she demanded, 'Why are we not being trained with them?'

'Because,' Maxwell told her, 'you were recruited by F section. We answer to Colonel Buckmaster at Baker Street. They belong to DF, de Gaulle's lot. It's a different chain of command.'

'De Gaulle?' Nicole's usually glum face lit up. 'Then I should be with them.'

'Well, you're not, so make the best of it,' was the curt reply.

As the course progressed Nicole had become increasingly intransigent. She made no secret of the fact that she thought much of it a waste of time. 'When I get to France I shall behave like an ordinary person,' she was fond of saying. 'I shall not trap rabbits for food and if I wish to cross a river I will use a bridge, not some contraption made with ropes.' That evening Steve heard her arguing vehemently with Maxwell. She could not make out the words and Nicole refused to discuss it at bedtime, but the next day the French girl did not appear for morning parade. When Steve asked Maxwell whether she should go and look for her he replied, 'No point. She's gone to join the Gaullists – good riddance, as far as I'm concerned.'

As a final passing-out test they were given a night operation to complete. This involved crossing a river and a five-mile hike through the forest; paddling themselves across a loch in canoes, navigating by the stars; carrying out a sabotage operation on a mock-up of an electricity transformer station; and returning safely to base before reveille. All this to be accomplished without falling foul of patrols mounted by students from one of the other houses.

Initially, everything went according to plan. They avoided an ambush in the forest because Lomax spotted a trip-wire across the path and dodged a patrol after Steve's sensitive nose picked up the whiff of tobacco smoke from their cigarettes. The charge was set successfully and they were well on the way home before the time pencil fuse set off the explosion. Then things started to go wrong. Danny, so agile on land, hated and feared water and tended to panic when forced into a canoe. That night, of all nights, he managed to capsize and had to be hauled, spluttering and shivering, out of the icy waters of the loch. They managed to salvage his canoe and shepherd him across to the other side but it cost them valuable minutes and by the time they had hidden the canoes there was less than an hour of darkness left. More critical was Danny's condition. His lips were blue with cold and he was becoming increasingly lethargic. They had all been warned about the dangers of hypothermia.

The landing place was at the edge of a small village and as they passed the outlying houses Danny sagged down against a wall, his arms wrapped round his knees. Lomax bent over him for a moment and when he straightened up his face was grim.

'We've got to get Danny back in the warm, pronto. It looks as though we may have to abort the mission and call for help.'

'No we bloody well won't!' Price exclaimed. 'Why don't we leave the stupid little pansy here and push on? After we've gone he can knock someone up and ask for help.'

'No,' Lomax responded sharply. 'We're a team. We don't abandon one of our own.'

Jack had been peering down the village street. He touched Lomax's arm and pointed. 'How about we drive back to Garramor?'

Parked outside a house was a car, one of the few in the area, which they knew belonged to the local schoolmaster.

'It'll be locked,' Lomax pointed out.

Jack winked. 'No problem. You all stay back here. Then if I'm caught you've still got a chance of getting away.'

Huddled behind the wall, Steve watched him prowl down the street and crouch beside the car. Lomax was consulting a map by the light of a pencil-thin torch beam shining between his fingers.

'It's miles round by road. We'll have to drive cross-country.'

'It should be OK on the forestry tracks,' Steve said. 'But not so good in the valley. How do we cross the river?'

'There's a bridge – here, see? And some sort of farm track leading to it.'

'It's going to be very boggy down there,' Steve commented dubiously.

'I don't see that we have any alternative,' Lomax said.

At that moment they heard an engine start and seconds later Jack brought the car to a stop beside them and they all bundled in. The drive through the forest was bone-shaking but they reached the other side safely. Then Steve's fears began to be realised. On ground sodden by melting snow the car tyres repeatedly lost their grip, and when they eventually reached the bridge they saw that the track had been churned to liquid mud by passing cattle. Jack took a run at it but yards short of the bridge itself the car skidded to a stop. He tried to rock the wheels free by reversing and then going forward but to no avail.

'Let me have a go, for Christ's sake!' Price exclaimed. 'You need to give it a bit of stick.'

'If you do that you'll just bury us deeper,' Steve pointed out.

'You keep out of this!' he snapped. 'Get out, all of you, and push, damn it!'

They climbed out and put their shoulders to the back of the car. Price revved the engine violently, with the result that they were all covered in mud and the car sank deeper still.

'You!' Price pointed at Danny, who was still huddled on the back seat. 'Get in here and take the wheel. It needs someone with a bit of gumption to push.'

'But I can't drive,' Danny protested.

'For Christ's sake! Look here.' Price demonstrated brusquely how to put the car in gear and pointed out the accelerator and the clutch. Then, ignoring Danny's protests, he came to the back of the car. 'Out of the way, Steve! Let the real men get to work.'

Steve retired to a short distance, grinding her teeth. It was getting light and as she gazed around her something caught her eye. A short distance away at the top of a slight rise stood a dilapidated barn and through the open door she glimpsed a gleam of machinery. She compressed her lips to suppress a grin. She watched Price heaving at the car and waited until the spinning wheels had covered him in mud, like the rest of them. Then she turned and wandered away up the hill. The tractor was exactly like the one her father had . . . and the key was in the ignition.

The men, hearing the engine, looked round and waved frantically, obviously thinking that it was the farmer or one of his workers approaching. She saw Lomax's face break into a delighted grin. Price's expression was even more satisfactory.

The next day at morning parade Maxwell addressed them.

'You have all successfully completed this element of the course and tomorrow you will be moving on.'

'To France?' demanded Price.

Maxwell looked at him with an ironic lift of the eyebrows. 'Not yet. Next you are going to do what all nice young ladies are supposed to do. You are all going to finishing school.'

Chapter Three

SOE's 'finishing school' was situated in Hampshire, at Beaulieu, the country estate of Lord Montagu. Steve's group were accommodated in a pretty country house in the grounds called Boarmans, where climbing roses around the windows were just coming into bloom. Conditions here were a good deal more pleasant than they had been at Arisaig. The house was well appointed and they each had their own room. The food was better, too, at least for anyone who liked curry. The commandant in charge was an old India hand and liked his meals as spicy as possible. Spring was now well advanced and the weather was much warmer. Daffodils were in full bloom in the gardens and cherries shed carpets of pink blossom whenever the wind blew. They had little time to appreciate the change, however, for the next day the final phase of their training began.

For Steve, this proved to be the hardest part. Every day they were given lectures on what they learned to call 'trade craft'. They were expected to take copious notes and then to spend the evenings memorising them. She had never enjoyed academic work and now she felt that she was being asked to cram more information into her head than she had ever had to absorb before. To add to the strain, they were all instructed that from now on they must speak nothing but French and all lectures were delivered in that language.

The lectures dealt with security and how to cope with random police searches or detect whether their rooms had been disturbed while they were out. An instructor who had worked for Max Factor in peacetime showed them how to disguise themselves if their cover was 'blown'. Another lecturer, who assured them that he had been taught his craft by a very successful burglar, showed them how to pick locks and open safes.

Some of the most important lectures dealt with how to organise a resistance circuit and how to approach and recruit potential members.

'Agents normally work in teams of three,' the tutor told them. 'There will be a leader, a radio operator and a courier. The courier's job is to carry messages and sometimes equipment between different members of the circuit. As always, security is the first consideration. No member of the circuit should know more about the others than is absolutely necessary. The best way to achieve this is to break each circuit down into separate cells, which only have contact with the circuit organiser through an intermediary. That way, if one group is "blown", its members cannot give away anything about the rest of the circuit. Members of the community who are sympathetic but not actually involved in resistance activity can act as contact points and pass on messages. Doctors, dentists and priests are particularly valuable for such purposes, since it is easy for people to find reasons to visit them, but don't neglect such people as bartenders or waitresses, who also come into contact with a wide range of people.'

The students learned different methods of communication, including the use of invisible inks and 'dead letter boxes', which were places where a message could be hidden for someone else to collect. But the technique that Steve found particularly hard to master was radio communication. She had to learn basic Morse Code and how to use a WT radio set, which was difficult enough, but the business of encoding messages involved what, to her, were hours of mind-numbing drudgery.

Alongside all this they still had to keep up the physical training programme that had been instituted at Wanborough and Arisaig and to practise with the weapons they had learned to use. Most nights, Steve fell into bed in a state of physical and mental exhaustion.

When they began to put what they had learned into practice she felt happier. They were sent into local towns, usually Bournemouth, on a variety of missions. They were warned that they might be followed and told how to spot when they were being tailed and how to take avoiding action. They were also sent to spy on nearby military bases or airfields and warned that local police would be on the lookout for suspicious activity. If arrested, they were to try to bluff their way out and only as a last resort to reveal where they came from.

For one exercise Steve was paired, to her dismay, with Harry Price. They were instructed to travel separately to Bournemouth and take rooms under assumed names. There they were each to collect a message from a dead letter box and then to meet up at a pre-arranged rendezvous the following morning to exchange information. It sounded deceptively simple. Steve left first and guessed as soon as she boarded the train that she was being shadowed by a smart young woman in civilian dress. She lost her by taking a taxi from the station and then changing her instructions about her destination after they had started. Just to make sure, she went into Plummer Roddis's department store and left by another door. Then she made her way to a quiet boarding house in a road leading back from the promenade and took a room.

The message was where she had been told it would be, hidden under a pew in a local church. Having retrieved it, she returned to the boarding house and sat down to dinner in the sepulchral quiet of the dining room, which was occupied by two elderly couples who ignored Steve and spoke only in subdued murmurs. Then a young man in naval uniform came in and took the table next to hers. It was natural that he should start a conversation and Steve learned that he was convalescing after a bout of pneumonia, having been rescued from the North Atlantic when his ship was torpedoed. He was feeling better, he said, but very lonely, since he was far from family and friends. Would she, he asked, care to come out for a drink with him after the meal? She was tempted but she remembered that they had been warned to beware of friendly strangers and made the excuse that she had letters to write and wanted an early night.

The next morning she was at the appointed place, a bench on the sea front, in good time, but there was no sign of Price. She waited an hour then gave up and went back to Beaulieu. Later that day she was sent for by the CO, Major Skilbeck, to explain the failure of the mission.

'Lieutenant Price maintains that he went to the rendezvous and you weren't there,' Skilbeck said.

'That's not true,' Steve returned. 'I waited an hour. Perhaps I should have hung on longer. I don't know what happened to him.'

'Well, as it happens, we do,' Skilbeck replied grimly. 'You did well to shake off your tail. We didn't pick you up again until you went to the dead letter box. And you passed the test with the naval chappy – an actor, of course, as I expect you realised. Price didn't do so well. He let us follow him all the way to the Grand Hotel and then fell for the blandish-ments of . . . well, a young lady of doubtful reputation who lets us use her services from time to time. The reason he didn't show up at the rendezvous was because he was still sleeping off the drug she slipped into his nightcap the evening before.'

The next morning Price did not appear for breakfast and later in the day Steve learned that he had been seen loading his suitcase into the truck that had fetched them from the station. He was heading for the 'cooler', she thought, and could not find it in her heart to feel sorry for him.

One of the most nerve-racking parts of the course was practice at resisting interrogation.

'No one resists the Gestapo's methods indefinitely,' the instructor said, 'however brave they are. So you should make up your mind what you can reveal that will be least damaging to the organisation and hope that, once you have told them that, they may think it's all you know. But the best defence is not to fall into Gestapo hands in the first place. You may be picked up on suspicion or as part of a routine investigation. If you can convince the SD interrogators, or whoever it is holding you, that you are just an ordinary person going about your day-to-day business there is a good chance they will let you go. But to do that, your cover story must be absolutely watertight and consistent with any story your colleagues are telling.'

To reinforce this lesson they were sent out in pairs on a mission and told that they had to think of an innocent ex-planation for where they had been. Steve was sent with Danny to Portsmouth, with the task of discovering which naval ships were in harbour at that time.

'It's hopeless!' Steve said when they sat down to discuss their strategy. 'We'll never get into the dockyard.'

'Of course not,' Danny said with a grin. 'But there's more ways than one to skin a cat. What we need is an informant on the inside.'

'And how do we find that?'

'Where do sailors go when they get shore leave?'

'The pub?'

'Exactly.'

'So, you mean we just go into a pub and start asking questions?'

'I think we'll need to be a bit more subtle than that. It's a question of – how shall I put it? – making friends.'

'You want me to go into a pub and . . . and *pick up* a sailor? What about you?'

He made a face at her. 'Oh, come on, duckie, don't be naive.'

It was not hard to find a pub near the dockyard that was obviously a favourite with sailors. Danny went in first and Steve followed a few minutes later. It was a rough looking place, the sort she would never have dreamed of entering under normal conditions. The floor was of stone flags and the ceiling was yellowed with years of tobacco smoke, clouds of which already hung in the air although it was only just past opening time. Groups of men, mostly sailors, were sitting around or propping up the bar. Danny was already sitting at a table with three sailors. Steve was the only woman in the place except for the barmaid, and her appearance was greeted with a moment of dead silence followed by a chorus of wolf whistles. At Danny's suggestion she was wearing a short summer dress and plenty of make-up. It was not her style at all and she made her way to the bar feeling most uncomfortable.

Before she could order a drink a burly matelot standing at the bar exclaimed, 'Come on, love. What are you having?'

It was contrary to all her upbringing to respond but she forced a smile and asked for a glass of cider. In a very few minutes she was seated at a wooden table surrounded by five sailors.

'So what is a lovely lady like you doing in a place like this?' one of them enquired.

Steve shifted on her seat and looked around her. She was not used to play-acting. But she had agreed to the plan with Danny and now she must stick to it. When she spoke it was in the Buckinghamshire accent she had grown up hearing, hoping that none of her companions would recognise the difference between that and the local Sussex burr.

'I . . . I'm looking for a man I met at a party a week or two back.'

'Sailor, was he? What's his name?'

'Peter Wilson – least that's what he said.'

'Rank?'

'I dunno. He was like you – same uniform an' everything.'

'Able seaman, then. What ship's he from?'

'Goodness, I don't know. But he said he was on leave while it was in dock here.'

The sailor raised his voice. 'Anyone here know a Peter Wilson?'

To Steve's dismay a voice from the other end of the bar called back, 'Tall guy, fair hair, tattoo on his left wrist?'

'Could be,' Steve agreed doubtfully.

'Never heard of him!' came the reply amid shouts of laughter.

'You don't seem to know much about him,' commented one of the men at her table.

Steve giggled. 'Well, I was a bit drunk at the time.'

'What do you want to bother with him for, anyway?' The man who had bought her the drink put his arm across her shoulders and breathed beer fumes into her face. 'You can take your pick from us.'

Steve lowered her gaze. 'He . . . he promised me . . . he said he'd keep in touch.'

One of her companions nudged his mate and muttered, 'Reckon he's got her in the family way?'

The first man grinned at her. 'Cheer up, love. We'll ask around, see if we can find him for you. Drink up and have another one.'

They seemed a friendly crowd and after a little Steve relaxed slightly. To divert them from asking her too many questions she began playing up the innocent, slightly stupid country girl.

'What's your ship called, then?' . . . 'What sort of a ship is that, then?' . . . 'A cruiser? Is that a big ship?' . . . 'Your mate's got a different name on his cap. What sort of ship is that, then?' . . . 'How long you going to be in dock, then?' Meanwhile, she was memorising the names of the ships on the sailors' caps. It was surprising and rather alarming how much information she was able to collect.

Then she felt a hand on her thigh, creeping higher. It was the sailor who had first accosted her. When she pushed his hand away he muttered, 'Come on, love. We all know your sort. Don't play hard to get.'

'You've got it wrong,' she said, trying to remain calm in spite of a rising sense of panic. 'I'm not like that.'

'Oh yeah? Tell that to the marines. Come on, my ship leaves port tonight. Give a lonely sailor something to remember.'

He put his arm around her and pulled her towards him, trying to kiss her. His cheek was rough against hers and he smelt of ripe sweat. His companions cheered him on and she was not strong enough to resist. For a moment she was tempted to employ one of the techniques she had learned from Major Sykes but she knew that would blow her cover completely. She twisted away from him, looking for Danny, but he had disappeared.

It was the barmaid who came to her rescue, marching over to the table.

'Knock it off, you, or I'll ban the lot of you. And you,' with a jerk of her head at Steve, 'out! We don't want your sort in here.'

Steve extricated herself from the sailor's embrace and headed for the door without further argument. In the street she found she was shaking all over and the trembling did not stop until she reached the station.

Standing on the platform waiting for the train, she began to feel calmer. The mission had been accomplished and soon she would be back in the security of Beaulieu. Then both her arms were gripped from behind by strong fingers and a voice said quietly in her ear, 'Now then, miss. No fuss please. Just come along with us.'

Steve swung her head from side to side. Two men stood beside her in civilian dress – raincoats and trilby hats – their faces expressionless.

'What do you want?' she demanded. 'Let go of me!'

'Now then, miss,' the taller of the two murmured. 'We don't want a scene, do we? Just come along quietly.'

'Come where? Who are you?' She tried to free her arms but their grip merely tightened. She felt herself being inexorably moved towards the exit. She wondered whether she should struggle, or cry for help, but there was something about the two men's calm assumption of authority that made her feel it would be useless. 'I don't understand,' she protested. 'What do you want with me? I haven't done anything.'

'Then you've got nothing to worry about, have you,' said her captor.

As they passed through the booking hall a man in petty officer's uniform turned away from the ticket desk and stood in their way.

'What's going on? Are you all right, miss?'

One of her captors reached into a pocket and flashed some kind of warrant card at him and he immediately drew back with a muttered apology. So they were official, then. Who could they be? Plain-clothes police? Special Branch? MI5? But what did they want with her? The answer was easy. She had been seen in a pub trying to wheedle sensitive information out of a group of sailors.

Outside the station she was pushed into the back of a waiting car and driven to an anonymous-looking brick building on the outskirts of the town. The car drove round to the back and a door opened as it drew up. Steve was marched along a stone-flagged passageway and then down a steep flight of steps to a basement area where several doors opened off a narrow passage. Her captors opened one and shoved her forward into a small, white-walled, windowless room. A man was sitting behind a table, in front of which was a single chair. The only illumination was from a bright spotlight standing behind him, so that his face was in shadow. She was pushed to a position in front of him and then released.

The man behind the desk spoke quietly. 'We know where you have been and why, so there is no point trying to deny it. What we want to know is, who are you working for?'

Steve swallowed, trying to conjure some saliva into a mouth suddenly parched. 'I don't know what you're talking about. I haven't done anything wrong.' She had had time to think in the car. She had been warned about this situation.

She was expected to talk her way out of it. To admit her real identity and purpose would be to fail. 'You can't keep me here,' she went on boldly. 'I'm a British citizen and I know my rights. You don't frighten me.'

'Don't I?' The tone was silky. He got up and came round the desk to stand in front of her. 'Perhaps this will change your mind.'

He struck her sharply across the face. It was not a very hard blow but enough to rock her on her heels and make her cheek sting. She found herself biting back tears of mingled pain and fury. There was a chill at the pit of her stomach. These people were not playing games.

'You can't treat me like this. I'll complain to the authorities.'

'Don't give me that!' The voice was sharper. 'You are a German spy, sent to collect information useful to the enemy. You have no rights here. What were you doing in that pub?'

'I was looking for my boyfriend.'

'Your boyfriend?'

'Yes. At least, I've only met him once, at a party just before I came here.'

'What made you think you would find him in Portsmouth?'

'He's a sailor – on HMS *Defiant*.' It was the name on the cap of one of the sailors in the pub. 'It's in dock there.'

'How do you know?'

'He wrote to me.'

'Show me the letter.'

'I didn't keep it.'

'And did you find him?'

'No. I couldn't get near his ship and the guard on the gate wouldn't even let me send in a message.' She hoped that she sounded sufficiently aggrieved.

'So what did you do?'

'I went to the pub. There were sailors there. I asked around to see if anyone knew him but no one did.'

'You seem to have gone to great lengths to find this man. Why was it so important?'

'I just wanted to see him, that's all. I liked him.'

'I'm sorry. That doesn't sound a sufficient reason to me.'

'All right. I'm in love with him.'

'After one meeting?'

'Yes.'

'I don't believe you. Now, why don't you tell me the truth and then we can avoid a lot of unpleasantness.'

'That is the truth.'

Behind her she heard the sound of footsteps and then unmistakably Danny's voice raised in protest. She swung round in time to see him being marched past the open door. Then the door of the next room opened and slammed shut.

'Never mind what's going on out there,' her inquisitor said sharply. 'You concentrate on me. It's no good going on lying to me. Tell me why you were so anxious to find this man. I don't think a girl like you would go running after a sailor.'

Steve hesitated. She had not wanted to use the next bit of the story.

'Look, if you must know, I was drunk at the time. I'm afraid he may have . . . I might be . . . I could be pregnant.'

'Ah.' There was a long pause. 'I suppose you realise that I could send for a doctor to verify that?'

Steve swallowed. Would they go to such lengths? She felt sure that they would if they felt it necessary. 'He couldn't tell. It's too soon. Anyway, I could be mistaken. It's only just over a month.' She felt herself blushing.

'And if the doctor discovered that you were virgo intacta?'

Oh, that was clever! But not quite as clever as he thought. The thought of undergoing such an intimate examination revolted her but she forced herself to remain defiant. 'He wouldn't.'

The interrogator sighed. 'I see we are going to have to resort to less civilised methods. I'll give you a little time to think it over. Sit down.'

Steve lowered herself on to the single upright chair.

'Cuff her,' he ordered.

Her hands were pulled behind the back of the chair and she felt handcuffs snap closed around her wrists. The wood of the chair dug painfully into her arms and her shoulders were wrenched backwards but she was unable to ease her position. The inquisitor looked at her for a moment.

'Think carefully. The sooner you decide to tell us the truth the less unpleasant it will be for you.' Then, to the men who had brought her in, 'You two can go.'

She heard them leave. The interrogator snapped off the light and walked to the door and she heard it close. Without the light the room was in total darkness. She sat tensely, straining her ears. Had he gone, or was he still standing behind her? Several minutes passed with no sound and she came to the conclusion that she was alone. The basement room was cold and in her light summer dress she was beginning to shiver. Also she was suddenly aware of an urgent need to pass water. Her shoulders ached and the darkness seemed to press on her eyes. Then she heard a sound, a quiet rustle, then a scuffling. She caught her breath. Mice! Or possibly rats. Mice were not dangerous, she told herself. Nor were rats, unless cornered. Nevertheless, the thought of them running around her feet in the dark was unnerving.

A new sound put the thought out of her mind. The door of the next room opened and slammed and she heard voices, first quiet, then raised in anger. She could not make out the words but it was not hard to guess that Danny was being interrogated. Then there was a noise like a chair being overturned and a sudden yell of pain. Danny's voice, she was sure of it. The voices went on, hectoring in tone, the words still indistinguishable. Then came a silence, broken by a scream of agony. Steve jerked against her bound wrists in a desperate effort to free herself. What were they doing to him? What would happen when her turn came?

There were no further noises and she became aware again of her own pain. The strain on her shoulders and arms was becoming unbearable and to her shame she realised that she had lost control of her bladder. Her skirt was saturated and she could hear the urine dripping on to the floor. Time passed. She stopped shivering. Her body seemed too chilled for that. She found that she was keening aloud through clenched teeth in reaction to the pain in her shoulders. What should she say when they came back? Should she confess the truth and hope that they would believe her? When she rehearsed the story in her mind it seemed even more unlikely than the one she had already told. And even if she could convince them, it would mean the end of her career with SOE and six months in the 'cooler' with Harry Price for company. That thought alone was enough to stiffen her resolve.

The door opened and steps crossed the room. The light was switched on, blinding her, and her interrogator's voice said, 'Well, are you ready to tell us the truth now – or do we have to give you the same treatment we gave your colleague? He didn't last long, I can tell you.'

Steve raised her head, screwing up her eyes to focus on his face. From deep within her anger replaced fear. 'You bastards! When I get out of here I'm going to sue you for assault. I'll see that you're dragged through the courts. Do what you like, I won't give you the time of day!'

He stepped closer and took her chin in his hand, forcing her face up to his own. For a minute he looked down into her eyes and for the first time she saw a flicker of humanity. At length he said, 'Well, you've got guts. I'll give you that.'

He walked to the door and she felt her stomach liquefy at the prospect of what might follow. There was a pause, then new footsteps approached. She tried to twist her head to see who was coming but she could not turn far enough.

Jeanne Borrel's voice said softly, 'It's all right, *ma chère*, it's all over now. Well done! Well done!' Hands fumbled with the handcuffs, which dropped away with a clatter, and a blanket was draped around her shoulders. Jeanne was on her knees beside Steve, rubbing her numb hands between her own. 'There, there, *chérie*, you're safe now. It's all over.'

Steve stared down at her uncomprehendingly. 'How did you know I was here?'

Jeanne met her eyes. 'Of course we knew. We have known all along. It was a test, and you passed with flying colours.'

'A test! You mean you put me through all that . . . deliberately?'

'It's only a faint hint of what the Gestapo will do if they catch you. We had to be sure that you could hold out, for a while at least.'

'Those men – who are they?'

'Oh, they're sent down specially from Baker Street.'

Steve caught her breath. 'Danny! What did they do to Danny?'

'No more than they did to you.'

'But I heard him scream.'

'No, my dear. You heard a recording made by an actor. Danny is all right. You can see for yourself soon.'

Steve pulled her hands away from Jeanne's. Feeling was beginning to come back into her arms and her mind, too, was losing the numbness of shock. 'You let them put me through all that. How could you? Don't you know how it feels?'

Jeanne sighed. 'Oh yes, *chérie*. I know very well. We have all been put through it. It's terrible, I know, but it's necessary. Come, let me help you up. There's a hot bath waiting for you and a change of clothes.'

Bathed and dressed, she was taken down to the car that had brought her and found Danny installed in the back seat with a vivid bruise on one cheek. It was plain that he had been hit considerably harder than she had.

'Are you all right?' she asked.

He shrugged. 'I've had more comfortable afternoons.'

On arrival at Beaulieu they were both called to the chief instructor's office. Major Skilbeck greeted them with a smile.

'Congratulations, both of you. You both stuck to your stories and they were consistent throughout. I'm sorry we had to put you through some pretty rough handling but I'm sure you understand that it's nothing to what you might expect from the Gestapo. The question remains, did you get any useful information. Well?'

It transpired that they both had a good list of ships that were in harbour and when they were due to sail and Skilbeck congratulated them on their success. In the days that followed Steve realised that she had got off relatively lightly. Danny was not the only man to appear with nasty bruises as a result of their interrogations.

At the end of six weeks they came to a parting of the ways. Danny was going to the SOE signals training unit to learn to be a radio operator. Jack was off to join the 'boffins' whose job it was to devise new means of sabotaging enemy factories and equipment. That left Steve and Lomax. They were going to the parachute training school at Ringway Airport outside Manchester.

On the last evening there was a riotous party at Boarmans and Steve, for the first time in her life, got really drunk.

They were accommodated at Dunham Massey, yet another of the grand houses that had been taken over by SOE. It was a common jest among members of the service that the letters stood for 'Stately 'Omes of England'. To begin with Steve did not find the training too difficult, since it consisted largely in learning to fall without hurting yourself, something they had been taught as part of the unarmed combat course at Arisaig. Then, on the second day, they were taken out on to the airfield and up to the top of a ninety-foot tower. There was a contraption there consisting of a long rope passing over a pulley, with a harness at one end and a means of attaching sandbags at the other. They had all been weighed beforehand and the idea of the sandbags was to act as a counterweight that would simulate the drag of a parachute.

As she stood in line and watched Lomax being strapped into the harness, Steve was shocked to discover that her legs were beginning to tremble. A glance downwards over the edge of the tower made her head spin.

'Ready, number one?' came a shout from the sergeant in charge on the ground below.

The corporal who was fixing the harness leaned over and gave him a thumbs-up sign.

'Jump!'

Lomax disappeared over the edge of the platform. Steve

could not watch to see how hard he hit the ground. She stood with her eyes shut, feeling the sweat trickling down her neck and between her breasts. Then it was her turn. The corporal must have felt her trembling as he attached the harness, for he winked at her and said, 'You'll be all right, miss. Easy as falling off a log.'

He leaned over and raised his thumb to the sergeant and Steve stepped forward to the edge of the platform. Bile rose in her throat at the vertiginous drop in front of her feet.

'Jump!' the sergeant shouted.

Steve felt as if her feet had taken root in the planks she stood on. *It's all right,* she told herself. *You won't be hurt. Just jump. You've got to do it!* But her feet would not move.

'Jump, number two!' yelled the sergeant. 'Are you going to stand there all day?'

Steve took a deep breath. In her mind she had already jumped, but her feet were still on the platform.

'Number two, either piss or get off the bloody pot!' the sergeant roared. Then, as Steve remained immobile, 'OK, get out of the way and let someone else have a go. You get down here.'

'Don't worry, miss,' the corporal said as he undid the harness. 'Happens to a lot of people.'

Steve climbed down the ladder, her legs shaking so much that she was afraid she might fall.

The sergeant looked at her. 'Sorry about the language, ma'am. Didn't realise it was a lady up there.' He jerked his head towards the temporary huts housing the admin offices. 'Major Henley will want to talk to you.'

Steve wanted to go and hide herself. She felt she would never be able to look the others in the face again, but as she trudged towards the hut Lomax ran after her and put a hand on her arm.

'Bad luck! It could have happened to any of us.'

'But it didn't, did it?' she snapped, torn between shame and fury at her own weakness. 'I let you all down.'

'No, you didn't. It was only a practice jump. You couldn't help it. It's nothing to be ashamed of. It's just one of those things.'

She forced a wan smile. 'Thanks, Graham. But that doesn't help. If I can't learn to parachute I'm useless, and that's all there is to it. I'll have to go. The CO wants me.'

Major Henley kept her waiting for ten minutes while he talked to the sergeant. She spent the time with her head in her hands, struggling to come to terms with what had happened. How could it be that she, always the daredevil, the one to climb to the top of the tallest trees and jump the most difficult fences, had suddenly been stricken with such cowardice?

When she was finally summoned into his office the major leaned back in his chair and looked her up and down.

'I hear you funked the jump.'

'Yes, sir. I'm sorry, sir.'

'What went wrong?'

'I'm just terrified of heights, sir.' She caught her breath. 'But I can get over it, sir. Let me try again. Please, give me another chance.'

Henley shook his head. 'No can do, I'm afraid. We can't risk sending someone out on a mission who might freeze at the crucial moment. Dropping agents is a tricky business at the best of times. If someone doesn't jump at the precise split second the green light goes on they could end up miles from the correct dropping zone. And they might cause other people to be dropped in the wrong place, too. In the worst case, it could mean the whole mission being aborted.'

'But if I can't drop I won't be able to get to France.' Steve almost wailed the words. 'I've done all the training. I can't pull out now.'

'Nonsense!' said the major, but his tone was gentler. 'There are other ways of getting there, you know. There's a chap called Déricourt who is organising regular flights in Lysanders. They can land on a pocket handkerchief, and I hear he's got a number of men and women in that way, and brought people out too. You could be sent in by that route. Or there's always the possibility of going in by sea.'

Steve drew a breath of relief as the spectre of total rejection faded, but at the core of her being there was still a nagging sense of failure. She might be able to continue with her mission, but she would always have the memory of that moment of cowardice at the top of the tower.

She said, 'That's good news, sir. Thank you very much. But even if I'm not going to be dropped, I'd still like to prove I can do it. Please let me try once more.'

The major studied her in silence for a moment. Then he said, 'OK. One more try. But if you mess up this time you're off the course. Right?'

'Understood, sir.'

He picked up the telephone. 'Sergeant, the ensign wants to try again. Get the equipment ready for her, will you.'

Steve swallowed. 'Now, sir?'

'Now. You know what they say about getting back on the horse, don't you?'

Steve knew very well. But she had never had any difficulty with climbing back on to her pony after a fall. This was different.

Walking out to the tower, she felt a strange numbness, as if she had taken a powerful soporific. She could hardly believe that she had insisted on going through the trauma she had just experienced for a second time. The sergeant saluted as she approached.

'Come to have another go, ma'am? Good for you.'

Her feet felt like lead as she dragged herself up the ladders. At the top she stood well back from the edge while the corporal fastened her into the harness.

'You'll be OK this time, miss,' he assured her.

She heard him shout down to the sergeant. 'Ready, Sarge!' Then came the instruction, 'Jump!' Steve closed her eyes, stumbled forwards a few paces and stepped into thin air. As she felt herself begin to fall she screamed aloud, partly from terror but also out of an upsurge of defiance. She would not be beaten!

The sergeant's voice came up to her. 'Keep your bleedin' feet together, ma'am!'

Steve opened her eyes and realised that she was falling but not hurtling out of control. She just had time to remember what she had been taught about letting her knees give and rolling with the impact before she hit the ground. She let herself go limp, rolled over and got up, amazed to find herself unhurt. From just behind her there was a round of applause. Lomax had obviously seen her walk back to the tower and had come out to watch.

He patted her on the back. 'Well done! I knew you wouldn't let it beat you.'

The next day they went up to make their first jump from an aircraft. They sat in a line with some other trainees from a different unit along the side of a superannuated bomber as it circled laboriously upwards. Steve was placed last, in case she froze again when the moment came. She was shivering with fear so violently that she was grateful for the noise of the engine, which prevented the others from hearing her teeth chattering. Suddenly she found her hand gripped in a warm male fist. It was Graham Lomax. Nothing was said, but he continued to hold her hand until the dispatcher got up and opened the door in the side of the plane.

They all stood up and clipped the lines that would open their parachutes to the running line along the side of the fuselage. Steve kept her eyes averted from the opening, fixing her gaze on the red light above the door. There were no windows so she could not see how far above the ground they were. She edged forwards, following the others as the leader moved to stand in the open doorway. The wait seemed interminable. Then the light went green and the first man disappeared. After that there was no time for thought. The men in front of her vanished, there was a shove on her back and she was out, falling through space. She wanted to scream, to shout for help, but the wind took her breath away. Then her parachute opened and suddenly she was not falling but floating, and below her the airfield and the surrounding countryside were laid out like the toy farm she had played with as a child. She threw back her head and uttered one word.

'Yes!'

She watched the ground coming up towards her, remembered her drill and landed neatly. As she battled to get her billowing parachute canopy under control Lomax came running over to her.

'Well done, Steve! It wasn't too bad, was it, after all?'

She agreed that it wasn't but later, when the euphoria had worn off, she found herself shaking again. She knew she had to make four more jumps, one of them in the dark, and she wondered whether she would be able to do it.

Somehow she got through the next two days, but instead

of getting easier it seemed to be harder each time to force herself to jump. Before the last night-time jump she was physically sick and spent the whole time while the plane circled to gain height worrying that she was going to throw up again. But when she was out and the 'chute was open she experienced an almost surreal sense of bliss. She was floating in a dark world with pale stars above her and below her the earth, where not a single pinprick of light showed. There was nothing by which to measure her rate of descent and she had the illusion that she could stay there for ever, suspended between earth and sky. She was so absorbed by this sensation that she failed to realise how close she was to the ground until it was almost too late. She landed awkwardly and felt one of her ankles give under her. When she got up, she discovered that to put any weight on it sent an arrow of pain up her leg.

She had to be helped into the truck that came to pick them up and had to grit her teeth to stop herself from whimpering aloud. All the effort and strain of the course, which had lasted for three months, and the terror of the last few days, came together with the pain in her leg and the thought that if her ankle was broken it might all be for nothing. It was too much.

The MO examined her ankle and sent her for an X-ray, which showed that she had suffered a bad sprain but there were no broken bones. She was given a sedative and put to bed in the infirmary.

When she rejoined the others at Dunham Massey the following morning she was told that an officer from SOE's HQ in Baker Street was waiting to see her.

A smart, pleasant-faced woman in captain's uniform rose from behind a desk as Steve hobbled into the room.

'I'm Vera Atkins, Intelligence Officer for F section. You seem to have had a bit of a rough time.'

'My own silly fault,' Steve said. 'I was daydreaming and not looking where I was going. I've made a bit of a duffer of myself, haven't I.'

'No,' Atkins said firmly. 'What you have done is show a very high degree of courage. Your instructors are in no doubt about what it cost you to go through with the course and they are united in their praise for you. In fact, all your instructors, all through the course, have had very positive things to say about you. They all agree that you are admirably suited for the work in front of you.'

'Then I will still be able to go?' Steve asked eagerly 'In spite of this?' She indicated her bandaged leg.

'Of course, but not until it is completely healed. But that doesn't matter. You are due for two weeks' leave anyway. Then there is final briefing to be carried out and last-minute checks. The earliest we could send you over is during the next moon period in the first few days of June. The MO tells me your leg should be perfectly fine by then. Where will you go for your leave?'

'Home, I suppose,' Steve murmured. It had never occurred to her that she might get another chance to see her parents before she was sent to France.

'What will you tell your parents about your injury?'

'Oh, that's no problem. I'll say I tripped over something in the blackout.'

'Fair enough. So, you can leave any time. I've made out a pass and a rail warrant for you. At the end of your leave you are to report to this address.' Vera rose and handed her a slip of paper. She held out her hand. 'Have a good leave – and a good rest. I'm sure you need it, and you certainly deserve it.'

In the common room Steve found Lomax preparing to leave, and it occurred to her for the first time that they might not meet again. They had been warned at Beaulieu that agents were rarely dropped to work with someone they already knew, for security reasons. They were both going south, so they shared a taxi to the station and caught the London train together.

On the platform at Euston Lomax said, 'Well, I guess this is it. I'll miss you, Steve. I wish you were going to be part of my team. Any chap who gets you as his courier will be very lucky.' Out of habit, they were both speaking French.

'I'll miss you, too,' she said. 'Thanks for everything, Graham. I don't think I'd have got through the course if it wasn't for you.'

'Rubbish!' he responded. 'You were never in danger of failing.'

Steve held out her hand. '*Bonne chance, mon ami.*'

'You too,' he said. He took her hand. 'Perhaps we'll run into each other again, when all this is over.'

'Yes, I hope so. Take care.'

'Don't worry, I will. *Au revoir,* Steve.'

'*Au revoir, mon cher.*' She leaned up and kissed him on the cheek and then turned and hurried towards the exit, so that he would not see that she was blinking back the tears. She took a taxi to Marylebone and caught the train to Princes Risborough.

Chapter Four

It was evening by the time she reached home. The light summer nights had arrived and the afterglow of the sunset was still staining the sky pink behind the beech trees, where rooks were cawing loudly as they squabbled over roosting places for the night. The dew was falling and the air smelt of freshly mown hay. Steve breathed deeply. This was the smell of home and it would be a long time before she smelt it again. She picked up her case, tucked her crutch under the other arm, and limped round to the back door. Her mother would probably be in the kitchen, and even if she wasn't the door would not be locked.

She pushed the door open and hopped over the threshold. 'Coo-ee! I'm home!'

Then she stopped short, staring. Roddy was standing on the far side of the kitchen table. He was in uniform and she could see that he was thinner than she remembered. His cheeks were hollow and there were lines around his eyes that had not been there the last time she had seen him. His face was deeply tanned and his hair, which had always been the colour of pale corn, was bleached almost silver, but it still fell forward in an unruly quiff over eyes that were the deepest cornflower blue.

All this she took in in the split second of silence while they faced each other. Then she said, 'Roddy! What are you doing here?'

'Your mother telephoned. I'm stationed at Cardington. It's only a few hours' drive.'

'I thought you were still in Malta.'

'Well, you would, wouldn't you.' His voice was tense. 'We seem to have lost touch. Why haven't you answered my letters?'

'What letters? I didn't get them. I've been on a course.'

'A bloody long course, by all accounts.' He took a step towards her. 'What's happened to your leg?'

'I fell over. Tripped over something in the blackout. It's just a sprain.'

He was gazing at her with puzzled, wounded eyes, and the sight sent stabs of anguish through her heart.

'Diana, darling, what was that last letter all about? I've been worried sick since I got it. What did you mean by saying that I shouldn't wait for you? That if I met someone else I shouldn't feel bound.'

'I didn't want you to miss out on being happy with someone else, that's all. If anything happened to me, I mean.'

'But why should it? After all, I'm much more likely to be killed than you are.' He searched her face. 'Are you trying to tell me you've found someone else?'

'No! No, there could never be anyone else for me. You know that.'

'But you know there could never be anyone else for me. We've always said that, ever since we were kids. I don't understand what's going on.'

Steve shook her head. She was tired and her ankle was hurting and she felt unable to cope with an emotional scene. 'I just wanted you to know that we might not see each other for a bit and you shouldn't hang on waiting for me if you found someone else.'

He came round the table. 'What do you mean, we might not see each other? What are you planning to do?' He gripped her by the arms and her crutch fell to the floor with a clatter. 'My God, you've volunteered for something, haven't you?'

The temptation to pour out the whole story was almost too great. She gazed up at him through eyes blurred with tears and shook her head dumbly. 'I can't.' The words forced themselves from her throat. 'Please, don't ask me!'

His expression had changed and she saw dawning comprehension. 'You speak French like a native. Fool that I am, I should have guessed! I've met chaps who were shot down over France, who escaped with the help of agents out there. But surely to God they are not sending women to do that sort of work, are they?'

Again, she could only shake her head. He pulled her into his arms and held her tightly. 'It's all right. It's all right, my darling. You don't have to say anything. I understand. But why did you have to do it? Isn't it enough for one of us to be risking his life?'

'Why did you volunteer to fly Spitfires?' she asked, her voice muffled against his tunic. 'Why should I sit at home safely?'

He loosened his hold on her and drew back so that he could look into her face. 'I should have known. You've always been a daredevil. My sweet, brave love!'

He kissed her and she felt the tension drain out of her body. 'Don't let's have any more nonsense about finding someone else,' he whispered. 'I'll wait till the crack of doom if there's the faintest chance of us being together.'

'So will I,' she answered. 'You know that.'

They kissed again and then he murmured, 'But we don't have to wait, do we? Here we are, now. I have to go back tomorrow but tonight is all our own.'

She clung to him, feeling his body mould itself to hers. More than anything else, she longed to give herself up to him, to spend the night in his arms. And after all, why shouldn't she? Thousands of other girls were dispensing with the formality of a wedding ring and snatching what few hours of happiness the war allowed them. Then she remembered. She could not let it happen. If she did, he would know that she had been unfaithful to him. And then what would all her protestations be worth? He would be terribly hurt. He might reject her altogether. How could she risk that happening when they were both about to go back into danger?

She pulled away. 'No, Roddy, we can't.'

'Why not?'

'My parents would find out. Where are they, by the way?'

'They went to bed. They're dying to see you but they had the tact to realise that we needed some time together. Do you honestly think they would blame us?'

'I don't know. Perhaps not.' She was desperately trying to think of an excuse that he would believe. 'But we shouldn't. It's not right.'

'Oh, darling! It could be our last night – the last for a long time, anyway. Surely even God couldn't regard it as wrong.'

He was holding her, caressing her face, kissing the side of her neck and her resistance was almost at an end. She pushed him away, almost violently.

'No! Listen. There's something I have to tell you.'

He looked into her eyes, frowning. 'There is someone else.'

'No! Well, not really – not anyone that matters but . . .' She dropped her eyes, focusing on a button on his tunic. How could she make him understand? She went on, her voice scarcely more than a whisper. 'There was someone. It was only once and I wasn't in love with him. But he was going to France the next night and he was so frightened and so lonely . . .'

She looked up, her eyes begging his forgiveness. She could not tell from his expression what he was feeling. He said slowly, 'You slept with him?'

'Yes.'

'Did you . . . was it good?'

'No, not really. He was very sweet, but it was his first time too. But I know it meant a lot to him so I'm glad I did it – I think I'd do the same again. But I've felt so guilty ever since, about us. Can you . . . can you forgive me?'

'Is that why you volunteered?'

'Partly. No, I was already thinking about it. I suppose it just gave me the push I needed. But I thought, if anything happened to me, you need never know.'

'And did you really think I would rather have some . . . some idealised memory of you, rather than the real, living person?'

'I was afraid when you knew you wouldn't want me any more; and I couldn't bear that.'

He put his hands on her shoulders. 'Darling, I'm no saint. I know we promised to be faithful to each other but we've hardly seen each other for four years. I'm flesh and blood, after all.'

'There have been other women?'

'A couple. No one I really cared about. So if you can forgive me, I've certainly no right to blame you. I think you did the right thing.'

The release of tension was so great that she almost collapsed. He pulled her close, stroking her hair. 'Poor girl. You're absolutely done in. I shouldn't ask you to do anything tonight. Come on, bed's the place for you.'

Before she could protest he swept her off her feet and carried her to the door. She wrapped her arms round his neck and hid her face in the angle of his neck, breathing in the smell of him. He carried her up the stairs and into her room and laid her on the bed.

'I'll get your case.'

When he came back she said, 'Wait for me while I have a wash, will you?' He put his head on one side and lifted an eyebrow quizzically and she went on, 'Oh, that's not fair of me. It's asking too much.'

'I'll wait,' he said.

When she came back from the bathroom he was sitting on the end of her bed and her heart lurched at the sight of his drooping head. She sat beside him and put her hand in his.

'It's our last chance, darling – for a while, at least. I'm not that tired.'

Steve woke the next morning to find the room full of sunshine and her mother standing by her bed with a cup of tea. She looked at the other side of the bed and was relieved to find it empty. She could not tell from her mother's expression whether she had guessed what had happened or not. She sat up, feeling as she used to feel on the first day of the summer holidays from school. Whatever was ahead of her, she had two whole weeks of leave, the sun was shining and Roddy loved her. It was enough.

Roddy had to leave after lunch. She went out with him to the shed where he had garaged his car, the 'old banger' that had once let them down so badly when she had gone AWOL from preliminary training at Overthorpe, and they clung to each other and kissed.

'Till the crack of doom, remember,' he said.

'Yes, I won't forget,' she answered.

'We'll get through this,' he said, with conviction. 'I can feel it. One day the war will be over, and it can't be much longer now. All we have to do is hang on.'

'Yes,' she whispered, 'that's right. Just hang on.'

He kissed her once more and began to say 'Good . . .' but she put her fingers on his lips.

'Don't say goodbye, please. And don't say good luck, either. Do you know what the French say when . . . well, when someone is leaving and they might need a bit of luck? They say *merde*. It's vulgar, I know, but it's a bit like people in the theatre telling each other to break a leg.'

'All right.' He smiled down at her. '*Merde* it is, then.'

She watched him get into the car and stood gazing after the dust cloud it raised as he sped away down the farm track.

For the first few days of her leave Steve felt as if she were living in a dream. After the struggles and tensions of the past months the peaceful life on the farm seemed unreal, all the more so because she was unable to be part of it as she always had been. She wanted to plunge back into the routine that she knew so well, helping with the milking, feeding the hens, giving a hand with the haymaking, but her damaged ankle prevented her. Instead she spent those days sitting in a deckchair in the garden with her foot up on a stool. When they could spare the time her mother or father or one of the Land Girls came and chatted to her, but there was a lot of work to do on the farm and very often she was left alone for long periods. In many ways that was a relief. They had all got used, from the time she first joined the FANY, to the fact that she could not talk about her work, so no one asked her awkward questions. Nevertheless, she was still on edge in case she let something drop that would indicate that she was about to embark on a much more dangerous mission.

She tried to read but could not concentrate and found it easier to lie back and listen to the bees buzzing in the blossom of the apple tree above her head and inhale the scent of lavender from the nearby border until she drifted into a light doze. It was only when her lassitude began to evaporate after three or four days that she realised how much the course had taken out of her.

As soon as she could put her foot to the ground without too much pain she limped into the kitchen to help her mother with the constant task of preparing meals for hungry farm workers. Then, as she grew stronger, she began to wander round the farm, renewing her acquaintance with the various dogs, cats and pigs who inhabited the farmyard and then venturing farther to greet the placid Friesian cows, every one of which she knew by name. Eventually, she made it up to the paddock where her beloved mare Scheherazade was grazing. The horse welcomed her with delighted whinnies, and it occurred to Steve that she could have gone riding, but her mother had done as she had suggested and the mare had been turned out to grass and her shoes had been removed. Steve turned away with a sigh and told herself that after all it was probably better not to get back into the habit, when she was going to be away again so soon.

At night she dreamed of Roddy and went over in her mind every moment of their night together. He had aroused in her a passionate response that Philippe's fumbling attempts had never touched. He had been tender and – she had to admit it to herself – skilled. She had not asked him to elaborate on his previous experiences but she came to the conclusion that rather than feeling jealousy she should be grateful. There was something else to be thankful for, too. She had no worries about becoming pregnant. He had taken care of that.

As the days went by, her initial relief at being home was replaced by a growing impatience to get back to the real business of life. Also, she found it more and more difficult to find things to talk about with her parents when there were so many subjects she could not touch upon. Saying goodbye all over again was hard, but it was a relief when her leave came to an end and she could set out for London.

The address she had been given was a private flat in Richmond Court, Bayswater. From behind closed doors leading off the hall she could hear the murmur of a number of voices. The flat was like a beehive, every cell buzzing with activity. She was ushered into a room that appeared to double as a bedroom, where she found Vera Atkins and Jeanne Borrel waiting for her. They greeted her warmly and enquired about her ankle. Then she heard a door close somewhere nearby and Vera said, 'I think Colonel Buckmaster is free now. Come this way.'

She opened a door and stood back for Steve to pass. She stepped through and found herself, to her embarrassment, in a bathroom – a very glamorous bathroom, to be sure, all fitted out in black marble, but hardly the place she expected to meet her commanding officer. Buckmaster rose from a folding stool and offered his hand.

'Sorry about the unconventional surroundings. Every room in the place is being used for one purpose or another.'

He was younger than she had expected, a tall man with a long nose and a clear, steady gaze. He invited her to take a seat on another stool opposite him and took up a manila folder.

'Now then, let's get down to business. You'll be aware from your training that a very important part of your life from now on will be your cover story. You may not also have realised that in fact you will have two aliases. One, the name under which you will live in France and the other the operational code name by which you will be known here and to your fellow agents. Let's deal with that first. Would you like to choose something – just a single French Christian name?'

Steve had been prepared for this by her experience with agents at Gaynes Hall. 'I'd like to be called Suzette, if that's all right.' She had chosen the name because crêpes Suzette had been the first dish she had learned to cook in Paris.

'Suzette?' Buckmaster nodded. 'That sounds fine to me. Vera?'

Vera Atkins, who was standing in the doorway, nodded in return. 'Yes, we don't have anyone else on our books using that name.'

'Suzette it is, then. Now, to the more complex question of your cover story. We've given a lot of thought to this, naturally. It must, of course, be consistent with the circumstances in which you might find yourself when you arrive in France. You will need to have some means of subsistence, some reason for being where you are, if you are to avoid suspicion. Our first thought, in view of your background, was that you might work on a farm, but then we realised that there is no way you would pass as a simple peasant girl. You are quite obviously a young woman of good education and, if I can use a rather dated term, good breeding. So we have come up with a story that we feel bridges that divide very nicely.' He opened the file and passed her a small buff-coloured card headed *Carte d'Identité* and bearing the name Marguerite Duclos. The space for the photograph was empty. 'So,' Buckmaster went on, 'from now on you are Marguerite Duclos, the daughter of the late M. Bernard and

Mme Marie-Louise Duclos, of the Manoir de Belmesnil in Normandy. All this is verifiable by the Germans should they wish to check. The Duclos family did indeed live at that address and they did have a daughter named Marguerite, whose birth was registered at the mairie in Rouen. We even have a copy of the birth certificate.' He passed another piece of paper to Steve. 'The Duclos family were prosperous landowners and Marguerite grew up at the Manoir, where she would no doubt have had a very similar childhood to your own. But Bernard Duclos was not a farmer. He was a member of the Diplomatic Corps, and when Marguerite was twelve he was posted to Geneva as an attaché at the French embassy there. His wife and daughter went with him and Marguerite was enrolled at a boarding school in Vevey. This gives credence to the fact that your French has a slight Swiss intonation. She remained at the school for the next five years. Then, tragically for them but fortuitously for us, in 1938, when Marguerite was just eighteen, the whole family was killed in a motoring accident. It took place near Geneva and was reported in the Swiss newspapers but, as far as we have been able to ascertain, not in the French press.' He passed a small sheaf of newspaper cuttings across the desk. 'Now, this is where we begin to depart from the truth. Our story is that you, Marguerite, were not in the car at the time. You were ill in bed or staying with friends, I leave it to you to make up the details, but in any case you survived the crash.'

'Won't there be a death certificate, then, as well as a birth certificate?' Steve queried.

'Of course, but in Geneva and the Swiss guard their neutrality with great punctiliousness. I cannot see them allowing the Nazis to check their records. This is where Marguerite's story fits in so well with our requirements.'

'So what did she . . . what did I do after my parents were killed?'

'Well, there is one more piece of the jigsaw to be put in place before we discuss that. It seems that M. Duclos was an inveterate gambler and when he died he left behind him massive debts. So there you are, Marguerite, an orphan and destitute. You returned to France, to your childhood home, and sold off most of the land to pay your father's debts, but you did manage to retain the manor house itself until the outbreak of war. Then, in the early months of the war, the house was requisitioned and became the HQ of a battalion of the Lancashire Fusiliers – which, of course, is how we come to be so well informed about the affairs of the Duclos family. In reality, all the property went to a cousin but it is unlikely the Gestapo would enquire that deeply. After Dunkirk the Manoir was taken over by the German army but, again fortunately for us, it was completely destroyed by Allied bombing the following year. You, meanwhile, I would suggest, had been forced to find work on a local farm. Recently, you have become increasingly unnerved by rumours of an imminent Allied invasion and, realising that western France is likely to be fought over again, you decided to try to make your way back to old friends in Switzerland. Of course, when you reach the border you are not allowed to cross, so now you find yourself stranded on the French side of the border and in need of a job to survive.'

'Is that where I'm going? Eastern France, near the border?' Steve asked.

'You will get the precise details of where you are being sent nearer the actual time, but in general terms that is what we have in mind at the moment. Does that suit you?'

Steve considered. 'I've never been to that area. But perhaps that's just as well. No one is likely to recognise me.'

'There's one more thing,' Buckmaster went on. 'It struck us as unlikely that a young woman like yourself would not have a husband or at least a fiancé by now. So we have provided you with one.' He passed a photograph of a young man in the uniform of a lieutenant in the French army across the desk. 'His name is Claude Montauban and he was killed in the retreat to Dunkirk.'

Steve turned the picture over. On the back was written in French, 'To my dearest love, Claude'. Where did this come from?' she asked.

'You don't need to know. Suffice it to say that he was the fiancé of a young woman who is now working for us. She has allowed us to use it.' He closed the folder and passed it across to Steve. 'All the relevant information is in there. I want you to take it away with you and study it until you are familiar with every detail. Any gaps, you must fill in from your own imagination. Jeanne will help you but over the next few days you have to become Marguerite Duclos. Her life must be as real to you as your own – more so, in fact. You must think her thoughts, dream her dreams. Your memories must become her memories. Do you understand?'

Steve took the file and stared at its anonymous cover. A dead woman's shoes. It seemed like theft to appropriate them for her own purposes, but she knew it was necessary. 'I'll do my best,' she said.

'I know you will,' Buckmaster said with a smile. 'Now, there are various other formalities to be gone through. First of all, you have an appointment with the dentist.'

'My teeth are fine,' Steve said, surprised. 'I had a check-up just before Christmas.'

'Do you have any fillings?' Vera Atkins asked.

'One or two.'

'Perhaps you don't know that English dentists fill teeth with amalgam, while French ones always use gold. One look in your mouth would prove to any interrogator that you are not a Frenchwoman.'

'One of them was done in Paris.'

'In that case you're lucky, but any others will have to be replaced. After that, Jeanne will take you to the flat where you are going to stay for the next few days. Tomorrow, you have an appointment with Mr Marks, our head of coding, at eleven o'clock to establish your personal code. Do you have any questions?'

Steve shook her head. She was already struggling to assimilate all this new information.

'Well, if there's anything else,' Buckmaster said, 'there will be plenty of opportunities to ask later. I think that's enough for now.'

The visit to the dentist was not a pleasant experience. As he drilled away at two perfectly sound fillings Steve found herself reflecting that this might only be a foretaste of what she had to endure in the months to come. It was a relief to get away to the pleasant flat that was to be her home for the time being and to relax in Jeanne's easygoing company.

Next morning a photographer arrived and Jeanne helped Steve to dress her hair in a more typically French style before he took her picture. After him came a tailor, who measured her for new clothes. Then, at eleven, the doorbell rang again and Jeanne ushered in a slight, dark-haired young man.

'Suzette, this is Leo Marks, our head of coding.'

As they shook hands Steve studied him with interest. So this was the man whose brilliance Frankie had spoken of with such enthusiasm. As they sat down she asked, 'Do you mind my asking, are you connected with the Marks of Marks and Spencer?'

He laughed softly. 'Only remotely. Actually my father is in the antique books trade. He has a shop in the Charing Cross Road, number eighty-four. You may have seen it?'

Steve shook her head. 'No. I'm afraid not. I'm not really a bookish sort of person.'

'So.' He leaned slightly towards her. 'What are your interests? Tell me a bit about yourself. I ask for a reason that will become clear shortly.'

Steve told him about growing up on the farm, about her horse and her love of the countryside, and after a little he nodded and opened a file he had brought with him.

'I'm sure you will have been introduced to the mysteries of coding at Beaulieu, so you will know that each agent has an individual code based on a few lines of poetry that they have committed to memory. You take five words at random from the poem, give each letter a number and then, using the code sheets I shall give you, you transpose those numbers into different letters, which can then be transmitted in Morse. The trouble with that is that most people choose a fairly well-known piece, which means that if the German cryptographers, who are at least as well versed in English literature as most agents, can break a single word they can usually guess the whole poem. And that in turn means that they can decode any subsequent messages. So what I have done is to ask various people to come up with some lines of verse that are completely new and will be known only to themselves, the agent concerned and the people whose business it is to decode that agent's messages.'

Steve smiled. 'Yes, I know about that.' Then, seeing Marks looked slightly alarmed, she explained, 'I have friends in the FANY who worked at Grendon Underwood.'

'Ah.' Marks nodded. 'Well, to proceed. I try to select

verses that will have some meaning for the individual concerned and I think I have just the thing for you. It's not great poetry, admittedly, but I think you will find that the sentiment behind it is something you can relate to.'

He handed Steve a slip of paper and she read:

> *This land I love is green and fair*
> *With hills and fields and rivers running by.*
> *This land I leave will still be there*
> *So I'm saying au revoir and not goodbye.*

A week later Buckmaster came to the flat.

'I've come to tell you that you'll be going out during the next moon period, probably the first or second of June. So, it's time to brief you on exactly where you are going. The first thing to say is that, in view of the accident to your ankle, we have decided not to risk dropping you by parachute. Instead, we are going to send you in by Lysander.'

Steve caught her breath. She was not going to have to parachute again. Thank God! *Thank God!*

'The disadvantage of that,' Buckmaster went on, 'is that the Lysander doesn't have the range of the aircraft we use for *parachutages* so you will have to be landed somewhere well short of your target and make your way there by train. Let me show you . . .' He unrolled a map of France on the table. 'This is where you will be working, in the Jura, to the east of Chalon-sur-Saône. We're sending you to a well-established *réseau* called Acrobat. You'll be aware that all the circuits have code names that are trades or professions. The man in charge of Acrobat is one of our best agents. His code name is Bob. But the Lysander will land you here.' He pointed to an area on the map just north of the Loire. 'The *réseau* that deals with Lysander operations is called Farrier and you will be met by a man calling himself Clément. He will take you to the nearest railway station and see you on your way. You will take the train to Chalon and then from there to Louhans – here.' His finger stabbed at the map. 'When you get there you must make your way to a café in the Rue St Honoré called the Bar du Centre. I shall give you a street map of Louhans so you will have no difficulty finding it. In the bar you will ask the waiter if he knows the address of Mme Marie Arnault. That is the password. He will then let Bob know you are waiting. When he comes Bob will say, "I'm sorry, but Mme Arnault has left to visit her cousin in Dijon." That way you will know that he is the right man. Now, don't look so alarmed. All this is written out for you on this sheet detailing your mission. You will have time to commit it to memory before you leave.'

'What will I be doing with the Acrobat *réseau*?' Steve asked.

'Your job is to act as a courier. Bob already has one girl, Paulette, working with him but his *réseau* is growing and now covers quite a wide area. He has asked for someone else to help. He will find a safe house for you and you may need to adjust your cover story to fit in with whatever he has in mind. He's an experienced agent, so you can trust his judgement implicitly.'

He stayed for a short while longer, going over details, and finally said, 'Now, I can't tell you exactly when you will be leaving. That is in the hands of the RAF. On the day, you will get a phone call some time before noon and then a car will collect you at five o'clock. If you haven't heard anything by midday that means you are not going that night, so the rest of the day is your own.'

The following morning Vera Atkins arrived at the flat with a suitcase.

'These are your clothes for France.'

She opened the case and laid the garments out on Steve's bed. There was a dark grey jacket and skirt, clearly not new, but of good-quality fabric and bearing the labels of a well-respected Swiss tailoring firm.

'We thought Marguerite would probably have hung on to one good outfit from her palmier days in Switzerland,' Vera explained.

With the suit there was a cream silk blouse and a smart little green hat. Then there was a navy summer dress patterned with small white sprigs of flowers, a pair of brown corduroy slacks, two shirts, a jersey, an overcoat and two pairs of shoes, one with a small heel, the other a pair of stout brogues. At the bottom of the case were two sets of flannelette underwear, not glamorous but practical. Examining all these items, Steve was impressed by the attention to detail. All the labels were either French or Swiss and every seam and button spoke of Continental tailoring.

There was a second case, a small attaché case. This held a sponge bag containing soap and toothpaste and such items of make-up as were available in France at the time, a hairbrush and comb, a nightdress and some handkerchiefs. Lifting them out, Vera showed Steve that there was a hidden compartment inside the lining and in that there was a Colt .32 and a sum in French banknotes that made her gasp. There were also, wrapped in tissue paper, a set of the crystals needed to operate a short-wave radio set.

'The money is mainly for Bob,' Vera said. 'Five million francs. The rest is for you. You will need to appear to have a job, to back up your story, but there is no need for you to rely on that financially. You may need money to bribe people, or to travel or for emergencies. The crystals are needed to replace the ones in the Acrobat circuit's radio. As you know, they are very fragile. Obviously, if the Germans were to search you in anything more than a cursory fashion they would find these and there is no way you could talk your way out of possessing them. So, if there seems to be any likelihood of a thorough search you must ditch the case. Hide it if you can, somewhere you may be able to return to, but if you can't, just try to leave it somewhere so that you can deny all knowledge of it.'

'What about the money?' Steve asked.

'Don't worry about that. You are much more valuable to us. The money can be replaced if necessary. Now, you will only have to carry this until you meet up with Bob. After that, you can just take your share of the money. This is a money belt, which you can wear next to your skin if you need to carry large sums. Otherwise, find a safe place and hide most of it. Remember, Marguerite is not well off. Don't draw attention to yourself by spending too freely.'

As she was leaving Vera said, 'Oh, by the way, wear those clothes from now on. You must feel at home in them.'

There was one more job to do. Vera had brought with her a bundle of postcards, all bearing Egyptian scenes – pyramids and camels and the Sphinx from various angles.

'This is where your family will be told you have been sent,' Vera said. 'You must write the cards and we will see that they are posted at intervals from Cairo.'

It took Steve an hour of chewing her pen to compose enough suitably anodyne remarks to fill them all.

Two days later the call came. Steve was to be ready to leave that evening. Jeanne watched carefully as she dressed and packed, making sure that she put nothing on or in her case that was not French. Together they checked her papers for the hundredth time and went over what she would say to anyone who challenged her on her way to the rendezvous with Bob.

At five a large black car slid to standstill outside the block of flats and Steve was surprised to see Colonel Buckmaster and Vera get out. Vera rang the bell and Steve followed Jeanne down to the street. It was a warm summer evening and she felt overdressed in the corduroy trousers, which she had chosen as most suitable for the journey. Buckmaster greeted her and then took a small package out of his pocket.

'We like to give everyone a little parting gift. Something to tell you how much we value you and that you might be able to pawn if you ever needed to raise some cash in a hurry.' He shook her hand. 'You are a remarkable young woman and we are all in your debt. Good luck.'

Steve found it hard to respond because her throat was suddenly tight, but a moment later she found herself in the back of the car, with Jeanne beside her and Vera sitting up beside the driver. She had always imagined that she would leave from Gaynes Hall, as she had seen so many others leave, but instead the car headed south out of London and was soon making its way through the Surrey countryside. It was the most beautiful time of the year. Lilac trees were heavy with blossom in the cottage gardens and in among the garden plots, most of which had been dug over to grow vegetables, delphiniums and lupins showed blue and purple. Farmers were out in the fields, making the most of the good weather to bring in the hay. Steve watched it all going past the car windows but it was like watching a film – pretty but unreal. The words of her code poem came back to her and she repeated silently, 'I'm saying au revoir and not goodbye.'

She remembered the package that Buckmaster had given her and opened it. It contained a solid-gold powder compact. She held it up to Jeanne.

'What am I supposed to do with this?'

'Use it. Don't worry. We all get one. The men get cuff links. It's a little insurance policy. And after all, Marguerite might well have been given such a thing, before her father died.'

At the airfield they were conducted to a mess hut where a table was laid ready and they were served with an excellent meal. Steve tried to do it justice but her throat was dry and everything tasted like sawdust. When they had eaten, Vera took her into a small room with curtained windows.

'Now, this may seem very strange but I'm going to search you. I know you've dressed and packed very carefully but we have to be sure that you have absolutely nothing on you that could give the Germans a clue that you're not French. You'd be surprised how many times we find that agents have kept on their own underwear because they don't like the stuff we've provided. Or they have English cigarettes or London bus tickets in their pockets. So you understand why I'm doing this?'

Steve had to take off her clothes and Vera examined every item, checking the labels and turning out pockets. Then she checked her cases in the same manner. When she was satisfied and Steve was dressed again she was given a set of fleece-lined overalls to put on over her clothes and a pair of lined boots. Then they went out in the fading evening light to where the Lysander was parked on the tarmac with its propellers turning lazily. It looked absurdly small to Steve, with its two cockpits one behind the other, like a child's toy.

The pilot, a lanky young man with a cheerful grin, shook hands with her and said, 'Happy to have you aboard.'

Vera shook her hand, too. 'Take care, Suzette. Good luck.'

Jeanne gave her a hug. *'Merde alors!'*

Steve climbed into the rear cockpit and her cases were piled in behind her. The pilot gave her a flying helmet to wear and showed her where to plug in the leads that came out of it so that she would be able to hear and speak to him. The cockpit cover was slid shut over her head, the pilot climbed in and she heard him asking ground control for permission to take off. The engine roared and Vera and Jeanne waved. Then they were taxiing across the grass, picking up speed. There were a few bumps, then she felt the nose of the plane lift and the ground dropped away beneath them.

It had all happened with a dreamlike inevitability. She realised that at the back of her mind she had always had the feeling that there would be a moment when she would be able to make the final decision, to go or not to go. But now she understood that that moment had passed months ago, in that dusty room in the Northumberland Hotel.

Chapter Five

After a while the pilot's voice came over her headphones. 'Just crossing the coast now.'

Steve looked down. It was almost dark by this time but she could make out the white line of the breakers. *My last glimpse of England*, she thought, and tried without success to conjure up some emotion. They flew low over the Channel to escape detection, and by the time they reached the French coast it was night and the full moon was rising in a clear sky.

The pilot said, 'Might get a bit of flak for the next few minutes. Don't worry if the old girl jinks about a bit.'

Almost as he spoke two white cotton-wool puffs appeared to their right and a second later Steve heard two low detonations. For the next few minutes she had to hold on tight as the little plane dived and climbed and banked and the white puffs exploded around them. Then the plane levelled out and the anti-aircraft fire was left behind them and she realised that she had not been afraid in the same way that she had been afraid of the parachute jumps. In fact, it had been rather exciting, like a ride at the funfair.

The plane flew on over the darkened countryside and Steve found her eyelids drooping. The tension of the day, together with the large meal, was having its effect. She let herself doze until the pilot's voice roused her.

'Should be over the landing ground any minute. Look out for the lights.' Steve scanned the ground below them. They were flying very low now and she could make out a wide, level plain, broken by the occasional darker patches of woodland. Over to her right she could see the broad ribbon of the River Loire reflecting the moonlight. She had driven across this area before, on the way to holidays in the south, and remembered the level plateau between Paris and Orleáns. It would be growing maize and wheat now, and she wondered where they would find a place to land.

'There they are, the beauties!' the pilot exclaimed.

Steve looked ahead and saw the lights; three tiny pinpoints laid out in a straight line and two others at right angles at one end. She had learned at Beaulieu how to do this. The straight line marked the landing strip and the two at right angles were at the up-wind end. Below them another light began to flash. *Dot, dot, dot, dash. Pause. Dot, dot, dot, dash.* The Morse sign for the letter V. It was the agreed code signal.

She heard the pilot's voice again, but not speaking to her this time. He was talking on the S-phone, the latest invention that allowed pilots to communicate with a reception party on the ground. He said, 'OK. I'm coming in.'

They had overflown the lights by now and the little plane made a steep banking turn, circled once and dropped towards the lights, side-slipping to lose height. The wheels kissed the soil, bounced, came down again and ran on, bumping over uneven ground. They stopped short of the last light, turned, taxied back and turned again into the wind, ready for take-off. Steve was wide awake now, her fingers unfastening the straps that held her, pulling off the helmet. She knew that speed was vital at this point. Their approach might have alerted a German lookout post. The longer the plane was on the ground, the greater the chance of being caught.

Three dark figures were running across the field towards her. She pushed back the cockpit cover and struggled out, cumbersome in her bulky overalls. As she dropped to the ground the first man reached her.

'Suzette?'

'Yes. Clément?'

'That's me. Welcome to France.'

A second man pulled her cases out of the plane and dropped them down to her. The third gripped her arm for a second. 'Good luck! I'll give your love to Blighty.' Then he hoisted himself into the cockpit and Steve realised that the flight had a dual purpose, to take an agent home as well as to deliver her. It was a comforting thought. She pulled off her overalls and handed them up to him.

'Come.' Clément tugged her arm and picked up a case. She grabbed the smaller bag and moved away from the plane, which revved its engines and rolled forwards. In a moment it was airborne and they watched as it turned, gaining height, and headed for England, waggling its wings in farewell. Meanwhile, the second man had gathered up the stakes to which bicycle lamps had been fastened to mark the landing strip. The whole operation had taken no more than three minutes.

Clément led her to the edge of a small copse at one corner of the field and showed her three bicycles hidden among bushes beside a farm track. He fastened her suitcase to the carrier of one of them and the attaché case to another.

'You can ride a bike?'

'Yes, of course.'

'It's not far. There is a farm two kilometres away where you can rest. Keep close to me.'

Steve mounted her bike and they bumped away along the farm track, the second man following behind. They rode without lights, relying on the moonlight. Soon the track joined a narrow lane and the going was easier. Clément set a good pace and Steve reflected that it was just as well that riding horses had given her strong leg muscles. At a junction in the road the second man left them with a low-voiced *'Bonne nuit'* and shortly afterwards Clément turned off the lane into another track and dismounted in front of the dark bulk of a farmhouse. He whistled a few bars of *'Gentille alouette'* and a door opened and Steve was ushered into a long, low room with a range at one end and a scrubbed deal table in the middle. A hurricane lamp hung from the rafters, and apart from that the only illumination was the glow from the range.

The man who had opened the door was in late middle age, short and square with powerful shoulders and iron-grey hair that stuck out round a face the colour of mahogany. He held out his hand to Steve. 'Mademoiselle, we are honoured to have you under our roof. Anyone who is willing to help us drive *les sales Boches* out of our country has only to ask. Everything we have is at your command.'

His wife, a little round woman, stepped forward and shook hands in her turn. 'My husband speaks for both of us. But you do not want to stand here listening to speeches. Please, sit down. There is food and wine. Make yourself at home. *Faites comme chez vous.*'

Steve sat. She had been in many farmhouse kitchens, both at home and in France, and this one, with its hams hanging from the ceiling and its oak dresser displaying big, chipped plates that spoke of large family meals, seemed comfortingly familiar. Her hostess placed a plate of charcuterie in front of her and carved chunks from a big, round loaf. There was a dish of butter that would have represented a month's ration in England.

The farmer poured home-distilled Calvados into chipped glasses and they drank to victory and death to *les Boches*. Soon she began to feel sleepy again and had to stifle a yawn.

Seeing it, Clément said, 'You have to get the first train, at seven fifteen. The station is twenty minutes' ride from here and you have to buy a ticket, so we will leave here just after six thirty. Rest until then. I will wake you.'

It was almost 3 a.m. The farmer's wife showed her the earth closet in the yard and then led her through to a bedroom with a big, old-fashioned double bed in it. Steve lay down without undressing and fell asleep.

Clément roused her as promised soon after six and she went outside and had a quick wash under the pump. Then she changed into the dark suit, which seemed more appropriate for a train journey. After a breakfast of bread and honey and 'coffee' made from roasted wheat she said goodbye to the farmer and his wife and set off for the station with Clément.

Steve felt conspicuous as they cycled along the country lanes. The local people were up already, heading out to work in the fields.

'What will you say if someone asks who I am?' she enquired.

'You are my cousin, visiting from Orléans,' Clément replied.

At the little country station of Bellegarde, Clément unstrapped her suitcase from the carrier of his bike and took hold of the handlebars of hers.

'*Au revoir, ma cousine, et bon voyage,*' he said, and kissed her formally on both cheeks. Then he turned and rode away, leading her bike. Steve stood and looked after him for a moment, feeling suddenly very much alone.

She picked up her case and went into the station. There

were two men lounging against a wall and it struck her as she passed that they were not local people. They were dressed for the city, but something about them suggested they were the sort you would not want to encounter in a city street at night. They followed her into the station and queued up behind her at the ticket desk. She knew that she would have to change trains at Bourges but she had intended to buy a through ticket to Chalon-sur-Saône. Instead, she bought one to Bourges and heard the two men behind her ask for the same destination.

When the train came, they got into a compartment a little farther back. She wondered whether she was being paranoid, whether the training at Beaulieu had made her over-suspicious. But she could not rid herself of the feeling that the two men did not belong. She got up and carried her case into the corridor, and when the train stopped at Aubigny she let everyone else get off and new passengers get on. Then, just as the guard blew his whistle, she dropped her case on to the platform and jumped out after it. As the train gathered speed she saw one of the men looking out of the window and knew from his face that she had been right to be suspicious.

There was another hazard ahead of her. A young German soldier from the Feldgendarmerie was checking everyone's papers at the exit. Steve paused and drew a deep breath. She had been assured that her identity card was perfect, according to the latest information, but she had been warned, too, that these documents were frequently changed in order to catch forgeries. This would be the first time hers was put to the test. She took it out of her handbag and walked as confidently as she could towards the exit.

The soldier was obviously bored with his work. He glanced at Steve's papers, then looked up at her face and gave her the sort of smile a young man gives when he meets the eyes of an attractive woman. Then he nodded and she passed on. Outside the station she paused to check the timetable on a notice board. The next train was in one hour. She passed the time wandering round the town and drinking coffee at a pavement café.

The journey to Bourges was uneventful, and when she changed trains Steve felt fairly confident that no one had followed her. She had a shock, however, when the train pulled in. It was crammed with German soldiers. She struggled along the corridor for some way but came to the conclusion that she was not going to find a seat so she reconciled herself to sitting on her case for the rest of the journey.

A minute or two later the door of the nearest compartment opened and a soldier came out. He clicked his heels and said in broken French, 'Madame, we cannot see you sitting in the corridor while we sit in comfort. Please, take my seat.'

Steve hesitated. She had no wish to be taken for a collaborator, but on the other hand she did not want to antagonise the Germans. She concluded that the most natural thing to do would be to accept. The soldier put her case up on the rack and offered to put her attaché case with it but she thanked him and refused, saying that she might need something out of it. His companions moved up so that she could have a corner seat. They were all extremely polite. One offered her a cigarette, which she refused, another chocolate, which she accepted for fear that another refusal would seem rude. There was some attempt at conversation but none of them had a very good command of French and, to Steve's relief, they soon gave up. She sat clutching the attaché case on her lap, scarcely able to believe that she was sharing this small, confined space with seven of the enemy.

The train chugged slowly across the countryside. After a while Steve's eyelids began to droop. She told herself that she must not drop off, but she had had only three hours' sleep the previous night, the air in the carriage was warm and heavy and the rhythm of the wheels hypnotic. Once or twice she jerked awake and forced her eyes open but before long she gave up the struggle. She was woken by movement and a hand gently touching her arm.

'We are approaching Chalon, madame.'

'What? Oh, yes, thank you.' She mumbled the words and then froze in horror. Had she spoken in English? She stared round the compartment but the men were busy getting their gear together, apparently undisturbed. She looked down. The precious attaché case was still on her lap.

One of the soldiers insisted on helping her out of the train with her suitcase. Then he clicked his heels, saluted and went off to join his comrades. At the exit she asked where the bus to Louhans started from and twenty minutes later she was on the last stage of her journey.

It was evening when she arrived at her destination and she was immensely grateful to discover that the Bar du Centre was only just round the corner from where the bus had dropped her. It was a small, rather dark place with seats in booths and a long enamel counter down one side. Two boys were playing table football at the far end and a couple of old men were standing at the bar drinking red wine. Steve slid into one of the booths and when the waiter came over she ordered a *citron pressé*.

The waiter looked at her with raised eyebrows. 'I'm sorry, madame. That is not possible.'

Steve realised that she had committed one of the faux pas

she had been warned against at Beaulieu. Fresh lemons were obviously unobtainable.

'Of course,' she murmured. 'What a fool I am! I'll have a lemonade, please.'

The waiter moved away and she saw him speak to the *patron* behind the bar and they both looked at her. She reminded herself that this was supposed to be a safe place, and when he came back with her drink she said, 'I am looking for a Mme Arnault. Do you happen to know her address?'

The waiter's expression did not change. 'I will enquire, madame.'

He went off into a back room and a moment later a solidly built man in his thirties appeared and came over to where she was sitting. She waited for him to give her the agreed password but instead he rested his fists on the table and glared at her.

'*Mon Dieu!* First they send me a radio operator whose French is so execrable that I have to keep him locked up in a chateau so he doesn't give himself away, and now they have sent me a schoolgirl!'

Steve stared at him. This was a total breach of everything she had learned at Beaulieu. She did not know whether to be angry or scared. She sat up straighter and responded coldly, 'Forgive me, monsieur. I do not understand you. I am looking for Mme Arnault.'

His eyes narrowed and he drew back slightly. 'Mme Arnault has gone to visit her cousin in Dijon.'

Somewhat relieved, Steve said, 'You are Bob?'

'Of course. And you are Suzette, I presume.'

'Yes. And I am not a schoolgirl.'

'You are far too young for this job,' he replied curtly. 'Hasn't London any idea of what we are facing here?'

Steve looked round the bar. The *patron* and the waiter

were listening with undisguised interest to this exchange. 'Please, monsieur!' she remonstrated. 'Surely we should not be talking of this here.'

He gave a short bark of bitter laughter. 'She has been in the country how long? Twenty-four hours? And she is presuming to lecture me about security!' He sat down opposite her. 'Now, you listen to me. I have been running this circuit for the last five months. I know who I can trust and who I cannot, so I don't need a kid straight out of Beaulieu to teach me.'

'I'm sorry.' Steve could feel herself blushing. 'As you say, I'm new to all this.'

'Have you brought the money?'

'Yes.'

'Well, come on. Where is it?'

Steve looked around her again. It seemed ridiculous to hand over that amount of money in such an open manner. 'It's here, in the briefcase.'

'Let's have it, then.'

Steve opened the case and took the money from the secret compartment. Bob took it and thrust it into a paper carrier bag, which the waiter handed him.

'What about the crystals?'

'They're here.'

He examined them. 'Intact, thank God.'

'What do you want me to do now?' Steve asked.

'Nothing for the moment. I've found you a safe house. You are going to live with a Mme Monceau. She is a widow and a milliner. You are going to be her cousin from the country, come to be her apprentice.'

'A milliner!' Steve exclaimed. 'But I'm hopeless at anything like that. I thought I was going to work on a farm.'

'There are no farms in the middle of Louhans,' he said

sarcastically. 'And I need you close. You'll just have to learn, won't you.' He turned and called to one of the boys. 'Jean-Marc! Take Mlle Suzette to the house of Mme Monceau.' To Steve he added, 'Just keep your head down and get acclimatised. When I need you I will send a message by Jean-Marc here. Understood?'

Steve nodded and rose. All she wanted at that moment was a meal and a bed and, if possible, a bath.

Mme Monceau had a narrow, dark face and a thin-lipped smile. She greeted Steve without warmth and made it clear that she was taking her in out of duty rather than inclination. The meal was forthcoming, but it was a meagre one, and her bed was hard and lumpy, in a small room whose window was apparently welded shut by years of grime. There was no suggestion of a bath.

The next morning Mme Monceau made it clear that she expected Steve to earn her keep. In fact, Steve rapidly became convinced that the reason she had agreed to take her in had more to do with the chance of getting some unpaid labour than with patriotism.

She spent the next four days huddled over the workbench at the back of the shop, pricking her fingers and enduring Madame's sarcastic comments about young girls who thought it was beneath them to work with their hands. She knew that Bob had been right to tell her to lie low and 'get acclimatised'. She had been warned often enough that the most dangerous time for new agents was immediately after their arrival in France. But she was unable to see how being stuck in the shop was helping her to get to grips with everyday life in the occupied country. There were times when she wondered bitterly whether there had been any point in all the elaborate training.

She worried about Bob, too. Buckmaster had called him one of their best agents but it seemed to her that he was flouting all the rules of security they had been taught. There was an arrogance about him that made her uneasy.

On the fifth day Jean-Marc appeared in the shop. 'M. Bob wants you. Come to the bar at seven o'clock this evening.'

When Steve entered the Bar du Centre she was directed into a back room. Bob was there, surrounded by four other men in working clothes. They were bending over a map and her first thought was that anyone coming in would have recognised them immediately as conspirators – particularly since the possession of maps was forbidden by the German occupiers.

Bob looked up and said, without any preliminary greeting, 'I'm sending you north, to the Besançon area. We're expanding the circuit and there's a chap working up there already who has connections in the area. He needs a courier. His operational name is César. Go to Salins-les-Bains and take a room at the Hôtel des Thermes. It's still a popular spa town so no one will think twice about a woman staying there on her own. You might drop a hint that you are waiting for someone. The French love any hint of a romantic assignation. There's a train at ten fifteen tomorrow. César will meet you in the hotel bar at noon the day after. He will claim to have met you before, at the house of some people called Renard. In return, you must say it was at a party for their silver wedding. Got that?'

Steve nodded, her brain working overtime to assimilate all the information. 'Got it.'

'Right. Good luck.' With that he turned away and resumed his conversation. Steve hesitated a moment and then realised that she had been dismissed. It struck her as rude but on reflection she was glad to be moving on. At least it was a chance to get away from Madame Monceau.

Salins-les-Bains was huddled in a narrow valley between two steep escarpments, each crowned by a fortress above which flew the swastika. Ancient grey buildings, which spoke of a grandeur and prosperity now faded into genteel respectability, lined the main street and climbed the flanks of the hill on the eastern side. The hotel had the same air of slightly shabby gentility and seemed to be occupied by elderly ladies with small dogs. Steve booked a room, ate a solitary lunch and went out for a stroll. There were German soldiers in the streets and it still required an act of courage to walk past them, but she was reassured by the fact that their glances as they passed contained only the sort of appreciation she was accustomed to read on the faces of men she met and nothing more sinister.

As she wandered through the gardens by the river and past the ancient salt works that had given the town its name, it struck her that it would have been a pleasant place to spend a few days' holiday, in the right company. But she was not used to being alone and the afternoon and evening dragged. She was glad when bedtime came. It was a hot night and for some hours she tossed restlessly, until in desperation she stripped off her nightdress and stretched out naked on the sheet.

She was woken from the deepest pre-dawn slumber by the sound of voices shouting and doors being banged.

'*Raus! Raus!*'

The German voices startled her into a panic. Were they looking for her? She was almost certain she had not been followed from Louhans. Had Bob betrayed her? She grabbed a dressing gown and pulled it round her, her mind whirling. There was a balcony outside her window. If she went out that way was there any chance of reaching the ground? One glance told her that such an attempt would be useless. The Germans had posted guards outside for just such an eventuality. The only hope was bluff. What should she try to hide? She was still carrying far too much money for someone in her supposed circumstances. She grabbed up the money belt and pushed it under the mattress. Her Colt .32 was in her bag and for a second she was tempted to slip it into her pocket, but she thought better of it and pushed that under the mattress too. As she did so the knocking reached her door.

Steve stumbled across the room and then stood still for a second or two, desperately trying to control the panic that was causing her breath to come in gasps. The knocking came again and a voice shouted to her to open up. A young soldier stood on the threshold and her first thought was that he was in field grey, not in the dreaded black uniform of the SD.

'Your papers, please,' he demanded.

'Oh, yes! Yes, of course.'

Steve moved back into the room and scrabbled in her bag for her identity card. When she handed it to the young man she noticed that he looked uncomfortable and was fixing his gaze somewhere beyond her left shoulder. After a second she realised that in her haste she had not fastened the dressing gown, which had fallen open to expose a good portion of her right breast. She pulled it across.

'I'm sorry. I was asleep. You startled me.'

'Your name?' he asked, without looking directly at her.

'Marguerite Duclos.'

He glanced at her papers, then briefly raised his eyes to her face, and she saw that he was blushing.

'Thank you, madame. My apologies for disturbing you.'

He clicked his heels and turned away to knock on the next door. Steve closed her own and leaned against it, shaking and struggling to control hysterical giggles. It had been a routine check, nothing more. She had been warned that the Nazis carried out random checks like this, on the off-chance of catching someone without the proper papers. But she couldn't help wondering whether, had the young soldier not been so embarrassed, he might have carried out a more thorough investigation.

At length she straightened up and walked shakily back to the bed. She lay down and pulled the sheet over her but there was no possibility of getting back to sleep.

At noon the next day she was in the bar as arranged. The only other occupants were two middle-aged ladies and an elderly couple, so she felt that César would have no difficulty recognising her. At a minute past the hour a man walked in. He was around thirty, she guessed, dressed in a suit and tie that placed him among the *petit bourgeois*, with fair hair brushed straight back from a wide forehead. He ordered a beer, then leaned on the bar and looked casually around him. Their eyes met and his face lit up.

'Madame, what a delightful surprise,' he exclaimed, coming over to her. ' You remember me – Henri Rehmann? We met at the house of M. and Mme Renard.'

'Of course,' she responded, holding out her hand. He took it and bent his head over it. 'It was at their silver wedding party, wasn't it? Please, do sit down.'

He smiled and sat opposite her. He had lively deep blue eyes and a wide mouth that gave his face a humorous expression. She wondered whether he was really French, or another British agent, like herself. There was something about his accent that puzzled her. They made conversation for a few minutes, talking about the weather, the impossibility of getting a decent meal because of rationing, the appalling delays on the trains – the sort of things people on both sides of the Channel complained about. Then he suggested they might take a stroll before lunch. Steve was not surprised. She had been taught that it was better to talk in the open air, where there was less chance of anyone eavesdropping.

Outside he said, 'So you are Suzette. But what name should I use if I need to introduce you to other people? Those not involved in our work, I mean?'

Steve hesitated. She had been told that it was preferable to keep her two identities separate. On the other hand, she could see that if they were going to work together he would need to know the name on her identity papers.

Seeing her dilemma, he said, 'Of course. Why should you trust me? I could perfectly well be a double agent. What can I say to convince you? Does Gavin Maxwell up at Arisaig still smoke eighty cigarettes a day?'

Steve smiled. 'When he can get them.'

'And is Captain Hardy Amies still giving lectures on the finer points of German uniform?'

'Yes, he is.'

'Is that enough? But of course, you will have been warned that Gestapo agents are quite well informed about the staff at the various schools. What else can I say?'

'It's all right,' Steve told him. 'I'm convinced. But it's not what you've told me. It's your voice. I've just worked out what the accent is. It's North Country – Yorkshire or Lancashire, I'm not sure which.'

'Oh dear.' He sighed. 'And I really thought I'd got over

that. Still, if it's convinced you, it has served a useful purpose, I suppose.'

'Isn't it dangerous, though – for you, I mean?'

'Well, I'm hoping that German ears are not quite so well attuned to English regional accents filtered through the medium of French. It's Manchester, by the way.'

'What about the locals?'

'That's not so much of a worry. There are very few French people now who don't hate the Boche. They may not be actively engaged in the Resistance but they wouldn't willingly betray someone who was.'

'You really think that's true of the majority?'

'I'm sure of it. The Nazis have made themselves so unpopular, particularly since the introduction of conscription of young men for forced labour in Germany – what they call the *Service de Travail Obligatoire*. Recruits are flocking to us. That's why I need you.'

As they strolled through the gardens by the river he said, 'I've been in touch with a friend and I think we have found the ideal place for you. Bob told me that you were expecting to work on a farm. Is that right?'

'Yes. Or as a cook. Anything rather than millinery!'

'Right. There is a lady living not far from here, the Comtesse de Montmain. She is a widow and her only son had been taken for the STO. My friend is sure that she would be delighted to employ you as a companion and someone who would help out with the work on the estate. What do you think?'

'Will she know who I am – why I'm here?'

'Officially, no. The fewer people who know that the better. In practice, she will almost certainly guess. Stick to your cover story and she won't ask awkward questions.'

'So she is on our side – sympathetic, at any rate.'

'Definitely. My friend vouches for her.'

'It sounds ideal.'

'Good. Fetch your things and I'll take you over there now. She lives just the other side of the *côte*, near Arbois.'

When Steve came out of the hotel with her suitcase César was standing beside a strange-looking vehicle. It was a *gazogène*, a van that had been converted to run by burning a mixture of wood and charcoal, like most of the private vehicles in France. Emblazoned on the side of it was the name of a firm that sold and repaired farm implements.

'Where did you get this?' she asked when they were both settled in the front.

'Someone I knew before the war. It's perfect cover. I can travel around the area without arousing suspicion.'

'You certainly seem to have some useful friends.'

'And they will put me in touch with others. This whole area is ready to rise up against the Boches. All it needs is organisation and equipment. What I need you to do initially is to set up two dead letter boxes so we can keep in touch and also find one or two reliable people who will pass on messages or provide a place where we can meet. I'll call at the chateau again in a week to hear what you've organised but it won't do for me to be seen there too often.'

The chateau of Montmain stood in a pastoral landscape overlooking the valley of the Cuissance. Steve and César were admitted by a grey-haired women who doubled, Steve guessed from the state of her apron, as cook and parlour maid. She led them to a room at the back of the building, which was furnished as an office, and a slim, very beautiful woman rose from behind the desk to greet them. The comtesse had dark hair, lightly touched with grey at the temples, and a clear, porcelain-pale complexion. Her fine-boned face was enlivened by a pair of large grey eyes, around which a network of fine lines was beginning to form. She was, Steve guessed, around fifty years old, but as she came towards them Steve saw that she moved stiffly, dragging one leg.

'M. Rehmann? I am delighted to make your acquaintance.'

César took the offered hand and bowed slightly over it. *'Enchanté, madame.'*

Steve reflected that, though his accent might not be perfect, his manners were impeccably French.

The comtesse turned to Steve. 'And you are the young lady that our mutual friend mentioned.'

'My name is Marguerite, madame. Marguerite Duclos.'

'I'm very pleased to meet you. I am told that you are looking for somewhere to stay.'

'Yes, madame. And I shall be happy to help out in any way I can.'

'I am sure we shall get on extremely well,' her hostess said cordially. 'Now, you must be ready for some lunch. M. Rehmann, you will stay and eat with us?'

Lunch was a pleasant meal, during which nothing was said that might be in any way compromising, but Steve received a definite impression that the comtesse fully understood why they were there and wished to give them any assistance in her power. To César she said, 'You will already know many people in the area, of course. But do make sure that you call on M. Marsac at the cheese factory on the road to Quingey. And you will find M. and Mme Bardet at the Hostellerie Comtoise in Arbois very reliable.' Then, turning to Steve, 'And if you should need for any reason to visit the doctor I can recommend Dr Lefort at the Clinique Pasteur, also in Arbois.'

César left immediately after the meal. Steve was sorry to

see him go but she felt at ease with the comtesse and more optimistic than she had done since she had arrived in France.

'I expect you would like to see round and then we can decide what you are going to do,' her hostess said.

'Thank you, madame.'

'Oh, please, you must call me Sylvie. There is no need to stand on ceremony. Tell me, can you by any chance ride a horse?'

Steve's heart leapt. 'Yes, I can. I've ridden since I was a small child.'

'Oh, excellent! Please, come this way. There is something I want to show you.'

Sylvie led her out into a courtyard surrounded by farm buildings and then through a gate into a paddock where a large black gelding was grazing. The horse lifted his head and whinnied softly, then came towards them, stepping delicately and tossing his head.

'He belongs to my son,' Sylvie said quietly, 'but since Michel . . . went away there is no one to exercise him. I cannot ride any more, since I had a bad fall a few years ago. See how fat he is getting?'

'He's beautiful,' Steve said.

'Yes. He's an English thoroughbred.' Sylvie glanced sideways at her. 'Perhaps you know the breed?'

'Of course,' Steve replied. 'Everyone knows the English thoroughbred. What's his name?'

The horse had come to a stop a few feet away and Sylvie held out a handful of grain that she had picked up on their way through the yard. He stretched his neck, wanting the titbit but clearly not intending to be caught.

'His name is Mephisto, but he is not such a devil really. A

little wild, but not wicked. Do you think you can manage him?'

'I'm sure I can,' Steve answered.

Greed finally overcame caution and the horse advanced and took the grain from Sylvie's hand and allowed Steve to caress his neck. 'We'll get on fine, won't we, *mon brave?*' she murmured.

Chapter Six

Over the ensuing days Steve found it hard to credit her good fortune. Every morning she saddled Mephisto and rode him out across the fields and into the forests above the valley. She had some difficulty catching him to begin with, and when she was mounted he made it clear that he resented a stranger in the saddle, but once he discovered that he could not unseat her he settled down and they both began to enjoy themselves. It was the perfect way of exploring the countryside without anyone querying her presence.

In the afternoons she explored further on a loaned bicycle, using the excuse that she was running some small errand for Sylvie. It might be shopping in the little town of Arbois, or carrying a message or a gift to someone in a nearby village, knowing that all those she was meeting were people whom Sylvie regarded as potential allies. She liked Arbois, with its broad main street running uphill from the lively little Cuissance and its dignified houses clustering around the church, and was fascinated to discover that it was here that Louis Pasteur had practised medicine and made his great discoveries. She called in at the Hostellerie Comtoise, which sat by the bridge over the river, and introduced herself to the proprietor and his wife. She also made a point of visiting the doctor on the pretext of a sore throat and told him that he had been recommended by the comtesse. They talked about the war and the occupation and Steve hinted at a hatred of the Germans and a wish to do anything she could to make life uncomfortable for them. The doctor indicated that his sympathies lay in the same direction but pointed out with a shrug that his professional position meant that he could never become actively involved. After a little more verbal fencing it was agreed that, should a man calling himself César ever want to get in touch with her, the doctor would be prepared to pass on a message.

The dead letter boxes presented no problem. By the time César called at the chateau she was able to identify two places. One was a small hut at the edge of an abandoned vineyard just outside Arbois, where a loose board could be lifted to conceal a message. The other was a large oak tree at a junction in the forestry tracks that criss-crossed the Forêt Domainiale de Mouchard. There was a hollow where the trunk forked and in this Steve placed an old tobacco tin.

When she told him what she had arranged César declared himself well satisfied.

'We'll keep the doctor for emergencies but I'll make a point of going in and introducing myself. We need a couple of other places where we can meet. I suggest the hostellerie in Arbois and the cheese factory that Madame la Comtesse mentioned. If I need to see you, or the other way around, we can leave a note in one of the places you've found. We'll call the hostellerie point "A" and the cheese factory point "B".'

One night Steve woke to the unmistakable drone of heavy bombers passing overhead. In the distance the airraid warning sounded. She got out of bed and went to the window. It was the dark of the moon and she could not make out the outlines of the aircraft but they were heading east. Away in the distance she saw flak begin to burst, and soon after that she felt rather than heard a series of heavy detonations. It was obviously an Allied raid and she tried to think what the target might be, over there almost on the Swiss border.

Every morning, during her rides, she checked the two letterboxes. Two days after the raid there was a note in the tin. 'Must see you. Meet at "B" Tuesday, 9 a.m.' To anyone happening to find the note it could have been an innocent lovers' tryst.

Steve set off on her bicycle in good time for the rendezvous. It was a longish ride but she was enjoying the cool morning air and whistling happily as she pedalled. Turning a corner, she found herself suddenly confronted by a checkpoint manned by members of the Milice, the paramilitary police force made up of local men who had decided to throw in their lot with the occupiers. They were regarded by the Resistance as a greater threat than the Gestapo, since they knew the area and would be quick to spot any strangers or unusual activity. A short, dark man with a heavy moustache, carrying an automatic rifle, waved her to a standstill. Her heart started to thump. What had she been whistling? She was almost sure it was 'The Lincolnshire Poacher'. Would he recognise that as an English folk song?

'Name?' he demanded.

'Marguerite Duclos.'

'Papers?'

Steve handed over her identity card.

'You're not from round here. What are you doing in this locality?'

'I'm a refugee. My home was bombed by the British. I'm staying with Madame de Montmain.'

'Where are you going now?'

'To the cheese factory to buy cheese for Madame.'

'It's a long way to go for a bit of cheese. What's wrong with buying it in Arbois?'

Steve shrugged and smiled. 'That's what I said – but Madame is very particular about her cheese. And I'm not in a position to argue.'

He stared at her for a long moment and she forced herself to meet his eyes and keep smiling. Finally he stepped back and jerked his head at the open road. 'You'd better get going, then.'

Steve mounted her bicycle, feeling her palms sweaty on the handlebars, and pedalled away.

She reached the cheese factory just after the appointed time and propped her bicycle outside the little shop attached to it. She found César in a back room, sampling the Comté cheese with the manager. After a few pleasantries the manager left them alone and went back into the shop to keep watch.

'I need you to go to St-Amour,' César began without preamble. 'I have an urgent message for London and the only radio operator within miles is Gabriel, the Acrobat *réseau*'s man.

'Gabriel?' Steve queried. 'Bob said something about a radio operator he had to keep shut up because his French was so bad. Is that him?'

César laughed briefly. 'His French is perfectly fluent. The only trouble is his Geordie accent is stronger than my Manchester one. Bob's put him into a chateau in St-Amour and won't let him budge. So I need you to go to him. You can get the train from Arbois. The chateau is a couple of kilometres outside the town, to the north. The lady who owns it is a Madame de Courville, a very staunch supporter.'

'What's the message?'

'Did you hear the bombers going over the other night?'

'Yes.'

'It was the RAF trying to knock out the Peugeot factory at Sochaux, near Montbéliard. The Huns have requisitioned it to make tank turrets. Unfortunately, it's built very close to a residential area and the bombs overshot. There was considerable destruction and loss of life but the factory remains unscathed.'

'So what can we do about it?'

'One of my contacts is a member of the Peugeot family. I've pointed out to him that as long as the factory goes on producing armaments for the Germans the RAF are going to keep trying to put it out of action. That means more innocent lives lost and, eventually, our boys will get lucky and his factory will be reduced to rubble. I suggested to him that it would be better all round if it could be put out of commission by internal sabotage. It only needs one or two essential parts in one or two key machines to be put beyond use and at the end of the war he will still have his factory.'

'That's brilliant! Will he do it?'

'He's prepared to consider it. But understandably he needs to be reassured of my bona fides. He wants to know that if he goes along with my idea the RAF really will leave him alone. So this is what you need to do. Tell Gabriel to send a message saying that if they want the Peugeot factory to stop production the BBC must broadcast the following message in the nine fifteen *messages personnels*. *"Les cerises de ma tante Adèle sont plus douces que les abricots de tante Marie"*.'

Steve knew about these broadcasts. Every evening at 6.15 and 9.15 the BBC broadcast a news bulletin in French. It was strictly forbidden by the Nazis for anybody to listen to them, but all over the country people tuned in to hidden wireless sets, risking arrest in order to get news untainted by

German propaganda. After each one there was a series of personal messages, sent by those who had escaped to England to relatives and friends still in France. Most of them were in some form of code and some were complete nonsense, inserted to confuse the enemy, but among them were vital coded instructions to agents and resistance groups.

'Got that?' César asked.

Steve nodded doubtfully. 'Yes, but I don't quite see the point.'

'My friend will be listening for that message. When he hears it he will know that I really am in touch with London and they agree to the plan. Now repeat the message.'

Steve did as she was bid and César continued, 'You must go at once. Get Gabriel to send the message on his next scheduled transmission. OK?'

'OK,' Steve confirmed. She hesitated a moment, then added, 'I know London think a lot of Bob. Colonel Buckmaster said he was one of their best agents. But I thought his security was very lax. I really didn't feel safe in Louhans.'

César's expression was grim. 'I completely agree with you. I couldn't get out of there fast enough. I know Bob has had one or two successes but I'm afraid they've gone to his head. He thinks he's invincible, and that's dangerous. But the good thing is, he's kept Gabriel at arm's length. You should be safe enough visiting him.'

On the way back to Arbois Steve pondered her mission. In spite of what César had said she felt she needed a plausible excuse for visiting Madame de Courville. Back at the chateau she broached the subject carefully with Sylvie.

'Madame de Courville?' her hostess responded. 'But I know her. You must take her a gift from me. Let me think – yes, I have it. A jar of my damson jam. In these hard times even such small presents are appreciated.'

It was after midday by the time she reached St-Amour. She paused as she left the station, glancing up at the sun to get her bearings, and then set off northwards. The road ran through the centre of the village and then out into countryside between slopes covered in vines, where the unripe grapes hung in tight green bunches. It was a beautiful day, the heat of the sun tempered a little by the altitude, and she had discarded her suit for the navy cotton dress. Walking through the peaceful countryside there was nothing to remind her that she was in enemy territory, and she realised how easy it would be to forget the need for constant vigilance.

The chateau stood at the top of a small hill, half hidden by trees. Her knock was answered by a skinny girl, and the expression on her face sent a tingle of foreboding through Steve's nerves. Madame was out, she was informed, and the girl could not say when she might be back. Steve's first instinct was to turn away and head back to the town. The girl looked like a frightened rabbit and it could hardly be due to the arrival of an unexpected visitor. But then she remembered how César had impressed on her the urgency of her mission. This was her first real test and she must not fail it.

'Since Madame is not here,' she said, 'perhaps I could speak to M. Gabriel.'

The girl's eyes swivelled from one side to the other, as if seeking a way of escape. Finally, she nodded dumbly and stood aside for Steve to enter.

'Up there,' she said, indicating a staircase. 'He's right at the top.' Steve mounted the stairs to a landing, saw a second flight and climbed again and came to a spiral staircase that obviously led up to one of the towers that crowned the roof.

She mounted slowly, silently, her ears alert to any sound from above. What if the Gestapo had located Gabriel's transmissions? That would account for Madame's absence and the little maid's terror. Perhaps they were waiting with him, to see who else might fall into their net. But surely the girl would not have let her walk into a trap without trying to warn her – unless she was too simple to understand what was going on.

She reached the door and stood listening. There was no sound from inside. She remembered the exercise at Garramor and wished she had her Colt in her pocket. She never carried it, reasoning that if she was stopped and searched its discovery would condemn her out of hand. Could she remember enough of what she had learned from Major Sykes to overpower any German officer who might be waiting for her? At least she had the advantage of surprise.

She turned the handle silently and flung the door open. There was only one man in the little turret room. He was sitting at a desk with his back to her and he was in civilian dress. But as Steve held back a gasp of relief he swung round and leapt to his feet and she found herself being covered by a Webley automatic. She instinctively threw up her hands.

'Don't shoot! I'm a friend of César's.'

He stared at her and she saw that he was sweating. 'Who are you?'

'I'm Suzette.'

'Suzette? Bob mentioned you. What the hell are you doing here?'

'I've got a message from César. What's wrong? Has something happened?'

'You haven't heard?'

'Heard what?'

'Bob's been arrested.'

'How? When?'

'Yesterday. The SD raided the bar. He tried to make a run for it but they shot him.'

'Was he killed?'

'No, only wounded, but they've got him.'

'How do you know about this?'

'Paulette came and told me. She's lying low and she said I should do the same.'

Steve's legs felt suddenly weak. If she had stayed in Louhans she might be in the hands of the Gestapo herself by now.

'Can I sit down?'

Gabriel laid his pistol on the desk and nodded briefly. Steve found a chair and looked round the room. To her surprise it was furnished as an artist's studio and a half-finished watercolour of the view from the window stood on an easel.

'You're a painter?'

'I dabble a bit and it's good cover. I get a good signal from up here and I can see anyone coming for miles while I'm transmitting. Then, if necessary, all the gear goes away under the floorboards and here I am – a poor artist whom Madame has taken in out of the kindness of her heart. At least, that was the theory – until today.'

'Do you transmit from here all the time?'

'Yes.'

'Isn't that very risky? I thought radio operators were supposed to keep moving around so the detectors can't pick them up.'

'Bob thought I was safer here. He was afraid I'd give myself away because of my accent.'

Steve found herself for once in agreement with the circuit

organiser. Gabriel's Geordie-accented French would have been funny if the situation were not so serious.

'But now I don't know what to do,' he went on. 'I've been expecting them to come for me at any moment.'

'Bob won't tell them where you are,' Steve said.

Gabriel shook his head in disbelief. 'Everyone talks, sooner or later. Forty-eight hours you're supposed to keep shtum. After that it's assumed that all your associates will have gone underground.' He lit a cigarette and she saw that his hands were trembling.

His panic produced an opposite reaction in Steve. After the initial shock she felt that her brain had moved into a higher gear. 'You mustn't stay here, that's obvious.'

'But where am I supposed to go?'

'You must come north with me. I'll contact César and he will find you another safe house. But first you must send this message. It's absolutely vital. When's your next sked?'

He glanced at his watch. 'In just under an hour.'

'Good. Then there's time for you to encode this. As soon as you've sent it we'll leave.'

He looked at her, wild eyed, and for a moment she thought he was going to refuse, but then he pulled himself together and sat down at the desk. 'What do you want me to say?'

Steve dictated the message and while Gabriel worked over his code sheets she stood by the turret window, watching the road that led from the village. She expected at any minute to see a fleet of the black Citroën *traction avant* cars that the Gestapo favoured heading their way, but the road remained empty except for a few of the local farm workers returning to the fields after the long midday break.

Eventually Gabriel said, 'That's done. Give me a hand to get the radio set up, will you?'

He lifted a floorboard and Steve helped him to extract the

wireless set, then, while he connected it to the mains, she draped the aerial round the room and pushed the end out of the window, where it was hidden among the ivy growing up the tower. Gabriel sat tensely by the set, watching the hands of the clock. At last the scheduled time arrived and she saw his hand move on the Morse key, sending out his call sign. The rattle of the key seemed unnaturally loud and she felt sure that it could be heard all over the house, and outside.

Eventually Gabriel removed his headphones. 'Right, that's gone. Let's pack this lot up.'

As they packed the equipment into the innocent-looking suitcase Steve said, 'There's a train at four thirty. Take a ticket to Arbois. That's the only time you will need to speak. When you get there go to the Hostellerie Comtoise. It's on the outskirts of the town, as you cross the river from the station. The owners are a M. and Mme Bardet and they can be trusted. Take a room and stay there until César comes to find you. I'll leave here first. You follow in five minutes and don't give any sign that you know me. I'll carry the set and look after it until you are settled somewhere. That way if the Boches do pick you up you won't have anything incriminating on you.'

She knew that carrying the set increased her own risk a hundredfold but it was axiomatic that a radio operator never carried his own set from one safe house to another, to minimise the risk of both set and operator being captured.

'Are you sure about this?' Gabriel asked, handing her the case.

'Of course. It's routine procedure.' She picked up the case and then reached out and touched his arm. 'Good luck. I'll see you again soon.'

It was a good job, she reflected as she lugged the heavy

case along the road to the village, that her years growing up on the farm had given her strong arms. The wait for the train seemed interminable and she had never felt so exposed. If Bob had broken under interrogation the Gestapo could arrive at any minute. She was thankful that she had never told him her cover name, so everyone in his circuit knew her only as Suzette. There was no reason why the Gestapo should be looking for Marguerite Duclos, but at the same time she knew that any random check would reveal the wireless set and result in her immediate arrest. Gabriel arrived and sat farther along the platform, not looking at her. By the time the train arrived the shock was beginning to take effect and her throat was parched. She realised that she had not eaten or drunk since breakfast.

When the train stopped at Lons-le-Saunier soldiers of the Feldgendarmerie boarded it and started checking papers. Steve left the precious case on the luggage rack, where she could disown it if necessary, and went and stood in the corridor. It was market day and the carriage filled up with men and woman carrying baskets of produce and bundles of various shapes and sizes. To Steve's relief her case soon disappeared under a pile of other luggage. If the soldiers had intended to search the travellers' possessions, they gave up the idea when they saw the enormity of the task. One of them glanced briefly at Steve's identity card and passed on.

At Arbois she extricated her case and carried it out to where she had left her bicycle, but instead of heading for the chateau she pushed the bike up the hill to the doctor's house. Evening surgery was just coming to an end and she was the last patient.

The doctor offered her a chair and enquired, 'How can I be of service, mademoiselle?'

'Has M. César been to see you?'

'Yes, he came the other day.'

'I need to get a message to him urgently. Can you help me?'

For a moment he hesitated and she guessed that he was weighing up the risks of becoming involved. Then he nodded. 'I can make a house call. The lady with whom he is lodging has a bad heart. It would not seem unusual.'

Steve let out a breath of relief. 'Thank you. Please tell him that I must see him, as soon as possible.'

'Come here tomorrow at ten o'clock. Tell the receptionist that you are collecting a prescription for Madame la Comtesse.'

The ride up to the chateau took the last of her energy. Sylvie met her in the hall.

'Something has happened, yes? It's all right, say nothing. I see you have some luggage with you. Let me show you where you can keep it.'

She led her to a boxroom, crammed with old suitcases, a broken sewing machine and a set of golf clubs. 'Put your case there, with the others,' she said, adding as Steve deposited her load, 'When you wish to hide a grain of sand, the best place is on the beach, *n'est-ce pas!*'

Steve did as she suggested and then took her hand and squeezed it.

'Thanks, Sylvie. I don't know where I'd be without you.'

Over the weeks she had developed a great affection for her hostess and she sensed that it was returned. Sylvie was always dignified and self-contained, a natural aristocrat, but beneath the façade Steve sensed a deep loneliness. Her husband had been killed in a climbing accident ten years earlier, leaving her to manage the estate and bring up Michel, their only son. It was obvious from her occasional remarks that she and Michel had been very close and his absence was a constant source of distress to her. Once or twice Steve had tried to bring up the subject of the STO and what Michel might be doing but Sylvie always shied away from the subject and Steve had concluded that she found it too painful. She knew that Sylvie understood perfectly why Steve was there and the risks that involved, although they never spoke of it, and she admired her quiet courage.

The next morning the doctor ushered her through a connecting door into his study. César was waiting for her.

'What's happened? Weren't you able to send the message?'

'Yes, it's gone,' she reassured him. 'But Bob's been taken by the Gestapo.'

'*Merde!*' She saw the muscles clench in his jaw. Then he said, 'Well, I'm not surprised. He was asking for it. What has happened to Gabriel?'

'I brought him here. He's at the hostellerie.'

'And his set?'

'Hidden at the chateau.'

His face relaxed and for a moment he gripped her arm. 'Well done! I knew I'd struck lucky when I met you.' He let her go and stepped back. 'So, we need to find a new hiding place for Gabriel. I think I know just the spot. I'll go and see him and as soon as he's settled I'll let you know. Then you can take his set to him. Thank you. You've done a great job.'

Steve felt a warm glow. The intensity of it surprised her and forced her to recognise that she was beginning to develop something more than respect for this capable, quietly spoken man.

'You'll let me know how things work out – at the factory, I mean?'

'Yes. I'll get a message to you in due course. Now, you'd better slip out. We shouldn't be seen leaving together.'

That night, as every night, Steve and Sylvie huddled over the wireless set in an endeavour to make out the British announcer's words through the hiss of static and the boom of German jamming. To Steve's delight in the middle of the *messages personnels* she heard the phrase that was engraved on her memory. *'Les cerises de ma tante Adèle sont plus douces que les abricots de tante Marie.'*

Forgetting for a moment that Sylvie was supposed to be unaware of her activities she let out an exclamation of triumph. Sylvie looked at her and cocked an eyebrow.

'This is good news, yes?'

Steve grinned at her. 'Yes, it's very good news.'

Two days later Dr Lefort paid an unexpected house call at the chateau, 'to see how Madame la Comtesse is finding the new medication'. Steve met him in the hallway and offered to conduct him to Sylvie and on the way he slipped a small piece of paper into her hand.

'Your friend has a new address. I have written it here for you.'

As soon as she was alone Steve unfolded the paper and memorised the address. It was in Lons-le-Saunier, a town about halfway between Arbois and St-Amour. She destroyed the paper, explained to Sylvie that she had to visit a friend, collected the suitcase from the boxroom and took the train south. Lons was a larger town than either Arbois or St-Amour and she had to carry the case for some distance through the streets before she found the house. There was a German garrison there and a cold sweat of fear broke out between her shoulder blades every time she had to pass a soldier, but no one stopped her and she eventually reached a tall, grey stone house on the edge of the town. An ancient lady dressed in black admitted her. Her scalp showed pink through her sparse white hair and she was bent almost double with age, but her black eyes were as sharp as a bird's.

'Go up,' she said, in answer to Steve's request to see Gabriel, 'he's right at the top. I can't manage the stairs any longer.'

Gabriel was installed in an attic room, where he had once again spread out his painting materials. He pounced upon the suitcase with relief. Then he pulled a heavy chest away from the wall and showed her where he had broken through into the eaves space to form a hiding place. It had involved removing some bricks but he had concocted a paste of flour and water to look like mortar and once the bricks had been replaced it formed a *cachette* that would pass all but the most thorough search.

'What about the old lady?' Steve asked.

'As far as she's concerned I'm a penniless artist. And she never comes up here.'

Steve made her way back to Arbois feeling that she had been relieved of a heavy weight in more ways than one. The next day there was a note hidden in the hut at the abandoned vineyard. 'Meet me at "A" 12 noon tomorrow.'

Arriving at the hostellerie she found César sitting in the kitchen with M. and Mme Bardet.

'You can speak freely in front of Pierre and Yvonne,' he assured her. 'They are working with us.' Over a plate of charcuterie and glasses of the local white wine he went on, 'First of all, you will be glad to hear that all production at the Peugeot factory has stopped and is not likely to be resumed in the near future – if at all.'

'How did you manage it?' Steve asked.

'I didn't. My friend the director introduced me to one of his foremen. He took me on a tour of the factory and I was able to point out certain key machines and suggest certain . . . modifications, mostly involving the use of small quantities of *plastique*. Some essential parts have been completely destroyed and replacements are very hard to find these days.'

He spoke dryly but there was a triumphant glint in his eyes and they all laughed and clinked glasses in congratulation.

César went on, 'I'm afraid it means another trip to Lons for you. We must let London know that the operation has been a success. But there is more to tell them. We need to arrange a *parachutage* of arms and equipment. You must be aware from the contacts you have made and passed on to me that there are potential *résistants* in every village. Indeed, there are villages where the whole population is in sympathy with the Resistance and just raring to have a go at the Boches. Also, I hear rumours of several *maquis* groups hiding out around the area, though I haven't managed to contact any of them yet. But we can't do anything without arms.'

'I've heard of the *maquis*,' Steve said, 'but I'm not sure what the term means.'

'They are outlaws – bandits,' Pierre Bardet said dismissively. 'Better to leave them alone.'

'Some of them are, I agree,' César said, 'but not all. When the Germans introduced the *Service de Travail Obligatoire* quite a lot of young men took to the hills rather than be sent to Germany. The term *maquis* is taken from the rough scrubland in the south where some of the first groups took refuge. Naturally, they are all fanatically anti-German. If there are local groups they could be very useful, but their efforts need to be coordinated and they need equipment.'

'Aren't the nights too short for a parachute drop at the moment?' Steve put in. 'I was told before I came out that they can't make drops this far east during the summer months because by the time the planes get here there are not enough hours of darkness left to hide the stuff.'

'That's true,' César agreed 'But we're well into August now. By September the nights will be getting longer. I want to get my request in early.'

Two days later they met again at the hostellerie and Steve was able to tell him that London had promised a drop of supplies during the September moon period.

'Excellent!' he responded. 'Now we have to find a suitable dropping zone. That's going to be your job. Got any ideas?'

'Yes,' Steve said. 'But I'll have to confirm them. When do you want to meet again?'

'Soon,' he said. 'I've been thinking. This idea of keeping everything at arm's length, using cut-outs, and so on, is all very well. But we really need to be in closer touch now that things are starting to move. An idea occurred to me. Would you find it an insult if we were assumed to be – what's the term? – "walking out" together?'

Steve laughed. 'Of course I wouldn't find it an insult! I think it's a very good idea.'

'In that case,' he said, 'I shall make a habit of calling at the chateau whenever I'm passing and I don't see why we shouldn't enjoy a few cosy dinners together here.'

Steve set about finding a suitable area for the arms drop. The countryside around Arbois was too hilly and well forested but north of the forest was the level plain carved out by the River Loue. It was arable land, given over to the cultivation of maize and wheat and vegetables, and offered few obstacles on which parachutes might snag. She made a visit to a local farmer whom she knew to be sympathetic and through him got an introduction to the mayor of the village of Chissy. By evening they had picked out a suitable field and recruited local men who would be prepared to build the necessary signal fires and transport the supplies when they arrived. They would even provide the 'platforms', the flat, horse-drawn carts used to carry the harvest, which were ideally suited to moving the containers in which the weapons would be dropped. Every house in the village had on the ground floor a huge, barn-like room entered through massive double doors, where grain and farm implements and even animals were kept. They could be used to hide the containers until such time as they could be broken open and their contents divided among the groups that needed them.

There was only one snag. Before finally agreeing, the mayor insisted on meeting her chief. Negotiating with a woman was one thing, but the final deal had to be made between men. It reminded Steve that this was a society where women did not have the vote. In some rural areas like this they did not even sit down to eat with the men but stood behind their chairs and waited on them.

Two days later César called at the chateau and took her out to dinner at the hostellerie. The restaurant was set out in booths and Pierre would have conducted them to one at the far end of the room, away from prying eyes, but César halted near the door.

'I think it would be better for us to sit where we can be seen,' he said. 'Then everyone will be able to see that it is an innocent, romantic dinner and not a meeting of conspirators.'

It was early and the restaurant was almost empty – not that it was ever full in these hard times. The clientele consisted mainly of those who had, in one way or another, done well out of the Occupation. Pierre settled them at their table and placed a 'Reserved' sign on the one next to it.

'I'll be behind the bar,' he murmured. 'If anyone seems to

be taking an interest in your conversation I'll bring over a beer you haven't ordered.'

César smiled at Steve. 'Well, there's no reason why we shouldn't mix a little pleasure with our business. What would you like to drink?'

She asked for white wine and Pierre brought them a bottle of the local vintage. Even here in rural France rations were getting shorter and Yvonne's culinary efforts were limited. They ate the *menu du jour*, which consisted of a thin vegetable soup, followed by a portion of one of the local sausages with *pommes vapeurs*. Together with these Pierre brought a covered dish, which he presented with a sly grin and a finger laid against his nose in warning. It was filled with deliciously aromatic field mushrooms, and Steve understood the gesture to mean that it would not be served to the other guests.

Over the food she reported to César what arrangements she had made with the men of Chissy and he agreed to come with her the following day to confirm them. They talked of what they hoped the *parachutage* would provide and how it was to be divided among the groups they had established. Other people came into the restaurant but the table behind them remained empty and they were able to converse without anxiety against the general hum of conversation.

At the end of the meal César produced a packet of cigarettes but checked himself in the act of offering them. 'Sorry, I forgot. Women are not allowed to smoke, not in public, anyway.'

He began to put the pack away but Steve said quickly, 'I don't, anyway, so you go ahead.'

He lit a cigarette and then reached across the table and laid his hand over hers. She was taken by surprise and her heart skipped a beat. César was smiling at her, his eyes warm and intimate, and she smiled back. Then the door behind her opened and she saw three men pass out of the corner of her eye.

When the men had passed out of sight to the rear of the room he withdrew his hand. 'Forgive me. I happen to know that two of those chaps are in the Milice. I wouldn't want them to start wondering why we're here together.'

Steve caught her breath. She had no wish to arouse the curiosity of the hated paramilitaries.

'That's all right,' she responded, but the loss of contact had left her feeling oddly bereft.

When they got up to leave, he took her arm with an old-fashioned formality that might have been assumed but might, she thought, be natural to him. As they walked back to the van she found herself enjoying the feel of the hard-muscled arm in hers and the warm proximity of his body. They drove back to the chateau in pleasantly companionable silence, and when they reached it he got out and came round to open the door for her.

'Thank you for tonight,' he said, offering his hand with Gallic courtesy. 'Business aside, it's been most enjoyable.'

For a moment she thought he might be going to kiss her, and her pulse quickened. Then he turned away and got back into the van. She went into the house, feeling a hot blush suffusing her face. How could she have even thought of that, after what had happened with Roddy? Of course César was right to keep things on a purely professional base. What was so shameful was that she had been disappointed.

Chapter Seven

Once the final agreement had been reached at Chissy, Steve travelled to Lons again to give Gabriel the coordinates of the dropping zone to transmit to London, and returned with confirmation of the date and the news that they were to expect fifteen containers.

'What do you want me to do on the night?' she asked.

'I want you to keep well away,' César responded. 'You're taking quite enough risks as it is.'

Steve had conditioned herself to obey orders but this time she rebelled. 'I want to be there. I'm tired of taking a back seat. I want to see some action. After all, I might have to organise a *parachutage* myself one day.'

César considered for a moment. Then he said, 'Very well. It's true that it might be useful to have someone else who knows the ropes as our operations expand. I'll pick you up in the late afternoon. We'll have to get to Chissy before the curfew and lie low there until it's time.'

That evening, listening to the BBC news, Steve and Syvlie heard that the Italians had surrendered and the Americans had landed at Salerno. They hugged each other ecstatically and Sylvie broke out one of her few remaining bottles of champagne to celebrate. At last there seemed to be a real prospect of victory.

'Now the Allies must launch a Second Front here in

France, surely?' Sylvie said. 'That way, they will have the Boches caught between two fires.'

'Yes, it can't be long now,' Steve agreed. 'Just think! It might all be over in a matter of months.'

The message confirming the parachute drop was broadcast the next day and by the following evening César and Steve were sitting in the kitchen of the mayor's house in Chissy, being regaled with the most lavish meal the village could provide. There was a huge tureen of *soupe à l'oignon* in which floated slices of crusty bread oozing melted cheese. After this came omelettes flavoured with morels picked in the surrounding forest, and the main course was a casserole of hare in red wine. They finished with more of the local cheese and juicy pears from the mayor's orchard. Up till now Steve's contacts with potential resisters had been tentative, as both parties felt their way to an understanding. Now she found herself treated as an honoured guest, a heroine prepared to risk her life for La France. Several of the men who were going to help with the drop were present and the party became quite rowdy as the jugs of wine went round. César had to remind their hosts more than once that they all needed to keep a clear head.

He need not have worried. At midnight the lamps were extinguished and the men moved silently down the village street. A harvest moon hung low and yellow over the fields. Steve felt a shiver of excitement, but it was different from the cold fear she had experienced on her lonely journeys. She knew what they were doing was dangerous but the company of these solid, good-natured men and the general air of purpose emboldened her.

The field she had chosen lay beside the river and was bordered by a narrow strip of trees. Beneath these, in the preceding days, bundles of firewood had been prepared and these were now dragged out and carried to places around the field which had been marked out in a pre-arranged pattern. One man stood beside each bonfire, a petrol-soaked faggot and matches ready at hand, while the rest remained in the shadow of the trees. The 'platforms' were drawn up in a small copse some distance away, in case the noise of the aircraft panicked the horses. Time passed. The plane was due at two o'clock but César had warned them that it might be late and they must be prepared for a long wait. An owl hooted, the river gurgled between its banks and the wind sighed in the branches. Steve pulled her overcoat closer round her. The nights were growing cooler.

Then, just before the appointed time, she was thrilled to hear the low drone of an aircraft engine. The men around her, who had been sitting on the ground or lounging against the tree trunks, stood upright and there was a low murmur of excitement. César stepped out into the field and flashed his signal lamp towards the men by the fires. Instantaneously flames began to leap up from all corners. Steve stood scanning the sky as the plane came closer. Suddenly it was there, lower than she had expected, a great shadowy shape skimming the treetops. César was flashing his light skywards now, sending the recognition letter J. A light blinked back in response. The plane over-flew them and then banked and turned in a circle, and as it came back Steve had a clear vision of its silhouette against the moon. Dark blobs appeared below it, which blossomed suddenly into parachutes. The pilot knew his job. The precious packages almost all fell within the circle of the fires, except for one, which disappeared into the waters of the river.

Before the parachutes reached the ground the field became a scene of frenetic activity. Men ran in all directions to grab the containers and detach them from the canopies.

Those who had waited with the 'platforms' brought them up to the edge of the field and the containers were heaved on to them. Two men even waded into the river to retrieve the one that had fallen there. Those in charge of the bonfires quenched them with buckets of water and threw the telltale embers into the river. Then they scattered straw over the blackened patches where the fires had been, to conceal them from German spy planes. Within minutes the field was empty and the carts were creaking back along the road to the village. There, doors were thrown open and the containers disappeared inside, to be hidden behind stacks of firewood or bales of straw.

When everything was safely stowed and the men had trudged off wearily to their homes, Steve and César made their way back to the mayor's house, where they shared a final glass of *marc,* the potent local spirit, with their host. After he had retired to bed, they sat on by the embers of the fire. They could not leave until dawn, when the curfew ended.

In one of the containers they had found two sealed packages, one labelled for César and one addressed to Suzette. César passed Steve's to her and she opened it, feeling like a child on Christmas morning. It contained a selection of small luxuries that were unobtainable in France – chocolate and coffee and a packet of English tea. Best of all, there was a sealed envelope full of letters. They had been opened and all references that might identify her removed but she understood the need for that. On top were four letters from her mother.

Dearest ▓▓▓▓

    Thank you for your PC. It must be so exciting to be in Egypt. I do hope you are getting some free time to explore all the fascinating sights. Do write and tell us all about it . . .

The rest of the letter was given over to local affairs. There were snippets of information about the farm, bits of gossip from the village, references to people she had known and some whose names meant nothing to her. The other three letters were similar. The harvest had been good; one of the Land Girls had accidentally stabbed the other in the thigh with a pitchfork but the wound had not been serious; Mrs Evans's son who was serving in the Far East had been invalided out of the army after a severe bout of malaria. The images they conjured up seemed as remote and unreal to Steve as the illustrations in a book of fairy tales. But there was one recurrent theme – a plea for her to write a proper letter, rather than the cryptic postcards she had composed before leaving London. Steve bit her lip, stabbed by the anxiety, the unspoken reproach, in the careful phrases.

One of the letters contained a postscript. *'I'm enclosing a letter from Frankie which was addressed to you here.'* The letter was dated 21 July.

Dear ▆▆▆▆,

I don't know if you will ever get this but I promised to keep in touch, so here goes. I'm still having a wonderful time! Nick was posted back here so we have been able to see a lot of each other. In fact, we spend all our free time together, swimming and sunbathing during the day and dancing at the officers' club or going to parties in the evenings. He's such a lovely man, Steve – clever and funny and kind and brave – 'a very parfait gentle knight'! And he seems to be really keen on me. Nothing's been said yet – about the future, I mean – but I suppose I mustn't try to rush things. I'm just making the most of this lovely summer.

Speaking of summer – it's really, really hot now. It makes it hard to concentrate on work, even though we have electric fans going all the time. But I must tell you one thing. I'm learning to parachute! Nick arranged for me to join a course they do here and I'm really enjoying it. Of course, I shall be scared to death when I make my first real jump but it's dead exciting – sorry, I mean really exciting.

I feel guilty, telling you all this when I know things can't be anything like as good for you. I think about you a lot and worry about what's happening to you. I wish you could write back and let me know you are OK. Please take care of yourself.

Love,
Frankie

Steve put the letter aside with a smile and a shake of the head. Trust Frankie! Was there anything that girl was not prepared to try? It occurred to her that if Frankie had spoken French rather than Italian she would have been much better suited to the sort of work she, Steve, was doing, rather than sitting behind a desk decoding messages.

At the bottom of the pile was a letter whose handwriting made her heart jump.

My darling,

It's so hard to write, not knowing if you will ever receive this or whether I shall ever get a reply. I think of you all the time and miss you with every breath I take.

Don't worry about me. We've been posted to Cornwall to guard the Western Approaches and it's pretty dull, routine stuff. The chaps in the squadron are starting to get bored, particularly as there isn't a great deal of entertainment locally.

*I keep telling myself this will all be over soon and we shall
be able to have the life we've always dreamed of – the house
in the country, dogs, horses, kids. One day it will all come true
for us, my darling. I know it!*

Please take care of yourself.

With all my love,

Roddy

Steve folded the letters and put them carefully back in the
envelope. César had finished reading his own and stood up
to put his glass on the table. Then he paused beside her
chair.

'A good night's work.'

She smiled up at him. 'Yes. It went well, didn't it?'

He crouched beside her, bringing his face level with hers.
'Can I just say something? I think you are the most remarkable woman I have ever known.'

She looked away quickly, into the fire. 'Oh, nonsense.
What on earth makes you say that?'

'It's true. When I think of you tonight, out there pulling on
parachute lines and helping to load the containers – so calm
and practical, in spite of the danger. And then I look at you
now. I know it sounds corny, but in the firelight you look so
. . . well, so feminine. I would never have believed a woman
could do what you're doing.'

Steve felt herself blushing. A moment before her whole
being had been filled with longing for Roddy and yet now in
spite of herself she felt her body responding to this other
man's closeness. 'There are dozens of other girls doing the
same thing,' she mumbled. 'I'm nothing special.'

'You are to me,' he said. He put out a hand and stroked
her cheek. Then he sighed. 'If I wasn't a married man . . .'

She turned her eyes to him. It had never occurred to her

to wonder whether he was married. 'I didn't know . . .'

'No.' He smiled ruefully. 'We don't know much about each other at all, do we?'

'Do you have children?' she asked.

'Two daughters – one two and the other only a few months old.'

'A few months! But you've been here . . . '

'Since just before she was born. I only found out about it through one of the *messages personnels*. I'll never forget it. *"Clément ressemble à sa grandmère"* We'd agreed the code before I left, of course – grandpère for a boy, grandmère if it was a girl. Good old BBC!'

'It must have been so hard to leave, just at that time,' Steve said. 'How could you bear it?'

'It was hard,' he admitted. 'Even harder for my wife. But I'd been waiting for so long – ever since January. I suppose we both had time to get used to the idea.'

'What did you do before the war?'

'I was a schoolmaster – and a committed pacifist. Then I found out about the concentration camps. My father was part Jewish. I realised then that pacifism just wasn't an option in this conflict. How about you? What were you doing?'

'Not much, I'm afraid. Helping out on my father's farm, helping my mother to organise the village fête – just hanging around waiting for something to happen, really.'

'I guess you're not married.' He touched her left hand. 'But there must be someone waiting for you to come back.'

She swallowed hard and nodded. Their eyes met and then he leaned forward and kissed her. But it was not a kiss of passion. Rather it was one of sympathy and gentle regret.

He drew back and stood up. 'You must be very tired. Try

to get some sleep. There are still a couple of hours before dawn.'

From that night onwards the operation entered a new phase and Steve found herself working at a much greater intensity. The circuit was expanding, and as news spread on the underground grapevine that arms and equipment could be obtained through the agency of the mysterious César more and more recruits came forward. César, mindful of the lessons in security they had been taught at Beaulieu and of the disaster that had overtaken the Acrobat *réseau*, did his best to keep the different cells in ignorance of each other. He selected three men to be his lieutenants and made each of them responsible for groups in a certain area. They in turn appointed leaders for each group, but none of these had any direct contact with César. It was necessary, however, for messages to be passed and equipment to be shared around, and this task fell to Steve.

She kept up her morning rides, checking the dead letter drops every day, but as well as this she found herself cycling ever greater distances to deliver instructions and sometimes weapons to the various cells. Shorter messages she memorised but sometimes the information had to be written down. One day, heading for a group in a neighbouring village, she was stopped by a patrol of Milice. They were used by now to seeing her cycling around the countryside but she was often stopped and treated to an interrogation that was teasing but at the same time intimidating. She guessed that it gave them pleasure to have an attractive young woman at their mercy. She had countered this by flirting with them in return, though she was careful not to be too obvious. It would not do for other people to see her as a collaborator. That day it was harder than usual to maintain an air of innocent good humour. On a piece of paper rolled up and concealed in the handlebars of her bicycle were detailed instructions for assembling and firing a Sten gun. By the time they had had their fun and let her pass her knees were shaking.

When it came to transporting arms the bicycle was no longer practical. Sylvie's car had been requisitioned by the Germans but in one of the stables Steve found an old pony trap. There was another horse in Mephisto's paddock, typical of the comtois breed, deep chested and round bellied. With the help of Georges, an old man who worked as a handyman for the comtesse, Steve pulled the trap out of the stable and cleaned off the cobwebs. The axle needed grease, which was provided by boiling down some pig fat, but apart from that it was perfectly serviceable. Georges created a false bottom, leaving a space some ten inches deep beneath it. With the old horse harnessed between the shafts Steve had a vehicle that was unlikely to cause suspicion on the country roads.

The first time she took the trap out she was careful to carry nothing incriminating. As she expected, the first patrol she met stopped her.

'What's all this? Bike broken down?' the leader asked.

'No, but my legs might if I have to keep cycling up and down these hills,' she replied.

'What have you got in there, then?'

'Firewood for old Ma Furneaux. She's got no one to collect it for her since the Germans took her grandson to work for the Fatherland.'

The man jerked his head at one of his underlings, who climbed into the cart and threw the bundles of wood about in a cursory manner.

'Nothing here,' he said, and she was allowed to proceed.

Next time the cart was full of baskets of apples from the orchard at the chateau. The *miliciens* helped themselves and let her go, which was just as well since the bottoms of the baskets were full of hand grenades and plastic explosives. On other occasions she had passengers, local people glad of a lift to visit friends or relatives, unaware that the secret compartment under their feet concealed Sten guns and rifles. The trap became such a familiar sight that the patrols no longer bothered to search it.

One day she was summoned to a meeting with César at the cheese factory. When she arrived, she found him in the company of a dark-haired, olive-skinned young man whom he introduced as Pedro. Pedro, she was told, had fought against the Fascists in the Spanish Civil War and had now volunteered his services in the same cause for this one. London had sent him to act as César's second-in-command.

'It seems London is pleased with us,' César said with a smile. 'We are now an independent, officially recognised circuit. We're to be known as Stockbroker.'

'Stockbroker?' Steve responded. 'Well, I hope it means they think we're a good investment.'

It was obvious to Steve from the start that Pedro's experiences in Spain had given him a passionate hatred of all fascists, but there was something fanatical about his dedication to the cause which made her uneasy. He had a volatile temper and she felt much more at ease with César's quiet, ironic manner. He soon proved his determination by organising their first major sabotage attempt. He made contact with the local railway workers, who were anti-Nazi to a man, and together they blew up a vital signal box outside the station at Mouchard, an important junction on the line going towards the German border. César was pleased with this boost to morale but he had mixed feelings about the wisdom of the exercise. Rumours were beginning to circulate about German reprisals in other areas, where men had been selected at random from villages suspected of harbouring what the Nazis termed 'terrorists' and shot in front of their families.

'The time when we are really going to be needed is after an Allied invasion. We should conserve our supplies for an all-out effort then, to disrupt supply lines and stop reinforcements being sent to the front. If we make ourselves too much of a nuisance now the Boches will come down on us like a ton of bricks and disrupt all our careful organisation. But I can see that some of the firebrands need to see a bit of excitement and I suppose a few good bangs will keep their spirits up.'

'Will the invasion come soon, do you think?' Steve asked.

'It had better,' he replied grimly. 'I don't know how much longer we can keep ourselves out of the clutches of the Boches at the rate we're going.'

She soon began to appreciate the force of his words. German patrols became much more frequent and their searches were more efficient than those performed by the Milice. Twice she was stopped and the trap and its contents examined but mercifully the soldiers never suspected the existence of the false floor.

On the slopes above the Cuissance the *vendange* was over and in the forest the leaves were falling and the wind in the bare branches made the trees hum like a gigantic musical instrument. Steve cantered Mephisto briskly along one of the rides, revelling in the movement and the cool air whipping her cheeks. Then, slowing to a walk, she turned off into a smaller path where the leaves lay fetlock deep. Mephisto arched his neck and snorted at the rustling, and Steve breathed in the moist, rich autumnal smell. It reminded her of autumn rides in the beech woods near her home.

That was the only trouble with these solitary morning rides. They gave her too much time to think, and as the exhilaration of speed subsided, memories welled up. She thought of her parents and the farm. Harvest would be over and they would be able to take life a little easier, after the long days of rising before dawn and working until the last glimmer of light to bring in the food the nation so desperately needed. The Land Girls would be out digging mangel-wurzels for the cattle's winter feed. Her mother would be making bramble jelly and storing the last of the apples, while her father got on with the autumn ploughing. She knew they would be worrying about her and her heart ached at not being able to let them know that she was all right. She thought about Roddy. He was safe now, or as safe as a fighter pilot could be in wartime – but for how much longer? Her longing for him was a physical need, like hunger or thirst. She dreamed of going home.

'Halt! Stand still. We've got you covered.'

Mephisto stopped dead, throwing up his head, and Steve came out of her reverie with a jolt. A man was standing in the pathway in front of her, a rifle in the crook of his arm. There was a rustling among the undergrowth on either side of the path and she saw four other men, all of them armed and all with their weapons trained on her. She berated herself for her foolishness. She had been miles away and had ridden straight into a trap. But the language and the accent had been French and the man before her was not in uniform. Recovering from her shock, she studied him. He was young, perhaps in his mid-twenties, and dressed in trousers that might once have been khaki and the sort of jacket that a well-to-do landowner might have worn for a hunting trip, except that it was ripped in two places and patched with mud. He had a lean, fine-boned face and large grey eyes that looked somehow familiar.

'What are you doing with that horse?' he demanded.

'Exercising him for Madame la Comtesse,' she responded. 'I'm staying with her, helping out.'

'Who are you?'

'My name is . . . ' She hesitated and made a quick decision. 'My name is Suzette. And you are . . . ?'

'Never mind who I am.'

Something fell into place in Steve's mind. Once or twice she had tried to get Sylvie to talk about her son – the son who was supposed to have been taken to Germany for the STO – but she had always been strangely evasive. And then there were those grey eyes. As if to confirm her suspicions, Mephisto suddenly took a few steps towards the man, extending his head and nickering with pleasure.

'You're Michel de Montmain, aren't you?' Steve said. 'You haven't gone to Germany. You've joined the *maquis.*' He started and to one side of her she heard a gun being cocked. 'Don't worry,' she went on urgently. 'I'm on your side. Have you heard of a man called César?'

He looked at her warily. 'I've heard rumours. What about him?'

Steve loosened her reins and swung out of the saddle. Mephisto was nudging the young man's shoulder.

'Tell me who you are and why you are here,' Steve said, 'and I will tell you who I am. If you're not satisfied . . . well, there are five of you and you have guns.'

He took hold of Mephisto's bridle, staring at her intently. 'You have told me your name. What more is there?'

'Are you Michel de Montmain?'

'Yes, that is my name.'

'And these are your *maquisards?*'

'What if they are?'

'I can help you. I am an English agent, working with César. You must have heard rumours that weapons and explosives are being dropped by parachute and given to the Resistance?'

Around her she heard the leaves rustle as the other men moved closer, but she kept her eyes on Michel.

'Rumours, yes. How do I know they are true?'

'I can prove it to you if you will trust me. I will bring César to meet you. If he believes that you want to help in the fight against the Boches he will give you weapons.'

It was a high-risk strategy but worth it for the possible gain.

'And if I let you go, how do I know that you will not go straight to the Germans, or to the Milice?'

'I am riding your horse. That proves that I am working for your mother, doesn't it? Why would I betray her son?'

'Does she know who you really are?'

'We have never spoken of it. It is better for her not to know. But she understands perfectly.'

For a moment he stood in silence. Finally he said, 'Very well. Bring this man, César, here tomorrow at this time. Bring him alone. If we see anyone else, if we get the slightest hint that the Boches are looking for us, I will come to the chateau and shoot you. Understand?'

'I understand,' Steve answered. 'But tomorrow may not be possible. I have to contact him first. Let us say the day after.'

He frowned at her, then nodded. 'Very well. Go now – and remember, I shall find you if you betray us.'

He patted the horse's neck and briefly rubbed his cheek against its nose. Steve felt a lurch of pity for him. How hard it must be to live as an outcast, so near to home and yet so far, and to see a stranger riding your beloved horse. She mounted and looked down on him with a smile.

'Don't worry. You can trust me. I promise.'

He stood aside and jerked his head in the direction she was going. She nudged Mephisto with her heels and he walked forward. She kept walking, not looking back, feeling the rifles aimed at her spine, until she rounded a bend in the path.

She rode straight to the oak tree where she had hidden the tobacco tin, glad that she made a point of always carrying a pencil and a small slip of paper. She wrote, 'Must meet. 10 a.m. point "B" tomorrow (Thursday).' Then she folded the paper and put it into the tin.

Two days later César picked her up in his *gazogène* van and they drove to a crossroads in the forest. From there, she led him deeper into the trees until they came to the little path she had followed before. He was carrying a basket containing a baguette and some cheese and a bottle of wine. If stopped, they were two lovers going for a picnic. Underneath the food nestled two British-made hand grenades, earnest of their good faith.

They had not gone far before they were challenged. This time the first warning they had was a sudden movement in the undergrowth and the barrel of a rifle pressed between their shoulder blades. They both stopped and Steve put up her hands.

César said quietly, 'Don't make me drop the basket. The results could be explosive.'

Michel stepped into the path in front of them.

'Le Pointu, take the basket. Bring them.'

A tall, very thin boy, obviously the owner of the nickname, stepped forward and took the basket from César, and Steve felt the gun prod her back. Michel led them farther along the path and then stopped suddenly and appeared to uproot a dead bush, revealing an opening that gave access to a narrow track leading down into a natural hollow. In the hollow were four rough shelters roofed with pine branches. A small spring welled up at the rear and trickled away through a narrow declivity, and in the centre of the hollow were the blackened remains of a fire. Three more men were lounging on the ground beside it.

Michel stopped in front of the largest of the shelters and faced them. 'What's in the basket, Pointu?'

The boy unpacked the bread and cheese cautiously and lifted the napkin that lined the basket. His face broke into a delighted grin.

'*Deux oranges, mon capitaine!*'

Steve had learned already that *orange* was the slang term for a hand grenade.

Michel stepped forward and examined the grenades. 'These are British?'

'Yes.' César spoke in his usual even tones.

'You have more?'

'Some. More will come in due course.'

'And you will give them to us? And guns? And ammunition?'

'If I am convinced that you will make good use of them.'

Suddenly Michel grinned too and thrust out his hand. 'You can be sure of that! I am Michel. And you are the one they call César?'

The two men shook hands and then Michel turned to Steve. 'Forgive me for the other day. I am glad my mother has found someone to ride Mephisto. I think he likes you.'

'I like him,' Steve said with a smile. 'It's a great privilege to ride such a magnificent horse.'

Michel gestured around him. 'Welcome to my *maquis*. I should like to offer you lunch but we dare not light a fire during daylight hours in case a Boche spy plane comes over. But we have a little wine and some cheese.'

They sat around on couches of pine branches and le Pointu poured the wine into enamel mugs and they drank to victory and death to the Boches. They shared the baguette augmented by rounds of flat bread baked in the ashes of the previous night's fire, with the cheese and some dried ham that Michel hacked off a lump hanging up under one of the trees. It was a frugal meal, but by the end of it Steve knew that they had found some useful allies. These were men who lived outside the law and who had nothing to lose and everything to gain from driving the enemy out of their country.

Chapter Eight

They received another *parachutage* during the October moon period, and this time Michel and his men were on hand to help. At César's request, as well as weapons and ammunition it included several pairs of boots, some warm clothing and two tarpaulin sheets. The *maquisards* would have some protection from the coming winter weather.

With Bob in captivity, César was trying to keep the Acrobat circuit going as well as his own. It was a relief when, on one of her visits to Gabriel, Steve learned that there had been a message from London telling them to expect a new leader to take over the circuit. It would mean that César had less responsibility and less travelling to do.

Early in November Steve headed for Lons with a report from César for Gabriel to transmit. César had moved Gabriel again, to an abandoned farm in a nearby village, and arranged for a young girl who lived there to go in and cook for him. Steve took a bus from the station to the village and set out to walk to the farm. She passed the house where the girl, Claudette, lived with her grandfather and younger brother, but she had gone only a hundred yards farther when she heard a bicycle behind her and Paul, the brother, skidded to a stop at her side.

'Madame, you must come back to the house. My sister needs to speak to you. It is urgent.'

Steve felt a shiver of anxiety. 'What is it, Paul? Has something happened?'

The boy shook his head mutely and turned his bike towards the house. Steve followed him. Claudette met them at the door, her thin face pale and taut. She beckoned Steve inside and closed the door behind her.

'What's happened, Claudette?' Steve asked.

'M. Gabriel has gone, and Mlle Paulette with him. The Boches came and took them away.'

'When?' The word came out of Steve's mouth in a gasp, as if someone had hit her in the stomach.

'Two nights ago. M. Gabriel was expecting a friend, he told me. He asked me to make a meal for Mlle Paulette and himself and the visitor. I was in the kitchen when the friend arrived and I heard them talking. He had brought a letter for M. Gabriel from his wife. They sounded happy – like good friends. I was just going to serve the meal when the new man said he must leave to see to some business in Lons, but he promised to return shortly. So I served the meal to M. Gabriel and Mlle Paulette and cleared away and then they told me I could go home. It was almost time for the curfew and Mlle Paulette said she would stay the night. I had just got home when two cars passed me – the big black *tractions avant* the Boches like. They went up to the farm, so I crept back and watched from behind the hedge. There were four men in each car and one of them was the man who was there earlier – the man who called himself a friend. They banged on the door and went in and in a minute I saw them come out again with M. Gabriel and Mlle Paulette. They were in handcuffs and the Boches pushed them into the two cars and drove away.' The girl's eyes were full of tears. 'I wanted to help, madame, but I didn't know what to do. I have been watching for you, to stop you going to the farm in case they are waiting for you.'

Steve put her arm around the bony shoulders. 'Thank you, Claudette. That was the only thing you could do. I'm very grateful.' She felt as if she was going to be sick, or perhaps burst into tears herself, but she forced herself to breathe deeply and stay calm. There would be time for shock and grief later but now she must be practical. 'Did any of them see you?'

'No, madame. I stayed in the kitchen while the man was there.'

'Does anyone in the village know that you have been working at the farm?'

'Yes, but they will not say anything to the Boches.'

'And the Boches have not been here or asked you any questions?'

'No, madame.'

'Good. I don't think they will bother you now. But if anyone should ask you, tell them that all you know is that M. Gabriel was an artist. He was very poor and lived alone and he asked you to cook for him. That is all you need say. Do you understand?'

'Yes, madame.'

Steve looked at her watch. She just had time to catch the next bus back into Lons.

It was vital to contact César at the earliest possible moment. 'I have to go now. You won't hear from us again. Here . . .' she scrabbled in her handbag and took out all the spare cash she was carrying. 'You must be owed some wages. Take this. It's all I have on me.' The girl looked at the money and Steve saw her eyes widen. It was more than she would normally earn in a month. But she shook her head.

'No, madame, thank you. I did not do it for the money. I did it for La France.'

'And La France is grateful,' Steve told her. 'Take this as a sign of her gratitude.'

Claudette hesitated a moment longer, then reached out and took the money. Steve said goodbye and walked back to the bus stop in the centre of the village. At every corner she expected to see one of the black cars waiting for her or a man in the long raincoat and slouch hat that the Gestapo affected hanging about, trying to look inconspicuous. But she reached the village square without incident, just in time to catch the bus.

On the way back into Lons, Steve struggled to come to terms with what had happened and its possible consequences. Gabriel had been in Gestapo hands for forty-eight hours. That was the limit of the time that agents were asked to hold out, to give their colleagues a chance to get away. Perhaps he would manage to hold out longer. Perhaps he would never speak, no matter what they did to him, but she remembered the words of the instructor at Beaulieu. 'Everyone speaks, sooner or later.' So what were the greatest dangers? He had known her only as Suzette, so with any luck her identity papers as Marguerite Duclos were still safe. But people had seen her going to the farm and, whatever Claudette might believe, there were always one or two who could be suborned by threats or promises into giving information. Her description might already be on file with the Gestapo.

César was in greater danger. Steve knew that he had been in regular contact with Gabriel, since Bob's arrest. Her first priority must be to warn him.

She passed the train journey in a state of nervous tension so great that it was almost impossible to stay in her seat. At every station she expected to see the sinister figure of a Gestapo agent boarding the train, or hear the tramp of boots as soldiers of the Feldgendarmerie invaded the carriages, demanding to see documents. But the journey passed without incident and as soon as she reached Arbois she made her way straight to Dr Lefort's surgery. It was mid-afternoon and she found the doctor in his study enjoying a post prandial snooze. His look of surprise as the house-keeper showed her in turned to one of concern as he saw her expression.

'Something is wrong. Is it Madame la Comtesse?'

'That's what I told your housekeeper but it's not true. I must contact M. César urgently – today. It is a matter of life and death.'

This time there was no hesitation. 'Very well. I shall call on the old lady. Shall I tell him to come to the chateau?'

'Yes. No – tell him to meet me at the hostellerie. I'll be there until just before the curfew.'

'Very good. Now, sit down and let me pour you a little restorative. You look exhausted.'

Steve shook her head. 'Thank you, but I must go. And please, go at once to find César!'

The doctor put down the bottle he had taken up and ushered her to the door. 'I shall go immediately. Don't worry.'

She found Pierre and Yvonne Bardet in the kitchen, eating their own lunch after having served their guests. She told them about Gabriel's arrest, adding, 'You two have no connection with Gabriel except through César, so as long as he is free you have nothing to worry about.'

They pressed her to eat lunch but she had no appetite. Pierre gave her a glass of *marc* and some ersatz coffee and then there was nothing to do but wait. She kept telling herself that César was probably out and would not get the doctor's message until he returned. By then it might be dark.

She began to regret the stress she had put on the urgency of a meeting. The last thing she had intended was for him to risk breaking the curfew. She wished that she could go and find him, but he had always been careful to keep his address a secret. She knew that it was good security, but in the circumstances it meant she could do nothing more to warn him of the danger.

Just as the light was beginning to fail at the end of the short November day there was a knock on the back door of the hostellerie and Steve jumped up hopefully. A young boy, whom she recognised as Laurent, the doctor's son, stood outside panting and bright eyed with excitement at being entrusted with an important mission.

'Madame, my father asks you to come at once to the surgery. It is very important'

With her nerves stretched almost to breaking point, it took every ounce of self-discipline Steve possessed to follow the boy up the street without betraying the rising panic that threatened to overwhelm her. He led her in by the back door to the doctor's study, where she was greeted by a sight that made her cry out in dismay. César was sitting in a chair by the doctor's desk. His right eye was blackened and his lip cut and swollen, his right arm was in a sling and his shirt-front stained with blood.

Steve ran across the room and dropped to her knees beside him, catching hold of his free hand. *'Mon Dieu!* What has happened to you?'

He squeezed her hand and attempted a grin that ended in a grimace of pain. 'Don't worry, it looks worse than it is. But my cover's blown. In fact the whole circuit may be completely *brûlé*. I've got to make a run for it.'

'What happened?' Steve asked again.

'I went to call on one of our men – Jean, he's a teacher in

Salins. When I knocked on the door it was opened by an SS officer with a pistol. It turned out Jean had been arrested and they'd left this man behind, as they do, to see who turned up. I managed to convince him that I'd just called to borrow a book but he said I'd have to wait with him until his relief arrived and then go with him to Gestapo HQ while they checked out my story. I knew if I ever got that far I'd never get out again, so I persuaded him that we might as well have a drink while we were waiting. He sat down at the table and I fetched a bottle of wine and when I passed behind him I hit him over the head with it. Stupid fool that I am! I didn't hit him anything like hard enough. He swung round and fired at me. Funnily enough, I didn't feel anything at the time. I thought he was firing blanks until I saw the blood on my shirt. I managed to knock the gun out of his hand and then we started the most ridiculous sort of wrestling match. He nearly throttled me but I managed to break free and winded him and then I ran for it. But he's got my identity card, so by dawn tomorrow every patrol in the area will be on the lookout for me.'

'This man, Jean – how much does he know?' Steve asked.

'Only the identity of the people in his immediate cell. And me, of course.'

'Did he know Gabriel?'

'My God, yes! He's taken messages to Gabriel for me. We must warn him!'

'Too late,' Steve said. I think it must have been Gabriel who put them on to Jean.' She told him what she had learned that morning. 'But I can't make out who the stranger was who led the Gestapo to him,' she added. 'If he brought a letter from Gabriel's wife he must surely be the new man London promised to send out.'

'Well, either that man is a double agent, or the real one

was captured and the Gestapo got someone to impersonate him. The letter would have been enough to convince Gabriel he was genuine.' César's head drooped. 'Either way, the whole circuit's gone.'

'No,' Steve said. 'You kept us all separate. The people in this area aren't implicated. If you can get away there's no reason why we shouldn't carry on. Pedro can take charge. What are your plans?'

'The good doctor here is going to drive me to Montbéliard. I have friends there who can smuggle me over the border into Switzerland.'

'Suppose you are stopped on the way?' Steve asked, looking up at the doctor. 'It's asking for trouble to be on the roads after curfew.'

'Not for a doctor,' he pointed out. 'I have a special pass. I shall bandage our friend's face so that he cannot be recognised and if I am stopped I shall say that he has been in a serious accident and I am taking him to the hospital in Montbéliard. His injuries will be enough to convince a routine patrol.'

'That's brilliant!' Steve said.

César gripped her hand. 'Come with me. The doctor can say you are a nurse. You are in danger, too. Come to Switzerland with me.'

For a moment Steve almost yielded to the temptation, but then she shook her head. 'Someone has to warn Pedro. And if he is going to take over the circuit he will need help. I'll go underground for a while. No one in the circuit knows my cover name except you. Once you are out of reach of the Gestapo I'll be safe enough.'

The doctor moved forward, a roll of bandage in his hand. 'Come, it is time we were on our way. Let me bandage your face.'

In a moment César's head was swathed in bandages, leaving only one eye exposed. Steve put her arm around him and kissed the only part of his cheek that was visible. 'Good luck, *mon cher* I shall miss you.'

'And I shall miss you,' he answered. 'Shall we meet again, do you think?'

'One day, back in England.'

'I shan't know how to find you.'

'Ask Maurice Buckmaster, or Vera Atkins. They'll be able to tell you.'

'Come,' the doctor repeated, taking César by the arm

As they were about to leave César stopped. 'How are you going to get home now? The curfew has started.'

'Wait!' Dr Lefort commanded. He disappeared for a minute into his surgery and returned carrying a small bottle. 'If anyone stops you, tell them that Madame la Comtesse is suffering from her arthritis and sent you to fetch some medicine to ease the pain.'

He opened the door and scanned the street briefly, then helped César into his car. Steve shook his hand, full of admiration for his calm efficiency. She had had doubts when they first met but now she saw that, once having committed himself, Lefort was a man who would rise to any emergency.

'Thank you, Doctor,' she said, then stooped to take a last look into the car. '*Merde alors,* César.'

'Look after yourself,' he answered. Then the doctor started the engine and the car pulled away.

Steve collected her bicycle and rode slowly back to the chateau. Sylvie met her in the entrance hall and immediately took her by the arm.

'Something is wrong. Come and sit down and tell me.'

She led her into her private sitting room and poured her a glass of Macvin, the local aperitif.

'Now, tell me what has happened.'

Steve struggled with the impulse to blurt out the whole story. She was certain that she could trust Sylvie implicitly but her training told her that the less her hostess knew the safer it would be for both of them. In the end, she said, 'A friend of mine has been taken by the Gestapo and they almost got César too. He got away but they know his identity.'

'Where is he now?'

'Someone – a friend – is taking him to the Swiss border.'

'And you?' Sylvie looked into her face. 'Are you in danger, too?'

'I'm not sure. The Gestapo won't have my name but I may have been seen. They may have a description.'

'Then we must change the way you look.' Sylvie stood up. 'Come and have something to eat. After dinner we will see what can be done.'

Steve ate without tasting her food but afterwards she felt calmer. When the meal was over Sylvie led her up to her bedroom and produced a bottle of hair dye from the back of a drawer.

'I bought this when the first grey started to appear, but then the war came and it seemed stupid and frivolous to bother about such things. Perhaps *le bon Dieu* intended me to keep it for just this moment. But first I think we must cut your hair. Sit here, at the dressing table.'

She took up a pair of scissors and began to snip Steve's hair. Half an hour later, when her hair had been dyed and towelled dry, Steve sat in front of the mirror again. Sylvie had wrought an amazing transformation. The conventional English rose with her dark chestnut hair neatly rolled back from her face had been replaced by an urchin with a tousled black mop combed into a fringe above her blue-green eyes.

'You look quite *gamine, n'est-ce pas?*' Sylvie remarked approvingly. 'I think you will not fit any description they have of you now.'

'Thank you, Sylvie,' Steve said. 'You've done a wonderful job. But I can't stay here, you know. Too many people have seen me and know what I used to look like. Tomorrow I must find somewhere else to live.'

'But where will you go?'

'I'm not sure yet. I have to get a message to someone. He may have ideas about that.'

There was nothing more to be done that night, but before she slept Steve packed a few things into her case and retrieved her gun and what remained of the money she had been given from where she had hidden it behind an old-fashioned wardrobe. Most of it was still intact, since Sylvie had asked nothing from her for her board and lodging. It seemed probable, however, that she might need it soon. She put the case by the bed, where she could grab it quickly, and peered out of the window. The room had a small balcony and the drop to the ground was not great. She reckoned that in an emergency her parachute training would enable her to jump down without injury. Her last waking thoughts were of César. She knew that there was a good chance that she would never see him again, and for the first time she realised how deeply she had come to care for him.

After a broken night, during which she had imagined or dreamed five or six different scenarios for César's capture, Steve woke to find everything normal, except for the image that greeted her in the mirror. The sun had just risen from behind a bank of cloud. It was going to be a beautiful day, and she thought wistfully that on any previous morning she would have gone straight down to the stable to saddle

Mephisto for her morning ride. Now she would never ride him again.

At breakfast she said to Sylvie, 'As I told you last night, there is someone I must contact but I don't know how to do it.'

'Do you have an address for him?'

'No, but we have two places where we leave messages. I know he will check them every morning. But I am afraid to go to leave the message in case I am being watched.'

'Then write your message and I will send Georges's grandson with it. You can tell him where the hiding place is. He can be trusted. Tell your friend to come here.'

'I don't like to involve you,' Steve murmured.

'Listen, you say the Gestapo do not have a name or an address for you. It will take time for them to trace you from a description. Your friend can come here quite safely, I think.'

'What will you say, if they eventually come looking for me?'

'That you left without explanation yesterday. I took you in, out of pity because you were a refugee, and I am shocked to discover that you abused my hospitality.' Sylvie smiled. 'I can be quite convincing when I want to be.'

Steve wrote a note to Pedro, saying that Suzette needed to see him urgently at the Château de Montmain. Sylvie sent for the boy and talked to him gravely about the privilege of being allowed to serve his country and swore him to secrecy. Steve instructed him carefully about where to leave the message and half an hour later he returned, grinning happily, to announce that the letter had been duly concealed.

Pedro arrived at midday, driving a *gazogène* similar to César's but bearing the name of a local *vigneron*. He stared at Steve for a moment as if he failed to recognise her and then she saw his face darken as he guessed the implication of her disguise. She gave him a succinct outline of the events of the previous day and for a moment or two he paced the room in silence, pinching the bridge of his nose between finger and thumb. Then he turned and faced her.

'I have heard nothing to suggest César has been arrested, but we must assume that he has and act accordingly. You must leave here at once. You have done a good job of changing your appearance but are your documents still valid?'

'No one knows my cover name except César but the photograph is wrong now, of course.'

'Of course. Well, there is a man in Besançon who can put that right for you but until then you must stay out of sight. I know a place. There is a little bistro in Besançon called the Brasserie Vauban, quite close to the railway station. The owner is a Louis Choquin. He and his wife are supporters and I have often used their place as a rendezvous. I will take you there and I know they will look after you.'

'What then?' Steve asked. 'What about the work?'

'That must go on, of course. I shall take over the *réseau* and once we can get you new papers you can start working as my courier again. The worst thing is, we shall have no radio contact with London. Without that we cannot organise *parachutages*. I will send someone west, to the Yonne area. I know there is a *réseau* operating there which has a radio operator. I will ask them to contact London to let them know what has happened and put in an urgent request for a new operator for this circuit. That is all we can do for now. Come, the sooner we leave here the better.'

Sylvie was waiting for them in the hall. Steve went to her and took her hands.

'Goodbye, Sylvie. I can never thank you enough for everything you have done.'

'I have done nothing,' the older woman replied. 'It has given me great pleasure to have you here and I shall miss you very much.' Her grip tightened. 'Before you go, tell me one thing. Have you had any word of my son, Michel?'

Steve squeezed her fingers. 'Yes. I have seen him. I can't tell you where he is or what he is doing, but he is well and among friends.'

'Thank you.' Sylvie's eyes filled with tears. She put her arms around Steve and hugged her tightly for a moment. 'Take care, my dear. And promise that you will come back and see us when all this is over.'

'If I possibly can, I will,' Steve promised.

She went out to where Pedro was waiting by the van. 'What if we get stopped?'

'I'll show you,' he said, and opened the rear doors. The van was full of wooden crates containing wine bottles, but at the far end, nearest to the driver's cabin, there was a space just big enough for someone to sit, out of sight. Steve climbed in and coiled herself into it. It would not pass a thorough search but to a casual glance the van's cargo would appear to be exactly what the name on the side suggested. Pedro slammed the doors shut and in a moment the engine started and Steve felt herself being carried away – away from the chateau, which had begun to feel almost like home, and once again into an unknowable future.

The Brasserie Vauban was a less sophisticated establishment than its name suggested and not as cosy as the hostellerie in Arbois. There was a long bar and a dozen small tables with stained check tablecloths. The clientele, as far as Steve could judge when she passed through on her arrival, were mainly workers from the railway marshalling yard across the road. Louis and Jacqueline Choquin were in the back kitchen. He was a squat man with a thick neck and very large hands and she was small and neat with dark hair coiled on top of her head and a face that had once been pretty but now had the faded look of a flower that was past its best. Pedro explained rapidly what had happened and Jacqueline clucked sympathetically while Louis greeted the news with a phlegmatic shrug. Neither of them had ever had any contact with César, since he had left the organisation of the Besançon cell to Pedro. They were sorry to hear about his arrest but not personally concerned. Steve could not help contrasting Louis' dour manner with Pierre's sly humour but it was clear that were staunch supporters of the Resistance and agreed without hesitation to take Steve in.

'There is a spare room at the top of the house,' Louis said, 'and she can help out in the kitchen or waiting at tables for her keep.'

As they were talking a girl arrived with a basket of goods from the market.

'This is our daughter, Juliette,' Mme Choquin announced.

Juliette was in her late teens, as far as Steve could judge, and had all the attractiveness that her mother must once have possessed. Her large dark eyes sparkled with vitality and her slightly upturned nose and curving mouth gave her face an expression of mischievous enjoyment.

Her mother explained briefly the reasons for Steve's sudden arrival and Juliette impulsively took her hand.

'Don't worry. You will be safe here. You can trust us.'

Steve smiled at her, cheered by her open warmth. 'I'm sure I can.'

Jacqueline looked critically at Steve. 'Those are country clothes, not right for the town. Juliette is about the same size as you. She can lend you something for the time being.'

Steve was wearing the trousers and sweater that had been provided for her in England. While she was at the chateau Sylvie had lent her clothes – jodhpurs for riding, and summer skirts and blouses for the warm weather – but she had left them behind, and the dark grey suit no longer seemed to fit her character. Juliette took her up to her room and laughingly laid out the contents of her small wardrobe.

'You have to look like a waitress now, not a young lady. See, try these on.'

'These' were a black skirt and a dark red blouse. Steve was slightly taller than Juliette and fuller in the bust, so the skirt was short and the blouse clung tightly over her breasts.

Juliette clapped her hands. *'Ooh-la-la! C'est magnifique!* You will have all the men after you!'

Looking at herself in the mirror Steve saw a complete stranger. The original Marguerite Duclos had been not unlike Diana Escott Stevens, but now the well-brought-up young lady had vanished and been replaced by a coquette with spiky dark hair and a provocative figure. She found the prospect oddly liberating. The instructions she had been given by the expert from Max Factor came back to her. It was not enough to disguise yourself physically. You must learn to live the part. So be it. This would be her new character. Marguerite Duclos had fallen on hard times but had recreated herself as a waitress with a sexy smile.

Chapter Nine

A light breeze sighed through the forest and ruffled the waters of the River Doubs. Steve got off her bicycle and sniffed the air. It smelt of fertility and rebirth. Above her the sky was a clear, pale blue and the forest was full of the sound of trickling water from the melting snow. It was February, and for the first time she sensed that spring was not far off. It had been a difficult, frustrating winter, though there was much to be grateful for. Most importantly, there had been no hint that the Gestapo had captured César. Pedro had contacts in the French gendarmerie but none of them had picked up any rumours of an arrest. Steve had managed to get a message to Sylvie through one of her contacts and had learned that no one from the SD or the Gestapo had been to question her and that Dr Lefort had returned safely to Arbois. Since there had been no further repercussions she had to assume that César had escaped, but she longed for definite news. Pedro had put out feelers, too, in an attempt to discover the identity of the man who had betrayed Gabriel and Paulette, but he had come up against a brick wall. They had no way of knowing whether he was the man sent out by London, who had been 'turned' by the Gestapo, or whether the real agent had been captured and an impostor had taken his place. Without any contact with London there was no way of finding out. The only consolation was that, as the winter months passed without incident, it seemed that they were safe for the time being.

In recent months, recruits had been coming forward to join the Resistance in ever increasing numbers. Now that it seemed inevitable that Germany would lose the war and that the Allied invasion, which would drive the occupiers out of France, must come soon, more and more people were feeling emboldened to take up the cause. There were others, more self-interested, who were beginning to realise that it would be politic to make it clear that they had had a part to play in ousting the hated enemy, lest they should be labelled collaborators when victory finally arrived. The problem, as far as Steve and Pedro were concerned, was to supply these increasing numbers with what they most craved – weapons and ammunition. It had been a winter of storms and high winds, which had rendered any possibility of a *parachutage* out of the question. The equipment they had received earlier had been distributed among the existing groups, and now they had nothing with which to prove their good faith and potential usefulness to the new cells that were growing up all around them. Worst of all, they still had no radio operator and no radio set, so they were unable to communicate with London. The emissary whom Pedro had dispatched to the *réseau* in the Yonne had returned to report that the message had been delivered, but since then there had been no sign that their controllers in Baker Street were even aware of their existence.

Steve had spent the winter bicycling around the area from one group to another, encouraging, reassuring, making promises that she herself was not sure would ever be honoured. She had had no difficulty in moving around since her explanation, if challenged, was that she was foraging for supplies for the restaurant. With rations growing shorter by the month most of the population of the cities spent their free time combing the countryside for eggs or milk or flour or any other produce that the *cultivateurs* in the villages were prepared to part with at black market prices. Her identity card had been replaced with one bearing her new photograph, though she had seen no reason to change the name on it. In the evenings she waited at tables in the restaurant or helped Jacqueline in the kitchen.

Juliette had become her closest confidante; in fact the younger girl stuck to her like her shadow. Early on she had begged to be allowed to help but Steve had been hesitant. She knew that the Choquins' support consisted in providing a safe meeting place for members of the Resistance but did not extend to active participation, and she was uneasy about involving their daughter any further, but Juliette would not be denied.

'You must understand,' she exclaimed, gripping Steve's hand, her dark eyes glowing. 'I hate the Boches! When I see them stalking around my city as if they owned it I want to scream and throw things at them. Sometimes I think if I can't do something useful I shall explode.'

On reflection, Steve decided it was better to channel the girl's enthusiasm into areas she could control rather than risk her throwing herself into some foolhardy enterprise that would endanger them all.

In spite of the shortage of explosives, Pedro had insisted on continuing his campaign of sabotage. Trains had been derailed, bridges blown up and enemy patrols ambushed. Steve worried about this. She remembered how insistent César had been that they should keep a low profile and conserve their supplies until they received the messages that would tell them that the invasion was imminent. It was then that an all-out effort would be required to disrupt the German communications. She had argued the point with

Pedro but he maintained that for the sake of morale it was necessary for the *résistants* to feel that they were, at least, making things uncomfortable for the enemy. That they had succeeded in doing this was evidenced by increasing activity on the part of the SD. Villages had been searched and people arrested and taken for questioning to the citadel in Besançon. Steve feared that they were stirring up a hornets' nest and that the whole *réseau* might be destroyed before the crucial invasion happened.

In the course of her travels around the area she had learned of the existence of two more *maquis* hidden in the forest of Caux, which stretched for some thirty kilometres along the south side of the River Doubs. When she made contact with them she found that both were small groups, eight men in one and twelve in the other, and they were in a pitiful state. Like many of the *maquisards*, they had taken to the forest for a variety of reasons – some to escape the STO, some because they were wanted by the police, a few for purely patriotic reasons. None of them had any experience of living rough and it struck Steve that they would be lucky to survive the winter. They were hungry, ill clad and filthy. When she reported their existence to Pedro he made the decision to incorporate them into the much better-organised group controlled by Michel de Montmain. He had persuaded Michel to move his people north to a camp that was better placed to attack the essential rail and road links between central France and the German border, which ran through Besançon. It was to this new camp that Steve was headed that morning.

Having caught her breath, she remounted the bicycle and pedalled slowly up the hill. Eight months of cycling around the broken country of the Franche Comté had given her calf muscles like those of a dray horse, but this was still hard work. Before reaching the top of the hill she got off the bike again, as if to take another rest, and stood gazing around her. When she was quite sure that the road was empty in both directions she heaved the bike across a roadside ditch and concealed it behind some bushes. Then she set off on foot along a path that led deeper into the woods.

After half a kilometre or so she stopped again, standing stock still and listening for any sound of movement. Then she ducked under some overhanging branches, and scrambled down a slope and across a little stream to gain another, narrower trail that slanted steeply up the face of an escarpment. A hundred yards from the top she stood still again, steadied her breathing and whistled the opening bars of 'Auprès de ma blonde . . .'. There was a rustle in the bare branches of a tree just ahead, then a thud as the lanky form of le Pointu dropped on to the path.

'Salut, Mlle Suzette!' he said, grinning broadly and raising two fingers to his temple in a rough salute.

'Salut, Pointu,' she responded. 'Ça va?'

'Oui, ça va. Come. The captain will be glad to see you.'

She followed him along the path to where it opened out on to a small plateau. At the rear, where the hillside rose sheer, was a cave, and under the trees that fringed the plateau on both sides were several sturdily constructed huts, roofed with tarpaulins and covered with a thatch of pine branches. It was a well-chosen spot for, though the surrounding forest sheltered the huts from view, the front of the plateau was open and commanded a clear view down to the valley of the Doubs and the main road and railway between Dole and Besançon. A little farther down the slope a spring provided the camp with fresh water.

Thirty or more men were sitting or lounging outside the huts, cleaning rifles and chatting. They rose as Steve appeared and called greetings to her and she responded warmly, addressing many of them by name and making enquiries about matters she knew concerned them.

'*Bonjour, Claude*. Did you manage to get a message to your wife? Is she all right?' . . . '*Salut, Charles*. I hear you've just become a father. Congratulations!'

Michel came out of the cave, which he had adopted as his private quarters, and greeted her with a kiss on both cheeks.

'I'm glad you're here. I have a surprise for you.'

'A surprise?'

'We have a visitor.'

'Where from? Who is he?'

'Ah, that is exactly the question. He *says* he's English, but I leave it to you to confirm that or otherwise. He turned up in Arbois a couple of days ago and went to the hostellerie, asking for you or Pedro. Pierre didn't know what to do with him but by good luck I'd given Marcel permission to visit his mother, who's ill, and he happened to drop into the hostellerie for a drink. Pierre told him about his problem and Marcel brought the stranger here. I told him he'd have to stay with us until I could get in touch with you.'

'Who sent him to look for me?'

'The same people as sent you, he says.'

Steve moved towards the cave entrance, her heartbeat quickening. She had not forgotten how Gabriel had been betrayed. The entrance to the cave was partly shielded by pine branches. Inside, the floor was of fine sand and a fire burned in the centre. The group had discovered that the smoke filtered out through a number of fissures in the rocks above, so dissipated that it was unlikely to be seen from a distance and give a clue to the location of the camp. It meant that the *maquisards* could cook proper meals and during bad weather there was a warm place for them all to shelter.

As Steve entered, a slight figure rose from the far side of the fire and came towards her. 'Suzette?'

The dim light, after the bright day outside, meant that for a moment she was unable to make out anything other than the outline of the visitor's body, but there was something familiar about the voice. She took a step or two closer, screwing up her eyes.

'Danny! *Mon Dieu!* It's you! I can't believe it!'

He came forward, peering at her. 'I'm sorry, I don't think . . . Steve? It's not, is it? Good God, I didn't recognise you.'

She laughed and held out her arms to him. 'I'm not surprised. Oh, Danny, I can't tell you how glad I am to see you.'

As they embraced Michel remarked dryly, 'I take it you two know each other.'

Steve turned to him. 'It's all right, *mon ami*. I can vouch for him. We trained together. Danny, this is Michel. Michel meet . . . oh, but . . .' She looked back at Danny. 'I'm sorry. Baker Street must have given you an operational name.'

He shrugged. 'Yes, I believe they did want me to call myself something ridiculous, like Desiré. I told them Daniel was a perfectly good French name and I didn't see any need to change it. Anyway, it's a bit late for introductions, considering we've been sleeping together for the last two nights.' Then, in response to a grunt of protest from Michel, he added mischievously, 'On opposite sides of the cave, I hasten to add.'

Steve laughed. 'You haven't changed. Still doing everything your own way. But why are you here?'

'What do you think?' he asked, nodding towards a package in the corner. 'You asked for a new radio operator, didn't you?'

Steve recognised the familiar brown leather suitcase and gave an exclamation of joy. 'Of course! Well, you couldn't be more welcome.'

Danny looked at his watch. 'I ought to have contacted London an hour ago. I've missed my last two skeds, but our friend here wouldn't let me transmit from his camp.'

'Quite right too,' Steve said. 'We don't want the Boches picking up your signal and descending on everyone here.' She was thinking hard. 'I'll take you to somewhere where you can work in safety, as far as that's possible. Do you have any transport? How did you get here?'

'By bicycle,' Danny said, wrinkling his nose. 'The least comfortable form of transport ever devised.'

'The bike was loaned by Pierre's son,' Michel put in. 'I had to send it back.'

'Well, in that case, it's Shanks's pony, I'm afraid,' Steve said. 'But the place I have in mind is only about five kilometres away. Shall we go?'

They said goodbye to Michel and Steve led the way back to where she had left her bike. As they walked she said, 'What's your cover story – just in case we run into a patrol?'

'My name is Jean Poignand and I'm a refugee from Marseilles. I worked as a clerk to a shipping company but now I'm looking for a job and prepared to turn my hand to anything.'

'So, what are we doing together?'

'Good question. Any ideas?'

Steve thought. 'Yes, got it. You went to Pierre Bardet at the hostellerie in Arbois, looking for work as a waiter or in the kitchen. He didn't have anything for you but he sent you on to his friend, Louis Choquin at the Brasserie Vauban in Besançon. That's where I'm working at the moment. There was no work for you there either, but now I am taking you to another friend, M. Carrez, the baker at Montferrand-le-Château. He needs an assistant – he doesn't know it yet but I'm sure he'll cooperate. You can live with him and his wife, but there's a place I'll show you close by where you can transmit from. Are you happy with that?'

'I shall be quite happy anywhere as long as I can stay in one place for more than a day or two. There are parts of my anatomy that haven't recovered from that bicycle ride yet.'

Steve retrieved her bike from the bushes and strapped the suitcase on to the carrier. Then they set out for Montferrand-le-Château, keeping to the narrow lanes that criss-crossed the hills. They reached the baker's house without incident and Steve introduced Danny – or rather Jean. Gilbert Carrez had proved himself a staunch supporter of the Resistance over the past months and as she had expected he agreed to take Danny in without asking questions. They ate lunch with Gilbert and his wife Marie, and then Steve led Danny up a track behind the house, towards the ruined castle that stood on the hill above. Just below the ruins there was a wooden hut that had been used at one time by the lumberjacks who made a living from the forest. That trade had dwindled over the years and now the hut was used occasionally as an overnight shelter by locals cutting timber or looking for mushrooms. The *maquisards* hid out there from time to time, on the way back from sabotage operations. There was a stove at one end and a long table occupied the centre of the space, with rough bunks along either side and a cupboard containing some basic crockery and a few bottles of local wine.

Steve set a bottle of wine and two glasses on the table between them and sat down. 'So, tell me what you've been up to since we left Beaulieu.'

'Oh, this and that. I was in Paris for several months but then things got too hot and they had to pull me out.'

'Too hot? How?'

'No one seems to know exactly what went wrong but there were some ugly rumours. Somewhere along the line someone gave some names to the Gestapo. A lot of our people were picked up. I was lucky to get out'

'What then?'

'They gave me a stint as a Conducting Officer. Funny business, seeing it all from the other side, if you see what I mean.'

'How are things back home?'

'Much the same as usual, when I left – blackout, rationing, miserable weather. Oh, hang on a minute. I've got something for you.' He turned away and opened the rucksack in which he was carrying his personal possessions. 'Here.'

He handed Steve a large sealed envelope. She slit it open and tipped out a small sheaf of letters in her mother's handwriting.

'Did Baker Street give you these?'

'Yes. They thought as you hadn't had a *parachutage* for some months you'd be glad to hear from your people.'

'But suppose you'd been stopped and searched with these on you?'

He shrugged. 'If that had happened they'd have found the radio set so my chances of passing as an innocent civilian would have gone up in smoke. A packet of letters would be neither here nor there. And I couldn't have told them anything about you. I didn't know who you were or where to find you. And you'll notice that Baker Street have blacked out any details that might have given the Gestapo a clue. Aren't you going to read them?'

'Yes,' Steve said, 'but first things first. When's your next sked?'

'In about an hour's time.'

'Right. We'd better get a message ready to go out.'

Danny took out a pad and pencil and became businesslike. 'What do you want to say?'

'Tell them you've met up with me and that Stockbroker is still functioning with Pedro as leader. Tell them we've had new recruits flooding in all winter and we are desperate for supplies. Make it clear that we can make things really uncomfortable for the Boches but we must have a *parachutage* at the earliest possible moment.'

'Do you have the coordinates for the dropping zone?'

'Not at the moment. Tell them I'll let them have them as soon as we have a definite date for the drop.'

Danny was looking at her with a grin. 'Well, well. It's not just the hairstyle that's changed. Are you sure it's Pedro leading this circuit?'

Steve blushed. 'Of course it is. I'm just telling you what I know he would want you to say.'

'Right,' Danny agreed, still smiling.

As he settled down at the table with his coding sheets, Steve opened her letters. There was the usual chit-chat about the farm. It had been a hard winter. One of the Land Girls had gone down with bronchitis. Rationing was getting worse and people were becoming dispirited with the progress of the war, after the brief euphoria of the Italian surrender. And, running through all the letters, was the same thread. *'Why don't we hear more from you? Why can't you write a proper letter?'*

There were letters from Roddy, too. He had been awarded the DFC for his exploits in Malta and promoted to squadron leader. He was now in charge of a new squadron based somewhere on the south coast. He missed her and lived for the day when the war would be over and they would be able to start their life together. Steve read the letters with a strange numbness. She found that she could no longer picture Roddy's face, or hear his voice in her imagination. Her most vivid memory was the physical sensation of his arms around her and his body close to hers, but even that seemed unreal, like something she had dreamed.

Underneath her mother's letters Steve found one from Frankie, dated 20 September.

> *Dear* ▬▬▬
>
> *I'm sorry I haven't written for some time but we've been snowed under with work here. It has got to the point since the Italian surrender where we have had to abandon normal shifts and all of us are working round the clock.*
>
> *Things are not quite so rosy here as when I last wrote. Nick has been posted. I can't tell you where, of course, but you can guess it's not anywhere safe. I'm worried out of my mind about him but there's nothing I can do . . .*

The letter went on but Steve found it hard to concentrate. All Frankie's concerns seemed so distant from the reality of her own life, yet she felt guilty about her lack of interest.

She folded the letters and started to put them in her pocket. Then, reluctantly, she carried them over to the stove and set light to them. When she was quite sure that they were all reduced to ashes she stirred the pieces into dust and turned to Danny.

'How's it going?'

'Ready. Let's get the aerial deployed.'

They draped the wire around the cabin and Danny settled himself at the table and put on his earphones. Steve stood at the door, watching the track. The chances of a detector van operating in this remote spot were small but she was taking nothing for granted. From time to time she glanced back at

Danny as he twiddled knobs and tapped at the Morse key and after a few minutes, to her delight, he gave her a thumbs up signal.

When he finally removed the headphones and switched off he said, 'They've acknowledged but there's no message. That's not surprising because they didn't know I'd made contact with you. The next sked is tomorrow morning. There will probably be a reply then.'

'I'll come back tomorrow, then,' Steve promised. 'Meanwhile, we'd better hide that set. And I'll arrange with M. Carrez for one of his kids to come and act as lookout while you're on air.' She looked at her watch. 'If I don't go soon I shan't get back before curfew.'

'You go,' he said. 'I can hide this and find my own way back to the village.'

'Sure?'

He grinned at her. 'I found my way halfway across France, didn't I? I can manage this by myself. Go on, off you go.'

She grinned at him. 'See you tomorrow, then.'

Steve cycled back to the city in a strange mood. The letters from home had saddened her, not so much by their content as for the sense of distance and dislocation they produced. On the other hand, Danny's arrival and the re-establishment of contact with London was a source of hope. By the time she reached the Brasserie Vauban her thoughts were concentrated on plans for the immediate future.

As soon as she entered the kitchen her optimistic mood evaporated. Louis and Jacqueline were sitting at the table, white faced and tense. Both of them started violently as she entered and then sank back in relief.

'What's going on?' she asked.

'It's bad,' Louis told her. 'There's been another *rafle.*'

Rafle was the slang term used to describe the Germans' periodic sweeps, intended to pick up suspected 'terrorists', as they termed the resistance fighters.

'How bad?' Steve demanded.

'We're not sure yet. So far it's only rumours. But we know they've got Paul Baverel and Georges Bey and Robert Nicholas, and if they've taken them somebody, somewhere, must have squealed, so there are bound to be others.'

'*Merde!*' Steve muttered. She sat down heavily at the table. 'Did they know about you – those three?' she asked.

Louis shook his head. 'Pedro never brought any of them here. They used to meet in the Café Bregille. I found out from Jacques, who works over the way in the marshalling yards. His lot always have their ears to the ground.'

'No one has been here, then?' Steve asked.

'No, and they're not looking for you, as far as Jacques knows.'

Steve quelled a rising sense of panic and forced herself to think. She recognised the names of the three men but she had never had any direct contact with them. Pedro had always dealt with them himself. It was possible that she and the Choquin family might not be implicated.

As if to shatter that fragile sense of security the back door slammed open and Juliette flung herself into the room. Her hair was wild and her face streaked with tears. She saw Steve and threw herself into a chair, grabbing her hand.

'Oh, thank God you're here. Something terrible has happened. Pedro is dead.'

'Dead?' Three voices gasped the same word.

'How?' Steve asked hoarsely.

'He was in the Café Bregille, with some other men. The Gestapo came for him. He pulled a gun and tried to shoot his way out. They shot him dead.'

'And the others?'

'The Gestapo took them away.'

Jacqueline began to weep. 'Oh, *mon Dieu! Mon Dieu!*'

Steve pressed her hands to her face. Her instinct was to jump up and run out of the house, to get on her bicycle and ride as far and as fast as she could, but she knew that that would be the worst thing she could do. Besides, she had a responsibility to these people who had taken her in.

'Listen,' she said. 'It seems that the Besançon cell has been blown. You say Pedro never brought any of them here. He was very security conscious. He kept people separate as far as possible. It's highly likely that he was the only person who knew of your involvement, or mine. You're sure he was killed, Juliette, not just wounded?'

'I wasn't there, but that's what I heard in the market.'

'Well, dead, he can't reveal anything. And the rest can't tell what they don't know. The chances are that we are all safe. The best thing we can do is stay quiet and not do anything that might draw attention. Business as usual, yes?'

Jacqueline swallowed. 'Yes,' she said huskily. Louis nodded.

Juliette fixed her eyes on Steve's face. 'You won't leave us, will you?'

Steve looked at her. Although she was only seventeen she had proved herself reliable and she was well known in the town and the surrounding countryside and able to carry messages without arousing suspicion. She was aware that it was not entirely patriotism and implacable hatred of the occupiers which motivated the younger girl. She had been head girl at her school and was familiar with the phenomenon of hero worship. It had always made her uncomfortable but she knew that, whether merited or not, such adoration imposed certain obligations on its object.

'No,' she said, 'of course I'm not going to leave.'

'And the work? Can we carry on without Pedro?'

'We shall have to. We can't stop now.'

Steve spoke almost without thinking. It was only after she had uttered the words that the enormity of their implication struck her.

It was a nervous evening. Somehow the food was prepared and served without the clients being aware that all four of them froze every time the door opened. Many of the customers were workers from the railway depot across the road, who belonged to or sympathised with the FTP – the Francs Tireurs et Partisans – a communist organisation which ran its own campaign of resistance, independently of SOE. Their conversation that night was mainly about the arrests, and from that Steve learnt the full magnitude of what had happened. By the end of the evening she knew that fifteen members of the Besançon cell had been arrested.

That night, unable to sleep, she went over and over in her mind the implications of what had happened. Only Pedro had known her as Marguerite Duclos and known where she worked. And Pedro was dead. It occurred to her that she should be mourning him but all she could think of was that, dead, he was no use to the Gestapo torturers. She told herself that her sense of relief was as much for his sake as for hers. Those who had been arrested, if they had heard of her at all, knew her as Suzette. She had seen some of them, once or twice, when she carried messages to Pedro but she doubted very much that they had taken much notice of her. Certainly none of them had any idea that she was a British agent. The question that worried her most was whether the *rafle* had extended beyond the city. Out there, there were plenty of people who knew her position in the circuit and who could give a good description of her. But on the other hand, they had no idea of her cover name or where she could be found. Again and again she asked herself how it could have happened that the Gestapo were able to pick up so many members of the circuit in one go. Either their intelligence had been much better than Pedro had guessed, or there was a traitor somewhere in the group. If so, who and where?

As the hours crept by Steve was almost overpowered by a sense of isolation. She had not liked Pedro particularly, but he had been someone to turn to, someone to carry the ultimate responsibility. There was Danny now, of course, but he would take his orders from her, not the other way around. She was oppressed by the realisation that out there there were dozens of people, perhaps a hundred who would look to her for leadership – people who were prepared to sacrifice everything for the cause and who would depend on her for its success, perhaps even for their lives. If she was the next person to be picked up, would she have the courage to endure without betraying them? She could not convince herself that she would. Eventually, exhausted, she comforted herself with the reflection that if the Gestapo knew about her they would have arrested her by now and at least she was in touch with London again. On that thought she fell asleep.

The next morning she woke with one thought uppermost in her mind. Danny! Was it possible that the *rafle* had included M. and Mme Carrez, and if so might Danny have been picked up too?

As soon as the curfew was lifted she mounted her bicycle and rode out to Montferrand-le-Château. To get there she had to cross the River Doubs, and she knew that all the bridges were guarded. She approached with her heart thumping so hard she felt sure it must be visible to any observer, but the soldier at the barrier merely gave a cursory glance at her identity card and nodded her through. There was the early morning rush of people going to work in the city, and in the lanes beyond the river men and women were heading out to their fields, but she saw no sign of unusual German activity. Montferrand was as quiet as ever and women in black dresses were gossiping unconcernedly as they queued outside the baker's shop. Steve waited her turn and then asked Mme Carrez whether the baker had any flour to spare for the brasserie.

'Go through to the back and speak to my husband,' the woman said.

In the bakery M. Carrez greeted her with a smile. 'Your friend is already at work, up above.'

Steve left by the back door and walked quickly up the track leading to the woodsman's hut. As she approached she saw Eloise, the Carrez's twelve-year-old daughter, get up from a log at the edge of the trees and scamper ahead of her. It was obvious to Steve that she had been set to watch the track and warn Danny of anyone's approach, but to a casual observer she would have been just a young girl out playing in the woods.

Eloise was waiting for her at the door of the hut. Steve thanked her and sent her home. When she entered Danny was on his knees, stowing the radio set into the space beneath the floorboards. He got up, dusting his hands, and greeted her with a broad smile.

'Congratulations. Baker Street are delighted to hear that Stockbroker is still in business and wish to extend their best wishes to you and Pedro. And you can expect a *parachutage* during the next moon period.'

Steve sank on to one of the benches beside the table. 'I'm

afraid things are not quite as rosy as I told you yesterday,' she said.

He sat opposite her and she told him as briefly as she could about the arrests.

'*Merde*,' he muttered. 'So what happens now? Do you want me to cancel the drop?'

'No!' Steve said quickly. 'No, we must have the supplies.'

'Who's going to organise it, then?'

'I am. I've been on enough *parachutages* to know what I'm doing.'

He grinned at her. 'Bravo! Does that mean you're taking over the circuit, then?'

'I suppose it does,' she agreed. 'Listen, I can't stay. I'll let you have the coordinates of the DZ as soon as I can but right now I've got to find out what has happened to the others. Are you all right here?'

'Happy as Larry,' he assured her. 'M. Carrez bakes very good bread!'

She stood up, then stooped to kiss his cheek. 'Thank God you're here!'

She made her way back down the hill to where she had left her bicycle and set off to find out what remained of her circuit.

Chapter Ten

The German sweep had extended farther than Steve had anticipated but it had been somewhat haphazard in its effects. Certain villages had been targeted, two men being arrested in one, three in another, one in a third, but others had escaped completely. Over the following days she made use of all her contacts to find out what had happened to those who had been taken. Many of the local gendarmes were sympathetic to the Resistance and information soon began to filter back to her. The men had been taken to the citadel, where the Gestapo ruled, not to the local police cells. There were rumours of screams heard in the night and then of executions by firing squad but there were no further arrests. It seemed the prisoners had gone to their deaths without speaking. Steve was fearful of the effect these events might have on other members of the circuit, but even in the villages that had been hit the remaining resisters were more determined than ever to continue the struggle. Some of them had already taken to the hills to set up their own *maquis*. The news that they could now expect a supply of arms and equipment from London came as a tremendous boost to morale. The information that Steve was now taking charge of the circuit was greeted with rather less enthusiasm. It was bad enough losing the appointed leader. That his replacement was a woman did not inspire confidence.

Steve's first task was to organise the reception for the

parachute drop and for this she turned to Michel and his *maquisards*. To her great relief, she found that his camp had remained untouched and he was unaware of the *rafle* going on in the villages below. He was disturbed by the news but agreed at once to her request for help. She chose, this time, a stretch of level ground beside the Doubs almost immediately below Michel's camp. It would take about an hour for his men to walk there through the forest, somewhat longer for them to return carrying the equipment, but the whole thing could be easily accomplished during the hours of darkness. The site was not far from a village where Steve knew she could rely upon some of the farmers for the use of their carts, and had the added advantage that the Doubs would make an easily identified landmark for the incoming aircraft. Its only drawback was its proximity to Besançon with its large garrison, but she reasoned that even if the plane was spotted they would have time to clear the field and conceal the equipment before anyone could reach them.

On the appointed day Steve cycled to Michel's camp during the afternoon, to be sure of getting there before the curfew. Michel had a battery-operated radio set and they huddled over it at 9.15 waiting for the message from the BBC to confirm that the drop was going ahead, but it did not come. Steve spent an uneasy night on a makeshift couch of branches in the cave and cycled back to Besançon the next morning, feeling stiff and frustrated. The next night they had better luck. The message came through the crackle of static. *'Celine m'a donné une fille.'* The *'une'* was significant. It meant that the plane was due at one o'clock.

At eleven Michel assembled his men and they set off in silent single file down the steep path through the forest. The full moon cast dappled shadows through the still-bare branches and the wind made a noise like a distant cataract.

Steve walked behind Michel. Normally, she did not carry a weapon but tonight she had the little Colt .32 strapped to her thigh inside her trousers and she found its weight comforting.

Michel's men had prepared the firewood in bundles at the edge of the forest and began to build the fires as soon as they reached the field. There was a moment of alarm as six shadowy figures appeared from the darkness but a whispered password identified them as men from the local village. The carts were ready in the lane a few hundred yards away. As the minutes ticked by they waited, tense and shivering, in the shadows, ears straining for the sound of aero engines. Then someone whispered, 'Listen!'

In the distance they could hear planes approaching, but it was not the sound of the single aircraft they were expecting. They heard the air-raid warning go off in Besançon and then the planes were overhead, eight of them, Lancaster bombers, flying up the valley.

'Should we light the fires?' Michel asked.

Steve shook her head. 'No, these aren't for us. Looks like a raid on Montbéliard.'

The planes passed over and a few minutes later they heard the sirens in the distance and then the heavy crump of explosions.

'Does that mean our plane won't come?' Michel asked.

'I'm not sure,' she replied. 'This could just be a diversion, to confuse the enemy defences.'

Whether that was true or not, the words were hardly out of her mouth before they heard the drone of another plane and almost immediately it appeared, flying very low along the river.

'Brilliant!' Steve exclaimed. 'The Huns will think it's just one of the bomber squadron that got left behind.'

She signalled for the fires to be lit and began flashing the code letter she had been given with her torch. An answering light blinked from the aircraft and it turned and swooped over them. The parachutes blossomed beneath it and then it was gone, with a farewell waggle of its wings. Already men were running to intercept the packages and the precious parachute silk was gathered in and consigned to the bonfires. Some of the men had objected to this order, until Steve had pointed out that the discovery of a scrap of such material could send the possessor to a concentration camp. Some of the canisters were opened on the spot and their contents distributed among Michel's men. The rest were loaded on to the carts and taken to a disused quarry, where they were stacked under an overhang of rock and hidden with bundles of brushwood. By dawn, the field was empty and all traces of the fires had been erased.

It was a long slog back up the hill, and by the time they reached the camp Steve was almost sleepwalking. At Michel's suggestion she lay down in the cave, but only on condition that she was woken after a couple of hours. There was a great deal to be done in the next few days.

The first problem was how to transport the weapons and explosives to the various resistance cells in the outlying villages. When she was based in Arbois there had been Sylvie de Montmain's pony and trap and the atmosphere had been comparatively relaxed. Now the German controls were much more rigorous. Any vehicle had to have a permit from the occupying authority and might be stopped and searched at any time. During the interval between Danny's arrival and the *parachutage*, however, Steve had been busy. There was a baker in Thalaise who owned a van with valid papers and the vet in Courtfontaine had a car and a trailer that he used to transport sick animals. His permit allowed him to travel over a wide area, even at night in an emergency. Local craftsmen had been put to work on both these vehicles, so that now there was a hidden compartment behind the racks of loaves in the baker's van and another under the floor of the vet's trailer, concealed by a good layer of straw and manure. After several visits to the quarry by both men the arms were distributed over a wide area to the south and west of Besançon.

Steve followed up each delivery to check that the equipment was safely stored and that the recipients knew how to use and maintain it. Some of the units had received training from Pedro or one of his lieutenants but, inevitably, there were others who had never encountered anything more sophisticated than a shotgun. To be instructed in the use of a Sten gun or a modern rifle by a young woman was something that many of the men found hard to stomach.

This was particularly true of a group based in Quingey, which was led by the local schoolmaster, a man in his forties named Raoul Villiers. The weapons allotted to this group had been stored in a loft above the village school, and Steve asked Raoul to assemble his cadre one Sunday afternoon so that she could explain their use. There were four of them, apart from Raoul – Thomas, who ran the local bar; Emile, the blacksmith; Simon, the butcher; and Jean-Pierre, his apprentice. Steve had had dealings with them before but always as a messenger, bringing orders from a higher authority. Now that she presented herself in the role of leader she sensed an undercurrent of antagonism. She tried to adopt a conciliatory approach but at the same time she knew she had to establish herself as someone worthy of their respect.

'What's this?' Raoul demanded, hefting a shapeless lump of material.

'Plastic explosive,' Steve told him.

'*Plastique?*' He looked at it doubtfully. 'What are we supposed to do with this?'

'Blow things up – trains, mostly.'

'We are supposed to blow up trains with this? It's no good to us. We haven't the faintest idea how to use it'

'Then I shall show you,' Steve responded.

'You know how to use this?' His scepticism was obvious. She was aware of the men around her exchanging glances. Jean-Pierre started to giggle and then stifled the sound at a glare from his boss.

'Bring it down to the schoolroom and I'll show you how to make up a charge,' she said. 'Do you have any sticky tape?'

'Tape? Yes. What for?'

'I'll show you. Bring that – she indicated the *plastique* – 'and that box of bits and pieces. Right. Come on.'

She led the way down the ladder to the schoolroom and the others followed, setting down their burdens on the teacher's table.

'Now,' Steve said, 'watch closely. You will have to do this for yourselves and perhaps teach others.'

She began to assemble a charge suitable for derailing a train. As she worked she remembered how the instructor at Arisaig had held her efforts up to ridicule because she was so clumsy. She was not even sure that she could still remember the techniques she had learned a year ago. But, miraculously, her fingers seemed to recall the actions they had performed over and over again in that classroom and in a few minutes the charge was complete. It was no work of art, but she was pretty sure it would do the job. She talked as she worked, explaining the use of detonators and time pencils, instructing them as to the best way to position the charge, but all the time she could feel them looking at each other, exchanging covert smiles. It was as clear as if they had spoken the words. *'This girl is going to show us how to blow up a train? What a joke!'*

'There,' she said, finally. 'That's ready.'

'Will it work?' Raoul asked.

She met his eyes. 'There's only one way to find out.'

'You want us to blow up a train?'

'Yes. I'll come with you, as it's the first time.'

'When?'

'I'll let you know. First I have to check what trains are due in the next few days. We want to blow up something that will disrupt the German war effort, not a passenger train carrying our own people.'

They saw the sense in that and the equipment was stowed away in a rather different atmosphere. Steve left them soon after, promising to return with definite plans in a day or two.

Back at the brasserie she waited for Jacques to come over from the marshalling yard for his evening beer and invited him into the back room. He listened to what she was proposing and responded with a wink.

'You're in luck. There's a freight train coming through from Mulhouse, day after tomorrow, and it's mainly tankers full of petrol and diesel, heading south for the army down on the Mediterranean. That'd go up with a fair old bang!'

'How come they are bringing fuel from Germany?' Steve asked. I thought they were short of oil.'

'Seems they've got some chemical process for producing petrol and diesel from coal,' Jacques said. 'Don't ask me to explain it. That's just what I heard. Now, let's have a look and see where the best place to stop it would be.'

He produced a plan of the local rail network and a copy of the timetable for the normal train service, and for half an hour he and Steve bent their heads over it. It was not long before they agreed the ideal spot, a bridge spanning both the Doubs and the Canal du Rhône et Rhin, which ran alongside the river. It was only a few kilometres from Quingey, and a train derailed there would have the added advantage of blocking the canal, which was used to transport coal and other heavy goods. Jacques calculated the time at which the freight train would reach it as around 10 p.m., which gave them enough time after dark to fix the charges. There was only one snag. A passenger train going the opposite way, from Lons-le-Saunier to Besançon, was due to pass that spot at 9.50. The timing was tight, but Jacques assured her that the freighter was more likely to be late than early.

Two days later Steve cycled to Quingey and told Raoul to call his group together. When she explained the plan to them their eyes widened with a mixture of excitement and disbelief. They knew that the line was patrolled by *gardes voies*, Frenchmen conscripted to watch the lines for signs of sabotage, and Steve sent Thomas and Simon to watch the line and time the patrols. They returned to report that they passed roughly once every half-hour. She told them to make up a second charge, just to be on the safe side and to make sure that they had taken in her lesson, and then there was nothing to do but wait for darkness to fall.

At eight o'clock they left to cycle to the bridge, Thomas going ahead as a scout in case there were German patrols on the road. They reached the place without incident and concealed themselves among bushes at the base of the embankment, where they had a clear view of the bridge. They waited until the patrol passed, two men, chatting together and clearly bored by the task. They were paying so little attention to the lines that Steve thought they would not have noticed if there had been a dead body lying there.

As soon as they were out of sight Steve beckoned to the

men with her and they scrambled up the embankment and made their way out on to the bridge. It took only a few minutes to attach the charges and unroll the command wire that would set them off. Since they could not be sure of the exact moment when the train would pass, the use of a time pencil was out of the question. The charges would have to be detonated manually. They connected the wires to a detonator hidden in the bushes and settled down to wait.

Half an hour later the *gardes voies* returned. To the horror of the six watchers, they decided to stop in the middle of the bridge for a smoke. Steve could feel her heart thumping. They were so near to one of the charges that they could almost have fallen over it, but they were both leaning on the parapet gazing along the river. She prayed that when they finally turned round their attention would be anywhere but on the ground beneath their feet. She looked at her watch: 9.45. Surely they wouldn't go on standing there much longer! The passenger train from Lons should be through any time now. She strained her ears. It was a quiet night and noises carried but she could hear no sound of a train.

At last the two guards straightened up, threw their cigarette butts into the river and wandered on along the track. Steve breathed a sigh of relief, but even as she did so another sound set her nerves jangling. Somewhere to the north a train whistle sounded. The freighter was on its way – and it was early.

'That's it!' Raoul whispered. 'It's coming.'

'Yes, I heard.'

'How long before it gets here?'

'Your guess is as good as mine. Soon. What's happened to the nine fifty?'

'God knows!'

As if in answer, they heard a second whistle, this time

from the south. The passenger train was coming. Steve made frantic calculations. If the freighter got to the bridge first there might still be time for the passenger train to be halted before it ran into the ensuing chaos. But if they both arrived at once . . .

'What do we do?' Raoul hissed. 'Do we abandon the plan?'

Steve was visualising the map of the railway that she had studied with Jacques. 'No!' she said. 'You stay here. If the freighter gets here before the passenger train, blow the charges. Emile, you come with me.'

Emile was the youngest, apart from the boy Jean-Pierre, and the fittest. Steve scrambled down the bank, with him close behind her, to where they had hidden their bicycles.

'Where are we going?' he asked.

'Signal box at Byans,' she replied, 'fast as we can get there.'

Byans-sur-Doubs was just over a kilometre away, in the direction of Lons. If they could reach it before the passenger train passed they might still be able to avert a disaster. Steve had never pedalled so hard in her life. Over the panting of her breath she could hear the distant chugging of the train. She was not sure whether it was scheduled to stop at Byans. She prayed that it was. The road followed the curve of the river, taking them temporarily away from the railway line. When it swung back they both saw the train standing in the station. Forgetting all attempt at concealment, Steve pedalled the last hundred yards to the signal box, flung her bike aside and raced up the steps, drawing her Colt .32 as she went. The signalman jerked round in surprise as she crashed through the door.

'Stop the train!' Steve gasped. 'Don't let it leave the station.'

'I can't do that,' he protested.

Steve levelled the gun at him. 'Do it! If you let that train go you will be responsible for the deaths of everyone on it.'

He stared at her, then comprehension dawned and his face broke into a grin. He raised his hands. 'OK, sister. I get the message. No need to wave that thing at me.'

He turned away and pulled a lever and Steve heard the signal clank into the Stop position. She looked down the line at the train, still waiting in the station, and a sudden idea came to her. She turned to Emile, who had followed her into the signal box.

'Watch him. Make sure the signal stays red.'

Then she ran down the steps and along the platform to where the engine stood. The fireman peered down at her.

'What's going on?'

Steve waved the gun at him. 'Get down.'

'What?'

'Get down and uncouple the engine.'

'Why?'

'Just do it!'

Slowly the man descended and the driver poked his head out. 'You can't do that. What about the passengers?'

'Believe me, they're safer where they are,' Steve told him. 'Come down and give your mate a hand.'

The driver descended. Curious heads were beginning to appear from the train windows. The guard came trotting up to find out what was happening.

'Shut up!' the train driver told him. 'It's none of our business.'

The coupling parted with a clank and the fireman looked at Steve. 'Now what?'

Steve pocketed her gun, knowing that these men, like most of the workers on the railway, were on her side. 'Has she got a good head of steam up?'

'Pretty good. Why?'

'Get up and open the throttle,' Steve told the driver. 'Then let off the brakes and jump out, quick.'

'Why?' The man looked scandalised. 'She'll go off the rails.'

Steve hesitated for a second. There wasn't time to explain. She remembered how they had learned to drive the little engine at Arisaig. She swung herself up into the cab and scanned the controls. They seemed much the same as the ones she had learned on. With a sense of growing excitement she opened the throttle, let off the brakes and then, as the engine began to move, jumped down to the ground. There was a slight down gradient between them and the river and the engine quickly began to gather speed.

Just as it was about to disappear from sight they all heard, or rather felt, a low concussion, followed immediately by another. Steve felt a surge of triumph. Both charges had gone off. A second later a brilliant flash lit the sky in the direction of the bridge, followed by a huge explosion, and a blast of warm air fanned their faces. The whole lot had gone up, and now the night sky was scarlet with the resulting conflagration. And the runaway engine was on its way to add to the chaos.

Behind her there was a confusion of voices as people jumped out of the train to see what was going on. It was time to disappear. She ran towards her bicycle and as she reached it Emile came clattering down the steps of the signal box.

'Bravo, *patronne! C'est magnifique!* What an explosion! Let's go and have a closer look.'

'Are you mad?' she asked him. 'The whole area will be swarming with Boches in a matter of minutes. Do you really think they are going to believe that you're just an innocent bystander? Get home and go to bed, in case they decide to drag the whole village out and take a roll-call. I'll contact you tomorrow.'

'What about you?' he asked.

'Don't worry about me. I've made my own arrangements. Go now, quickly.'

She turned away to her bike, then looked back. 'Well done, Emile. Thank you.'

He grinned. 'Thank *you, patronne.*'

She watched him start to cycle away, smiling. *Patronne* – 'boss'. She could have asked for no greater accolade. She mounted her bike and pedalled slowly away from the railway, her senses alert for any sound of movement ahead of her on the road. It was too dangerous to cross the Doubs during the curfew but Montferrand-le-Château was not far away, on her side of the river. At the baker's house she tapped softly on the back door. Danny was waiting to admit her.

'Well? How did it go?'

'Fantastic! The whole lot's gone up in smoke.'

She felt light headed, euphoric, yet at the same time oddly detached, as if she were watching herself playing a part. M. and Mme Carrez sat her down at the kitchen table and plied her with bread and cheese and red wine while she told her story.

When she ran out of breath Danny said quietly, 'I suppose there was a driver and a fireman on the freight train, too.'

Steve stopped, her glass halfway to her mouth. She had known this but had kept the thought at bay until now. 'Yes,' she said slowly, 'of course. And probably German troops to guard the contents. But what about all the extra lives that might have been lost if the train had got through? The men who might have been killed by the tanks, if they had had fuel. The women and children who might have been bombed if the aviation fuel had reached the planes? We're fighting a war, Danny. You may say you have never killed anyone. I admire what you do, sitting here on your own, day after day, with your radio set, risking capture every time you transmit. But just remember, without your radio messages we wouldn't have the explosives to blow up the trains.'

He lowered his eyes. 'You're right, of course. We're as guilty – or as innocent – as each other.'

Shortly afterwards Mme Carrez led her upstairs to the room where Eloise slept and moved the sleepy girl into the bed she shared with her husband so that Steve could use hers. She pulled off her outer clothes, crawled under the blankets and slept instantly, to wake the next morning to the smell of fresh bread and the chatter of voices in the bakery.

She waited until mid-morning and then set off for Quingey. At the railway bridge a crowd of rubber-necking locals lined the road. Steve propped her bike against a tree and wandered casually over to them.

'What happened?' she asked a woman at the edge of the crowd.

'A train was derailed. They're saying it was sabotage.'

Steve edged closer, until she could see into the river. What had started out as a simple demonstration to prove that she knew what she was talking about had resulted in a truly spectacular pile-up. The engine of the freight train had careered on across the bridge and then rolled down the embankment on the far side, and the first wagon had fallen on top of it, spilling its volatile contents into the firebox. The resulting explosion had more or less destroyed the bridge. The rest of the train had fallen across the river and the canal, blocking both. And then the runaway engine of the passenger train had plunged into the wreckage, ripping away the rails and the balustrade on the remaining portion of the bridge. It would require a railway crane to remove the wreck, and Steve knew that there was only one of those in the area. It would be weeks before the Germans could use that route to get fresh fuel and ammunition to their troops again.

She cycled on into Quingey and found Raoul at the school. Class was still in session and she could hear him reading to the children in steady, measured tones. When the children went home for lunch she slipped inside and shortly afterwards the rest of the group joined them.

'So,' Steve said, cocking an eyebrow at Raoul. 'The charges went off, then.'

He had the grace to look slightly embarrassed. 'Yes, they went off. But where did that other engine come from?'

Emile chimed in, clearly still excited. 'That was the *patronne*'s idea. We stopped the train. Then she made the driver and the fireman get out and uncouple it and she got in and made it go. It was magnificent!'

'You started the train?'

'Yes.' Steve shrugged casually, as if to imply that driving a train was just one of the many accomplishments expected of a British agent.

'*Nom du diable!*' was the muttered response.

From that day on Steve was treated with great respect by the Quingey cell – and not only by them. The story of her exploits that night seemed to spread by osmosis from village to village, and before long she was generally acknowledged as '*la patronne*' by all the groups in the circuit. She resisted all requests to repeat the performance, however, insisting that from now on they should all save themselves and their supplies for the expected invasion. Some of them ignored her instructions and went ahead with small-scale acts of sabotage anyway, but they were limited and sporadic and the area settled into an uneasy calm.

In April they had another *parachutage* and this time it included a 'body' – SOE's term for an agent. This turned out to be a young Frenchman with aristocratic looks and a manner to match, who went by the name of Albert. He had been sent, the message from HQ informed her, to take over Stockbroker. Steve knew she should be relieved but her first emotion was one of resentment. In the two months just past she had come to think of the circuit as 'hers'. She took Albert back to the brasserie and there, over a late dinner – or early breakfast – she gave him a comprehensive account of the situation, without mentioning specific names or places. He listened, and when she had finished his face broke into a smile that completely transformed him.

'You have obviously done a splendid job and have got everything well in hand here. I suggest you carry on as before. I have to go south to see what can be retrieved of the circuit around Lons. It's a big area and I'm going to have my work cut out. I'll take overall responsibility, of course, but it'll be a relief for me to know that there is someone I can trust to keep things going around here. But we need to be able to get in touch. Is there anyone you can suggest, between here and Lons, who might be able to carry messages?'

Steve suggested Dr Lefort and also gave him the address of the cheese factory. The next day he went south in a *gazogène* van owned by a friend of Louis Choquin's.

Albert had brought good news. The invasion would happen soon and he had detailed instructions from London about what was required when it started, and also two messages that they were to listen out for from the BBC. The first would tell them to stand by, because the invasion was imminent, the second that it had actually begun. Steve set off on her rounds again. By the end of April every group in the area had been allotted a specific target, to be attacked as soon as the messages came through.

A strange hiatus ensued. Summer was coming and the days were growing longer and warmer and there was nothing more to be done. The nights were already too short for more *parachutages* so there was no more equipment to distribute. Instead, Steve had time to explore the beautiful old city of Besançon, couched in the crook of the Doubs, or stroll along the elegant promenades that fronted the river. She would have liked to visit the citadel, which occupied the crag above the river, but that was where the German garrison was housed and no one could pass within its walls without a permit. Often Juliette came with her, or took her off to a '*plage*' farther upriver where the locals swam. Steve loved the water but she was astonished to discover that, while Juliette enjoyed splashing in the shallows, she had never learned to swim. They had grown closer than ever over the past months and Steve took strength from the younger girl's inexhaustible energy and *joie de vivre*.

With time on her hands Steve began to take more interest in the food she helped to prepare and serve. Louis was a good cook but his ambitions did not extend much beyond the basic dishes that were the staples of local cuisine, and the shortage of ingredients limited him further. Steve found relief from the tensions of her mission in experimenting with what was available to introduce more variety into the menus. She was so successful that the reputation of the restaurant began to spread, to the extent that they began to be patronised by German officers, who normally ate only in the more sophisticated establishments in the centre of the city. To begin with, Steve was uneasy about this development, but she reasoned that if the Germans took it into their heads to conduct another purge of suspected 'terrorists' they were less likely to come looking for them in a place where they were accustomed to receive a welcome and a good meal.

The ultimate accolade was bestowed on her efforts when Colonel von Klimt, the officer commanding the garrison, came with two other officers to sample the food. Their arrival threw the entire establishment into a state approaching hysteria, but Steve insisted that they be treated as honoured guests and given the best the house could offer. The colonel was a powerfully built man with a strong, patrician face and dark hair liberally flecked with grey. At first sight Steve found him intimidating, but then he smiled and she saw that his brown eyes were alive with humour. For a brief second she was reminded of her own father.

She served the party herself and, while the younger officers were ogling Juliette, the colonel engaged her in conversation. His French, like his manners, was impeccable. When she cleared the plates after the main course he said, 'That was excellent. Please thank the chef for me – or better still, if he can spare the time, ask him to come out here so I can thank him myself.'

Steve felt a small glow of satisfaction. 'That won't be necessary,' she said. 'As it happens, I cooked it myself.'

'You did? Well, I congratulate you. You are obviously a very talented young lady.' He looked around the room. 'Tell me, is this a family business? Are you the proprietor's daughter?'

'No,' Steve said, picking up his plate. 'I just work here.'

The colonel came again, the next evening, and this time

he was alone. She had cooked rabbit in red wine and she waited by the table until he had tasted it.

He dabbed his lips with his napkin. 'Delicious! Tell me, where did you learn to cook?'

Steve thought quickly. Her own experience in Paris did not fit with Marguerite's life story. 'Oh, from my mother mainly.' It was true in part. She had used her mother's recipe for jugged hare for that dish.

'Your parents are also in the restaurant trade?'

'Oh, no. My parents are dead – a car accident before the war.'

She saw genuine sympathy in his eyes. 'I'm so sorry. Do you have any other family nearby?'

'No, I'm not from round here. My home was in Normandy, until it was requisitioned by the English at the start of the war. Then it was taken over by your people and finally it was destroyed by British bombing. I'm a refugee.'

His look of concern deepened. 'How tragic! To lose both your parents and then your home.'

'I'm one of thousands,' Steve said tartly. 'If your people hadn't started the war none of us need have suffered.'

She had spoken more honestly than she intended and she went back to the kitchen biting her lip. She had set out to work on the attraction she read in his eyes, but now she had probably antagonised him instead. When she took him his dessert he said quietly, 'You know, there are some of us for whom this war is as unwelcome as it is to you. But what can we do? We have no choice in the matter. I am not a military man. I should be much happier looking after my estates in Bavaria. I'm too old to be cannon fodder, so I shift piles of paper. But I think myself lucky to have been sent here.'

'I'm sorry,' Steve said. 'I didn't mean to be rude. I know you can't be blamed.'

Clearing up after the guests had left, she recalled the look in his eyes. He was a good man, she thought, caught up like the rest of them in a situation he could not control.

In mid-May Albert reappeared, bringing with him a middle-aged man with a moustache and watery blue eyes, whom he introduced as Colonel Biondel.

'I represent the FFI,' the colonel told her. 'The Forces Françaises de l'Intérieur. This force has been set up by General de Gaulle. All resistance units are now expected to join. I shall be in command in this area and I am empowered to issue commissions to any local leaders who are deemed worthy.'

'It has been agreed in London,' Albert said, 'that we should cooperate with the FFI and accept its authority.'

Accordingly, Steve took the colonel to meet all the local groups. He was much impressed by Michel's *maquis*, and on learning that he had been a lieutenant before the French army was disbanded promptly promoted him to captain. Michel received this honour with a faintly sceptical smile, since he had been in total command of his men for over a year and the official rank did nothing to increase his authority. It would, however, the Colonel assured him, guarantee that he received proper recognition once France had been liberated.

The only people who refused to have anything to do with the Colonel or the FFI were the communists of the FTP, who had their own command structure. When Steve reported this to Albert he sighed.

'I'm afraid we are seeing the pattern of things to come. General de Gaulle is establishing his power base for after the liberation, but the communists are not going to let him have it all his own way. It will be a fight to the finish.'

'You don't mean civil war!'

'It won't come to that. The general will make sure of that. Anyway, all that matters for now is to get rid of the Boches. We can all unite in that effort.'

Chapter Eleven

As the days lengthened further towards midsummer Steve found it increasingly difficult to restrain the impatience of the men and women in the different resistance cells. The constant demand was, 'When are the Allies coming? Why don't they invade?' Every evening she and Juliette tuned in to the BBC, hoping to hear the message that would tell them the invasion was imminent. All over France, she knew, small groups were doing the same thing, in spite of the draconian penalties imposed by the Germans for anyone found listening to the broadcasts from London. In one of the villages Steve visited, a whole family had been arrested, only weeks earlier, for exactly that crime. At last, on 1 June, they heard the words they were waiting for. The coded message informed them that the invasion would take place within days and they should be ready to act. On 5 June the second message came. The Allied troops were on the move and every resistance group was required to do everything in its power to impede the German efforts to repel them.

When Steve explained the meaning of the coded messages to her, Juliette grasped her hand, her eyes shining. 'It's happening! At last they are coming. Soon we shall be free.'

Steve squeezed her hand in return but her mood was sober. 'It's good news, but don't get your hopes up too high. The Germans are not going to surrender easily and you have to remember that we shall probably be among the last people to be liberated. It's a long way to this area from the Channel coast.'

'But at least it's started!' Juliette's excitement was undiminished. 'What do we do now?'

'We sit tight and do nothing,' Steve replied, and saw the other girl's face fall. 'Every group has its orders and they will all have been listening for the message. They have the arms and they know how to use them. There's nothing to be gained from us running around the countryside, drawing attention to ourselves.'

She spoke with confidence but inwardly she, too, longed to be out there, checking that the targets she had assigned each group were being attacked as planned. She need not have worried. By dawn crucial rail junctions and signal boxes all round the area had been disabled and vital bridges blown up. It would be days, perhaps weeks, before the Germans could move reinforcements through the valley from the border at Mulhouse.

After the first flurry of activity there was a hiatus, which left Steve, and she guessed many others, with a sense of anti-climax. Instead of the unstoppable sweep of the victorious armies that they had all expected, the Allied troops remained bottled up in their Normandy bridgehead, and it was obvious that the Germans were going to fight for every kilometre of French soil. Undeterred, the various cells Steve had set up kept up their campaign against German communications, and as fast as the enemy repaired bridges and tracks they were destroyed again.

Before long it became necessary to redistribute some of the equipment. The more active units were running out of explosives, while others had a surplus. One day Steve was stopped by a sentry guarding one of the bridges across the

Doubs. Most of the regular garrison were used to seeing her pass, as she combed the countryside ostensibly in search of supplies for the restaurant, but this was a newcomer, a young man obviously keen to impress his superiors with his efficiency.

'Your papers, please,' he demanded. Unlike most of his compatriots he seemed to speak reasonable French.

Steve got off her bicycle and handed them over.

'What have you got in there?' He indicated the basket on her handlebars.

Steve lifted the cloth covering the basket. 'Eggs. I work as a cook at the Brasserie Vauban and I've just bought these from a farmer in Boussière.'

'This restaurant – it is in Besançon?'

'Yes.'

'So why are you going this way? Besançon is behind you.'

Steve sighed wearily. 'I know. But now I have to go to Damperre. I've heard that there is a farmer there who has mushrooms to sell. If I can get some I can make mushroom omelettes.' She smiled at him. 'I make a very good omelette. You should come and try one.'

This slightly flirtatious approach usually worked well but not this time. The young soldier glared at her.

'Don't try that line on me. Let's see what else you've got in that basket.'

'It's just eggs.'

'I'd like to be sure of that. Take them out.'

Steve looked at the basket. The eggs nestled on a bed of straw and under the straw was a slab of plastic explosive wrapped in sacking.

'How can I?' she asked. 'I've got nothing to put them in. If I try to take them all out I'm bound to drop some and break them.'

'I'll break the lot of them if you don't do as I tell you!' he retorted. 'Get on with it.'

At that moment a car drew up beside them and a voice called, 'It's Mademoiselle Duclos, isn't it? Good afternoon.'

Steve turned and saw the colonel waving to her out of the rear window. She went over to him.

'Is there a problem?' he asked.

Steve allowed a slight tremor to come into her voice. 'This man wants me to take all these eggs out of my basket. I've cycled such a long way to get them and I'm bound to break some if I do.'

He smiled at her. 'Don't distress yourself, mademoiselle. Your eggs are quite safe.' He beckoned to the young sentry, who came forward a pace or two and snapped to quivering attention. 'You must learn that there is a difference between being efficient and being officious. This young lady is well known to all of us. She is not a threat to security. She cooks at a local restaurant, where I often eat myself. In fact, I shall not thank you if the eggs are broken and she is unable to make my favourite crêpes Suzette. Let her pass.'

The sentry saluted and stepped back but Steve caught the glint of fury in his eyes. She had made him look a fool in front of a superior officer and she knew he would not forgive that. The colonel wound up his window and the car drove on.

Steve mounted her bike and pedalled away as steadily as her shaking legs permitted. She understood a good deal more German than she ever let on, and as she went she heard the corporal in charge say, 'Now you've done it! Why did you have to go and stop the colonel's bint, of all people?'

Her first reaction was annoyance. She was not 'the colonel's bint'! Then she smiled inwardly. It could do no harm for the soldiers to think that – in fact it might come in useful.

Two days later an orderly arrived at the brasserie with a message. The colonel would be delighted if Mlle Duclos would dine with him in his apartments in the citadel. An escort would be sent to conduct her through the barriers at seven the following evening. For a moment Steve was terrified. Could this all be part of an elaborate plot to entice her into the citadel, where she might be imprisoned and tortured for information? Then common sense reasserted itself. If the colonel suspected her of involvement with the Resistance he could have had her arrested without resort to subterfuge. There remained the possibility that he intended to seduce her, but it seemed out of character. And anyway, there was little choice in the matter. To refuse would be to court suspicion.

At seven the next evening she was ready, dressed in the navy-and-white dress she had been given in England, the last vestige of the well-to-do Marguerite who had been reduced to waiting in a back-street restaurant. A smart corporal presented himself at the door in a staff car and drove her up the steeply winding approach to the main gate. The citadel of Besançon occupied a superb strategic position on a plateau a hundred metres above the River Doubs, which curled around it in an almost complete circle. The car was halted at the entrance to an arched gateway in the perimeter walls while a sentry inspected her pass and then they drove on, across a moat and through another gateway into a central courtyard. Here the car stopped and the corporal handed her out. Steve looked around her and felt a shiver of horror. To one side stood three stout stakes, almost the height of a man. The Germans had made no secret of the fate that had befallen the conspirators who had been arrested in February. They had been shot, and Steve knew that she was looking at the place where they had met their end.

The corporal led her up a winding staircase to the door of the colonel's apartment. He was waiting to greet her, with the same formal courtesy, she sensed, that he would have shown had she been a titled lady rather than a waitress. The room was spacious and elegantly furnished, with windows giving a wonderful view over the town to the river and the wooded hills beyond.

Seeing her gaze, he said, 'It is beautiful, isn't it? Such a superb position. And it is, of course, the *chef d'oeuvre* of the architect Vauban, after whom your restaurant is named.'

'It is beautiful, yes,' she agreed. 'But such ugly things happen here. I saw those stakes in the courtyard. Is that where you shoot your prisoners?'

He looked as if he had received a physical wound. 'That was not my doing. You have to understand that prisoners in Gestapo custody do not come under my jurisdiction. The Gestapo are a law unto themselves and anyone who crosses them may find himself having to reckon with Herr Himmler. Not a pleasant prospect, whatever your rank. I'm too old to survive a posting to the Russian front.'

Steve sensed that he was as horrified by the executions as she was and regretted her brusqueness. 'I'm sorry. I don't understand how the chain of command works in your army.'

He gestured to a chair. 'Please, sit down, and let us try to forget the war for a minute. Can I offer you a glass of champagne?'

He was a good host and Steve found herself thinking that

if they were not at war he would have fitted in perfectly at one of her parents' dinner parties. It was difficult to think of him as 'the enemy'. Over dinner he asked her about herself and she told him Marguerite's story, which she had almost come to think of as her own. In return, he spoke nostalgically about his home in Bavaria and the estate that had been in his family for generations. She was surprised by how much they seemed to have in common. Like her, he loved the countryside and he spoke lyrically of the area around his home, and she had to make a conscious effort to refrain from a similar description of the Chiltern hills where she had grown up. Like her, too, he was a keen horseman, and at one point she found herself giving him an enthusiastic account of the thrill of the hunt, with hounds in full cry and a big fence ahead.

He laughed. 'You sound like one of those English fanatics!'

For a moment cold fear gripped Steve's stomach but she forced a laugh in response. 'We hunt in France, too, you know – but we have the sense to hunt something you can eat, like deer. Only the English are mad enough to go chasing after foxes.'

'I have ridden with an English hunt, the Beaufort,' he amazed her by saying. 'Oh, there's no need to look so surprised. Before the war I had many friends in England.'

Later in the conversation he remarked that he was surprised that she was not married, or at least engaged.

'I was engaged,' she replied. She opened her bag and took out a photograph, but as she looked at it she experienced a sudden sense of dislocation. This was not the face she had in her imagination – the face of a young man in RAF uniform. It was a stranger, in the uniform of the French army. The sensation passed in a second and she pulled herself together, but a lingering ache remained. She handed the photograph to her companion. 'His name is Claude Montauban. He was killed in the first months of the war.'

He looked at it and handed it back. 'I'm sorry,' he said, and she had the impression that it was not just an expression of sympathy but an apology on behalf of his nation.

Over coffee he reached across the table and touched her hand lightly. 'I want you to understand one thing. I have not asked you here in order to seduce you. That thought must have crossed your mind.' Steve opened her mouth to deny it but he went on, 'I have a wife and a daughter almost your age. A son, too, three years younger. For a year now I have been cooped up with only men for company. Of course, the baser needs can always be accommodated, but I miss the society of women. This evening has given me great pleasure. I hope, perhaps, that we can repeat it.'

At ten o'clock he rang for his driver and instructed him to take her home.

As the car descended through the empty, darkened streets, Steve was bewildered by the variety of her reactions. Suzette, the secret agent, was reckoning the possible risks and advantages that might accrue from friendship with such a senior officer. Meanwhile, Marguerite was torn between guilt at fraternising with the enemy and a warm appreciation that not all of them were as brutal as the popular imagination painted them. What Diana Escott Stevens, daughter of an English gentleman farmer, might make of the situation she could no longer imagine.

Juliette continued to be Steve's invaluable assistant, taking instructions to different groups or carrying messages to Danny in Montferrand to be transmitted to England. But Steve never allowed her to carry arms or explosives, which would immediately have condemned her in case of a search. Nevertheless, when she failed to return from Montferrand in time for the curfew one evening her parents were understandably anxious.

Steve tried to reassure them. 'She's a sensible girl. She will have realised that she didn't have time to get back before curfew and stayed the night. Marie Carrez will have given her a bed.'

Juliette was still missing when the curfew was lifted the next morning and it was clear that something more serious had happened. Steve mounted her bicycle and rode out to Montferrand, only to learn that Juliette had left there the previous evening.

'She insisted on waiting until my last sked,' Danny said, 'to see if there was a message from London. But she had enough time to get back before curfew – just about.'

Back at the brasserie there was still no sign of Juliette, so Steve decided to enlist the help of a local gendarme who had proved before now that his loyalties lay with the Resistance. She guessed he would be having his lunch break and found him in the café he frequented near the police station. She sat down at his table, making it look as if the assignation had been pre-arranged, and told him in a low voice what had happened. He promised to make enquiries and bring the results to the brasserie when he came off duty.

At 5.30 he came into the restaurant and Steve saw at once that he had bad news. She took him through to the kitchen, where Louis and Jacqueline were trying to concentrate on preparing the food for the evening.

'I've got a mate who works at the prison,' he said. 'That's where they take people who've been caught infringing the regulations – breaking the curfew or selling on the black market, you know the sort of thing. He says Juliette was brought in last night and they put her in a cell, planning to deal with her in the usual way in the morning. Then, first thing today, a Gestapo officer came and insisted on taking her up to the citadel for interrogation.'

Jacqueline gave a cry of horror and Steve felt the blood draining away from her heart.

'But why?' she exclaimed. 'Why should the Gestapo suspect her?'

The gendarme shrugged. 'You can probably answer that better than I can.'

'What shall we do?' Jacqueline sobbed. 'We must do something.'

Steve ran her hands through her hair, forcing down her rising sense of panic. Only one possibility occurred to her and it was a slim chance. 'I'll go and see Colonel von Klimt. He's the only person who might be able to help.'

Half an hour later she presented herself at the outer gate of the citadel, carrying a basket of *rillettes,* which she knew were a favourite of the colonel's.

'I want to see Colonel von Klimt,' she told the sentry. 'I have a gift for him.'

'Pass it in to the guardhouse,' was the response. 'They'll see he gets it'

Steve gave him her most seductive smile. 'But I want to give them to him. He may want to thank me – personally.'

The man hesitated, then called his sergeant. After some consultation Steve was passed on to a higher authority within the citadel and then further up the chain of command until she finally encountered a captain who had dined at the brasserie with the colonel.

'*Rillettes,* eh?' he said with a grin. 'Well, I hope there are enough for us all to have a taste.'

'I expect the colonel will be generous,' Steve murmured demurely.

An orderly took her up to the colonel's apartment, where she found him sitting behind a desk with a pile of papers in front of him.

'Mlle Duclos! What a pleasant surprise. Please come in.'

As soon as the orderly had closed the door Steve set her basket on the desk and leaned towards him. 'The *rillettes* are just an excuse. I need your help, Herr Colonel.'

'In what way?'

'You remember the girl who serves in the brasserie with me – Juliette?'

'Of course. How could anyone forget such a pretty face?'

'She has been arrested and for some reason the Gestapo have brought her here. It was just a violation of the curfew. She'd been to see friends and must have left it too late to get home.'

'What would the Gestapo want with her?'

'I can't imagine. They must think that she's somehow mixed up with these acts of sabotage we keep hearing about.'

The colonel spread his hands in a gesture of disbelief. 'A girl like that? She can't be more than seventeen or eighteen. She's a child!'

'I know.' In some deeply buried part of her conscience Steve sensed a revulsion at deceiving this kindly man but she suppressed it. 'It's ridiculous. But I can't bear to think of her in the hands of those thugs. She must be terrified. Can you help . . . please?'

The colonel sighed deeply. 'You know I have very little power over the Gestapo. However' – she saw him straighten his shoulders – 'I am, nominally at least, in command here. Perhaps it's time I exercised my authority.'

He got up. 'I can't make any promises but I will do what I can.'

He laid his hand on Steve's arm and led her to the door. 'Go home and wait. And try not to worry. I am sure that even those *dummkopfs* will realise before long that they've got the wrong person.'

That night the restaurant did not open. Three tense hours later a staff car drew up outside and Juliette tumbled out of it, white faced and tearful but apparently unharmed. As they huddled round the kitchen table, with her mother's arm around her shoulders, she grew calm enough to answer questions.

'I knew I was late leaving Montferrand but it would have been all right if I hadn't got a puncture. It took me ages to mend it and by then it was nearly time for the curfew. I got across the river just in time and I thought if I kept to the back streets I might get away with it but then I saw a patrol coming. I suppose I should have tried to bluff my way past them but instead I tried to hide. But they saw me and I suppose that made them suspicious. I told them I'd been visiting my boyfriend and had forgotten the time but they marched me off to the prison and shut me up in a cell. Then in the morning the Gestapo came and took me to the citadel.'

'Did they harm you?' her father asked.

'They searched me.' She shivered. 'It was horrible. There was a doctor there and he . . . '

'Hush,' Steve murmured. She had been told that in such circumstances no orifice was left unexplored, but she saw no reason to add to Juliette's trauma by making her relive the experience. 'You weren't carrying anything incriminating?'

'No, thank God. I had a message from London for you but when I saw the patrol I ditched it in a waste bin. I'm sorry.'

'You did the right thing. Danny will have kept a copy. That's not a problem. What happened next?'

'They kept asking me the same questions. What was my boyfriend's name? Where did he live? How long had I known him?'

'What did you tell them?' Steve knew that Juliette did not have a boyfriend.

'I told them it was Jean-Claude from Boussière.' Jean-Claude was an active member of the *réseau* and only a few years older than Juliette. 'I thought if they questioned him he would back me up, but I knew it was a risk. I couldn't think of anything else.'

'What happened next?' Steve asked.

'The man who was questioning me said, "You are lying to me now but eventually you will tell me the truth. Think about it," and then he left me alone. I seemed to be there for hours. No one came near me and I was hungry and cold and desperate for something to drink. Then I suddenly heard shouting from somewhere near by. I recognised the colonel's voice. It sounded as though he was having a furious argument with someone. Then the man who was questioning me came back and just said, "You can go."' She choked back a sob. 'I couldn't believe it. I was sure they must know something. And when I got out into the courtyard the colonel was there and he put me in his own car and told the driver to take me home. I tried to thank him but I couldn't find the words.'

Jacqueline was crying too. 'We must all thank him. How can we express our gratitude?'

'It might be best to say nothing,' Steve said. She was deeply moved by the colonel's action, knowing what the consequences for him might be. 'He has taken a risk, over-ruling the Gestapo. We don't want to rub their noses in it.'

*

On 15 August there was good news at last. A second Allied force had landed on the south coast, between Nice and Marseilles, and in the latter city resistance fighters had come out of hiding and taken to the streets. To add to this, they heard over the BBC that the Americans had broken out of the D-Day bridgehead and were heading for Le Mans and the Loire.

It was a day or two later that a stranger appeared in the restaurant, a middle-aged man, better dressed than the majority of their clientele. Steve served him and he remarked casually that the restaurant had been recommended by a friend.

'Oh yes?' she responded. 'Who would that be?'

'Dr Lefort, of Arbois. He is a colleague. My name is Matthieu Maufroy. I am the doctor at Arc-et-Senans.'

Steve's pulse quickened. 'And how is the good doctor's grandmother?' she asked. 'Has she recovered from her shingles?' It was the recognition formula she had agreed with Albert for any messenger passing between them.

'She is much better, but still weak. She finds the heat trying.' It was the correct response. The man continued, 'I am looking for someone called Suzette. Is she here?'

'I can pass on any message,' Steve replied. 'What does the doctor have to tell her?'

'Her friend wishes to meet with her. He will be at the cheese factory on the Mouchard road at noon the day after tomorrow.'

When Steve reached the cheese factory the manager showed her straight into the inner room. In the doorway she stopped short in amazement. Albert was not alone. There were three men with him and they were all in uniform. One was a major in the American Marines, one wore the uniform of a captain in the Free French forces and the third was a sergeant in the Royal Engineers. As she stared speechlessly, Albert came forward with a smile.

'Let me introduce you. This is Major Clarkson, who prefers to be called Hank. This is Capitaine Pierre Poignand and this is Sergeant Bill Watts. They form what is apparently known as a Jedburgh team. Gentlemen, this young lady prefers to be known simply as Suzette.'

There were handshakes all round and the American said, 'We've been hearing great things about the work you guys have been doing in disrupting German traffic. Congratulations.'

They were all speaking French, though Steve reflected that the American would reveal himself the moment he opened his mouth – but presumably that no longer mattered, since they were making no attempt to conceal their nationalities.

'Forgive me,' she said, 'I don't understand why you are in uniform. Aren't you taking a terrible risk? The Germans are still in control of this part of the country.'

'We know that,' he said with a broad grin. 'But not for much longer. We don't intend to show ourselves to them, don't worry. We're here to show your people that we're right behind them and to offer what assistance we can, wherever it's needed.'

Over wine and good Comtois cheese they settled down to discuss the situation. The Allies were advancing on both fronts. Marseilles and Grenoble had already fallen and the Americans were heading up the Rhône valley towards the Jura region.

'What we need now from you guys,' the major said, 'more than anything else, is intelligence. Which units are stationed where, and in what strength? What troop movements are taking place and in which direction? The Huns are starting to retreat and our guess is they will want to withdraw as many as possible of their men to guard the Fatherland. So keep up the good work on the roads and railways. The harder you can make it for them to get away, the better chance we have of trapping them before they can cross the Rhine.'

'How do I get the information to you?' Steve asked.

'I'm told you have radio contact with London. Send it to your people there and they will see that it's passed on to the relevant commanders.'

Back in her own area, Steve visited every unit to spread the news that there were Allies in uniform among them and that soon the Americans would be here in force. She asked them to report all troop movements to her. Then she compiled and encoded a summary of all the forces stationed in and around Besançon and took it to Danny to transmit to London.

On the 6 p.m. bulletin from the BBC on the 25th they heard the wonderful news that General Leclerc had entered Paris at the head of the liberating army. It was champagne all round for the clients of the Brasserie Vauban that night. People were no longer afraid to express their hatred of the occupiers, though they were careful to do so only among friends and were not yet quite ready to rise up against them. Technically, France might now be free, but here on her eastern borders the Nazis were still very much in charge.

Chapter Twelve

It was at the beginning of September that the baker from Montferrand-le-Château came into the kitchen of the brasserie with a tray of loaves. Underneath the paper lining the tray was a note in code from Danny. Steve took it to her room and painstakingly decoded it. It read: *'We have good intelligence that General von Helmstadt will be passing through your area. He has called a conference of local commanders at Salins-les-Bains for Sept. 6th and will then proceed to Germany for an important meeting with Hitler. Most desirable he does not reach his destination. Use all available means to prevent this'*

Steve spent some time studying her map of the area. It was possible that the General might be travelling by train, but in view of the disruption that her people had caused to the railways she thought it more likely that he would go by road. In which case, there was only one possible route – along the main road from Mouchard to Besançon and then north-west towards Montbéliard. He would obviously be travelling in a well-guarded convoy and there was only one unit in her area capable of mounting the sort of ambush necessary to attack it. She folded the map, got out her bicycle and set off for Michel's *maquis*.

He listened to her explanation of what was required and nodded. 'I think I know just the spot. Come with me and I'll show you.'

A half-hour walk through the forest brought them down to

the main road at La Roche-de-Valmy. Here the road ran close to the Canal du Rhône et Rhin, bordered on its other side by the steep rocky outcrop that gave the place its name.

'We'll set charges to blow up the leading vehicles,' Michel said, 'and have a tree almost cut through farther back, so we can fell it behind them. My men will be hidden up above among the rocks, able to fire down on to the convoy with Stens and rifles. I'll have some others stationed on the far side of the canal, in case anyone tries to escape that way.'

'Excellent,' Steve agreed. 'But can you be sure of getting the general?'

'Don't worry,' he told her. 'I'll have a special squad ready to rush in as soon as we've got the Boches pinned down. I'll lead them myself.'

'What will you do, snatch him?'

He looked at her. 'What would we do with a prisoner? I can't afford men to guard someone day and night and there is nowhere to lock him up.'

Steve met his eyes and felt a chill in her stomach. Usually she was able to close her mind to the fact that every success for the Resistance meant the death of at least one German, probably many more. But she had never had to plan a cold-blooded murder like this before. Suddenly the excitement and optimism engendered by the Allied invasion and the prospect of victory seeped away, leaving her exhausted and sick. From the bottom of her heart she hated this war, and all it entailed.

September 6th was two days away. There was no way of knowing whether the general would move on that evening or wait until the following day, but they assumed he was likely to want to sleep at Salins. Michel planned to have his men in position from the evening of the 6th, however, just in case.

Once she was satisfied that they had made their plans as foolproof as possible Steve went back to Besançon. Part of her wanted to stay, arguing that it was cowardly to leave Michel and his men to face all the danger, but she knew that it was more important that she should carry on with her work of coordination rather than risk a stray bullet or, worse still, capture.

By the evening of the 6th she was in a state of high tension and finding it difficult to keep her mind on the job of cooking and serving at the brasserie. Her nerves were stretched even tighter when three of the officers from the garrison came in to dine. They were in jovial mood, chatting with Steve and flirting with Juliette.

'What's happened to the colonel tonight?' Steve asked. 'I hope he's not ill.'

'No, no,' one replied. 'He's gone off to a meeting in Salins. But he's expected back here tonight.' He winked at Steve. 'I'm sure he'd rather be eating here but we are expecting an important guest.'

Steve understood then the full force of the cliché 'her blood ran cold'. For a moment she thought she might drop the tureen of soup she was holding. She put it down hastily and some of it slopped on to the tablecloth.

'Hey, careful!' one of the officers exclaimed. 'Are you all right, mademoiselle?'

'I'm sorry,' Steve mumbled. 'I . . . I'm not feeling well. I think I may be coming down with something.'

In the kitchen she grabbed hold of a chair-back to support herself. To have planned the murder of an unknown German general was one thing, but to allow the colonel who had been so good to them to fall into the same trap was insupportable. He was a kind, honest man forced to override his human instincts by an inhuman machine. He had saved her, unwittingly, and then knowingly risked his own position, perhaps his life, to save Juliette. Steve was under no illusions about what a posting to the Russian Front might mean for a man his age. And she had used his innocence and good nature to deceive him. Was she now going to allow him to go to his death in an ambush she had prepared?

She caught Juliette by the arm. 'Take over for me! I've got to go out. Tell them I'm ill and I've gone to bed.'

'You can't go out!' the girl protested. 'What about the curfew?'

'To hell with the curfew!' Steve exclaimed. Then she pulled herself together. 'I have to go, Juliette. I'll keep to the back streets. There aren't so many patrols these days.'

'But why? Where are you going?'

'I'll explain tomorrow. Just cover for me with that lot in there.'

She grabbed her coat and went out to where her bicycle was parked in the yard. The streets of the city were dark and deserted and there were no lights on her bicycle but there was just enough moonlight to enable her to see where she was going. Once she had to skid to a halt as a German patrol passed across a junction just ahead of her, and a few minutes later the sound of approaching engines forced her to take refuge in a narrow alley, where she stood with a pounding heart as an armoured car and two motorcycle outriders drove by.

Once out of the city she felt safer, but ahead of her was what threatened to be an insurmountable barrier. To reach the place they had chosen for the ambush she had to cross the river. She chose a route that would take her across one of the less used bridges, with the hope that perhaps it would not be guarded during the hours of curfew, but as she approached she saw a glimmer of light from the blockhouse.

She scanned the road ahead but could not see a sentry. Perhaps, if she was lucky, he was warming himself in the guardhouse. She considered putting her head down and pedalling as fast as she could across the bridge, in the hope of getting across before she was spotted, but decided instead to try a stealthy approach. She got off her bicycle and pushed it slowly forward. In the silence of the night the ticking of the bearings sounded heart-stoppingly loud. She had drawn parallel with the blockhouse and was just beginning to think that perhaps her luck was in when a figure stepped out of the shadows and a torch was shone in her face.

'*Halte!* Where do you think you're going?'

With a sickening sense of despair Steve recognised the sentry who had challenged her once before. He obviously recognised her, too.

'It's Mademoiselle Duclos, isn't it? Don't tell me you're off to buy mushrooms at this time of night!'

On the ride, Steve had had time to think up a story, though she knew it was a pretty thin one. 'I'm going to see my boyfriend. He lives in Pugey and I've just heard he's very ill. Please let me pass. I must see him.'

'Boyfriend, eh?' The sentry's lip curled in disbelief. 'Does the Herr Colonel know about this?'

'It's nothing to do with him. The colonel likes my cooking, that's all. My private life is my own.'

'So what is this boyfriend's name, then?'

'Claude Montauban. I can show you a photograph, if you like.'

'I'm not interested in your boyfriend's photograph. You've no business being out during curfew. So just turn around and get back home, and be thankful I don't arrest you.'

'Please!' Steve begged. 'He's terribly ill. He might die. I have to see him.'

'Tough! You'll have to wait till tomorrow.'

'All right!' Steve changed her tone. 'So it was a lie! Suppose I were to tell you that I'm going to meet the colonel himself? He's on his way back from Salins-les-Bains and we've arranged a secret rendezvous.'

He laughed harshly. 'Now you really are trying my patience. Why would the colonel do that? Go on, get out of here. Push off, before I change my mind about arresting you.'

Steve realised that this time she was not going to be able to talk her way through. The only solution was to resort to the methods she had been taught at Arisaig.

'But I've got a pass – he gave me a letter to show if I was stopped.'

'A likely story! Let's see it, then. Hand it over.'

Steve moved towards him, pushing her bike with her left hand, while her right groped in the pocket of her skirt, reaching for the Colt, which she had strapped to her thigh before leaving the brasserie. When she was within arm's reach she shoved the bike forward, ramming the front wheel between the soldier's legs with all the force she could muster. As he doubled up with a gasp of pain she withdrew her right hand, holding the gun, and hit him as hard as she could on the back of the head with the butt. He collapsed across her handlebars and then hit the ground with a thud as she yanked the bike backwards. For a moment Steve stood looking around, straining her ears over the sound of her own panting. She could hear a low murmur of voices from the blockhouse where the rest of the guards were sheltering but no sign of alarm. She looked down at the body slumped at her feet and the words that had been dinned into her by the 'heavenly twins' at Arisaig came back to her. 'Go for a quick, clean kill. A wounded man can recover and a prisoner is a liability. You must finish him off.' She looked at the gun in her hand. A shot would undoubtedly rouse the men in the blockhouse. She had no knife but she knew that there were blows she had practised that were guaranteed to kill. For a moment she contemplated the physical sensation of bringing the edge of her hand down on the unprotected neck and a wave of revulsion swept over her. At that instant the man at her feet groaned and simultaneously there was a shout of laughter from the blockhouse.

Steve shoved the Colt back into its holster and mounted her bike. A second later she was over the hump of the bridge and pedalling hell for leather towards a bend in the road. For the next couple of kilometres she continued to ride as fast as she could, expecting all the time to hear the sound of pursuit behind her, but the silence remained unbroken except for the swish of her tyres on the road and the rustle of leaves in the night breeze.

She now had a new source of anxiety. Could she reach the place appointed for the ambush before the convoy got there? As she drew nearer she strained her ears, expecting to hear the sound of engines and then the explosion that would signal the start of the fighting. But still the forest remained silent. When she reached the place she dismounted and stood still, looking about her. For a moment she wondered whether there had been some change of plan, or whether she had mistaken the spot, so little sign was there of any other human being in the vicinity. She steadied her breathing, pursed her lips and whistled the opening bars of *'Auprès de ma blonde . . .'*. There was a pause, then a rustle in the undergrowth beside the road and the lean figure of Michel moved out into the moonlight.

'Suzette?' He peered into her face. 'What is it? Has there been a change of plan?'

'Yes . . . no,' she gasped. Now that she was here she realised suddenly how useless her attempt must be. 'The general is on his way. He plans to spend the night in Besançon.'

'Excellent! We shouldn't have long to wait, then.'

'But it mustn't happen.' She was gabbling, trying to make sense of a flood of conflicting feelings. 'We can't do it. We must abandon the plan.'

'For God's sake, why?'

'Because there's someone else in the convoy. Someone who doesn't deserve to die.'

'What? Hostages? Women and children perhaps?'

'No, nothing like that. Colonel von Klimt, the commander of the garrison in Besançon, is with the general.'

'So much the better. Two birds with one stone.'

'No, you don't understand. He's a good man. He comes to the brasserie. I've had dinner with him in the citadel. He doesn't like this war any more than we do.'

Michel leaned closer, searching her face in the dim light. 'You are lovers?'

'No! It's not like that. We're friends, that's all.'

He took hold of her arm. 'Come off the road, in case someone comes along. Then we can talk.'

He lifted her bicycle into the ditch and led her deeper into the forest, to a place where she could sit on a flat rock. Then he crouched beside her and put his hand over hers.

'Suzette, you must realise how impossible this is. We have a mission. We have to go through with it.'

'I know,' she said, her voice rough with distress. 'It seems so wrong that a good man should have to die.'

'He isn't the first, or the last,' Michel commented grimly.

'And I've heard stories about this General von Helmstadt. Farther south they were getting a lot of trouble from saboteurs. He surrounded the nearest village, assembled all the men between twelve and sixty and shot the lot in cold blood. If we can take him out, at least he will never be able to perpetrate another atrocity like that.'

Steve put her head in her hands. The realisation was dawning on her that she had betrayed all her training. She had acted out of emotion instead of reason and had put not only herself at risk but perhaps also Michel and all his men. It was quite possible that the sentry at the bridge had raised the alarm and that she had been followed. Even now German troops might be moving stealthily through the forest to surround them.

A shrill whistle from somewhere above them brought her out of her reverie with a start.

Michel pressed her arm reassuringly. 'It's all right. That's Pierre. I posted him at the top of the hill to keep watch. It means he can see the convoy approaching. Here, come with me.'

He half led, half pushed her farther up the slope until she was behind a rocky outcrop.

'Stay here and keep your head down,' he instructed. 'This ought to protect you from any stray bullets. I must leave you now, but I'll be back when it's all over.'

He disappeared into the darkness and all around her Steve could hear the rustle of branches as his men moved quietly into position. Even in her distressed state she was able to appreciate the degree of discipline he had instilled into his heterogeneous troop. Very soon she could also hear the noise of engines as the convoy approached. Unable to resist the temptation to watch, she squirmed to the top of the rock and peered over. She saw the two motorcycle outriders who led the group, followed by an armoured troop carrier. Behind that were two saloon cars, presumably carrying the general and his staff, and at the rear was a second troop carrier. The motorcyclists passed her position and for a second or two she thought that the explosive charge that was supposed to halt the convoy had failed to go off. Then it exploded, with perfect accuracy, immediately beneath the leading troop carrier. Bodies and shards of metal flew into the air, there were screams and shouts and the squeal of brakes. Then Michel's men opened fire with Sten guns and rifles, aiming down into the confused mêlée on the road.

Within seconds the survivors among the German troops had reacted, throwing themselves down at the side of the road and spraying answering fire into the forest. For the first time in her life Steve heard live bullets sing over head and the thwack and whine as one ricocheted off the rock just below her. She cowered lower, but not so far that she could not keep her eyes on the road. Amidst the rest of the noise she heard the crash of a tree being felled, and the rear troop carrier, which had begun to reverse followed by the two cars, came to an abrupt stop. Then she saw two groups detach themselves from the shadow of the trees and run forward, six men in each, close knit into a single wedge. The windows of the two cars were open and she could see the muzzle flashes of guns from inside. One man in the leading group fell but the rest ran on. Then the cars were surrounded and she could no longer distinguish what was happening. Moments later, she saw the men running back into the trees.

The soldiers at the side of the road were still firing but the return fire from the *maquisards* had diminished. Michel materialised abruptly at her side, grabbing her arm.

'Come on. Time to get out of here.'

He began to drag her up the slope. She shook her arm free and climbed beside him, aware that around her the other men of the *maquis* were withdrawing too. At the top of the hill they stopped, panting, and listened. There was still sporadic firing from below but no sound of pursuit.

'Good,' Michel said. 'We've given them enough to think about to stop them coming after us. But it won't be long before reinforcements arrive. We must keep going.'

'The general?' Steve asked, as she followed him along a faint track.

'Dead,' he responded, and then before she could ask anything else, 'and everyone else in the cars.'

Steve clenched her teeth and concentrated on keeping up with his rapid stride. They had to take a roundabout route back to the camp, keeping to scarcely visible paths through the forest to avoid any chance of encountering the German troops who would by now be searching for them. Once or twice they came to a halt as a dark figure appeared ahead of them, until a soft whistle of recognition identified the newcomer as one of Michel's men, but most of them had dispersed, melting away in true guerrilla style to make their own way back.

By the time they reached the camp Steve was dizzy with fatigue. Michel led her to the cave and sat her down on his bed and gave her a glass of *marc*.

'Rest here. I have to check on the men.'

When he came back she was sitting with her head in her hands, staring blankly at the ground between her feet, but she roused herself to ask, 'Are there many casualties?'

'Two dead,' he responded tersely. 'Four wounded, only one seriously. They've taken him to the doctor in Arc-et-Senans.'

Steve looked up. 'Who died?'

'Jean-Louis and Jacques Leblanc.'

'Jean-Louis? He was just a kid. Oh God . . .'

He knelt in front of her and took her hands. 'Suzette, this is war. I grieve for them as much as you do but it could have been much worse. We have scored a great success. You must concentrate on that. London will be delighted when you tell them we have taken out von Helmstadt. He was a very able commander. Removing him will make it that much easier for the Americans to force their way up the Rhône. It could shorten the whole war.'

She nodded, but she could not feel any sense of triumph. At his suggestion she lay down and slept uneasily for what remained of the night, waking to sunlight slanting in through the mouth of the cave and the sound of men moving about outside. She found Michel breakfasting on acorn coffee and day-old bread and discovered she was hungry.

'What now?' he asked.

'I must get to Montferrand to give Danny the news to transmit – but my bike's back there by the road.'

'Damn! Can it be traced to you?'

'I don't know. Possibly.'

'You should stay here until we're sure.'

'No, I must make sure the message goes out on his next sked. And then I must go back to Besançon. The Choquins will be worried. I'll make my way on foot by the forest paths. It will be safer than going by road.'

Michel sent one of his men to escort her as far as the village. The forest tracks were quiet, though she could hear tanks and armoured vehicles moving on the main road. She reached Montferrand without incident, but when she entered the kitchen at the bakery she was shocked to find Juliette waiting for her, with M. and Mme Carrez and

Danny. The young girl's face was white and streaked with tears and she flung herself on Steve, babbling hysterically.

'Oh, thank God! Thank God you are safe, at least. I was afraid I would not catch you. This is the only place I could think of to come. You mustn't go back to the city.'

'Why not? What's happened?' Steve gripped her by the shoulders and shook her.

Juliette caught her breath in a gasp and Steve could see her struggling for control. 'We're *brûlé*. Completely blown! The Gestapo came this morning, very early. They arrested Papa and Maman. I only escaped because I had gone out to buy bread. Lucien from next door came to find me and tell me not to go home. They're looking for us, both of us. They asked for you by name.'

'By what name?'

'Marguerite Duclos, of course.'

Steve let go of the girl and sank down on the nearest chair. This was all her fault. First she had let sentiment govern her instead of logic and then, at the crucial moment, she had lacked the nerve to carry her actions through to the proper conclusion. The sentry had recovered and had given her name to the Gestapo and now the Choquins were paying the penalty. She felt that finally her reserves of courage had run out and she wanted to put her head on her arms and weep. She looked around the room, from Juliette's tear-stained face to those of M. and Mme Carrez, taut with anxiety, and then to Danny. They were all waiting for her, expecting her to take command and tell them what to do next.

'How did you get here?' she asked Juliette.

'I didn't know where else to go. I took a chance and crossed the river straight away, with all the people on their way to work. I hoped the Boches would not have had time to circulate my name and my description. I suppose I was lucky. Anyway, they didn't stop me.'

Steve heaved a deep sigh. She felt sick and exhausted but somehow she had to make decisions and find some comfort for her friend. She reached out and took the younger girl's hand. '*Ma chère*, I'm so sorry about your parents. But with any luck they will be able to convince the Gestapo that I was deceiving them, as well as the authorities. As far as they knew, I was just a refugee who needed a job and somewhere to stay.'

'What will you do now?' Gilbert Carrez asked.

'Juliette and I will join the *maquis*,' Steve said. 'It's the only answer. And I'll take Danny with me. You've sheltered him long enough and I don't want the trail to lead to you, too. The Americans are only a few miles away. Within days they will be here and then we can all breathe freely again.'

She went up to the woodcutter's hut with Danny to collect his radio set, thanked the Carrezes for their help and then set out with her two companions back the way she had come that morning.

Chapter Thirteen

It was the beginning of yet another new phase in Steve's clandestine existence, and in a strange way she found it a relief. Now she was living outside the law, among people who all knew her real status, though not her true identity. There had been a change within herself, too. She felt as if the last vestiges of softness had been pared away. The old, warm-hearted Steve was gone. Sentiment had led her to the brink of disaster. Now nothing was left but duty and determination to see the job through to the end.

Her greatest problem was the fact that she no longer dared produce her identity papers, which meant that she could not move around freely. As a precaution she decided to change her appearance once again. Over the last months she had succeeded in darkening her hair, first with the remains of the dye Sylvie had given her and later with a concoction of the grounds left over from making ersatz coffee, but lately her natural auburn colour had begun to show again at the roots. She went to one of the men in the camp who had once been apprenticed to a barber and got him to cut her hair to a length of half an inch. The result, she suspected, was bizarre, but since there were no mirrors in the camp she soon forgot about it. At her suggestion, Juliette too cut her hair, though not so radically, but without access to any form of cosmetics there was little else they could do to disguise her.

Juliette was the one chink in the armour Steve had built round her heart. She showed great determination not to give way but Steve could see that she was racked with anxiety about her parents. The lively, carefree girl she had grown so fond of became a silent shadow, despite everything she tried to do to cheer her.

Life in the camp was not too uncomfortable. Michel insisted on moving out of the cave and giving it over to the two women, which gave them a modicum of privacy. Facilities were primitive but no worse, Steve reflected, than she had experienced at pony camp as a child. Food was not a problem, since the *maquis* had good relations with all the local farmers, though the standard of cooking left much to be desired.

Danny settled in happily with his radio set, the more so since he rapidly struck up a flirtatious relationship with one of Michel's lieutenants, a piratical-looking character named Armand – an incongruous friendship that afforded Steve considerable amusement in her moments of relaxation. London's response to her message regarding the ambush on General von Helmstadt was fulsome in its congratulations.

'Get them to send us some more supplies, if they're so pleased with us,' Michel said, but the request fell on deaf ears. All available flights were being directed to areas closer to the Western Front.

As the Allies advanced the activities of the Resistance changed to match the new situation. Whereas they had been concerned with preventing reinforcements reaching the front line they were now concentrating on hampering the withdrawal of the German army. Michel and his men staged several ambushes, and although they concentrated on picking off small units and stragglers, the precautions that their activities forced the enemy to take had the effect of slowing their retreat. Other cells continued to derail trains, though bridges were now left intact. They would be needed by the advancing Allies, in due course. Unable to use the roads freely, Steve cycled along the many forest tracks that criss crossed the area or kept in touch with the different units by dead letter drops. Information about the disposition of troops came to her from all around, and she and Juliette spent long hours watching the roads through binoculars and making notes of numbers and types of vehicles. Sometimes they ventured down to the villages, mingling with the crowds on market days or helping to bring in the grape harvest, in order to pick up the latest gossip or spy on the cap badges or other insignia of troops passing through. It was risky but the only way of being sure that their information was correct in every detail. As a result Danny was able to send a steady stream of intelligence back to London.

As September drew on they began to hear evidence that the battle was drawing closer. In the distance there was an almost continuous boom of artillery. Then came the day when they heard from their scouts that the Americans had reached the banks of the River Loue, where they were temporarily halted by a determined German stand.

Steve squeezed Juliette's arm. 'It can't be long now. Once the Yanks are in Besançon they will set all the Gestapo's prisoners free and you'll be able to go home.' *And so will I!* she added to herself, scarcely able to believe it.

The next day Steve was busy encoding a message and Michel was checking the dwindling supply of ammunition when Pierre, who had been set to watch the main road below the camp, came running across the clearing.

'*Patron*, come! There is something here you must see!'

Steve and Michel followed him quickly to the vantage point and looked down. A long stream of military vehicles was crawling along the road from the direction of the city.

'They're evacuating!' Michel breathed. 'They are evacuating Besançon.'

'Thank God!' Steve responded. 'Do you think they are all pulling out?'

'It looks like it.' He turned away. 'This is too good an opportunity to miss. I'll get the men together.'

'Wait!' Steve said. 'We must let the Americans know that the city is undefended. We don't want them to start bombing it or shelling it, thinking the Boches are still there.'

'Radio London and let them know,' he said.

Steve shook her head. 'It's too slow. By the time the message gets there and is decoded and then passed on the Yanks could be here. They're only a few miles away. I'll have to try to contact them directly.'

'How?'

'I'll have to slip through the lines. It shouldn't be difficult. The Germans must be too busy to mount identity checks now.'

'It's too dangerous,' he protested. 'Let me go.'

'No, you're needed here. I'll go now and wait for darkness to cross the river. I can travel through the forest almost all the way.'

He continued to protest but she refused to listen. Now that liberation was so close she was determined to do something decisive. When she told Juliette what she intended, however, the younger girl insisted on coming with her.

'Suppose something happened to you – an accident perhaps. Or suppose you were wounded. You would need someone with you – someone who could carry the message. Besançon is my home. My parents are there, and my friends. It is important to me to keep it safe. I have the right, I think.'

It was an impossible argument to refute. Secretly not sorry to have company, Steve yielded and the two of them mounted their bicycles and set off along the forest tracks.

By evening they were at the edge of the forest, looking across the gently undulating plain through which the Loue flowed. The noise of battle was a continuous thunder, and they could see shells bursting on both sides of the river.

'There's a bridge just beyond Chissey,' Steve said. 'We'll wait until dark and then try to cross there.'

As night fell they cycled cautiously into the village. The streets were deserted and many of the houses had been hit by shells. Steve saw with a pang of regret that some of them belonged to men who had helped with that first *parachutage*. She guessed that most of the inhabitants had left to seek refuge in the forest. No one challenged them, though two shells exploded too close for comfort, showering them with debris and lighting up the area. For a brief moment Steve began to think that the Germans had evacuated the area and they might be able to cross the river unchallenged, but when they came in sight of the bridge they saw that there was a gun battery dug in right beside it. They got off their bicycles in the shadow of a ruined farm building and Steve searched her memory for other ways to cross.

'We'll have to try further upstream. It means going back through Chissey and then taking the road to Chamblay.'

It took them fifteen minutes to reach the next bridge, but there too their way was blocked, this time by an armoured car parked in the middle of the road. They stood in the darkness and took stock of the situation.

'There's an American battery just the far side of the river a little farther down,' Steve said. 'I can see the flashes. But there doesn't seem to be anything on this side. There's nothing for it. We'll have to swim.'

'But I can't swim,' Juliette protested. 'You know that.'

'Of course, I'd forgotten. OK. You stay and take care of the bikes. It's too dangerous here in the open. Go back to the crossroads and wait for me there. If I'm not back by dawn, make your own way back to the camp.' Juliette began to protest but Steve cut in. 'I've never tried to give you orders before but I'm giving you one now. Go back and wait for me.'

When Juliette had gone, leading the second bicycle, Steve made her way along the bank to a point where the river curled in a loop and a small tributary joined it. It was easy to understand why there was no gun battery sited here, since the ground was marshy. She stumbled through the dense undergrowth to the edge of the stream and crouched behind a bush, studying the river banks in both directions. The noise was deafening now, the roar of the guns combining with the express-train rattle of shells passing overhead, and the ground shook with the explosions. She could see the flashes from the American battery a little downstream but there was no sign of activity on her side of the river. She began to take off her shoes and trousers, glad that it was dark and she was alone – though it crossed her mind to wonder what she would do if she encountered an American patrol before she had time to dress herself on the other side. She pulled off the rest of her clothes, tied them in a bundle and hung her shoes round her neck. Then she slid down the bank, feeling her legs scratched by brambles and stung by nettles. The river was not wide or fast flowing and at this time of year the water was not particularly cold, but it was chilly enough to make her catch her breath. The water reflected the glare of exploding shells in crimson ripples.

Holding her bundle above her head, she waded deeper until in the middle of the river the current pulled her feet from under her and she was forced to swim. She struck out for the opposite bank, holding her bundle above her head with one hand, letting the current carry her downstream until she reached a place where she could scramble out.

Once on dry land she stood still, listening. This might be ground held by the Americans but she had no wish to fall victim to a bullet fired by a nervous sentry. There seemed to be no sign of movement near by, so she rubbed herself with her shirt, which she had managed to keep more or less dry, pulled on her damp garments and her sopping shoes and began to make her way cautiously towards the gun emplacement.

She had almost reached it when a figure rose out of the darkness and she heard the bolt of a rifle being pulled back.

'Halt! Who goes there? Advance and be recognised.'

The American voice made her want to laugh with delight. She raised her hands and walked forward slowly. 'Don't shoot. I'm English. I've got an important message for your commanding officer.'

A couple of minutes later she was being interviewed by a young lieutenant.

'Who are you? What the hell are you doing here?'

'I'm a British agent. I've been working with the Resistance in Besançon. Please take me to your CO. I have vital information for him.'

She was put into a jeep and driven to a house in the nearby village of Chamblay, where she found herself facing a colonel who looked as if he had not slept or shaved for days.

He listened to her message and then said wearily, 'Tell me why I should believe you. As far as I know you could be a

German agent or a collaborator. Can you prove you are who you say? Do you have any documents?'

'Hardly!' Steve retorted. Her wet clothes were clinging to her and she was beginning to shiver. 'I run the risk of being searched by the Boches every day.'

'Well, what can you tell me to make me believe you?'

'I could give you a radio wavelength and a code name, but it will take time to get an answer back.' She racked her brain for an alternative. 'Wait! I've had a thought. Have you by any chance come across a Major Clarkson? He's an American, over here as part of a Jedburgh team. You've probably overrun him by now.'

'Clarkson?' The colonel got up and strode across to the door. 'Hank?' he shouted. 'Would you come in here for a minute?'

Hank Clarkson looked as weary and dishevelled as his superior. He peered at Steve and for a moment she was afraid that he did not recognise her. Then his face broke into a grin.

'Jeez, Suzette! What happened to your hair?'

'I had to change my appearance. Hank, can you tell the colonel who I am? I've got some vital information.'

'Sure!' He turned to the other man. 'John, this here is Suzette. I don't know her real name but I know she's a British agent who's been working farther north – and doing a great job. All that useful gen about troop movements we've been getting has come from her.'

Things changed rapidly then. She was given a set of American fatigues several sizes too large while her clothes were taken away to be dried. An orderly brought scalding coffee laced with brandy – the first real coffee she had tasted in months – and peanut butter sandwiches. As she ate, she told the two Americans everything she knew about the situation in her area.

When she had finished the colonel said with a grin, 'Well, I guess you'll be about ready to start for home, as soon as your clothes are dry. We can put you in a jeep and send you back to Chalon and from there it shouldn't be too hard to find a plane going back to the UK. You could be back in London by tomorrow.'

For a moment the prospect made Steve feel faint with joy. She could go home! She could see her parents and the farm again, be safe, live a normal life – marry Roddy. Then the image of Juliette waiting at the crossroads dragged her back to reality.

'I can't,' she said. 'There are people waiting for me on the other side of the river. I've got to go back to them.'

'You're sure? It's going to get pretty rough over there in the next day or two. We're going to make a big push tonight.'

'I can't leave them to face it alone. Anyway, you'll be there soon. I'll be waiting for you when you roll into Besançon.'

'How are you planning on getting back across the river?'

'Same way as I came, I suppose – swimming.'

The colonel laughed. 'I guess we can do better than that for you.'

He gave some orders and sent an orderly to fetch her clothes, which by some miracle were almost dry. In half an hour she was back at the river, this time in the company of a sergeant of marines and three soldiers carrying a rubber boat. They paddled her across, helped her up the bank and wished her good luck, then disappeared silently the way they had come.

For a few minutes Steve stood looking back across the

river. Her throat was aching and there was a void where her stomach should be. Safety and freedom had been so close and she had let them slip through her fingers. The urge to call the men back and say she had changed her mind almost overwhelmed her. Then she took a deep breath and turned away to stumble across the marshy ground and out on to the road.

It was almost dawn when she reached the crossroads and found Juliette waiting for her. They fell into each other's arms, half laughing, half sobbing with relief.

'Did you find them, the Americans?' Juliette asked.

'I did. They're planning a big assault tomorrow. With any luck they'll be in Besançon by nightfall. And look! See what they gave me?' She emptied her pockets to display bars of chocolate and packets of chewing gum. 'Here, have some. I've already eaten.'

Juliette thrust the chocolate into her mouth with ecstatic murmurs and then they mounted their bicycles.

'Come on!' Steve said. Her anguished mood had been replaced by a dizzy euphoria. 'One last effort. Let's get back to camp and give them the good news.'

They had almost reached the far side of the forest and Steve was revelling in the crisp morning air and the growing warmth of the rising sun when they spun round a corner and almost ran into a party of German soldiers. They were gathered around the tailboard of a truck with mugs and mess tins in their hands, obviously having breakfast before moving on. Both girls braked hard but they were in the middle of the group before they skidded to a halt. All round them mess tins were dropped and rifles brought into the firing position. Harsh German voices demanded who they were and where they were going.

Steve forced a broad grin. 'Hello, boys. Got a hot drink to spare for a couple of thirsty girls?'

An officer appeared from the front of the truck. 'Who are you?' he demanded in French. 'What are you doing here?'

'We're just a couple of girls from back there,' Steve said, gesturing vaguely behind her. 'We're trying to get away from the fighting. It's terrible round our village.'

'Search them,' the officer ordered.

The search immediately revealed the American chocolate and gum.

'Where did you get this?'

'An American patrol came through. They gave us these. But then your men counter-attacked and the Americans ran away.'

The officer looked from Steve to Juliette, undecided but clearly still suspicious. 'Put them in the truck. We'll take them with us and hand them over to the proper authorities. Move!'

As they were manhandled into the truck Steve was gripped by a sense of disbelief. This could not be happening – not now, after all she had been through. Bitterly, she remembered that a few hours earlier she had been on the verge of going home. She had not slept all night and the sudden collapse from euphoria into despair almost undid her. But now she knew she must think clearly. Her own life and Juliette's depended on it.

She gripped Juliette's hand and murmured in her ear, under cover of the noise of the truck's engine, 'Don't worry. The Americans are coming. Just remember, we're two ordinary French girls running away from the fighting. Stick to that and we'll be all right.'

The optimistic attitude was hard to maintain as she

realised that the truck was headed away from the firing line. The hours passed and the truck ground on until she calculated that they must by now be well beyond Besançon. Eventually, they came to a standstill in the square of a small town she had never seen before, though she was relieved to see from the signs above the shops that they were still in France. The square was packed with German transport and soldiers were milling about or sitting on doorsteps and walls. The scene was chaotic, and it gave Steve hope that somehow in the middle of it all they might be forgotten. They were prodded out of the truck and taken into what appeared to be a garage or storage space attached to one of the houses. Here they were left under the eye of a guard, who refused to look away even when they were forced to relieve themselves in a corner of the room. No one else came near them, and they were offered neither food nor drink.

Eventually an SD officer came in and demanded to see their papers. Steve handed hers over, hoping that this man had come from somewhere outside her area and that the names of Marguerite Duclos and Juliette Choquin would mean nothing to him. In this respect, at least, it seemed they were in luck. He glanced at the names and then asked again where they had been going and why.

'You say you were running away from the fighting. How is it, then, that you were in that area when your identity cards give both your addresses as Besançon?'

Steve had had time to think about that. She gave a small shrug. 'All right, I admit we were trying to cross to the Americans. They have food to spare. We're starving in Besançon. We thought if we could get across the river we'd be better off.'

'So why were you heading back the other way?'

'We met an American patrol. They gave us the chocolate

and the gum. But then the fighting started again and we were frightened. We decided it was too dangerous.'

The officer stared at her in silence for a moment. Then he turned on his heel and went out.

Some time later a soldier brought them water and some thin soup and the guard was changed. It grew dark and they guessed that nothing more was going to happen that day. There were some old sacks in a corner and Steve spread them out and persuaded Juliette to lie down. Then she stretched out beside her, wrapping her arms around the girl's slight, shivering form, and fell into an uneasy sleep.

The next morning they were herded into the truck again and all day it bumped and swayed along the potholed roads. By the time it stopped Steve realised that they must be deep into Germany. They found themselves in the courtyard of a huge, grey building with windows that were no more than slits. Their guards marched them through a heavy, iron-clad door and into a bare room containing a desk and a single chair. They were left to wait for some time until a Gestapo colonel entered. He interrogated them briefly but Steve had the impression that his mind was on other things and their arrival was an unwelcome distraction. After a few minutes he went to the door and called a guard.

'Put them in a cell. I haven't got time to deal with them now. They can wait until I've dealt with more important matters.'

As the cell door closed behind them Steve put her arms around the weeping Juliette. 'Be brave. The war can't go on much longer and when the Germans surrender the Americans will let us out. All we have to do is hang on and stick to our story. We're just two innocent French girls who got mixed up in all this by mistake.'

Chapter Fourteen

Gina Franconi climbed out of the taxi outside the main door of Grendon Underwood, the SOE signals station where she had been based two years earlier. The old house looked much the same but there were more Nissen huts in the grounds than she remembered and the paths between them, which had been a sea of mud when she left, had been gravelled. The whole set-up, which had looked temporary and improvised when she arrived, now had an air of permanence. Weeds were growing up round the edge of the huts and there was moss on the roofs, so that they had acquired an organic look, as if they had sprouted up from the soil. In the grand hallway of the house itself the polished wood floor had been scuffed by boots and the wallpaper on the staircase showed the marks where equipment had been carried up and down. One thing remained the same – the institutional smell of boiled cabbage and polish.

Frankie dumped her kit and reported to the commanding officer. Captain Henderson looked up from some paperwork with the same expression of calm efficiency that Frankie remembered. She had changed very little, though perhaps the marks of fatigue on her face were a little more deeply etched. Frankie wondered whether the girls under her command still referred to her behind her back as 'Mother Hen'. She came to attention and threw up a salute.

'Lieutenant Franconi reporting for duty, ma'am.'

Henderson got up with a smile. 'Welcome back, Franconi. And congratulations on the promotion.'

She offered her hand and Frankie shook it. 'Thank you, ma'am.'

'Did you have a good leave? It must have been nice to be home for Christmas.'

'Yes, very nice, thank you, ma'am.' Frankie had no intention of going into the details of the fraught two weeks she had spent with her family.

Henderson returned to her seat. 'I've been looking at your file. It seems you've been making quite a name for yourself out in Italy. There's even a suggestion of a decoration.'*

Frankie felt herself blush. 'Oh, I don't know about that, ma'am.'

'Well, your last CO speaks very highly of you – though he does suggest that you prefer to use your own initiative rather than deferring to the chain of command.'

Frankie hesitated. 'Sometimes it was necessary, ma'am.'

Henderson looked at her quizzically. 'I'll take your word for that. Anyway, it appears there is at least one officer who may owe you his life. I hope he's duly grateful.'

Frankie resisted the temptation to feel for the engagement ring that she was wearing on its chain under her uniform. 'Oh yes, ma'am, I think so.'

For a moment their eyes met and Frankie had the feeling that she was being gently probed. She remained silent. Her relationship with Nick was nobody's business but their own, now that he was no longer in the service.

Henderson became businesslike again. 'Right. I'm putting

*For the full story of Frankie's adventures, see the same author's *We'll Meet Again*.

you in charge of B Company. You know the drill. We are still working two shifts, eight till two and then two till eight, and your job will be to supervise all the decoding work on your shift. Your lot are on the early shift at the moment. You'll find the work less pressurised than it was. Now that so many of our agents have been withdrawn we no longer have the French traffic to deal with.'

The remark brought a nagging anxiety to the forefront of Frankie's mind. 'Have we got any agents left in France, ma'am?'

'No. I gather that General de Gaulle was only too ready to see the back of them once he was installed in Paris.'

'So, did they all get back?'

'Not all, no.'

'Do we know what happened to the others?'

'Baker Street may do . . . though I doubt it. All we know is what we can glean from the messages we decode. Is there someone you're particularly interested in?'

'A girl I trained with at Overthorpe. Her name's Escott Stevens. I know she volunteered and was accepted for training but I haven't heard from her since.'

'Do you know what her cover name was? Or which circuit she was dropped to?'

'No, ma'am, I'm afraid not.'

'Then there's nothing I can tell you. But if she was back home, wouldn't she have got in touch by now?'

Frankie sighed. Her stomach felt hollow. 'I suppose so. I've been hoping perhaps there were still a few circuits operating and she might be with them.'

'No.' Henderson's tone was gentle. 'I'm sorry.'

Frankie pulled herself together. 'Oh well. Better get on, I suppose.'

'Yes. Ask one of the orderlies to show you where you're sleeping. You'll be pleased to hear that you get a room in the house, now you're an officer.'

Frankie settled back into the familiar routine of the signals station. It seemed strange at first to be sitting at the supervisor's desk, checking the work of the women in the decoding room, particularly as some of them were older than she was and had been at Grendon when she first arrived there two years ago. They seemed to accept her quite readily but she missed the friends she had grown so close to in Italy – Midge and Dickie and the others. She tried to concentrate on the work but she had to admit to herself that she was restless. After her brief foray behind enemy lines the previous summer everything else seemed an anticlimax. It was not that she had any wish to repeat the experience but it was frustrating to be back at Grendon, doing the slow, grinding work of decoding. She was fed up with the war and all it involved. And she missed Nick. She wrote to him every day, using the letters as a kind of diary and posting them two or three times a week.

He wrote back almost as often. He was becoming more and more immersed in politics and used the letters as a way of clarifying his own ideas about what needed to be done in the country once the war was over. Frankie had never thought much about the subject, but without fully realising it she absorbed a good deal of political theory in this way. It was not, however, what she really wanted to read about. Nick's letters were loving and he told her repeatedly how much he missed her but there was no definite reference to plans for their wedding or their future together. Frankie wanted to be able to imagine what their life would be like,

where they would live, what part she would play in his
career, but it seemed he was not ready to commit himself to
any definite arrangements.

She had been at Grendon for just over two weeks when a
letter arrived that had been sent originally to Italy and had
now followed her back. She could see at a glance that it was
not from Nick or any of her family, though the handwriting
was vaguely familiar. It was when she saw the postmark that
her stomach turned over. Princes Risborough! That was
where Steve lived, but the writing was not Steve's. She recognised it then as Steve's mother's, and that could only mean
bad news. Her hand shook as she opened the envelope.

Dear Frankie,

*I am not sure whether or not I should be writing this letter
but I feel you have a right to be told our news. Diana (Steve,
you would call her) has been posted missing. You remember I
told you in my last letter about the man who came to see us
from the War Office when we made enquiries about her? The
one in civilian dress who refused to give us his name? He
arrived without warning yesterday and told us. He wouldn't
say where or how it had happened – only that we should be
very proud of her. As if we were not proud of her already! Of
course, we had no idea that she was in any danger. We knew
she had been posted abroad but we assumed she was working
in some 'back-room' capacity well away from the front line.
As you know, we have received several postcards from her
with pictures of Cairo and the pyramids but I can't imagine
what she can have been doing there that was so secret.*

*I know you and she are both members of the same unit,
although you have been posted to different places, so perhaps
you will understand how she came to be in such a dangerous
situation. I'm not asking you to explain. I know you would*

not be allowed to put that sort of information in a letter. But perhaps when you come back to England you will come and see us and we can talk then.

It's hard to believe that we shall never see her again. Of course, 'missing' does not necessarily mean dead but the man who brought the news advised us not to hope for too much. She was such a lovely girl, so full of life and warmth, and our lives are going to be so empty without her. But there must be hundreds of families who are suffering in just the same way so we must come to terms with it somehow. We were told that what she was doing – whatever it was – was of vital importance to the war effort and that she had shown great courage. I suppose we must just have faith that in some way her sacrifice brings peace a little nearer.

I know you will be distressed by this news and I hope I have done the right thing in writing to you. Diana valued your friendship very highly so I think she would want you to know. Please take care of yourself and come to see us when you can.

Yours sincerely
Annabel Escott Stevens

Frankie sank down on the edge of the bed and gazed at the sheet of paper in her hand without seeing it. She wanted to weep but somehow the sobs seemed to be trapped in her throat. It was not so much that the news had come as a shock. She had guessed some time ago that Steve must have been either killed or captured. Now the thought that she would never see her friend again was subsumed in her sense of pity for Steve's parents. How could they bear such a loss? Steve had been an only child. How could they ever fill the terrible gap that her death left in their lives?

She knew she must get in touch with them but a letter seemed so inadequate. She ought to go and see them.

Princes Risborough was quite close, as the crow flew, but it was cross-country. To get there by public transport and back again in her time off was impossible. After some thought, she took her problem to Captain Henderson.

'I know it's too soon to ask for leave, ma'am, when I've just had a couple of weeks,' she concluded, 'but I really think I ought to go and see them and, like, express my condolences. But I'd probably have to get a bus into Aylesbury and then another one to Princes Risborough, and even then it's quite a walk from the village to their farm.'

'Can you drive?' Henderson asked.

'No, ma'am. I never got a chance to learn.'

Henderson looked amused. 'A FANY who never learned to drive! Now that would puzzle a lot of people.' She became serious again. 'Assuming you could, would it be possible to get there and back in your off-duty time?'

'Oh, yes. It would be easy by car.'

'What shift are you on at present?'

'The early one, ma'am – eight until two.'

'Right. I'll arrange for a vehicle and a driver to be available for you from two p.m. on Sunday. Just make sure you're back in time for lights out.'

Dusk was gathering in the branches of the leafless trees as the car wound its way up the narrow lane and turned into the drive of Hillfoot Farm. In the back seat, Frankie was gripped by a painful nostalgia. The last time she had come this way it had been with Steve, in a battered old truck smelling of sour milk and cow dung. She remembered her happiness at being with her friend and her anxiety about what Steve's parents would think of her. That was the weekend Steve had told her that she was planning to volunteer as an agent.

Overlaying these memories was a more pressing problem. What was she going to do with her driver while she was with the Escott Stevenses? She was a nice enough girl, only just eighteen and apparently rather over-awed by Frankie, but she certainly could not be allowed to sit in on their conversation. On the other hand, she could not just be left outside in the cold. Frankie wondered whether there was anywhere in the village she could send her, but the tea shop, if there was one, would soon be closed and the pubs were not open yet. She had never had to deal with a subordinate outside the confines of a military base and was not sure how to behave. She decided she would have to rely on Annabel Escott Stevens's superior knowledge and experience.

As the car drew up, Frankie leaned forward. 'Sit tight a minute. I'll let you know what to do.'

She had phoned in advance so she knew she was expected. Annabel opened the door to her in person and Frankie saw that she was attempting to conceal her grief beneath a mask of good manners.

'Frankie, it's good to see you! Thank you so much for coming.'

'I would have come sooner,' Frankie said, 'but your letter only found its way to me a couple of days ago.'

'Come in. You must be frozen. Have you come far?'

'Only from Grendon. I'm back there again.' Frankie paused in the doorway. 'I've got a driver outside. Is there somewhere she could wait?'

'Of course. The girls are in the kitchen having a cup of tea and a warm-up before the evening milking. She can sit with them. Just a minute . . .'

While her hostess went to the kitchen door and called one of the Land Girls, Frankie looked around the hall. On her last visit it had been decorated with swags of holly and evergreen, with a magnificent Christmas tree in one corner. Now Twelfth Night was long gone, and everywhere the Christmas decorations had been put away, but the bareness of the room seemed to Frankie like an outward sign of the loss the household had suffered.

When Frankie's driver had been escorted to the kitchen Annabel said, 'We're in the drawing room. Come in.'

Frankie remembered Steve's father as a big man with powerful shoulders and a weather-beaten face, and she was shaken to see the effect his daughter's loss had had on him. He seemed to have shrunk, as if some internal force had gone out of him, leaving his body loose like a badly fitting suit of clothes. They shook hands, wordlessly. The polite greetings and the question of Frankie's driver had glossed over the first minutes of meeting but now there was no escaping the purpose of her visit. Frankie took a breath, swallowed and turned to Annabel.

'Mrs Escott Stevens, I'm so sorry to hear about Steve – Diana. It must have come as a terrible shock to you – to both of you.'

She could see that now the subject had been broached Annabel was struggling to hold back tears.

'Yes, it did, of course. But we have to keep reminding ourselves that we're not the only ones to have lost someone. I suppose . . . I suppose it's the unexpectedness that makes it worse. We always thought that she was in no more danger than she might have been here, with the chance of being hit by a doodlebug. You understand what I mean?'

'Yes, of course,' Frankie responded. It was hard to know what else she could say.

'What we can't understand,' Mr Escott Stevens said, 'is what she can have been doing in Cairo that was so secret – and so dangerous.'

Frankie took a deep breath. 'Look, I'm not supposed to talk to anyone about this. But I do know Steve – Diana – probably wasn't in Cairo at all. She was working on something top secret and it was something that needed a lot of courage. I can't tell you any more but it's quite right that you should be very proud of her.'

Mr and Mrs Escott Stevens exchanged glances and nodded. He said, 'Thank you, Frankie. That confirms what we have suspected. Diana was fluent in French. Would I be right in thinking that that had something to do with it?'

Frankie hesitated, then nodded.

'You mean she was working as some kind of spy, or secret agent?' Annabel exclaimed.

Frankie met her eyes. 'I really can't talk about it,' she said, knowing that her look had said all that was necessary. 'But you shouldn't give up hope completely. It may be that she is . . . being held somewhere, and if so it won't be long before our troops find her and set her free. She might be home in a month or two.'

Mr Escott Stevens touched her arm lightly. 'Thank you. I won't embarrass you by asking any more questions. I suppose we shall have to wait until the end of the war to hear the true story.'

'When that happens, I will come and tell you what I know,' Frankie promised. 'It's not much, but it might help.'

'Thank you,' Annabel repeated. 'We're so grateful to you for taking the time to come and see us. Now' – she made a visible effort to pull herself together – 'you must be dying for a cup of tea. I'll just fetch the tray.'

Over tea Frankie said, 'What about Roddy? Does he know?'

'Yes, poor boy,' Annabelle said with a sigh. 'We telephoned him as soon as we heard the news. He's heartbroken.'

Frankie looked down at her plate to hide the tears that had come to her eyes. There was nothing she could think of to say. They talked platitudes while she finished her tea and then she sensed that the Escott Stevenses would be more comfortable dealing with their grief alone. When Mr Escott Stevens got up, saying it was time to attend to the milking, she took the opportunity to say goodbye.

'Please come and see us again,' Annabel said as she saw her to the door. 'Whether you have any information or not. We shall always be glad to see you.'

Frankie thanked her and got into the car. In the darkness, as they made their way with hooded headlights through the country lanes, she finally let the tears fall.

Chapter Fifteen

'Je suis Marguerite Duclos. Je suis Marguerite Duclos!'

Steve woke abruptly, unsure whether she had spoken the words aloud. The other three occupants of the cell were still asleep, so she assumed that she had not. A faint, grey light filtered in through the tiny window high up in the wall. The winter dawn was breaking. Steve sat up, pulling the one thin blanket around her shoulders and shivering. She ran a hand through her hair, which was no longer as short as a boy's. Her mouth tasted foul and she longed for a bath and a chance to clean her teeth.

She felt faintly reassured by the words that had been running through her mind as she woke. In the three months she had spent in this tiny space, where four of them were crammed into an area meant for two at most, the one comfort she had clung to was that no one suspected her real identity. As a Frenchwoman caught up by accident in the chaos of the German retreat she had a chance of remaining unnoticed. If her captors suspected for a moment that she was a British agent she knew that the best she could hope for was to be shot out of hand. Ever since her capture she had expected daily to be interrogated and had prepared herself to maintain her story, but for some reason the interrogation had never happened. Night after night she had gone over in her mind the history of Marguerite Duclos, filling in with her imagination any gaps in the narrative. Apart from a brief interlude in the American camp she had spoken nothing but French for eighteen months. She even thought in French. But she was still not sure how long she would be able to maintain the deception under pressure.

Some days after their arrival in the prison she and Juliette had been moved into this cell, which was already occupied by two other women, one of whom was serving a sentence for dealing on the black market and the other awaiting trial on a charge of prostitution. Steve realised quickly that they were in an ordinary civil prison and had somehow been mixed up with prisoners who had no connection with the security services. The town, she learned from the other women, was Karlsruhe, and she had begun to hope that she and Juliette might remain there, forgotten, until the war was over. Every day they hoped to hear news of a German surrender or the sound of Allied tanks in the streets, but it seemed the fighting had ground to a standstill and no one would tell them what was happening.

A more immediate worry was the wardress in charge of their wing. She was fully aware that neither of them had been charged with anything, and that they were incarcerated simply on the orders of the Gestapo, and it disturbed her sense of order.

'You two should not be here,' she told them frequently. 'This is not the right place for you.'

The cell door opened with a clang, startling the other three women out of sleep. The wardress, a large woman with arms like tree trunks, filled the space.

'You two, Duclos, Choquin! On your feet. Come.'

As they stumbled to their feet, Steve's heart began to pound and she saw in Juliette's face a look of rising terror. She pressed her arm and whispered, with false optimism, 'Perhaps they've finally realised there's no reason to hold us.'

They followed the wardress down a long corridor, through several doors that were unlocked and locked again behind them, out into the prison yard. The brightness of the winter light hurt Steve's eyes and the cold bit into her flesh. Both she and Juliette were still wearing the light summer clothes in which they had been arrested. A canvas-covered truck stood in the yard, with a couple of bored-looking soldiers beside it.

'Get in!' the wardress ordered.

'Where are we going?' Steve asked.

'You'll find out. Somewhere where people like you belong – and not before time.'

Steve was shaken to discover that it took all her strength to haul herself up into the back of the truck. Three months cooped up in a cell, on a diet that consisted of a cup of bitter ersatz coffee in the morning and a bowl of thin soup containing a few potato peelings, with a piece of dry bread, in the evening, had taken their toll. She reached down and pulled Juliette after her, aware that the younger girl was in an even worse state than she was. It had almost broken her heart to watch Juliette fading as the weeks passed. The physical deprivation, coupled with incessant anxiety about the fate of her parents, had reduced her to a pale ghost. In vain had Steve pointed out that the Americans must have liberated Besançon very soon after their arrest and so her parents would certainly have been freed.

As the truck drew out of the prison yard Steve gripped Juliette's hand and put her lips close to the girl's ear. One of the soldiers, an elderly man with a perpetual cough, was riding in the back with them but Steve took the chance that he either could not hear or did not understand French.

'There might be a chance to escape. Keep your wits about you and be ready to follow me if I make a move.'

The truck kept going at a steady pace, and through the opening at the back Steve caught glimpses of grey streets and bomb-damaged buildings, but there was no chance to escape. Eventually it turned into a large yard and came to a stop. The soldier guarding them rose and gestured to them to get out. Steve saw that they were at a railway station and that a large crowd of women and children was being herded on to the platform by soldiers with guns. With a prod of his rifle, their guard indicated that they should follow.

'Who are they all?' Juliette whispered. 'They can't all be like us.'

Steve shook her head to enjoin silence and they joined the crowd. Many of the women were weeping; some carried bundles, others had small children in their arms. Then Steve saw with a shock that all of them had a yellow star stitched to their clothes. She remembered the rumours that had been circulating in Britain about what was happening to the Jews in German-occupied territory, but this mass displacement of people puzzled and scared her. She swung round to look for the guard who had brought them.

'This is a mistake! We don't belong with these people!'

But the man had already turned away and was heading back to the truck. His job was finished. Another soldier shouted something at her in German and shoved her forward. She grabbed Juliette's hand.

'Stick close to me! We mustn't let ourselves be separated.'

A train stood at the platform and to her disgust Steve saw that it consisted of a long line of cattle trucks. Many of them were already filled with women and she and Juliette were forced into another, already so full that there was scarcely room to stand. The door was slammed shut and she heard bars being dropped into place across it. A few minutes later the train jerked into motion.

Steve had had plenty of chance to brush up her German while in custody and she made use of it to question the women nearest to her, but they knew no more than she did about their destination. 'A camp' was all she could get from them.

All day the train chugged along. Unable to sit, the women swayed and jolted against each other. There were no toilet facilities and the state of the floor suggested that others before them, whether human or animal, had been forced to relieve themselves where they stood. Children whimpered or screamed, women sobbed. Some of them had brought a little food with them, which they shared among the rest, but there was nothing to drink, and before long Steve was desperate for water. The only consolation was that the crowding produced a degree of warmth, though a bitter wind blew in through the gaps in the side of the truck.

Late in the afternoon they entered a tunnel and then the train came to a sudden halt. For what seemed like an hour they stood in pitch darkness, waiting. Then they heard the clang of doors being opened and the tramp of feet. When their door was undone Steve clambered down and saw that all the women were trudging back along the track towards the faint gleam of daylight at the end. She and Juliette stumbled along with the rest until they came out into the light. A long straggling line of women was moving ahead of them, up the slope of the embankment, urged on by the guards, who moved backwards and forwards along the line like anxious sheepdogs. At the top of the embankment they had a view over a wide plain, with a river running through it. It was bitterly cold and a light fall of snow had covered the ground. Black against its whiteness, the column of people was wending its way along a narrow road leading to a small village. Steve wondered whether perhaps that was their

destination for the night, but as they went forward she saw
that the head of the line had already passed the houses
without stopping. She put her arm around Juliette and
pulled her close, for warmth and support, and they plodded
along after the others.

The road crossed a bridge over the river and there the
mystery was revealed. Upstream, the railway bridge had
been destroyed, either by sabotage or by bombing. Farther
on, beyond a low hill, puffs of smoke revealed the presence
of another train, waiting to carry them on towards their
destination. It entered Steve's numbed mind that if they
were ever to escape, this might be their only chance.

They shuffled past the first houses of the village, aware of
silent watchers in the windows. In the village square there
was a water pump and as they approached Steve saw some
of the women break away and head for it, desperate for a
drink. Others followed and the guards ran after them, to
drive them back into line. In the temporary distraction Steve
saw her opportunity. They were passing a narrow alleyway.
She gripped Juliette harder and hissed, 'This way!'

The two of them stepped aside into the alley and Steve
tried the first door they came to. To her surprise it opened
and they found themselves in the kitchen of a little cottage.
There was a deal table with the remains of supper on it and
beyond it an elderly couple rose in consternation from their
seats on either side of the kitchen range. Steve put one hand
to her lips and then clasped both in a gesture of supplica-
tion. Whether the old people felt sympathy for the two
pathetic creatures in front of them or whether they were just
too frightened to react she could not tell, but they said
nothing.

After a few tense moments, the woman moved cautiously
forward to the table and pushed a jug of warm milk and two

mugs towards them. Steve drank and thought she had never tasted anything so delicious. Another pause followed, during which they heard the tramp of feet and the shouts of the guards slowly fade into the distance. Then the old man stirred himself abruptly and moved to the door. He opened it and looked out, then stood back and with a gesture invited them to leave. Regretfully, Steve drew Juliette towards the street. She longed to stay, to beg for shelter, but it was clear that the man had done all he was prepared to do and it would be useless and unfair to ask for more.

Darkness had fallen and the village was silent and, apparently deserted. Hand in hand, the two women headed back the way they had come. Steve had no idea where they were, or in which direction they should try to travel. She knew only that before the night grew even colder they must find shelter of some sort. On the outskirts of the village they had passed one or two buildings that looked like small farms and it was to them that she led Juliette, who stumbled after her in a daze. A barking dog warned them away from one house but a little farther on they came upon a barn that was some distance from any other buildings. Steve pushed open the door and found herself in what had once been a stable but was now empty except for a few old sacks and some wisps of straw. But at least the walls were sound and kept out the wind. Steve spread the sacks on the floor in one of the stalls at the rear of the building and pulled Juliette down on them.

'We'll stay here for the night. In the morning we'll be able to work out which way is west. If we keep travelling in that direction we must meet up with the British or the Americans somewhere.'

It was a faint hope, but the best plan she could think of. They lay down, huddled together for warmth, but Juliette's body was icy and nothing Steve could do seemed to warm her. As the night wore on she began to mumble incoherently and to beg over and over again for water. Steve had been taught the symptoms at Arisaig and knew that her friend was suffering from hypothermia and that if nothing was done she would probably die.

When the first hint of light showed through the cobwebbed window Steve roused herself from an uneasy doze. 'Listen, Juliette! I'm going to find us some warm clothes and something to eat. You must wait here. Do you understand me? I'll bring you something to drink, too. But you must stay here! Promise me you won't move. I'll be back soon.'

She opened the door and peered cautiously out. More snow had fallen during the night. She had no idea where she was going to find what she needed. She had to rely on luck. As she approached the farmhouse she froze in the shadow of an outbuilding as the door suddenly opened, emitting a shaft of light across the snow. A woman came out, bundled up against the cold and carrying a large bowl. She closed the door behind her and Steve watched as she made her way across the yard and into a paddock at the back. Then she heard the sound, so familiar that it brought a stab of nostalgia, of hens clucking as they were let out of their coop.

Guessing that the woman would be gone for a few minutes, Steve moved quickly across the yard and tried the door. It opened into a lobby, in which hung coats and scarves. Boots stood below them. Steve stood still, straining her ears. One of the coats obviously belonged to a man but there was no sign of anyone in the house. She remembered that every able-bodied man had been called up to defend the Fatherland so it was quite possible that the woman was running the farm single-handed. She unhooked one of the coats – presumably a spare one belonging to the woman. It would do for Juliette. She put the man's coat on herself. It came to her ankles but at least it was warm. The woman's spare boots would do for Juliette but there was no way Steve could walk in the man's. She would have to hope to solve that problem some other way. She wound a scarf round her neck and then hesitated.

Very carefully, she pushed open the inner door. The warmth of the room almost made her faint. On the table were the remains of the woman's breakfast – half a loaf of black bread and a hunk of cheese. Steve looked out of the window. She could see the woman's torch moving beyond the gate and guessed that she was collecting the eggs. She stuffed the bread and cheese into the pockets of the coat, filled a pitcher that stood by the sink with water and slipped silently out into the frosty morning.

Pushing open the door of the shed, she called softly, 'Juliette? It's all right, it's only me. Look what I've got! A warm coat for you, and bread and cheese.'

Juliette lay where she had left her, half hidden among the sacking. Steve knelt down and raised her head. 'Come on, *chérie*. Eat. It will make you feel better.'

She wrapped the coat around the girl and held her tightly, rubbing her hands to warm them and feeding her sips of water, alternating these with mouthfuls of bread and crumbs of cheese, and little by little she began to revive. Steve was aware that time was passing and it could not be much longer before her theft was discovered. She tried to formulate some kind of plan. From the train she had glimpsed little parties of refugees plodding along the roads carrying their few possessions, and she hoped that once they were away from the village they might pass unnoticed. They could walk by day and shelter in barns like this at night, and steal food to live.

The only thing that mattered now was to get as far away as possible.

Eventually she decided that Juliette was conscious enough to move. 'Come along, we can't stay here. You must make a big effort. I'll help you.'

She had just struggled to her feet when the door of the barn slammed open and a rough male voice shouted, 'Come on out! We know you're in there. Get out here where we can see you.'

Instinctively, Steve clapped her hand over Juliette's mouth. She put her lips against the girl's ear and breathed, 'Stay here. Don't make a sound.' Then she raised her hands and stepped out of the stall.

Three men stood in the doorway. One of them was in the uniform of the Feldgendarmerie and he was holding a pistol levelled at Steve's heart. Behind them she saw the figure of the woman from the farm.

'So there you are,' the policeman said. 'Did you think we can't count? Did you imagine we wouldn't miss the odd one? You made it easy enough for us to find you.'

Steve looked down. There in the new snow were her footprints, one clear trail leading away from the barn and back again. The overnight fall had wiped out any others.

Chapter Sixteen

February came and the first snowdrops forced their way through the frozen earth in the gardens at Grendon Underwood. In Europe the Allied forces were at last making progress. Early in the month came the news that the Americans had broken through the famous Siegfried Line and were advancing into Germany. By the end of it, they were across the River Roer and outside Cologne. At the news of each advance everyone expected to hear of the German surrender, but still they fought on. Reports began to filter through of horrifying discoveries made by the Russian forces on the Eastern Front and for the first time Frankie heard the name 'Auschwitz'. In early March the Allies crossed the Rhine.

One evening, after a day of blue skies and boisterous wind, Frankie was called to the telephone. It was Nick.

'Darling, I've got some good news. Two bits of good news, actually. One, yesterday I walked three steps unaided. And two, I've just been selected as the prospective Labour candidate for Portsmouth North. Let's do something to celebrate.'

'Nick, that's wonderful! Congratulations! What sort of something did you have in mind?'

'Let's get married!'

Frankie realised she was holding her breath and let it out with a gasp.

'When?'

'As soon as we can. Will you be able to get some leave?'

'I don't know. I expect so. But, Nick, you still haven't met my family – not properly.'

'No, that's true, I haven't. But now that I can walk a few steps, travelling will be a bit easier. See if you can get some time off and we'll go up to Liverpool. We can discuss the arrangements for the wedding then.'

Frankie had barely returned to the mess when she was called back to the phone. Assuming it was Nick again she said, with a laugh, 'So? What did you forget to tell me?'

'What do you mean, forget?' said her sister's voice. 'I haven't started yet.'

'Oh, Maria! I'm sorry. I just had a call from Nick. I thought it was him again. What's happened? Is there anything wrong?'

'No, don't panic. I've got some news, that's all. Michael's back. He's got two weeks' leave and we're getting married by special licence on Saturday. Can you make it?'

'Saturday!' Frankie's brain was working so fast it made her feel dizzy. 'I think so. I'm sure my CO will be sympathetic, under the circumstances. Listen, will it be OK if I bring Nick with me? I don't want to mess up your big day.'

'No, bring him, for Pete's sake! I'm fed up of hearing Mum say "we've not seen hide nor hair of this chap of your sister's". Mind you, I don't know where we'll put him. No offence, but I don't really fancy having to share my bedroom with you on the night before my wedding.'

'No, I can understand that. Don't worry, we'll work something out. There go the pips! I'll see what I can organise and ring you back tomorrow. OK?'

Nick had bought them first-class tickets for the train journey to Liverpool and Frankie passed the journey on a merry-go-round of conflicting emotions. It was wonderful to be with him again, specially wonderful to see him on his feet, albeit supported by crutches, when they met at Euston Station. The wheelchair was consigned to the guard's van and, seeing him seated in the carriage, no one would have known he was disabled. That had its darker side, too, and Frankie guessed that some of their fellow passengers were wondering what a man of his age was doing out of uniform. But what disturbed her more was the thought of the reception they might get when they reached their destination. Her parents had met Nick once, briefly, three years ago, when he had brought her home after rescuing her from a bombed-out shelter. Her father, still imbued with the traditions of his Italian parents, had been furious that Nick had proposed without asking his permission first, and her mother was devastated at the prospect of her daughter marrying a non-Catholic. When it transpired that her fiancé was 'a cripple' they were convinced that she was throwing herself away on a man who was unable to support her and wanted her only as a nursemaid. At least, she told herself, the news that he was going to stand for Parliament should dispel that idea.

It was late afternoon by the time they reached Liverpool. Nick had booked a room at the Adelphi, pointing out that he must be somewhere where there were lifts rather than stairs. It had come as a relief all round because Frankie knew that her mother felt they should offer him hospitality, while she herself just wanted somewhere where they could be alone together. When the bellboy had taken his tip and left they looked at each other for a moment in silence. Nick heaved himself out of his chair on to the edge of the bed.

'Come and sit down.'

She sat beside him, feeling a shiver of excitement. He put his arms around her and kissed her on the lips, at first gently, almost experimentally, then more confidently, his tongue seeking hers, flooding her body with liquid fire. She wound her arms around his neck and pulled him down until they were lying across the bed. He raised his head and looked down at her.

'Do we have time?'

'We'll make time.'

They had made love once, only once, and that had been eighteen months ago, on the night before he was dropped back behind German lines. Since then they had been together only when he was lying at death's door in the partisans' camp or recovering in an Italian hospital, except for those few days at his home before Christmas. That time, in the hot African night, they had stripped off their clothes and flung themselves down on the warm sand, consumed by the sense that this might be the first and last chance they would have. Now, in a chilly hotel room with daylight outside the windows, the whole business took on an awkward formality. Nick sat up and wriggled out of his jacket and began unfastening his trouser buttons. Frankie took off her tunic and skirt, embarrassed by her army-issue underwear. Then, seeing that Nick was in difficulties getting his trousers off, she went to him.

'Here, let me help.'

She tugged at the turn-ups, then realised that he still had his shoes on. Their eyes met and suddenly they were both laughing. He pulled her to him and rolled her on to her back, kissing her passionately. Somehow they pulled each other's clothes off and scrambled between the cold sheets. She caught her breath at the first contact of his bare skin on hers, then let his warmth enclose her and gave herself up to him.

*

An hour later they climbed out of a taxi outside Mr Franconi's shop. Nick looked at the name painted on the window and chuckled.

'Figaro the Barber! I remember now. Your father's an opera lover. I think we shall have a lot in common.'

I hope you're right! Frankie thought, but she said nothing.

They had left the wheelchair behind at the hotel since, as Nick pointed out, it would be no use to him in a first-floor flat. He heaved himself upright on his crutches and hobbled towards the front door. Before he reached it, it opened and Maria came out.

'You two took your time,' she observed. 'I've been watching out for you. Was the train very late?'

She looked past Nick and caught Frankie's eye and Frankie thought she winked. She met her sister's gaze inscrutably. 'Yes, very.'

Maria turned to flash a smile at Nick. 'Hello, I'm Frankie's sister.'

Nick propped himself on his crutch and held out his hand. 'I know. We've met before.'

'Oh, you remember? I was only a kid at the time.'

'How could I forget? A kid, maybe, but one who was obviously going to grow up to be a very beautiful girl.'

'Ooh!' Maria turned to her sister with a giggle. 'Talk about a smooth operator! Does he always go on like this?'

'No, he saves it for special occasions,' Frankie returned dryly. 'Are we going to spend the evening out here on the pavement?'

Maria held the door open. 'Can you manage?'

Nick looked at the steep staircase. 'I'll get there.'

Frankie handed her case and a paper carrier to her sister. 'Can you bring these up for me?'

With one hand gripping the banister and a crutch under

the other arm and Frankie supporting him from behind, Nick struggled upwards. Frankie was grateful that her parents had the tact to stay in the living room rather than waiting for him at the top of the stairs. It was not until they finally arrived in the hallway that her mother appeared. Frankie saw that she had had her hair done in a tight perm and was wearing the navy dress she wore for church on Sundays. She took one look at Nick's face and whatever formal greeting she might have prepared was forgotten.

'Oh, you poor man! Fancy having to struggle up all these stairs. We should have come to you.'

'No, not at all,' Nick responded, panting. 'It's very kind of you to invite me.' He held out his hand. 'I'm very pleased to meet you again.'

'And we're glad to see you,' Mrs Franconi replied, and it sounded to Frankie as if she meant it. 'Now, come along in and sit down. You look as if you could do with a drink.'

Mr Franconi rose from his chair as they entered. Frankie understood the gesture. It was not for him, as master of the house, to go running out on to the landing to greet his guest but rather to receive him with dignity in his own place. She tried to read his face, praying that the meeting would be a success.

It was Nick who took the initiative, hobbling forward with hand outstretched and launching into his perfect Italian. 'Signore, thank you for inviting me into your home. I am so glad to meet you face to face at last. I want to apologise in person for proposing to your daughter before consulting you but circumstances made it very difficult for me. I'm sure you will understand that.'

Mr Franconi took the offered hand. 'You explained your reasons in your letter and I accept them. You have behaved honourably. We will talk later. Please, take a seat.' Then, reverting to English, 'Ada, I'm sure our guest would like a drink.'

'Will you have a glass of beer, Major Harper? I'm afraid we've nothing stronger.'

Nick smiled at her, the smile that Frankie always found so irresistible. 'Beer would be wonderful, thank you. And please, call me Nick.'

They chatted for a while, about the war mainly, and then Mrs Franconi suggested that it was time to eat. The table had been laid in the dining room, a small, rather dark room looking on to the street, which they hardly ever used. Today, however, there was a fire in the grate and Nonna Franconi's best lace tablecloth on the table.

Ada Franconi said, 'I didn't know what to cook but then I thought you might like a taste of Italian food so I asked Nonna for her recipe for spaghetti bolognese.'

Nick paused at the door. 'Darling, where's that carrier bag?'

'Here.' Frankie fetched the bag and Nick held it out to Mr Franconi. 'This is a gift from my father, sir, with his best wishes. By pure good luck he happened to have laid down a couple of cases of claret before the war started and he's managed to make them last. I think it ought to go quite well with the spaghetti.'

The spaghetti was an inspired choice, turning the meagre meat ration into a savoury feast. Frankie, lifting the first forkful to her mouth, looked up and caught Nick's eye and knew that they were both remembering meals eaten round rough wooden tables in peasant kitchens.

Mr Franconi raised his glass. 'Here's to the future. Tomorrow Maria gets married and soon we shall have peace. Let us hope that there are happy times ahead for all of us. The future!'

When the meal was over the three women took the dishes to the kitchen and left the men settled in the living room with a cigar each, a celebratory gift from Mario Parisi, who owned the corner shop, and, Frankie guessed, strictly 'under the counter'.

As soon as they finished the washing up Maria exclaimed, 'Come into my room, Frankie. I'm dying to show you my dress.'

The dress was hanging on the back of the door, shrouded in a white sheet.

'There, what do you think?' Maria shook it out and whirled round with it.

For a moment Frankie was unable to answer. She was back in Italy, suspended over a dark valley, the glow of the signal fires beneath her and the canopy of her parachute above. Then Maria held it up against herself and the folds of parachute silk resolved themselves into a full-skirted dress, with a close-fitting bodice and ruched sleeves.

'Maria, it's beautiful!' she said, sincerely. 'You couldn't wish for a lovelier wedding dress.'

'It is, isn't it?' her sister responded. 'It's just what I've always dreamed of.'

'What are the bridesmaids wearing?' Frankie asked.

'Well, uniform, I suppose,' Maria said. 'You're not allowed to wear anything else, are you?'

'Me? You want me to be a bridesmaid?'

'Of course I do. You're my sister, aren't you?'

For a moment Frankie was inclined to argue. Then she realised that whatever reason she gave Maria would be hurt, so she smiled and kissed her. 'Of course, if that's what you want. I'll be happy to do it.'

Their mother was sitting at the kitchen table, but when they reappeared she said, 'Well, better go and join the men,

I suppose.' Frankie's heart was thumping but, to her relief, both men seemed relaxed. Her father looked across at his wife.

'Nick has been telling me that he has a very good chance of being elected to Parliament when the war is over.'

'Oh yes?' Mrs Franconi replied. 'That'll be nice.'

Frankie looked from one to the other and then at Nick, who responded with a faint lift of his shoulders. She understood that nothing had been formally agreed and guessed that her father did not want to say anything definite until he had been able to discuss it with his wife. She knew better than to push him for a decision. Shortly afterwards Nick got up and thanked her parents for their hospitality and Frankie went down to the street to find a taxi. Her father helped Nick down the stairs and shook hands with him. Then, seeing Frankie about to get into the taxi with him, he frowned.

'Where do you think you're going?'

'Nick needs a hand at the other end,' Frankie explained. 'I'll just see him back to the hotel.'

Her father glanced at his watch and she knew he was calculating how long it would take to get there and back. 'All right, but don't be late back.'

As the taxi drew away Frankie let out a sound somewhere between a growl and a laugh. 'My father! He still treats me as if I was fifteen!'

Nick took her hand. 'I expect he always will. He's a good man, darling. He really only wants the best for you.'

'And have you convinced him that that's you?'

He laughed and drew her close. 'I think he's beginning to get the message.'

Chapter Seventeen

Steve gritted her teeth and tried to prevent her legs from shaking. An icy wind was sweeping across the parade ground, cutting through the flimsy, striped pyjama-like uniforms they were all forced to wear and they had already been standing at attention for roll-call for over an hour. *Appell* started long before the winter dawn and it was still dark. This was nothing unusual. She knew that the guards kept them standing deliberately and were alert for any sign of weakness. She had seen women collapse and be dragged away, never to be seen again.

Already weakened by the long spell in gaol and the trauma of the train journey and the abortive attempt to escape, she had lost even more weight on the starvation diet in the camp but she recognised that she was still in a better condition than many of the other women, some of whom had been there for months or even years. When she had arrived, three weeks earlier, she had been horrified at the sight of these skeletal figures, so thin that it was hard to believe they still lived. And since then conditions had deteriorated, impossible as that seemed, with an influx of new prisoners, many of whom had been marched for days from camps elsewhere. Even the officers running the camp had apparently been overwhelmed by the challenge of accommodating still more bodies in the already overcrowded huts and had made no attempt to house the new arrivals, who wandered hopelessly, seeking shelter from the bitter weather. Steve already had to share a bunk with another woman, packed in like sardines in a long hut, and she knew she was lucky to have even that degree of comfort.

An officer was walking slowly along the lines of women, peering into each face. Steve recognised him as Haupsturmführer Schnabel, thickset, bull-necked and with a face the colour of raw meat, one of the most brutal in a camp staffed by sadists. As he drew level with her she held her breath, trying to suppress the violent shivering that racked her body, careful to look straight ahead and not meet his eyes.

'This one!' he snapped to the two female guards following him. 'Take her!'

Steve felt herself seized by both arms and half marched, half dragged out of the line. Her instinct was to struggle but she suppressed it. There was no point in giving them an excuse to rough her up. No doubt that would come soon enough.

As she stumbled across the parade ground between the guards she was filled by a fatalistic despair. So it had come at last! After all these months, the Gestapo had finally remembered why she had been arrested – or had someone betrayed her? Now she had to face the interrogation she had dreaded. Would she be able to withstand whatever torture they had in store for her? It crossed her mind that any information she could give would be useless now. France had been liberated and all her colleagues would have returned to their peacetime occupations, or at least be somewhere out of reach of the enemy. All except those who had been captured, like herself. She realised with a sickening lurch in her stomach that there must be others in camps like this against whom the authorities were keen to gather incriminating evidence. Were Paulette and Gabriel being held somewhere – perhaps even César? Would she have the strength not to give them away if confronted with them?

She became aware that she was not being marched towards the punishment block, as she had expected, but towards the little group of houses outside the main camp where the officers and their families lived. The Haupsturmführer stalked ahead of them and disappeared through the front door of one of them. Steve and her guards followed. She was taken along a hall and into a room furnished as an office, where the Haupsturmführer took a seat behind a desk.

He regarded Steve in silence for a long moment.

'How long have you been here?'

'Three weeks, Herr Haupsturmführer.'

'Why are you here? You're not a Jewess, are you?'

'No, Herr Haupsturmführer.'

'What's your name?'

'Marguerite Duclos, Herr Haupsturmführer.'

'Nationality?'

'French, Herr Haupsturmführer.'

He got up and came round the desk to stand close to her, looking her up and down. She gazed ahead, not meeting his eyes, aware of the sour smell of sweat and stale tobacco that came from him.

'Still quite strong,' he murmured. 'Must have been a good-looking woman once.' He spoke as if she were not present, or as he might have commented on an animal.

He returned to his desk, his tone businesslike. 'My wife is not strong. She is unable to fulfil her duties. You will do this work for her.' He jerked his head at the two women who still stood on either side of her. 'She's filthy. Take her upstairs and clean her. When she's ready you can take her to the kitchen and hand her over to my orderly.'

Steve was led up to a bathroom. One of the guards ordered her to strip while the other filled the bath. When she stepped into it she screamed. The water was almost scalding. The two women laughed and pushed her down into it. She almost passed out but found that if she kept still it was just bearable. They stood over her while she scrubbed herself with coarse kitchen soap and washed her hair with the same stuff. It was humiliating but she didn't care. Once the initial shock of the hot water had passed she revelled in it. It was the first time she had been clean for months, and at last she was rid of the lice that had infested her ever since her arrival in the camp. They had shaved her head when she arrived, as a precaution against this, so they said, but it was pointless. There was supposed to be a delousing plant but it had not functioned for months and all the huts were overrun with lice.

When she was clean the problem of her clothes arose. Her prison uniform was as lousy as her hair had been. One of the guards left the room and returned with a cotton overall. There was no underwear and Steve felt very vulnerable in the skimpy garment, but at least it was clean.

As soon as she was dressed they marched her down to the kitchen where the Haupsturmführer's orderly was waiting. He was a middle aged man with sharp eyes and a super-cilious manner. Steve guessed that in civilian life he had been a butler or a senior domestic servant of some kind. He was obviously used to running the household and regarded Steve with distaste. He apparently did not regard washing up as part of his duties, however. The sink was stacked with greasy dishes.

He nodded towards them and said, 'You can start with that lot. When you've finished there's a basket of laundry to see to and then you can wash the floor.'

Minutes later Steve found herself alone in the kitchen. The warmth and the smell of stale food made her feel sick and giddy and she had to grip the edge of the table to steady herself. As her head cleared, she began to take stock of the situation. She was not suspected, not about to be interrogated. Moreover, she was clean and in a warm place, and a place where, presumably, there was food. She knew she would have to be careful. Any suspicion that she was helping herself would immediately result in a transfer to the punishment block. But this was her best chance of survival. Whatever it cost her in lost self-respect she had to keep this job!

She went to the sink and started on the dishes. As she worked she was suddenly transported back to Overthorpe, where she had done her preliminary training with the FANY. They had been made to wash dishes and scrub floors for the first couple of weeks, and how some of them had resented it! So this is what they were preparing us for, she thought – and for the first time in months she almost smiled.

She had almost finished when the door opened and a woman came in. Accustomed to the sight of her skeletal companions Steve's first thought was 'I don't see much wrong with you!' but a closer look changed her opinion. Frau Schnabel was plump, certainly, but she was the most colourless creature Steve had ever seen. Her face and hair were all of a uniform, lifeless straw colour, and the effect was completed by a shapeless shift of the same tone. Her eyes were so pale that Steve could not tell whether they were blue or hazel, and she gazed around the kitchen with a vacant, listless stare. Her eyes passed over Steve as if she were part of the furniture.

Steve reminded herself that she had resolved to do everything in her power to please her new employers, so she said politely, 'Good morning, Frau Schnabel.'

The pale eyes focused on her for a moment and the woman nodded vaguely.

Steve went on, 'I have almost finished washing the dishes, Frau Schnabel. What else do you want me to do? Would you like me to prepare a meal? I can cook.'

There was a pause, while Frau Schnabel appeared to be struggling to bring her thoughts to bear on the question. Then she shook her head.

'We have a cook. A man comes from the cookhouse.'

With that she turned and drifted out of the kitchen. The news that she was not required to cook was a blow. Steve could see that it would be much harder to help herself to anything with one of the soldiers in charge of preparing the food. When she was sure that Frau Schnabel was out of the way she made a tour of the kitchen, trying the cupboard doors. They were all locked. Never mind, she told herself. The thing to do was make herself useful to this cook, whoever he was.

A few minutes later the orderly reappeared.

'Coffee for the Herr Haupsturmführer. He likes it strong, black, with sugar. Quick now!'

'Where is the coffee?' Steve asked. 'The cupboards are locked.'

'Been trying them, have you?' the man sneered. 'You'd better watch out. He'll have you flogged if he catches you stealing.'

'I was looking for soap,' Steve said quickly. 'For the laundry.'

The man produced a set of keys and opened the cupboard where the coffee and sugar were kept. Then he stood and watched while Steve prepared it.

'Shall I make you a cup?' she asked.

'I get my own, in my own quarters,' was the response.

When the coffee was ready he locked the jars back in the cupboard and then followed Steve along the hallway to Schnabel's office. Schnabel glanced up from his papers, nodded for her to put the cup down and jerked his head towards the door. Steve returned to the kitchen. There had been no chance to take a sip of the drink or, as she longed to do, to stick her finger into the sugar and lick it.

She set to work on the washing, hoping that when the cook arrived he would be a little less suspicious, but lunchtime approached without any sign of him. Eventually, the orderly returned. Frau Schnabel wished for coffee. She did not take lunch and the Haupsturmführer always had his in the mess. Once again, all the ingredients were locked away as soon as the drink was prepared.

The afternoon dragged past. Weak with hunger, it took Steve a long time to finish the laundry. She washed her prison uniform as well and hung it all out in the small yard behind the house. Shivering in the open air, she had a momentary impulse to escape, but although the house was not in the same enclosure as the prison huts it was still in an outer compound surrounded by a high perimeter fence, and a glance at the watchtowers surrounding it told her that there was no chance of crossing the open ground beyond and reaching the forest without being seen and shot. She went back into the kitchen.

The cook turned out to be a sandy-haired youth with acne who clearly had no real interest in the job but regarded it as a way of keeping out of the firing line. He greeted Steve without surprise and proceeded to prepare a meal of pork chops and potatoes in as slovenly a manner as Steve had ever witnessed in any kitchen. When it was ready he said,

'You can serve it and wash up. The leftovers go in the bin for the pig swill, out the back.'

It was all Steve could do to carry the plates to the dining room without falling on the food herself, but she forced herself to be patient. The Haupsturmführer and his wife were sitting opposite each other in stolid silence. Steve set the plates in front of them and retreated to the kitchen.

When the bell summoned her to collect them she was overjoyed to see that on each one there was a bone from the chops and the rim of fat from the outer edge. Frau Schnabel had even left a potato. Back in the kitchen she seized one of the bones, chewing and sucking at it until it was as clean as if some carrion bird had picked it. The fat was beginning to congeal, but she ate that too and then licked the plate clean. She was about to start on the second bone when she remembered the other women in her hut. There was one young girl who had given birth two days after Steve's arrival, aided only by the ministrations of some of the older women. The child had survived, miraculously, but the girl had scarcely any milk for it and its thin, pathetic wailing had almost driven Steve to despair. She looked round the kitchen. In a bin she found the paper that the meat had been wrapped in. It was against every law of hygiene she had ever learnt to mix raw meat with cooked but that was the last thing to be considered now. She wrapped the bone, the fat and the potato in the paper and then she scoured the bin for further treasures and retrieved the potato peelings and the outside leaves of a cabbage. She put a pan on the stove and boiled them while she washed up.

When the peelings were cooked she ate half. They tasted foul but she forced herself to swallow. Every mouthful meant another day's survival. Then she wrapped the rest with the bone and the fat from the chop and looked for some

way of concealing the package so she could smuggle it back
to the hut. Her uniform, which consisted of a pair of
trousers and a loose-fitting jacket, was in the laundry basket.
It was still damp but she put it on, shivering as the clammy
cloth touched her skin, and then tucked the packet of food
into the waistband of the trousers. It was risky but she reckoned that unless they searched her the guards were unlikely
to spot it under the shapeless jacket. She had just finished
when the door was thrown open and two guards appeared
to escort her back to her hut.

The young mother's name was Elsa and her gratitude
when Steve unwrapped her gift was so pathetic that Steve
was almost reduced to tears. Even so, she was so weak that
it took Steve and the other women nearby all the patience
they could muster to persuade her to finish the food, for her
baby's sake. Though all of them watched every mouthful
she ate, no one begrudged it or attempted to take any for
themselves.

Lying in her bunk, Steve wondered how long she could
make her good fortune last. Surely the Allies must arrive
soon. Here in the camp they heard no news of the war, but
those who had survived the death marches told of rumours
of Allied advances and growing panic among the German
forces. If she could just keep herself alive for a few days or
weeks longer . . . and keep Elsa alive too . . . The girl
reminded her of Juliette. What had happened to her? For
days she had watched every new batch of arrivals, dreading
to see Juliette among them, but there had been no sign of
her. Was it possible that she had survived and escaped? Or
had she frozen to death in that barn?

Chapter Eighteen

Maria's wedding was everything Frankie had once imagined hers would be. The church was packed with family and friends and the bride floated down the aisle on her father's arm in a cloud of white silk. It was the first time she had seen her sister's fiancé, and she was pleased to see that he was a nice-looking lad with dark hair and a complexion burnished to a healthy tan by his years at sea. He seemed improbably young, to her eyes, but then so did Maria. Watching them as they took their vows, there was no doubt in Frankie's mind that they were deeply in love.

The reception was held in a room above a pub, within walking distance of the church. Frankie looked at the food spread out on the buffet table and exclaimed to her mother, 'How on earth have you managed all this on the ration?'

'Oh, folk are very good,' Mrs Franconi replied. 'As soon as the invitations went out people started popping round with a tin of ham or peaches or a packet of biscuits, giving up their ration points to help out. That's what happens when you get married in the place where you grew up.'

It was her only reference to Frankie's decision to marry someone from outside the tight-knit community around Scotland Road. In the bustle of getting ready for the wedding there had been no chance to ask what her parents' decision had been, and Frankie had been wondering all day about how to introduce Nick to the other guests. He had insisted that he could make his own way to the church and on from there to the reception, so that she could attend to her duties as a bridesmaid, which meant that no one had seen them together so far. During the ceremony Frankie had worn gloves, as uniform regulations required, and she had not removed the one on her left hand as she stood beside the bride and groom in the receiving line. Her father resolved the problem for her when Nick appeared, leaning on his crutches with another guest helpfully carrying his wheelchair.

'Everyone, meet my other prospective son-in-law. This is Gina's fiancé, Major Nick Harper.'

Frankie had just come off morning parade on her first day back at Grendon when she was told that Captain Henderson wanted to see her. The coincidence was convenient, since she had been just about to ask for an appointment.

Henderson greeted her with a smile. 'Come in, Frankie. Sit down. How was the wedding?'

'It all went very well, thank you, ma'am.'

'Good. Was this a younger sister, or an older?'

'Younger, ma'am. She's only seventeen.'

'Goodness, that is young!' Henderson's smile became mischievous. 'You'll have to look to your laurels, won't you?'

Frankie drew breath and was about to launch into the speech she had prepared when the CO went on, 'Now, to business. You'll be aware that we are coming to the end of our work here. Signals traffic has reduced to a trickle and the unit is going to be wound up very shortly. Most of the girls will be offered immediate demobilisation and that would, of course, include you. However, a job has come up that I think you might want to consider. Baker Street are looking for one or two bright, reliable girls to help with some of the essential work involved in winding up the organisation. How would you feel about a transfer to London?'

Frankie blinked. Her mind had been focused on her forthcoming wedding and the change of direction was destabilising. 'What would I be doing, ma'am?'

'I think the main emphasis is on tracing the whereabouts of agents who haven't made it back to this country. I remember you were concerned about a friend of yours so I thought you might like to take it on.'

Frankie could not think how to reply. Demob would mean she could get married and begin her life with Nick within weeks. But on the other hand, she was being offered the chance to find out what had happened to Steve, and she knew that if she turned it down the question would haunt her for the rest of her life.

'I'd like to do it, ma'am,' she said finally. 'There's just one problem.'

'Which is?'

'You were saying just now about my looking to my laurels. The fact is, I am engaged. I was coming to see you today to ask for leave to get married.'

Henderson sat back in her chair and surveyed her with a twinkle. 'Married, eh? Now let me see if I can guess the identity of the lucky man. It wouldn't be a certain Major Nick Harper, would it?'

Frankie gulped. 'How . . . ?'

Henderson laughed. 'Oh, I've heard the whispers on the grapevine. Grendon isn't completely cut off from the outside world, you know. Congratulations, my dear. From what I hear you deserve each other . . . and I mean that in the nicest possible way. Now, about this transfer to Baker Street. You're sure you want to do it?'

'Yes, ma'am, I'm sure.'

'When do you want to get married?'

'We were hoping for some time next month.'

'Well, suppose I let them know you'll be starting next week but that you've requested leave for your honeymoon. I'm sure they'll be agreeable to giving you some time off.'

Summoned by the Haupsturmführer's bell, Steve went to the dining room to collect the dinner plates. As usual, the Schnabels were sitting in silence. Steve had never heard him address a single word to his wife, and she seemed almost unaware of his presence. The Haupsturmführer's plate was empty, even the chicken bones picked clean, but Steve was glad to see that Frau Schnabel had left quite a bit on hers. Steve had noticed during the weeks she had worked in the house that the German woman seemed to eat less and less, without any apparent loss of weight, but the mystery had been explained when she had discovered a tin of chocolate biscuits under her bed. Over the weeks Steve had found that she was expected to take on more and more work around the house, cleaning and polishing, and Frau Schnabel had spent more and more of her time either in bed or sitting gazing blankly out of the window. How she had obtained such a luxury as chocolate biscuits Steve could not imagine, but it explained the other woman's loss of appetite. It was a state of affairs that suited her very well.

As usual, Frau Schnabel ignored her but, as she took his plate, the Haupsturmführer looked up from his paper and for a moment their eyes met. Steve experienced a sense of shock that surprised her, until she realised that for the first time he had looked at her as if she were a human being rather than an inanimate object – more alarming than that, he had looked at her as if she were a woman.

'Good!' he said. 'That was good.'

Steve lowered her eyes hastily. 'I'll tell Corporal Gunther.'

Gunther, the sandy-haired cook, was lounging with his feet up on the kitchen table, reading the newspaper. It had taken Steve less than a week to convince him that she was a better cook than he was and he could safely leave all the work to her. It was an arrangement that suited them both. He brought in the food and unlocked the cupboards and left her to get on with what he clearly regarded as a woman's job. Nevertheless, she had to be careful. He was suspicious and she often caught him watching her as she moved round the kitchen. Also, she knew that the orderly regularly checked the contents of the cupboards and would have noticed at once if she had started to help herself. The best she could manage was the occasional pinch of sugar, a sip of the Haupsturmführer's coffee before she took it in to him, a mouthful of milk. Whatever conditions might be like in the rest of the country, the officers of the SS wanted for nothing, but under the orderly's eagle eye any deficiency would be easily spotted. It was the leftovers which were the real bonus.

That day Gunther had arrived with a scrawny chicken. Left to himself he would have roasted it until it was the texture of leather, but Steve had discovered that the Haupsturmführer kept a good store of wine, so she had casseroled the bird in that, flavoured with rosemary from a bush she had found in the garden.

She said, 'The Haupsturmführer enjoyed his meal. I told him I would pass on his compliments.'

Gunther got to his feet and yawned. 'You'd better make sure it stays that way. I wouldn't want to lose this cushy little number. Right, I'm off. Make sure you get the washing up done before they take you back.'

As soon as he had gone she collected all the scraps together. She had removed the wing tips and the parson's nose before she served the chicken and she added what was left on Frau Schnabel's plate to them, keeping back one half-chewed chicken leg for herself. It took every scrap of will-power she possessed not to eat the whole lot, but she restrained herself. How Elsa would enjoy those wing tips! Steve was able to take back little enough to the hut for her, but it had made a difference. She had milk now, and the baby did not cry quite so much. And it was not only Elsa who benefited. Steve distributed what she could spare to the weakest of the other women in her hut. She knew that some of them resented her good luck and there had been dark murmurings about 'collaboration' and suggestions that she was Schnabel's mistress as well as his servant, and once or twice she had felt that she was in real danger of being roughed up. But the other women, led by Elsa, had stood by her, pointing out that she could very easily have eaten all the food herself and given them nothing. Steve recognised, with a sense of guilt, that her generosity was not motivated solely by compassion. It was a necessary part of her own strategy for survival.

She boiled the potato peelings and added them to the mix. Today there was an extra luxury. Together with the chicken Gunther had brought a bunch of carrots and, wonder of wonders, an onion. Steve had been forced to put most of them into the stew, because he was watching her, but she had managed to pop a few pieces of carrot into her mouth when his back was turned and had been unable to resist a slice of the raw onion. She could taste it now on the back of her tongue every time she breathed out. She would have to be careful the guards did not smell it on her breath when they came to collect her.

When the washing up was finished she parcelled up the scraps, using sheets from the newspaper that Gunther had left behind. There was still some gravy left in the casserole and she remembered there was a crust of bread remaining from the Schnabels' breakfast and used that to soak up as much of it as possible. It made a soggy package but she tucked it into her waistband and hoped it would hold out until she got back to the hut. Even then, there was still some liquid left so she picked up the dish and tipped it into her mouth, almost swooning at its savoury richness.

She was just filling the dish with water at the sink when she heard the door behind her open and close. She froze. It was not the guards. They always arrived with a loud tramp of boots along the wooden boards of the hallway. That sneaky orderly was on the prowl again, hoping to catch her out.

'Still at work?'

It was not the orderly's voice. Steve spun round to find the Haupsturmführer standing behind her.

She caught her breath. 'Forgive me, Herr Haupsturmführer. I didn't hear you come in.'

He looked at her in silence for a few seconds. Then he said, 'You have gravy round your mouth.'

Instinctively Steve put up her hand to wipe her face and he caught hold of her wrist.

'You have been stealing food. I thought you had put on weight since you came to work here. Now I know why. You are a thief.'

'It was only scraps,' Steve gasped. 'The bits left on the plates. It would only have gone into the pig swill.'

His little eyes glinted in the broad, beefy face. 'But the pig swill feeds the pigs and the pigs are needed by the German people for food. So by stealing from the pig swill you are stealing from the people of the Fatherland. And for that you must be punished. Unless you can make amends in some other way.'

'How?' He was standing very close to her and she found it difficult to get her breath.

'I will show you.'

He shifted his grip, grabbing her by the back of the neck and pressing his other hand into the small of her back, pushing his body against hers so that she could feel his erection. His mouth sought hers and she twisted her head in an effort to avoid it. Suddenly he gave an exclamation of disgust and pulled away.

'Your breath is foul! Filthy bitch! What have you eaten?'

Steve staggered back, feeling the edge of the sink pressing into her back. 'It's not having enough to eat that makes your breath smell.'

At that moment she became aware of a moist warmth against her stomach and a trickle of liquid ran down her thigh. Involuntarily she glanced down and saw to her dismay that a brown stain was spreading across the front of the striped prison jacket. The package of food she had hidden had burst under the pressure of his body. His eyes followed hers.

'What is this?' He grasped the front of the jacket and ripped it open, leaving her exposed from the waist up, the food in its soggy newspaper sticking out from the waistband of her trousers. 'Hah!' He pulled it out and threw it on the floor. 'Thieving bitch! Eating the scraps not enough for you, eh? Smuggling food back to your hut as well. Now you will have to pay.'

'Please,' Steve begged, 'it's for a young girl with a baby. She can't feed it. She has to have more to eat. The poor child is innocent. Why should it suffer?'

She saw a change come over the Haupsturmführer's expression. It was not compassion, however, but a sly, sadistic glee.

'You want to help this girl? You want me to let you take food to her? Very well, but there is a price.' He reached out and grasped her breast, pinching the nipple hard between his calloused fingers. 'You will pay for it. You understand me?'

Steve stared into his eyes. There was no choice. If she refused he could still force her, or send her to the firing squad. If she acquiesced there was still a chance of survival, for her and for Elsa. She lifted her chin. 'Very well. Do what you want.'

He gave a low, guttural laugh. 'I don't want your foul breath or your stinking body.' He was still gripping her by the back of the neck and his other hand was fumbling with the buttons of his flies. 'You can put your filthy mouth to a better use.'

Chapter Nineteen

As Frankie approached the building in Baker Street that housed the Inter Services Research Bureau, as SOE was known to the outside world, she experienced a quiver of trepidation. Then she smiled inwardly as she remembered her terror on her first visit. Seventeen years old, her first time in London, applying for a job the nature of which was swathed in mystery on the instructions of a man she had known for no more than three or four hours! No wonder she had been nervous! Now, at least, she had some idea what she was letting herself in for. She took a deep breath, pulled her shoulders back and marched confidently past the sentry at the door.

She was directed to the office of Captain Vera Atkins, who greeted her briskly.

'I've read your file. All your senior officers seem to think highly of you. I'm afraid what we are doing here is not going to be as exciting as some of the work you've been engaged on. I hope you won't be bored.'

'It can't be more boring than decoding messages, ma'am,' Frankie responded. 'And I'm happy to do anything I can to help trace our people who are still over there.'

'Good,' said Atkins. 'Then let's get to work. We have reams of reports and signals transcripts to go through. As the armies advance and prisons and POW camps are liberated the Red Cross and other organisations try to keep records but, of course, it's a mammoth task and it doesn't help that all our agents were operating under pseudonyms. Tracing them is like trying to follow one thread through a huge tangle of string.'

Frankie hesitated, then said diffidently, 'Did Captain Henderson mention anything about my request for leave to get married?'

'Oh yes, she did say something. I gather you're marrying Nick Harper.'

'Yes, ma'am.' Frankie wondered whether there was anyone in SOE who didn't know about her relationship with Nick.

'Well, you've got quite a catch there,' Atkins observed. 'I heard he was wounded. How is he?'

'Making good progress, thank you, ma'am.'

'Good. Now, about this leave. I'd really like to see some progress with this work before you disappear. Would the beginning of May do for you?'

Frankie had hoped for an earlier date but she knew she had to settle for that. She was given a small office along the passage from the captain's and a pile of files to work through, containing the names of agents, the operational names by which they had been known and the identities they had been given as part of their cover stories. There were reports from the organisers of the circuits to which they had been assigned and any information that could be gleaned from other sources about their last known whereabouts.

On the second day she opened a file labelled with the code name Suzette and saw the name Diana Escott Stevens. There followed transcripts of signals that mentioned her activities and a report by her circuit leader, a man who had operated under the pseudonym César.

'She is a young woman of exceptional courage and initiative. She has frequently undertaken dangerous missions with a calm efficiency that has been an example to us all. She has a warm, optimistic personality, and has established excellent relationships with local sympathisers. An outstanding officer.'

'That's my Steve!' Frankie muttered aloud, through a constricted throat.

The report was dated December 1943. After that, the file was empty. Frankie went through to Vera's office and showed it to her.

'Why is there nothing after the end of '43?'

Vera glanced at the file and said, 'Well, that's easily explained. César had to make a run for it in November that year, after his cover was blown. He got out through Switzerland and that report was part of his debriefing. I'm afraid the chances are Suzette was caught then. Several other members of the circuit were arrested at that time.'

'Who took his place?'

It took some time, sifting through the records, to come up with the answer. There had been no official leader for Stockbroker until April the following year, when it had been taken over by a Frenchman, the Comte de Brouville, code-named Albert.

'He belonged to RF, the section run by de Gaulle's people, so his file won't be here,' Vera said.

'Could we get hold of it?'

'Only if we went to Paris – and then I wouldn't give much for our chances. RF have never been very keen on co-operating. It seems we've struck a dead end.'

Frankie went back to her desk biting her lips with frustration. Two days later she was summoned to Vera's office and found her in the company of a tall man with a humorous mouth and hair brushed back from a broad forehead.

As Frankie came to attention Vera said, 'I thought you would like to meet Captain Ree. You know him from the files as César. Harry, this is Lieutenant Franconi. She's an old friend of the young woman you knew as Suzette.'

'César!' Frankie exclaimed, forgetting protocol as she grasped the outstretched hand. 'Please, do you know what happened to Steve?'

'Steve?' He looked puzzled and Vera put in, 'Suzette's real name was Diana Escott Stevens. Frankie and all her friends knew her as Steve.'

Ree's gaze sharpened. 'Frankie? Don't tell me you're the girl who wrote to her from North Africa! I always assumed it was short for Frances or Francesca or something.'

'So she did get my letters?' Frankie asked. 'I was never sure if they got through to her.'

'Well, she certainly got one. I remember her chuckling over it,' he said warmly. 'I think it gave her a lot of pleasure.'

'So do you know where she is now?' Frankie persisted.

Ree sighed. 'Alas, no. I haven't had any contact with her since the night I had to make a rather hurried exit from France.'

'Do you think she was arrested at the same time?'

'I hope not. I tried to persuade her to leave with me but she felt she had to stay to warn the others. I thought she would be safe. I was the only person who knew her cover name and where she was staying. I was convinced that she would still have been there when her area was overrun by the Americans and that she would be safe home by now. I came here today to ask Vera for her address.'

For a moment they looked at each other in silence and Frankie felt the hope that had briefly surged up when they were introduced ebbing away again.

Vera said, 'Look, I'm sure Frankie would like to hear everything you can tell her about Suzette. Why don't you both go and grab a cup of tea or something? I'd join you but I'm up to my neck here.'

Ree smiled at Frankie. 'Oh, I think we can do better than that.' He glanced at his watch. 'It's gone twelve. Can I take you to lunch?'

Over spaghetti bolognese in a little Italian restaurant Ree told her everything he could remember about Steve during the time they had worked together.

'She was a wonderful girl,' he concluded. 'I just wish to God I'd taken her with me when I left.'

'How did you get out of France?' Frankie asked.

'Well, I told you that the last time I saw Suzette – Steve – was in the local doctor's surgery. He drove me to Montbéliard, where I had friends. One of them was a *passeur* – I suppose you could say a smuggler. He used to bring car tyres across the border from Switzerland to sell on the black market. He knew how to get past the German patrols and he got me over. I gave myself up to the British consul, who was supposed to intern me, of course, since Switzerland was neutral, but after a few months he sent me to the south of France and from there I was escorted across the Pyrenees into Spain. The Spanish interned me there for a further month, but eventually the British ambassador got me out and I came home via Gibraltar. That was last summer. After France was liberated I went back to check up on some of the people who had helped me and make sure they were all right, but it never occurred to me to ask after Suzette. I assumed she was safely back home.'

Frankie sighed deeply. 'It's as if she vanished off the face of the earth. But there must be someone who knows, some record, somewhere.'

'Well, all I can suggest,' Ree said, 'is that you get in touch with Sylvie de Montmain. She lives just outside the town of Arbois and that's where Suzette was staying. If anyone knows what happened to her, she will.'

After he had paid the bill, he said, 'Did Suzette – Steve – have any family? I'd really like to go and see her parents and tell them what a wonderful daughter they had.'

'I'm sure they'd love to meet you,' Frankie replied. 'But they don't know what she was doing, and I'm not sure we're allowed to tell them.'

'To hell with that!' he said. 'The war's nearly over. What harm can it do? They deserve to know they had a heroine for a daughter.'

Frankie gave him the address and they parted in the street, promising to keep in touch. Frankie watched him walk away, thinking how well he and Nick would get on and wondering whether they could arrange to meet. She was glad Steve had had the support of such a man.

Back at the office Vera called her in. 'I've remembered something. We dropped a radio operator called Daniel Jardine to Stockbroker in February '44.' She handed Frankie a file. 'These are his signals.'

Frankie took the file back to her desk. There was a sheaf of signals in code, with the painstakingly decoded transcripts attached. She whooped aloud with joy as she read the first one, which announced that the circuit had been taken over by an agent code-named Suzette. There followed detailed reports from Suzette herself describing sabotage attacks and ambushes and then a flurry of signals itemising enemy forces. Frankie wondered which of the girls at Grendon had had the job of decoding the messages and she spent an hour working backwards from the decodes to find out what Steve's code poem had been. The irony of it

caught at her throat. *'I'm saying au revoir and not goodbye'.*
The last message reported that the American forces were
within a few miles of Besançon. After that there was silence.

Frankie took her findings back to Vera. 'So she wasn't
arrested when César had to make a run for it. We know she
was operating right up to the end. What happened to
Jardine?'

'We don't know. His file is blank from the time of that last
message. It seems he didn't get back either.'

Frankie returned to her office, grinding her teeth in frustration. Once again a hopeful lead had brought her only to
a dead end.

Steve gripped the edge of the kitchen table and forced
herself to her feet. The Haupsturmführer would be waiting
for his coffee. She staggered as she walked to the sink to fill
the kettle. Her head was throbbing and spasms of pain
twisted her guts as she straightened up. The room was
oppressively stuffy in this unseasonable April heat but in
spite of that she was shivering. She knew what the symptoms meant. She had seen enough of her companions
collapse and die in the last weeks. Elsa had succumbed, and
her baby. Every day working parties dragged the emaciated
bodies to the open burial pits at the edge of the camp, but
still the ground was littered with corpses. But Steve was
determined not to die, and her only chance was to keep her
place with the Haupsturmführer. Here, at least, there was
water. There had been no fresh water in the camp for days
and the air was filled with the stench of excrement.

Something was about to happen, she was sure of that.
Appell still took place at four o'clock every morning but the
attitude of the guards was different – they were no less
brutal but she sensed an unease and there seemed to be

fewer of them. Frau Schnabel had disappeared – Steve had no idea where she had gone, and the Haupsturmführer was edgy and abstracted. He had even stopped playing the sadistic games that had made her life a misery since the discovery of her theft. Until recently he had come to the kitchen every evening after Gunther had left and forced her to 'perform' in return for the scraps of food. His tastes were bizarre and cruel, and often he withheld the promised reward. He would snatch the food from her at the last minute and throw it into the bin, or force her to choose between eating herself and taking the minuscule amount he allowed her back to the hut. Lately, supplies had started to run short even for the officers, and without Frau Schnabel's leavings there was less to go round. In the camp itself rations were reduced to half a cup of thin turnip soup every day. There had been no bread for weeks. Steve knew that she was as skeletal as the rest of the prisoners now. She also knew that if Schnabel suspected she was ill she would be sent back to the camp, to Hut 48, where the sick were sent to die.

As she waited for the coffee to brew a noise from outside attracted her attention. The window overlooked the main compound and she saw that the prisoners there were all converging on the main gate, those who had the strength running, others dragging themselves. Then she noticed something else. The watchtowers were unmanned and the guards on the ground were standing around listlessly, as if waiting for orders. She craned her neck to see what was causing the excitement at the gate. The crowd was surrounding a vehicle of some sort. She could see arms waving, hands outstretched. A violent shuddering gripped her. Could this be what they had waited and prayed for for so long? Had the Allies finally reached them? Then the crowd parted for a moment and she saw the flag fluttering on the front of the jeep. It was the Union Jack.

The coffee percolator bubbled and Steve reached for a cup. Liberation was at hand but she had one last duty to perform. The Haupsturmführer would not die, of course. He would get proper medical attention. But she could make sure that he experienced some of the agonies she had seen her friends suffer. She poured the coffee, sweetened it, and then with careful precision she raised it to her mouth and spat into it. Then, supporting herself with her free hand against the wall, she stumbled down the hallway to her tormentor's office.

Chapter Twenty

Over the next weeks there was a stark contrast between Frankie's daytime work and the evenings. London was buzzing with optimism as victory came ever closer. In the spring weather the parks were full of young women walking out with soldiers on leave. The theatres and bars were thronged every night as people compensated for the gloom of the war years. Nick came up to town every few days and took her to restaurants and shows, giving her a taste of glamour and excitement such as she had not known since leaving Cap Matifou, where they had danced the night away in the officers' club. He was getting stronger all the time and was able to walk a little farther every time they met, though he still needed the wheelchair to go any distance.

Then came news that dampened everyone's spirits. On 15 April Allied troops entered the concentration camp at Bergen Belsen. Two days later they entered Buchenwald. As the reports came in, with the appalling photographs of the survivors, Winston Churchill encapsulated the feelings they all shared: 'No words can express our horror.'

On the day the news broke Frankie went into Vera Atkins's office.

'Ma'am, do you think some of our people could be in those places?'

Atkins looked at her sombrely. 'We're just beginning to

discover what the Nazis were capable of. Nothing would surprise me.'

The general mood soon recovered. There was good news to set against the bad. On the 23rd of the month the partial blackout that had remained in force was lifted and for the first time in nearly six years London's streets were bright with lights. On the 25th US and Russian troops met on the River Elbe and, of particular interest to Frankie and Nick, news came that the Allies had taken Milan and Venice. The same day, Mussolini and his mistress were shot by partisans and hung upside down from the façade of a petrol station in Milan. At the end of the month the Russians entered Berlin and rumours began to circulate that Hitler had committed suicide.

Frankie and Nick were married on 5 May. They could scarcely have chosen a more auspicious date for their wedding. The day before, Field Marshal Montgomery received the surrender of all German forces in western Germany.

Frankie's parents had arrived that evening and Frankie was delighted to find that the excitement of their first visit to London, combined with the euphoria of victory, outweighed any doubts they may have had about the wedding taking place away from all their friends and family. In fact, she sensed that they were relieved at not having to explain Frankie's choice of a register office.

As they had planned, it was a simple affair. Frankie wore uniform and Nick wore his slightly ill-fitting 'demob' suit. Guido Franconi was in the pre-war suit he had dug out for his younger daughter's wedding, which had become rather too tight around the collar and waist for comfort, and Ada wore the same navy dress but enlivened by a new hat in a tone of puce that clashed with her fresh complexion. She cried most of the way through the ceremony, but whether out of joy at her daughter's happiness or regret that she was not being properly married in the sight of God, Frankie could not determine.

Nick was accompanied by his father and a Lieutenant Colonel Mark Saxon, who had been his Conducting Officer during his training and who acted as best man. Among his guests, a complete surprise to Frankie, was Mrs Phyllis Bingham, the officer who had interviewed her when she applied to join the FANY and who had left the service and retired to Scotland some time previously. There was also, even more surprisingly, a full general, who was introduced to her afterwards as none other than Colin Gubbins, the head of SOE.

At the end of the reception the general came to shake hands with them. 'I know what you both did in Italy,' he said, 'and I hope one day we shall be able to give your courage and sacrifice due recognition. I wish you all the very best for the future. You deserve all the happiness and success that fate can bestow.'

They had planned to spend their honeymoon on the borders of Sussex and Hampshire, visiting Nick's favourite childhood places and looking around for a house somewhere in the constituency he would be fighting when the election was called. But these plans were amended when the announcement was made that 8 May would be celebrated across the country as VE Day – Victory in Europe. They both agreed that there was only one place to be on that day, and that was London. Early in the morning they joined the crowds around the Victoria Memorial in front of Buckingham Palace. They cheered as Churchill drove past to lunch at the

palace and listened in a respectful hush when the great
man's broadcast to the nation was relayed over loudspeakers
to the masses thronging the Mall and Whitehall. The war,
he told them, would officially end at midnight.

'Advance Britannia! Long live the cause of Freedom!
Long live the King!'

They cheered again and again as the royal family
appeared on the balcony.

When someone started the conga Frankie tried to push
Nick's chair out of the way but before she could move a
grinning sailor seized hold of the handles and Nick was
manoeuvred into the line that snaked round and round the
Victoria Memorial. Holding on to the sailor's waist, Frankie
experienced a euphoria she had never known before. It was
all over! The fear and the anxiety, the suffering, the killing
and the dying – all finished! Life stretched before her like an
endless summer.

In a tented hospital set up outside the perimeter fence of
Belsen concentration camp an American Red Cross worker
was making his way down the long row of beds. In each bed
lay an emaciated form just recognisable as a woman, and the
Red Cross worker stopped at each one to ask the same
questions, first in German, then in French. Name? What
was your last address, before you were sent here? Who is
your next of kin? Do you have any idea where they are now?
Is there anybody you would like us to contact? Sometimes
he received intelligible answers, which he noted down on the
clipboard he carried. Sometimes he was greeted with incom-
prehension or helpless tears. Some of the women called out,
begging for news of family or friends. Others cringed away
as he approached, terrified of any hint of officialdom.

Almost at the end of the ward, he stopped by a bed in

which the occupant lay still and silent, with closed eyes. The skin was stretched so tight over the skeletal face that it was hard to believe she still lived, yet the chest rose and fell with rapid, shallow breaths.

The Red Cross official bent closer and said in German, 'Can you hear me? I'm from the Red Cross. Can you tell me your name?' There was no response, so he asked the same question again in French. Still the eyelids did not flicker.

The nurse who was escorting him said, 'I'm afraid you won't get an answer. She hasn't spoken since she was brought in.'

He straightened up. 'Do we have any idea who she is?'

'I'm afraid not, except some of the other patients think she is called Marguerite.'

'French, then.'

'Probably – or Belgian.'

'Perhaps we should put her on the list to be transferred to a French hospital.'

The nurse shrugged. 'She's too weak to go anywhere at the moment. Typhoid on top of extreme malnutrition is too much for most bodies to cope with. I wouldn't worry too much about where to send this one. To be honest, we don't expect her to make it.'

The Red Cross official sighed and shook his head, then moved on to the next bed.

Chapter Twenty-One

By the end of her honeymoon Frankie was wishing that she had opted for early demobilisation, rather than accepting the job in Baker Street. There was so much in her own life now that demanded her attention. They had rented a little cottage in Shoreham in which to start their married life. Nick said it was only a farm labourer's dwelling, but to Frankie it had all the magic of the gingerbread cottage in the fairy story, with its dormer windows and its tangled garden. She longed to spend time there, doing domestic chores such as making curtains, activities that she would have scorned not so long ago. But underneath her own happiness the unanswered question of what may have happened to Steve still nagged at her conscience, and that forced her back to the pile of files in her office.

Nick had his career to think of, and when Frankie went back to Baker Street he headed for Blackpool, for the Labour Party conference. He knew how Frankie felt but he urged her to press for early release.

'I need you with me. I want you out on the doorsteps canvassing. We're going to have a real struggle to get people to come out and vote. They really don't want this election. They say a National Government got us through the war and they don't see why we can't go on that way. It doesn't help that both the main parties are promising the same things – new houses to replace all those lost in the bombing, jobs for the men returning from the forces, a proper National Health Service, better education. Our job is to convince people that Labour will actually deliver those promises, whereas the Tories will just drift back into the old pre-war ways.'

'But I don't know anything about politics,' she protested. 'I wouldn't know what to say.'

'Yes you do,' he insisted. 'You've seen poverty and deprivation at first hand. You've known families that wouldn't call a doctor because they couldn't pay his bill and bright kids going into dead-end jobs because they had to leave school at fourteen. You've seen what unemployment does to people. The folks round here may have a different accent but they still have the same problems.'

Frankie promised to do her best but for the time being she had no option but to return to Baker Street.

Vera Atkins greeted her with a brisk 'Good honeymoon? Excellent. Now, how do you fancy a trip to Europe?'

'Europe? Why?'

'We're not getting anywhere here,' Vera said. 'The only way we're going to find out any more is by going out there and trying to trace our people on the ground. We'll start by going through the records of the prisoners in those God-forsaken concentration camps. We know from Odette Sansom and one or two other survivors that a lot of our people were sent to them after they had been interrogated. I've managed to wangle us seats on an RAF flight going to Frankfurt. We leave tomorrow.'

'There's just one thing, ma'am,' Frankie said hesitantly. 'You know my . . . husband' – the word still sounded foreign and unlikely to her – 'you know Nick is standing for Parliament. He wants me to be with him when the campaign starts.'

'I can understand that,' Vera said, 'and I know you only agreed to this posting as a temporary thing. I promise you, when Parliament is dissolved and the election is called I'll let you go. Will that do?'

Frankie smiled. 'Yes, that's fine. Thank you, ma'am.'

Frankie thought she had seen the worst bombs could do in Liverpool after the May blitz, and then later in London, but nothing had prepared her for the devastation she saw from the plane as they flew over Germany. For mile after mile scarcely a building was left standing. Towns and villages had been reduced to heaps of rubble as the Allies had fought their way through them.

'Why on earth didn't they surrender sooner and avoid all this?' Frankie asked.

Vera shrugged. 'I suppose that's what happens when a madman takes over the country.'

They based themselves in a relatively undamaged hotel on the outskirts of the town, which had been taken over by the Red Cross. On the journey from the airfield Frankie watched in horror as they passed through streets where women and children and old men picked hopelessly over the ruins of their homes searching for . . . what? Food, clothes, anything they could sell or barter to keep themselves alive. The Red Cross personnel were snowed under with the struggle to reunite families and find homes for survivors of the concentration camps, but Vera and Frankie were given an office and access to all the documentation available.

It took them less than a day to realise that the task was hopeless. The camp commandants had ordered most of the records to be destroyed when they knew that the Allies were closing in so there was only the testimony of the survivors to tell them who had been incarcerated in each one.

Vera pushed a pile of files to one side with a sigh. 'We're not getting anywhere like this. We'll have to start somewhere else.'

'Where?' Frankie enquired doubtfully.

'We need to look at the Gestapo records. They will have files on everyone they arrested and presumably those will include what happened to them afterwards. We'll go to Paris, to Gestapo HQ in the Avenue Foch.'

Frankie said hesitantly, 'César – Captain Ree – suggested it might be worth contacting someone called Sylvie de Montmain. She lives near a town called Arbois and apparently Steve stayed with her. Is there any chance I could go there?'

'Excellent idea!' Vera responded. 'I'll see if I can arrange transport for you.'

In the hospital outside Belsen the same Red Cross worker was once again making a round of the women's ward. Many of the beds were empty now. Some of the occupants had been moved out to hospitals nearer their home towns or to centres for displaced persons. Others had died. But the woman called Marguerite was still there.

'She's hanging on, then?' he remarked to the nurse.

'Yes. She's a fighter, no doubt about it. We think she might make it after all.'

'Has she said anything? Do you know who she is?'

'She doesn't speak when she's conscious but sometimes she mutters in her sleep.'

'Can you distinguish the language?'

'Most of it is unintelligible, but I assume it's French.'

The Red Cross man bent over the prostrate figure and said in French, 'I'm from the Red Cross. I'm here to help you. Can you tell me your name?'

There was a pause, then the pale lips parted and a voice like a breath of wind in dry grass whispered, '*Je suis Marguerite Duclos.*'

The contrast between the destruction in Germany and the pastoral peace of the Franche Comté made Frankie feel as if she were on a different continent, rather than only a few hundred miles away. She had managed to get a flight on an American plane as far as Chalon-sur-Saône and had then taken the train to Arbois. The countryside basked in midsummer heat, and from the train window she saw orchards where cherries and apricots hung in heavy clusters and hillsides seamed with ranks of vines. In the valleys cattle and horses grazed in pastures just beginning to turn brown in the drought.

She had telephoned from Chalon to let the comtesse know she was coming, but she was anticipating the interview with some trepidation. Her Italian was perfect but she had only a smattering of schoolgirl French and she was not sure how they were going to communicate.

At the station a slender, dark-haired young man was waiting to greet her.

'*Bonjour!* I am Michel de Montmain. I'm delighted to meet you.'

'Oh, you speak English!' Frankie said, shaking hands. 'I'm so glad. I'm afraid my French is not up to much.'

'My English is rusty, I'm afraid,' he responded, 'but I spent a summer in your country before the war. This way. Let me take your bag.'

He led her out into the station yard and she noticed that he limped slightly. In the yard she stopped short, gazing at the vehicle that awaited them.

'What happened to your car?'

He laughed. 'It's what we call a *gazogène*. It has been converted to burn a mixture of wood and coke. There is still no petrol to spare for ordinary motoring. Don't worry. It's perfectly safe.'

As they drove Frankie said, 'You don't seem to have suffered much damage here.'

'No, thank God. The American troops passed through this area more or less unopposed. There was more fighting farther north, where they had to force the crossing of the Doubs, but we were lucky.'

Frankie remembered that the French army had been disbanded after the country surrendered and she wondered what part he had played in the war.

'Were you here then?' she asked.

'Not just here. I was up there, where the fighting was.'

'But I thought . . .'

He glanced sideways at her. 'With the *maquis*.'

'You were with the Resistance?' Frankie's heart lurched and she was about to ask whether he had ever come across an agent named Suzette when the car swung in through a gateway and drew up outside a building that looked to her like a miniature version of a fairy-tale castle.

Sylvie de Montmain was waiting for them in the hall.

'Lieutenant Franconi, I'm so pleased to meet you at last. You are a friend of Marguerite's?'

'Marguerite?' Frankie was confused for a moment. 'Oh, you mean Steve?'

The comtesse lifted her shoulders with a smile. 'Of course, we never knew her real name. To me she was Marguerite, but to Michel she was Suzette. We are looking forward to hearing from you who she really is.'

Frankie turned to the young man. 'You knew her, too?'

Before he could answer the comtesse broke in, 'But we are

standing here in the hall and you must be tired and thirsty after your journey. Come and sit down.'

She led the way out on to a terrace, shaded from the sun by a magnificent wisteria. 'Now, I'm afraid I cannot offer you tea, or even real coffee. Such things are still not available. But we make some good cider locally. Will you have a glass of that?'

Frankie accepted. She was longing to pursue the questions she had come to ask but knew that good manners required a little patience.

When the drinks had been poured the comtesse said, 'So. What news can you give us of Marguerite or – what did you call her – Steve? But surely that is a man's name.'

Frankie felt something like a blow in the region of her heart. 'I'm sorry. I've come to ask whether you can tell me what happened to her.'

'You don't know? She has not been liberated?'

'No. We know she was somewhere in the Besançon area almost up to the point when the Americans arrived, but after that we have no idea what happened to her.'

Michel leaned forward. 'I can tell you a little. I mentioned in the car that I was with the *maquis*. When César was betrayed Suzette – what did you call her? Steve? – moved to Besançon and took over the circuit there. She was magnificent. She even taught the men how to lay explosive charges and derail trains. But then, last summer, when the Americans were only a few miles away, the Gestapo found out who she was. They started looking for her and for a girl called Juliette, who worked with her. She was the daughter of the couple who ran the restaurant where Suzette was living. They had to go into hiding and they came to live with my *maquis*.' He paused and sighed. 'If only she had stayed with me she would have been safe.'

'You can't be sure of that,' his mother pointed out. 'After all, some of your people were killed and you were wounded in that last battle, trying to prevent the Boches from blowing up the bridge behind them.'

'And succeeding!' he said, with a momentary flush of pride.

'So what happened to Steve – Suzette?' Frankie asked.

'When we saw the Boches retreating she went to tell the Americans. We didn't want them to shell Besançon unnecessarily. I needed all my men to protect the bridges so Suzette went with Juliette. We never saw her again. We know she got through to the Americans. She could have stayed with them but she knew Juliette was waiting for her. They were arrested on their way back.'

'How do you know that?'

'From Juliette herself. She escaped – but she should tell you the story herself. After lunch I will drive you to Besançon. I know the family will want to meet you.'

Frankie felt the last traces of optimism draining away. She knew she should be relieved that her quest was at last bearing fruit but it was leading her only towards the final proof of what she already dreaded.

Over lunch she remembered something that might provide another clue. 'Do you know what happened to the radio operator who was working with her? His name was Daniel Jardine.'

'Ah, Danny!' A brief, nostalgic smile touched Michel's face. 'He survived – and he fought with us in that last battle to save the bridge. He always maintained that he was a pacifist but when it came to the final showdown he found he could lob grenades with the best of us. I think it was when Suzette failed to return that he changed his mind. But when it was all over he decided that the atmosphere in post-war

France would not suit him. I believe he and his friend Armand are somewhere in North Africa now.'

As soon as the meal was over Michel drove her to Besançon. As they crossed the calmly flowing River Loue he said, 'Juliette told us that Suzette had to swim this to reach the Americans. All the bridges were guarded and there were shells falling all round. She was a brave one, your friend.' And as they crossed the Doubs he said proudly, 'And this is the bridge we prevented the Boches from blowing up as they retreated. The last fight – but a good one!'

The Brasserie Vauban was closed but Michel took her round to the back door where they found M. and Mme Choquin enjoying a post-prandial siesta in the kitchen. When he introduced Frankie and explained why she had come she was greeted with a warmth that almost over-whelmed her. Madame hurried to the foot of the stairs and called and a minute later a slender girl whose dark eyes seemed too big for her pale face came running into the kitchen.

'You are a friend of Marguerite?' she exclaimed, seizing Frankie's hand in both her own. 'Oh, please, tell me she is all right! I owe her my life.'

Sadly, Frankie explained that she knew less than they did. Over the next minutes, crowded with questions and answers, she learned of the Choquins' arrest and their subsequent liberation by the advancing Americans and their anguished search for their daughter. Juliette told her about her incarceration in the jail at Karlsruhe with Steve and then the train journey and their escape.

'She gave herself up when they came looking for us, so that they would not search the barn and find me. That is why I owe her my life.'

'How did you get home?' Frankie asked.

'The woman who owned the farm found me, after the soldiers had gone. I think she did not know when she called the police who it was that had stolen her food and when she saw Marguerite she felt ashamed. She took me in and hid me until I was stronger. Then she gave me food and some warm clothes and I walked. There were other people on the road. They were all heading west, towards the Americans, because they didn't want to fall into the hands of the Russian army. I joined up with some of them. They didn't seem to care that I wasn't German. I don't know how many days I walked but in the end I stumbled straight into an American tank crew. The officer in charge spoke a little French. He sent me back to a first aid post and from there I went to a field hospital and they sent me to a hospital in Strasbourg. And from there I managed to get a lift to Besançon.'

'We had given her up for dead,' her mother said tearfully. 'It is only thanks to the sacrifice of your friend that she survived.'

Frankie found Vera in Paris, staying in another building requisitioned by the Red Cross, and surrounded by files, which she had wheedled with some difficulty out of the French authorities.

'This is going to take months,' she said, after listening to Frankie's report. 'But so far I haven't found any reference to Steve in these files. It's a real needle-and-haystack job. You might as well get back to England and help your husband with his campaign. I'll arrange for you to go on indefinite leave until your demob comes through.'

There was a tap on the door and a young woman wearing a Red Cross armband came in.

'I know you're busy, but something has come through that

I thought might be of interest. One of the names on the list you gave me has just turned up on a roll of displaced persons in a hospital in Lille.'

Both Vera and Frankie sat up sharply. 'Which name?' Vera asked.

The girl consulted her note. 'Marguerite Duclos.'

The hospital in Lille was run by nuns, and as Frankie followed the white-robed figure down the long corridor she felt a comforting sense of familiarity. She no longer accepted most of the teachings of the Church, was not at all sure that she even believed in God, but she had been happy at her convent school and the presence of the nuns and the familiar holy pictures on the walls soothed the nervous anticipation that had been building inside her ever since the revelations of the previous day.

The sister led her to a bed at the far end of a ward and drew the curtains around it to give an illusion of privacy. 'I'll leave you alone, but I'll be close by if you need me.' She spoke in English with an Irish lilt to her voice

Frankie looked down at the figure in the bed. Her heart was thumping. The nurse had warned her that 'Marguerite' seemed unable to communicate or to understand where she was, but Frankie had convinced herself that the sight of a familiar face would put an end to that. Now, as she gazed down at the wasted form and the closed eyes, she had a moment of terrible doubt. She could not be certain that this was Steve after all. The hair, which had once been a rich auburn, was lifeless and the colour of old straw, and the face, which she remembered as shining with health and good nature, was now a taut mask, the skin stretched so tight over the bones that it seemed it might split open with the slightest movement.

Hesitantly Frankie laid a hand over the thin fingers that rested on the coverlet. 'Steve? It's me, Frankie.' There was no response. 'Steve?' she persisted. 'Darling, it's all right. Everything's going to be all right now. You're quite safe. I'm going to take you home, back to England.'

There was still no answer but she saw the eyelids flicker and noticed that the lashes were still long and chestnut in colour. She leaned closer and stroked her cheek.

'Open your eyes, Steve. It's me, Frankie. Please look at me.'

Still there was no answer. Frankie sought desperately for some form of words that might pierce through to some still-glowing ember of memory. She found herself recalling the code poem she had so painstakingly reconstructed from the decrypts. If Steve remembered anything it must surely be that. Leaning closer she murmured, 'This land I love is green and fair, with fields and hills and rivers running by. This land I leave will still be there, so I'm saying au revoir . . .'

'Saying au revoir and not goodbye.' The words were a faint whisper, but as she spoke them the long lashes lifted and Frankie found herself looking into blue-green eyes that banished all doubt.

'Steve! Darling, I'm so happy I've found you! We've been so worried about you.'

The ghost of a frown creased the other woman's brow. '*Je suis Marguerite Duclos*,' she whispered.

'No!' Frankie said. 'No, you were pretending to be Marguerite. But your real name is Diana. Diana Escott Stevens. You're Steve, and I'm Frankie. Gina Franconi. Remember?'

'Steve?' She echoed the name as if it stirred a faint memory. 'What happened to Steve?'

'You are Steve. Marguerite Duclos does not exist. That is
the identity you were given when you were sent to France,
but it was all a pretence. You don't have to pretend any
more. The war is over and the Germans have been defeated.
You're perfectly safe. No one is going to hurt you. You're in
a French hospital but soon I'm going to arrange for you to
be taken back to England. Your mother and father will be so
happy and relieved. You will be able to go back to the farm.
You remember the farm? You remember the Chiltern hills
– and the cows and the dogs and your lovely little horse?
Scheherazade. That was her name. You must remember
her. And Roddy. Roddy is still waiting for you. He misses
you so much. Now you can be with him at last.'

She babbled on and saw the first hints of expression in the
lifeless face, like the first flickers of flame among damp
sticks. Then suddenly Steve's head jerked up from the
pillow. 'Juliette! I have to find Juliette!'

She began to claw weakly at the bedclothes in an attempt
to rise.

'No! Steve, you mustn't try to get up. Relax, it's all right.
Juliette's safe. I've seen her. She got home. She's with her
mother and father.'

Steve's eyes had closed again and Frankie could not tell
whether she had heard. She gripped her hand. 'Come back
to us, Steve. We love you and we want you back. Your
mother and father are longing to see you and so is Roddy.
Please, come back to us.'

Quite suddenly, Steve's eyes opened again and this time
the blankness had been replaced by a glimmer that seemed
to well up from deep within her, like a diver rising to the
surface of a lake.

'Frankie?' she said, as if she had only just become aware
of her presence. 'Frankie? Is that really you?'

Frankie found tears running down her cheeks. 'Yes, darling! Yes, it's really me!'

'You must go! They'll catch you. It's not safe . . .'

'Yes, it is! It's perfectly safe. The war's over. There's nothing to be afraid of any more.'

Steve gazed at her, frowning. Her lips moved as if she were trying to formulate a thought. Then she said, 'I'd like to go home now. Have you come to take me home?'

Chapter Twenty-Two

Steve opened her eyes and looked up through the leaves of the apple tree at the unblemished blue of the sky. It was a hot summer afternoon and even here in the shade the air was still and heavy with the scent of lavender. The hum of bees in the bushes along the path stirred some vague memory that floated across her mind and then vanished again. There was a movement near by and her mother knelt beside her deckchair.

'I've brought you a glass of lemon barley water, darling. I thought you might be thirsty.'

Steve took the glass and sipped. The drink was cool and sweet. Anything with sugar in it pierced her taste buds like an arrow after so long without. Memories lurked here, too – sweat and the hollow ping of tennis balls on rackets, laughter and sun on bare limbs. She looked at her mother's face.

'I used to play tennis.'

'Yes, darling, you did. You played a very good game of tennis. And you will again, soon.'

A cow lowed in a nearby meadow. 'Milking time,' Steve murmured. 'Where's Daddy?'

'Gone to bring the cows in.'

She struggled to sit up. 'I'll go and help.'

'Not yet, darling. You're not strong enough yet. One day, soon.'

Her mother stroked her hair and she lay back and let

herself sink into the half-sleep in which she spent most of her time. Images from the last weeks assembled themselves in her mind like elements of a kaleidoscope – her own bedroom, familiar photographs on the walls; the taste of good food; the brilliance of the sunlight and the colour of flowers; her little chestnut mare, which had been brought into the garden so that she could caress the soft muzzle and feel the warm breath on her cheek. Her father had carried her downstairs in his arms and she had smelt the familiar smell of tweed and masculine sweat, but she had had to hold her breath and clench her muscles to prevent herself from struggling. It had been the same with the doctor who had examined her when she reached home. The touch of a male hand or the smell of a man's body produced a nauseating panic which she was hardly able to control. She knew her father sensed it and it distressed her, but there was nothing she could do to stop it.

That train of thought led her inevitably to the one topic that she wished to avoid above all others. Roddy. He had arrived a few hours after her parents had brought her back from the RAF aerodrome at Northolt and had come bounding into her bedroom. But she had hidden under the blankets and refused to see him. How could she face him, after what had happened to her? How could she bear to let him touch her? Yet she longed for the comfort of his arms and wept inwardly at the thought of how he must feel. That had happened . . . how long ago? A week? Two weeks? She seemed to have lost the ability to keep track of time. What was she going to do about Roddy? The thoughts were too painful and she took refuge again in sleep.

Someone was stroking her hair again. The touch was familiar but it was not her mother's. There was a faint masculine scent in her nostrils but it was not her father's.

She opened her eyes and saw the long-dreamed-of face looking down at her, the blue eyes creased at the corners from gazing into the sun, the unruly lock of hair that fell across one eyebrow. With a convulsive movement she put her hands across her own face.

'Don't! Don't look at me! Leave me alone!'

'Darling, please don't hide from me.' His voice was breathy, trembling on the verge of tears. 'I can't bear it. I love you so much. Why don't you want to see me?'

'You can't. I'm ugly. You can't love me now.'

He took hold of her wrists and gently pulled her hands away from her face. She did not have the strength to resist.

'You're not ugly. You're thin and pale and I can't even begin to imagine what you've been through, but none of that makes any difference to the way I feel. I've waited for you for so long and I thought I'd lost you. All I want now is to take care of you and see you well again.'

She gazed up at him. She wanted to feel his arms around her but she knew she must not give in.

'You can't . . . I mustn't . . .' she muttered.

'Darling' – he caressed her hair back from her face and looked into her eyes – 'we've been through all this. Don't you remember? That wonderful night when you came home on leave. You told me about Philippe – about what happened between you – and I told you it didn't matter. That's all past history now.'

She rocked her head from side to side. 'No. Not that, not that! It's worse than that. You won't want me now.'

His hand became still, resting on her shoulder. 'Did something happen, in the camp? Did someone . . . do something to you?'

She closed her eyes, unable to sustain his gaze. Her voice was a monotone, scarcely more than a whisper. 'We were starving. One or two of the girls in my hut were very close to death. There was an officer in the camp . . . He took me to work in his house. When he found out I could cook he let me do that. I used to steal things – nothing that they would miss. The outside leaves of vegetables, bones from the meat. I took them back to the hut, hidden inside my clothes, for the others. One day he caught me. He said I could go on doing it provided I . . . What could I do? The bits I stole were all that was keeping the girls alive. What could I say?'

He sat back on his heels and took both her hands in his. 'He asked you to sleep with him? And you did.'

'Not sleep . . . no, I never slept with him. Other things.'

'Did he hurt you?'

'Sometimes. He liked to feel he had power over me. He made me do things . . . I hated him.'

He put his arms around her but she struggled and he let her go. 'Hush! It's all right. You don't have to tell me any more. You don't have to think about it. I understand. I can see why you don't want to be touched. I can wait. I've had plenty of practice over these last five years. I'm not going to lose you now, my darling. I'll wait until you're ready to come to me.'

'You still want me? You don't mind?'

'Mind! Of course I mind. I mind because you were hurt. What happened to the bastard who did this to you?'

'He's dead. When he knew the Allies were almost at the gates of the camp he wanted to shoot himself. I was in the house. I went into the room to take him a cup of coffee and he was sitting at his desk with the pistol in front of him. But he didn't have the guts to go through with it.'

'So what happened?'

'I went over to him, to give him the coffee. Then I picked up the gun. He saw what I was going to do. I think he was grateful.'

'You shot him?'

'Yes, so I'm a murderer, as well as everything else.'

'No. No more than I am or anyone else who's fought in the bloody war. You gave him what he deserved, that's all. And if you hadn't, if I thought the bastard still lived, I wouldn't rest until I'd tracked him down and killed him. And then I probably would have been accused of murder, so you've saved me from that.'

She put out her hand and tremulously touched his. 'I shouldn't expect you to wait for me. I don't know how long it will be before I can . . .'

'It doesn't matter. All I want is to make you forget it all. I don't mind how long it takes. I'll wait until you feel ready. Just let me be with you, that's all I ask.'

Her hands seemed to move of their own accord, reaching out towards him. Then his arms were around her, his lips kissing her eyes and her cheeks and finally her lips. And for the first time since she was arrested she found herself crying.

The church of St Margaret, Westminster, was crowded for the first big society wedding of the new post-war era, between the Hon. Marjorie Granville and Squadron Leader James Lampeter, eldest son of the newly created Baron Aston. Roddy leaned into the taxi and held out his hand.

'Come on, darling.'

Steve eased herself out of the seat and straightened up, clinging to his arm.

'OK?' he asked, and she nodded, taking deep breaths.

The day was hot but she was wearing a loose coat over her dress and a wide-brimmed hat that almost hid her face. She was still embarrassed by her gaunt cheeks and unnaturally thin arms and legs. It was a relief to see that most of the guests had already arrived and there were just a few late-comers hurrying up the steps.

Roddy said, 'We'd better go in, or we'll be arriving after the bride.'

An usher met them at the door and would have conducted them to one of the front pews but Steve held back and Roddy said, 'We'll just sit here at the back, if that's all right.'

Steve clasped her hands for a moment of silent prayer, as she had been taught to do, but the only thought that came into her head was 'Oh, thank God it's all over!' She decided that, under the circumstances, that was quite appropriate. She sat back and looked down the aisle. In the second row back on the left she could see a head of glossy black hair under a little crimson hat. That must be Frankie. And the dark-haired man next to her must be her new husband. Next to him she could see a familiar pair of square shoulders below a severe dark bob. Surely that must be Dickie Nightingale, another old friend from Overthorpe days.

Roddy nudged her gently. 'Who is this chap Midge is marrying? I've never come across him.'

'Jumbo? That's what they call him. Oh, it's quite a story,' Steve whispered back. 'Frankie told me when we were waiting for a flight back from Lille. They met in North Africa. He's a pilot, like you, but his job was to drop agents into southern France. He and Midge started an affair but when he proposed she turned him down because he told her his father was an engineer in the Midlands. You know what a dreadful snob she is. And she was brought up by her ghastly parents to believe that she had either got to marry money or a title. Then Jumbo got shot down and she realised what a fool she'd been. Luckily, he managed to bale out and got back through one of the escape lines the Resistance had set up, and when he asked her again she accepted. The irony of it is, it turns out his father owns a huge car factory and is one of the wealthiest men in Britain, and he's done so much for the war effort that he's been made a peer.'

Roddy chuckled softly. 'So she's got the money *and* the title! Good for her! I always had a soft spot for old Midge.'

The organ struck up 'The Entry of the Queen of Sheba' and they all rose. *Trust Midge to choose that*, Steve thought. *It fits her down to the ground.*

Midge looked wonderful, of course. Steve wondered what pre-war wedding dress or ball gown had been sacrificed to provide the yards of white satin that swathed the slender figure. And the lace veil must surely be a family heirloom. But it was the radiant face underneath the veil which drew the eye.

Steve had been to many weddings and always found the poetry of the service moving, but today it was almost unbearable. She sat gripping Roddy's hand and wondering whether she had been right to come. Her first instinct when the invitation arrived had been to refuse, as she had resolutely refused to see anyone but Roddy since her return. He had persuaded her, telling her that Midge had telephoned, begging him to try, and that it would do her good to get out of the house and see her old friends. She had agreed to please him.

It was a relief when Mendlessohn's Wedding March struck up and the bridal procession walked down the aisle. As they drew level Midge caught Steve's eye and blew her a kiss and suddenly Steve knew she was right to have come. They let most of the guests pass them, and then followed the wedding party into the sunshine. Steve's instinct was to slip away quietly but before she could move Frankie had pounced on her.

'Steve, I'm so glad you made it. You look so much better. How do you feel?'

'I'm making progress – as the doctors say.'

'I feel awful about not coming to see you, but life's been so hectic, what with the election campaign and everything.'

Dickie was behind her. 'What I want to know,' she interrupted in her usual forthright manner, 'is why we've all been kept in the dark. I've been back from Italy for nearly three weeks and I had no idea you were at home. We would have come to visit you.'

'I know, I just didn't feel up to seeing anyone – and I didn't want anyone to see me. You think I look dreadful now? You should have seen me a month ago!'

Frankie kissed her. 'Oh, darling, what does that matter! You're alive, that's the only thing that matters.'

'If we'd known you were going to be here today we could have arranged an extra celebration,' Dickie put in.

'I'm afraid I'm not up to anything like that yet,' Steve responded. 'I wasn't going to come at all but Roddy kept trying to persuade me and then Midge rang up and begged me to come. Oh' – she looked round at him – 'I haven't introduced you. Everyone, this is Roddy Faversham. Roddy, you have met Gina Franconi, haven't you? Frankie's the girl who sat up all night to let me back into Overthorpe, the night the car broke down. Remember?'

'Of course I remember.' Roddy laughed. 'Yes, we have met, at your house just after you got home.' He held out his hand. 'I never got round to thanking you properly, Frankie. God knows how long it might have taken to get her back if it wasn't for you. Should I call you Frankie, or do you prefer Gina now you're a civilian?'

'Oh, Frankie, please,' she said. 'But of course it's not Franconi any more. It's Harper.' She looked round to where

Nick was waiting, leaning on his stick. 'This is my husband, Nick. Darling, this is Steve – Diana Escott Stevens.'

Nick limped forward and took Steve's hand. 'Frankie's talked about you often. I'm so glad you're still with us.'

Steve looked from him to Frankie. 'So this is the mythical Nick Harper.'

Nick laughed. 'Sorry to disappoint you. Just flesh and blood, like everyone else.'

There was a stir among the crowd around them and Midge floated towards them in a cloud of white satin. She put her arms around Steve and kissed her on the cheek.

'Steve, darling, I haven't had a chance to come and say hello. The wretched photographer is behaving like Hitler. How are you?'

'Improving, thank you. And congratulations. I wish you and James every happiness.'

'Oh, we shall be all right,' Midge said. 'No one could be unhappy for long with Jumbo. Now, are you sure you won't change your mind about coming to the reception?'

'No, really. I'm not strong enough yet. But you must come and see us when you get back from your honeymoon, and bring that nice-looking husband of yours with you.'

One of the ushers edged his way through the throng. 'Midge, the guests are getting restive and the photographer is having a tantrum. They need you back for another picture.'

Midge sighed theatrically. 'Sorry, darling. I'll have to go. But look, if you're sure you won't stay I want you to have these.' She put her bouquet into Steve's hands. 'You'll be next, won't she, Roddy?'

'If I have my way.' He smiled.

'But you'll need them for the photograph!' Steve protested. 'You'll upset the photographer even more.'

Midge drew herself up to her full, elegant height. 'Bugger the photographer!' she said, with exquisite precision, and glided away to where the rest of the wedding guests were waiting.

Frankie looked around her. 'Isn't it glamorous? All the men in their morning suits, and heaven knows where the women found those gorgeous dresses. They didn't get them with clothing coupons, that's for sure.'

'The smell of mothballs is almost overpowering,' Nick said with a chuckle.

'Don't spoil it,' Frankie told him. 'I used to read about weddings like this in Picture Post when I was a kid and drool over the photographs. I never thought I'd actually be going to one.'

'Bit different from ours,' he commented. 'I hope you weren't too disappointed.'

She squeezed his arm. 'Our wedding was perfect. I married the man of my dreams. What more could I ask for?'

Roddy turned to Nick. 'By the way, congratulations. It's a pretty remarkable achievement, getting yourself elected to Parliament at your first attempt.'

Nick shrugged modestly. 'Well, I had a head start on a lot of other chaps, being demobbed early. And then I picked up the sympathy vote. I was still in a wheelchair on the day. And, of course, I had the best door-to-door canvasser in the business.' He took Frankie's hand. 'Frankie's absolutely brilliant. She can talk to anyone.'

'There you are,' said Dickie triumphantly. 'I told you once you could go far, do anything. You'll be standing for Parliament yourself soon.'

Frankie laughed. 'One politician in the family is enough to be going on with. I've got other things in mind – for the moment.'

Steve saw her glance down at her stomach and had a flash of intuition. 'Frankie! You're pregnant, aren't you?'

Frankie blushed. 'Three months. I didn't think it showed.'

'It doesn't. I guessed, that's all. I'm so happy for you.' She looked from her to Dickie and then across to Midge. 'So here we all are – after everything that's happened. Think how far we've all come since those days at Overthorpe. Did you ever imagine . . . ?

'Not in a million years,' Frankie said. 'Just fancy. Little Frankie Franconi from Liverpool, an MP's wife.'

Nick put his arm around her waist. 'Never mind the wife bit. How about Frankie Franconi, MP?'

Frankie squeezed his fingers. 'Who knows? One day, maybe. Right now I've got everything I ever wanted.'

'What are your plans?' Nick asked, looking at Roddy.

'As soon as Steve's well enough we're going back to France. I'm sure I can wangle a lift with one of my old chums in the RAF. We're going to see all the people she worked with out there, so she can really be sure that they're OK.' He put his arm around Steve. 'That's what you want most of all, isn't it, sweetheart? And then, if Steve's ready, we're going to get married and have the house in the country, and horses and dogs and kids, of course – just like we always dreamed, aren't we, darling?'

Steve leaned against his shoulder. 'I don't care where we are as long as we're together. No more goodbyes – ever.'

If you enjoyed *Never Say Goodbye* you'll love
Hilary Green's new four book series of love, war and
adventure spanning the whole of the Second World War.

Hodder & Stoughton are proud to publish
the first of the Follies series.

NOW IS THE HOUR

Available in paperback in May 2007

read on for an exclusive extract . . .

HODDER

Rose Taylor looked around the stage. Almost the entire company of the Fairbourne Follies had assembled, drawn together by fear and the need for mutual support. The theatre had the chill, damp feel that always seemed to seep up from the sea below during the night, not to be banished until the audience came in for the evening performance. The sea was rough today and Rose could feel the waves thudding against the timbers that supported the pier. After the September sunshine outside the single working light above the stage hardly seemed to penetrate the gloom.

Monty Prince, the company's proprietor and comedian, was trying to keep up spirits with a succession of gags. The holiday audiences, out for an enjoyable evening after a day on the beach, loved him, but this morning the wisecracks sounded tired and empty. His wife was sitting a little apart, stiffly upright on a wooden chair. Dolores da Ponte was a daunting spectacle, clad from chin to ankle in black, her once slender figure struggling against the confines of her corset, her hair, which was a little too dark and glossy to be natural, drawn back into a tight bun, scarlet lips clamped round a long cigarette holder, from which a dusting of ash fell on to her ample bosom. To most of the company she was Madame, though everyone knew she had been born simple Dolly Bridges somewhere in the East End of London.

Rose looked round at the other girls of the chorus line. Sally Castle was perched on the edge of the props table, swinging her long legs and painting her nails. Her sister Lucy crouched on the floor with her arm round Pamela Jones, who was crying softly. Near by, Barbara Willis, known to them all as Babe because her fresh face and golden curls made her look like a schoolgirl, stared into space, tense and pale. Down in the orchestra pit Franklyn Bell, the company tenor, who had obviously been drinking in spite of the fact that it was not quite eleven o'clock, was boring the boys in the band with his perpetual complaint about modern crooners, who sang through their noses and could not be heard without a microphone. His partner, Isabel St Clair, was sitting in the stalls, ignoring him. Rose found herself wondering why they stayed together, when they obviously fought on a daily basis. It was easier to think about that, a distraction from what might be about to happen.

'Anybody seen Chantal?' Monty Prince asked.

'Not since last night,' someone said.

'She'll be on the ferry by now, I should think,' Sally said. 'She's got family in France, hasn't she?'

Rose's gaze travelled on from one face to another. These people were like a second family. All summer they had worked together, shared lodgings, weathered the ups and downs in the company's fortunes, lent each other money, put up with the temperaments and petty jealousies inherent in the performer's life. Many of them had been together for two or three summer seasons. Now it struck her that she might be seeing some of them for the last time. There was one face she could not find. Then the pass door to the stage opened and closed and three young men came through. In front was the tall, gangling figure of Guy Merryweather, always ironically known as Merry, their pianist and musical director, his normally lugubrious expression more sombre than ever. Next in was handsome, blond-headed Felix Lamont, alias Mr Mysterioso, the conjuror and magician. And behind him Rose saw at last a dark head of wavy hair that no amount of Brylcreem could tame, and warm brown eyes beneath strongly marked brows met and held her own.

Richard Stevens came across the stage to join her. 'Have you been here long? Nothing's happened, has it?'

'No, not yet. We're still waiting for the prime minister's broadcast.'

'I'm sorry I'm late. We've been packing.'

'Packing? Already? You're sure this is it, then?' Rose felt a cold chill work its way through her guts.

'Not much doubt, I'm afraid.'

'What will you do, if . . . if the worst happens?'

He took her hand and pressed her fingers tightly. 'I'll have to join up. But I must get home first and see my parents. Then I'll probably sign up with the South Lancs – that's my dad's old regiment. The trouble is, if the bombing starts straight away as people seem to predict, there's no knowing what will happen to the trains. Felix has offered to give me a lift up to town immediately after we've heard Mr Chamberlain. That way I can catch the earliest possible train.'

'So you're going straight away? No time for . . . for anything else?' She felt as if the lump in her throat would throttle her.

He looked down into her eyes. 'I'm afraid not. Felix wants to go at once. He's desperate to get to Uxbridge and join the RAF.' He hesitated, then went on. 'Rose, I must talk to you – privately, before I go. Come over here a minute.'

He drew her into the wings where they were out of sight of most of the company. 'You know what I'm going to say, don't you?'

'Please don't,' she said. 'We've been through it all before.'

'But things are different now. I know you asked me to wait, until we were both sure, but I can't go off to fight and leave everything up in the air like this. I know I've no right to ask you to commit yourself, when there's a chance I may not come back. But at least promise me you won't forget me.'

'I'll never forget you,' she said. 'But it would be better if you forgot me.'

'But why?' he demanded. 'Why, Rose?'

'You know why. It wouldn't work, you and me. We're too different. You know this isn't the life for you. This summer's just been a bit of fun for you, but you told me yourself what you really want is to sing in opera. And with your voice and your background you can do it. I know you can. You can't waste all those years training in Italy.'

'But I don't see what that's got to do with you and me,' he said, and Rose could hear the desperation in his voice. 'What difference does it make?'

'Because that's not my world,' she replied, and her own voice was beginning to quiver. 'We come from such different backgrounds. I could never feel at home with the sort of people you'll be mixing with. You didn't want your mum and dad to come and see the show, because you knew they wouldn't approve. What do you think your mother would say if you went and married a cockney chorus girl from Lambeth?'

'That's not the point,' Richard protested. 'I could fall in love with a duchess and she still wouldn't be good enough for my mother. I've told you before, my dad may own the factory but he's just an ordinary working man at heart. It's my mum who's always thought of herself as being from a different class. She's always on at me to "better myself". But it's nothing to do with her. I know I couldn't do better than you. It doesn't matter what she thinks.'

'Yes it does. Families matter. You didn't get on with my mum and sister when they came down here.'

'I tried! I just didn't know what to say to them.'

'And they didn't know what to say to you. That's my point. The gap's too big, Richard, and it would pull us apart sooner or later.'

He stared down at her in silence for a moment, and the pain

in his eyes made her want to cry out and take him in her arms. At length he said, 'There's no point in going round and round over this. The chances of me making a career of any sort are pretty slim, in the present circumstances. Can we just agree to keep in touch? And when this war is over, if I'm still alive, I'll ask you again – and perhaps then you'll believe that I'm serious. Can we do that?'

'Of course we can,' she answered, and the tears she had been fighting back welled up in her eyes. 'But you mustn't talk about dying. You've got so much talent . . . so much to give to the world. You have to stay alive!' *And you have to stay alive for me!* she wanted to add, but she forced the words down.

'Quiet, everyone!' It was Monty's voice. 'The PM's speaking.'

Rose and Richard moved back on to the stage. Monty had brought in a wireless set and plugged it in in the wings. In the silence that followed they all heard the flat, exhausted tones of Mr Chamberlain.

'I am speaking to you from the Cabinet Room at Ten Downing Street. This morning the British ambassador in Berlin handed the German government a final note stating that unless we heard from them by eleven o'clock that they were prepared at once to withdraw their troops from Poland, a state of war would exist between us. I have to tell you that no such undertaking has been received, and that consequently this country is at war with Germany.'

For a moment the silence remained unbroken. Then Pam let out a wail. The sound seemed to release everyone else from some kind of trance and all around Rose people began to hug each other with tears in their eyes. She saw Felix give Merry a brief pat on the arm.

'Cheerio, old chap. Best of luck!'

He turned away and she saw the stricken expression on Merry's face as he looked after him and thought automatically, *Poor Merry!* So desperately in love, and with so little hope.

As the noise subsided the prime minister's voice became audible again. 'Now may God bless you all and may he defend the right. For it is evil things that we shall be fighting against, brute force, bad faith, injustice, oppression and persecution. And against them I am certain that right will prevail.'

Richard gripped Rose's hand. 'I'm sorry, Rose. I'll have to go. But perhaps it's just as well. I don't know if I could stand a lingering goodbye.'

She nodded, swallowed. 'Yes, you're right. This is the best way.'

He touched her cheek with his free hand. 'I'll never forget these last months.'

'Nor will I,' she answered.

He sighed. 'I have a feeling that one day we shall look back on this summer of thirty-nine as a kind of paradise.'

'And Adolf Hitler as the snake in the Garden of Eden?' she said.

'Exactly.' He gave her a tight smile. 'What will you do?'

'Go home to Lambeth, I suppose. The show will have to close if all you chaps are going to join up.'

He frowned. 'I don't like to think of you in London. Can't you find somewhere to stay in the country? After all, your sister's boys have been evacuated, haven't they?'

'Yes, poor little mites. I suppose it's for the best. But I'll have to stay with Mum. She won't leave the shop, I'm sure.'

'Try to persuade her,' Richard said urgently. 'London's going to be a very dangerous place if the Huns start bombing.'

'Don't worry about me. You take care of yourself, please!'

From the wings Felix called, 'Richard, are you coming?'

'Yes! Hang on a moment.'

He leaned down and kissed Rose once on the lips. 'Goodbye, my darling. Look after yourself.'

'And you!'

She watched him cross the stage, which was rapidly emptying. As he reached the wings she called, 'Write to me!'

He came back. 'I almost forgot! I don't have your home address. Here, write it down for me.'

He handed her a used envelope from his pocket and a fountain pen and she hastily scribbled her address.

'Give me yours.'

'Richard! Are you coming or not?' Felix was shouting impatiently from below the stage.

'Coming!' He looked back at her. 'There's no point. I shan't be at home. I'll write from wherever they send me and let you know how to get in touch.'

'Promise!'

'I promise.' He kissed her once more, very briefly, and hurried across the stage. In the wings he paused and looked back and she lifted a hand in farewell. Then he was gone.

Chapter One

Rose turned up her collar and pulled her coat around her, hugging her hands under her armpits. The night air was bitter. She thought that she could not remember a winter as cold as this and wondered for a moment, illogically, if the blackout could have something to do with it. The street was almost deserted and she could hear her own footsteps clicking sharply in the frosty air. They reminded her how much her feet ached. After two performances in the chorus line of *Babes in the Wood* it was not surprising, but that did not make them hurt any less. But in spite of everything, she hummed a song from the show as she walked. She was eager to get home. She had news – good news.

She reached her mother's shoe shop and fumbled her key into the side door that led to the flat above. Upstairs, in the sitting room, there was light and warmth and the table was laid for supper. Her mother and her sister Bet were waiting for her. They always waited up for her to come home after the show, although she'd told them there was no need.

'Oh, thank goodness for a fire!' Rose exclaimed, pulling off her coat. 'It's *freezing* out. Talk about brass monkeys!'

'Now, Rose, language,' her mother reproved her. 'Sit down, you look all in. I'll put the kettle on. I've kept your meal hot for you. I managed to get a nice marrow bone from the butcher so I made some soup.'

'Lovely, Mum.' Rose sat down at the table. 'Just what I need.'

Bet wrinkled her nose in disgust. 'Before the war marrow bone was something we gave to the dog, not something we ate ourselves.'

'There's nothing wrong with good marrow-bone soup, my girl,' her mother said. 'You wait till they bring in meat rationing, like they're promising. You'll be glad to eat it then.'

'Honestly!' Bet wailed. 'What are they trying to do, starve us? Four miserable ounces of butter every week, four ounces of bacon. I can eat that in a day!'

'Yes, and look what it's done to your figure!' Rose could not resist the jibe.

'That's what motherhood does for you,' Bet returned. 'You wait till you've had a couple of kids.'

'Good audience tonight?' her mother asked.

'Packed out. People seem to have made up their minds that the war's not going to stop them enjoying themselves.' Rose took a mouthful of soup and decided that this was the moment to broach the subject uppermost in her mind. 'Actually, I've got some news.'

'What sort of news?' her mother asked.

'I've been offered a new contract.'

'Who by? The panto's closing in a couple of weeks, isn't it?'

'Monty Prince. He was at the show tonight and came round afterwards.'

'But I thought there weren't going to be any summer shows this year,' Bet said. 'Nobody will be going to the seaside for a holiday while the war's on.'

'It's not a summer show. It's something called Entertainments National Services Association.'

Bet giggled. 'Blimey, that's a mouthful.'

Rose laughed in return. 'I know. I told Monty, that'll never catch on! Apparently it's got government backing. I think the idea is to take people's minds off the war.'

'He's not asking you to join up, is he?' her mother said suspiciously.

'No, Mum. It's a civilian outfit, nothing to do with the military.'

'So where would you be performing? Here, in London?'

'Oh no, I don't think so. Monty said we'd probably be touring. But it's a job, that's the main thing. I was beginning to be afraid I wouldn't find anything once the panto closed.'

'Oh no, Rose.'

Rose looked up from her plate. Her mother was frowning. 'What?'

'I don't want you going off again. Not while there's a war on.'

'Oh, don't be daft, Mum,' Rose said, smiling. 'It's not as if I'm going into the army. What harm can come to me?'

'You don't know what might happen. Suppose Hitler starts bombing London like they said he would? We could be bombed out and have to move. Or suppose there's an invasion? If you were at the other end of the country, how would we ever find each other again? We need to stick together at a time like this.'

'But there hasn't been any bombing!' Rose replied, trying to keep the exasperation out of her voice. 'There hasn't been any fighting at all. Everyone's saying it's a phoney war. It might all blow over in a month or two.'

'Well, if it does people will be able to go to the seaside again and the summer shows will start up and you can get a job in one of them.'

'But suppose it doesn't? I have to work, Mum!'

'No, you don't. There's a job for you here, helping out in the shop. I can do with an extra hand, now Fanny Carter's decided to go and live with her sister in the country.'

'But that's not a proper job!' Rose could feel a tide of desperation rising in her throat. 'I have to dance, Mum! You know that.'

'That's all you care about, your blessed dancing!' her mother grumbled. Her face was creased with anxiety and Rose felt a stab of guilt. 'I can't go through it all again, Rose. Not a second time.'

'Go through what again?' Rose demanded.

'What I went through in the first war, waiting every day for a telegram telling me your father had been killed. He came through it, thank God, but he was never the same again, you know that. The gas did for him in the end.'

'But I'm not going anywhere near the fighting,' Rose said. 'You'd have no need to worry.'

'But I would worry. And what about the shop? I can't manage on my own.'

'You've got Bet here.'

Her sister looked up from her knitting. 'Don't look at me! If the boys come home I'll be moving back into my own place. I'm thinking of bringing them back. I don't believe they're happy where they are. You can't rely on me.'

I never could! Rose almost answered, but she swallowed the words. She had always suspected that Bet had married at the age of seventeen in order to get away from the monotony of the shop and that now she was jealous of the freedom her younger sister's career on the stage gave her. Rose looked from her to her mother. Bet's face was sullen and obstinate; her mother looked ready to cry at any moment. She felt trapped.

She pushed her plate away with a sigh. 'Look, nothing's been decided. The show doesn't close for two weeks and anyway Monty's got to sort out the rest of the company and find a place to rehearse. He probably won't be ready to go ahead until next month at the earliest. Let's wait and see what happens, shall we?'

Her mother's face cleared. 'That's a good girl. I knew you'd see it my way. Things will all work out for the best, you'll see.'

Rose dropped her eyes to hide the anger in them. She knew

her mother's fears were genuine, but she felt, too, that she was being blackmailed.

'Oh, by the way . . .' Bet rose and took an envelope from the mantelpiece. 'There's a letter from your fancy man.'

'He's not my fancy man!' Rose protested, the anger she had been struggling to suppress rising to the surface.

'Fancies himself, if you ask me,' Bet replied.

'No he doesn't! Just because he's educated and well spoken you think he's putting on airs.'

'Oh, now, Rose,' her mother put in, 'you've got to admit he's a bit out of your class.'

'What's that got to do with anything?'

'What do you want with someone stuck up, like him?' Bet demanded. 'You should stick to your own kind.'

'Stuck up! You just can't bear anyone who isn't exactly like us. What's wrong with us all? Why are we afraid of people who are cleverer or better off? It's not him that's stuck up! It's us that's stuck down!'

As soon as the words were out of her mouth Rose heard how ridiculous they sounded.

Bet giggled. 'You make us sound like envelopes.'

Rose spluttered into her teacup, torn between laughter and tears of annoyance. 'Oh, you! I can't have a serious conversation with you.'

'Aren't you going to read your letter, then?' her mother asked.

Rose fingered the envelope. 'I'll read it later. You two get off to bed. You've got to be up early for the shop. I'll wash the dishes.'

When they had said goodnight and gone she slit the envelope. This was the fourth letter she had had from Richard since he had rushed off to join up. The first had informed her that he had joined the South Lancashire Fusiliers, and was undergoing basic training; the second that he was going on embarkation leave prior to leaving for some undisclosed destination; and the third that he was 'somewhere in France' but could not tell her more than that.

This letter was no more informative. He was still in the same place, conditions were bad . . . eighty men sleeping on the floor of a disused factory . . . *The MO came round and said there wasn't enough ventilation for that many men so they knocked two blooming great holes in the wall. That let the air in all right – and the wind, and the snow!* Food was monotonous and only relieved by occasional visits to an *estaminet* in the local village where the proprietress did a nice line in egg and chips. Nothing was happening and everyone was bored and fed up. The only bright spot had been a pantomime, which he and his company had staged for Christmas. *The adjutant found us a piano and there were a couple of chaps who could play a bit but they had no idea about arranging music for the assortment of other instruments we put together. How I longed for dear old Merry! (By the way, I had a letter from him last week. His regiment is still in England but, reading between the lines, I think he's pretty fed up with army life.) Anyway, we decided to have a go at* Aladdin, *with me as Abanazer and a young lad with quite a nice light tenor voice and the most amazing legs as the Principal Boy. We had a lot of fun rehearsing and I must say the performance seemed to go down really well. The CO invited some of the local bigwigs but I'm afraid they were totally bemused by the whole thing! The concept of a man dressed up in tights pretending to be a girl pretending to be a man was something beyond their comprehension.*

Rose chuckled to herself over that bit, but the letter left her with a feeling of emptiness. He addressed her as *my darling Rose* and wrote of how much he missed her and longed to be with her, so he hadn't forgotten after a few months apart, as she had been sure he would. She had convinced herself that, for him, this was just a summer romance. It seemed she had been wrong. She missed him far more than she had ever imagined and was beginning to regret what had been simple common sense at the time. But was he writing to the real Rose, or was it some imaginary ideal he had in his head? Distance makes the heart grow fonder, ran the old adage, but was that a basis for a real relationship?

In bed she tried to envisage his face, but she could not see it clearly. It was his smile that she remembered best, the wide, uninhibited grin of pure pleasure in being alive or the tender, dreamy smile when he looked into her eyes and told her he loved her. She remembered the tea dances at the Palace Hotel in Fairbourne, when their two bodies moved together in perfect harmony, and heard in her imagination the sound of his voice when he sang – powerful as a great river, warm as velvet . . .

She woke the next morning to a sense of loss, which she was unable to place at once. Was she grieving for Richard, or for the opportunity of a new job, which had been snatched away from her almost as soon as it was offered? *It's not fair!* she found herself thinking. *It's not fair!* Was she being selfish? She knew her mother had made sacrifices to pay for her dancing lessons. Perhaps she owed it to her to stay at home now the situation was so uncertain. The thought of being cooped up all through the summer in the little flat and the shop below made her almost frantic with frustration. It wasn't staying in London that she minded, or being with her family. Despite their differences they had always been close. It was not being able to dance that would drive her mad. Nothing gave her so much pleasure as dancing. Ever since she could remember it had been as natural to her as breathing. She sometimes felt that the urge to dance had been woven into her muscles while she was still in the womb; that her nerves were so attuned to the sound of music that at the first notes her limbs automatically began to move to its rhythm. Ballet, tap or modern, waltz, tango, samba or can-can – it made no difference. She loved them all. There was nothing to stop her ignoring her mother's objections and taking the job, of course. But she remembered her anguished expression and knew she would never forgive herself if anything happened to her or Bet while she was away. She could hope for a job that would allow her to stay in town, but she had combed the pages of *Variety* for weeks without seeing any hint of auditions for a new show. Monty was her only chance, and it looked as if she was going to have to turn him down.

Coming downstairs to breakfast, she found Bet weeping over a crumpled sheet of notepaper.

'Bet, what is it?' she exclaimed, going quickly to put her arm round the plump shoulders.

'Oh, it's just me being silly,' Bet answered. 'It's a letter from Billy, that's all.'

'Is there something wrong with him?' Rose asked.

'No, no. He says everything's fine. But I hate them being away from me, Rose. I wish I'd never let them be evacuated. There isn't any danger, after all. It's more than four months since I've seen them and even Billy's letters don't sound like him any more.'

'Let's see,' Rose requested, and Bet handed her the letter. It was written on good-quality notepaper and, from the absence of blots and spelling mistakes, Rose had the impression that it had been copied out, perhaps more than once.

> *Dear Mother,*
> *This is just to let you know that Sam and I are well and happy and to thank you for the presents. We had a good Christmas with plenty of good things to eat, but we missed you and Gran and Aunty Rose, of course. I am back at school now. There are a lot of children in my class, so we only go in the morning or the afternoon because there isn't*

*room for all of us at once. But when I cannot go to school I
do lessons here with Mrs Marshall. Sam sends his love. We
hope you are all well. Give my love to Gran and Aunty
Rose.*

Your loving son,
Billy

Rose laid the letter on the table. 'You're right. It doesn't sound
like Billy. He wouldn't call you "Mother", would he?'

'Not when he was living here,' Bet said, rubbing her eyes
with the back of her hand. 'He's being taught different ways,
Rose. When he comes home he'll be a stranger.'

'Or he's being told what to write,' Rose said grimly.

Bet stared at her. 'You mean that Mrs Marshall who's
looking after them won't let them write what they want?'

'Well,' Rose said, 'I reckon that letter's been corrected and
rewritten, don't you? Our Billy was never that hot on
spelling.'

'Oh!' Bet exclaimed. She was silent for a moment, taking in
the implications of the situation. 'Then we wouldn't know if
there was anything wrong, would we? Not if she was telling
them what to write.' Her eyes filled with tears again. 'Oh, Rose,
what are we going to do?'

Rose looked at her sister and the irritation of the previous
evening evaporated. Poor old Bet, she hadn't had much of a
life. Two kids by the time she was twenty, in a little two-up,
two-down house just round the corner from her mother's flat.
She had never known anything beyond the small corner of
south London where she had grown up. 'We'll go down there
and see them, that's what,' she said. 'And if they're not happy,
we'll bring them home.'

'How are we going to get there?' Bet wailed. 'It's right out in
the country, miles from anywhere. Oh, I wish I'd learned to
drive! Reg wanted to teach me, but I was too scared.'

'Me too,' Rose said. 'You know what, Bet? We've depended too much on men, and now they're not around we're blooming helpless. We've got to learn to stand on our own feet.'

'That's all very well to say,' Bet said miserably, 'but it doesn't answer the question.'

'There must be trains, buses, something!' Rose exclaimed. 'Where are they?'

'Little village called Hawkhurst, down in Kent.'

'Well, at least it's not the other end of the country,' Rose said comfortingly. 'We'll go round to Waterloo station and see what we can find out.'

At that moment their mother came running up the stairs from the shop.

'Hey, girls, guess what!'

'What?' they asked simultaneously.

'The river's frozen! Mrs Jackson from up the road just came in to tell me.'

'The Thames?' Rose said incredulously.

'Yes! Mrs J says it's the first time since goodness knows when.'

'Well,' Rose said, 'I told you it was cold last night. I didn't realise it was that cold!'

'What's the matter with you, Bet?' Mrs Taylor demanded, noticing her elder daughter's face for the first time. 'You look like you'd lost half a crown and found sixpence.'

Rose explained. Mrs Taylor nodded emphatically.

'Right! The sooner you get down there and sort it out the better.'

It turned out that there was a train that would take them as far as Etchingham, a neighbouring village, but as far as they were able to discover the bus service from there to Hawkhurst was infrequent at the best of times and did not run at all on Sundays, the only day when Rose was free. It seemed Bet would have to go on her own.

'I shan't know what to say!' she protested. 'This Mrs Marshall sounds like a right old dragon. I've never been much good at speaking up for myself, not like you, Rose.'

'Hang on!' Rose said. 'I've had an idea. I know who might help us out.'

'Who?'

'Monty Prince. He's got a car.'

'Oh, but we couldn't ask him, could we? I mean, he doesn't even know me.'

'He remembers you from when you came down to see the show. He asked after you and Mum last night. And he's a really good-hearted man. He gave me his card. I'll go down to the phone box now and ring him.'

She had not misjudged him. Monty agreed to come over the following Sunday and drive them down to Kent.

Promptly at eleven, the car drew up outside the shop and Rose and Bet climbed in.

'This is really very good of you, Mr Prince,' Rose said. 'You remember my sister Bet?'

''Course I do.' Monty twisted in his seat to shake hands with Bet in the back. 'And call me Monty, please. I'm not the boss now.'

'How's Madame?' Rose asked.

Monty shrugged. 'Busy, busy. We're looking after some refugees, relatives from Poland.'

'I didn't know you had Polish relations!' Rose said.

'Oh, distant, you know, distant. But we Jews have a strong sense of family ties. And some of the stories coming out of the country since the German invasion are very disturbing.' He turned to Bet. 'Your old man off in the forces?'

Bet nodded. 'He was called up early on. They want mechanics, people who can maintain trucks and such.'

''Course, they would,' Monty said, nodding as he started

the engine. 'Two million called up this month! It's starting to feel like the last shambles.'

They drove for a while in silence and then Monty said, 'You heard anything of the rest of the girls, Rose?'

'Sally and Lucy are in panto in Croydon,' Rose told him. 'Babe is at home, helping her mum and dad. They've got a market garden somewhere down in Dorset, you know. And Pam's working in a munitions factory. I get letters from them all when they can find time to write.'

'Pam in a munitions factory!' Monty said. 'It's hard to imagine, somehow.'

'Well,' Rose said with a grin, 'she reckons she's earning better money than she'd ever have made in the theatre. And it said in the paper the other day that women doing war work are demanding equal pay with the men.'

'Equal pay!' Monty chortled. 'Whatever next! Don't suppose you've any idea what happened to Chantal?'

'None at all,' Rose said, trying to keep her voice neutral. The less she thought about the company soubrette, who claimed to be the love child of a Scottish aristocrat and a French ladies' maid, the better for her own peace of mind. There had never been anything definite but she had been aware of the nudges and winks, immediately suppressed when she appeared. She told herself that she had only herself to blame. She had told Richard he must wait until they were more certain of their feelings, so she could hardly blame him for seeking consolation elsewhere. Sally Castle had tried to warn her, but then Sally's morals were no better then Chantal's and she had no intention of descending to their level.

The weather was still bitterly cold and as they left the city the roadside hedgerows were stiff with ice. The sky was overcast so there was no glitter or sparkle to the frost. The land was steel grey, as if the fields themselves had been camouflaged for war. Occasionally they had to pull over to allow a long convoy of tanks and trucks to pass, but apart from that there was very little traffic. Petrol for private motoring was in short supply and most people hoarded it for essential journeys.

Monty insisted on buying them both lunch at a pub, so it was early afternoon when they reached their destination. The house where the two boys had been placed turned out to be a mile or so outside the village in a narrow country lane. It was a tall, rather forbidding red-brick building, half hidden behind a thick laurel hedge. Bet was suddenly seized with panic.

'We ought to have written,' she murmured. 'Let them know we were coming.'

'Well, we're here now,' Rose said firmly, 'and we're not going home till we've seen the boys.'

She marched up the garden path and rang the doorbell. Bet followed hesitantly, with Monty tagging along at a discreet distance. There was a pause long enough for Bet to whisper, 'Perhaps they're out.'

Then they heard the sound of movement inside and the door was opened by a gaunt middle-aged woman, whose grey hair was drawn back so tightly into a bun that it appeared to pull the corners of her eyes out of shape.

'Yes?' she enquired.

'Mrs Marshall?' Rose knew it was no good expecting Bet to take the initiative.

'Yes.' The same flat, unwelcoming tone.

'I'm Rose Taylor. And this is my sister Bet . . . Mrs Barker. We've come to see Billy and Sam.'

For a second the woman's face remained blank, then her lips stretched in a smile that seemed to have no relationship with the rest of her face.

'Billy and Sam's mother! You'd better come in.' She stepped aside and they moved past her into a dim hallway. 'This way.' She opened a door and showed them into the front room, where an aged white-haired man wrapped in a tartan shawl was crouched over the single bar of an electric fire. Rose could understand why, for the room struck her as being scarcely warmer than the street outside.

'This is my father,' the woman said. 'I'm afraid he's rather deaf. This is Billy and Sam's mother and aunt, Father,' she said, raising her voice. 'They've come to visit.'

The old man glanced up and mumbled vaguely, but then relapsed into his former position staring at the fire and took no further notice of their presence.

'And is this the boys' grandfather?' Mrs Marshall enquired, with the brightness of a cracking icicle.

Monty looked slightly embarrassed and Rose said quickly, 'No. This is Mr Prince, a family friend. He drove us down.'

'Are the boys here?' Bet asked timidly.

A strange expression passed over the woman's face and her eyes darted from one side of the room to the other. 'No, I'm afraid they're not. They're out. What a pity you didn't let us know you were coming.'

'Out where?' Bet asked.

'They've gone out to tea. They were invited . . . Sunday afternoon, you see . . .'

Rose said, 'Perhaps you could give us the address and we could call in. We wouldn't want to miss seeing them.'

Once again the eyes flickered round the room. 'Well, it's a bit difficult. I'm not exactly sure of the address. They were collected, you see . . . by car. It's not people I know very well.'

'You've let them go off with people you don't know, to you don't know where?' Rose said.

'Oh, but they're quite safe. The people who invited them are very reliable. It's all arranged through the church, you know. A nice afternoon out for the poor little chaps.'

'What time will they be back?' Bet asked.

'I couldn't tell for sure . . . quite late, I should imagine.'

'We'll wait,' Rose said grimly.

Mrs Marshall's expression was becoming increasingly hunted. 'I don't know that that would be a good idea. I mean, there's no knowing how long they'll be. They might stay the night.'

Rose's heart was beating fast and there was a chill sense of foreboding in her stomach. She took a step closer to Mrs Marshall. 'You don't actually know where they are, do you?'

The woman stepped back and her nostrils flared. For an instant Rose was reminded of a frightened horse. Then the look of panic was replaced by defiance.

'No, I don't. And you know why? Because they've run away, the ungrateful little brats! After all we've done for them. They arrive here, a couple of dirty little guttersnipes, and I do my best to turn them into decent, well-behaved children with some sense of discipline, and this is what happens.'

For a moment Rose thought Bet was going to faint. The colour had drained out of her face and she took a couple of wavering steps forward. Then a red flush rose from her neck up to her hairline.

'They're not dirty! And they're not guttersnipes! How dare you call them that! What have you done to them, you old witch?'

'Old witch! Old witch!' Mrs Marshall was spluttering with fury.

Rose stepped between the two of them. She was not given to displays of temperament. Years of living and working with volatile 'artistes' had taught her to avoid confrontations. Now, however, her pacific nature had given way to a cold rage. 'How long have they been gone?'

Something in her tone seemed to quell the other woman's bluster. 'Since this morning. I took them to church, like I always do, and they went into the Sunday school. Then, when the service was over, there was no sign of them. I asked the girl who teaches the Sunday school and she said she hadn't seen hide nor hair of them. I thought they'd slipped off home but when I got back I found they'd taken their things and disappeared. And what's more,' the tone of righteous indignation returned, 'they've stolen food from the larder. Bread, and a whole week's ration of cheese!'

At this point Monty, who had been standing in the doorway, stepped forward. 'Have you informed the police?'

'No. There's no need to go bothering them. They'll turn up, soon enough. Once it starts to get dark they'll be back, looking for a warm bed to sleep in.'

Rose ground her teeth. 'Well, they won't be sleeping here, that's for sure! They wouldn't run away for no reason. As soon as we find them we're taking them home.'

'Taking them home!' Mrs Marshall exclaimed. 'At a moment's notice? You can't do that!'

'Oh yes we can,' Rose retorted.

Mrs Marshall drew herself up and sniffed. 'Well, I must say, I've never known such bad manners! Never a by-your-leave or a please or thank you. But I suppose I should have expected no better.'

'You can expect a great deal worse when the authorities find out how you've let them go wandering off without any attempt to find them,' Rose replied grimly.

'Come along, ladies,' Monty interposed. 'There's no point in standing here arguing the toss. Where's the nearest police station?'

'Up on the hill, the other side of the village,' Mrs Marshall said sullenly. 'But you won't get much help there. I happen to know Constable Hitchins is fed up to the back teeth with dealing with these refugee children. They've been nothing but trouble from the word go.'

Monty turned to leave, taking Bet by the arm.

'Just a minute,' Rose said. 'We need their ration books. Get them, please.'

'Ration books?' Mrs Marshall sounded as if she had trouble remembering what the words meant. 'Oh, well, I'm not sure I can put my hand on them right now.'

'Oh yes you can,' Rose said. 'I don't mind betting you and your father have been eating their rations and letting them go short. That's probably why you took them in, in the first place. Now, are you going to find them or do I have to tell the police you've stolen them?'

The threat produced the desired effect. Mrs Marshall disappeared into the kitchen and returned with the two little books of coupons. Rose snatched them from her and followed Monty and her sister out to the waiting car.

Since her outburst, Bet had relapsed into shocked silence, and as soon as they reached the car she burst into tears.

Rose put her arms round her. 'Don't cry, love! We'll find them. They'll be on their way home. They're probably back at your house by now.'

'But I'm not there!' Bet wept. 'They won't know where to go.'

' 'Course they will. They know where their gran lives, don't they? They'll be all right.'

Monty produced a hip flask of brandy from the glove box and after a sip or two Bet became calmer, but Rose could feel her shivering as they drove through the winter dusk.

Mrs Marshall had been right about the attitude of the local constable. He wrote down the boys' descriptions and grudgingly agreed to circulate them to other forces in the area, but he obviously took the same view as she had, that they would turn up as soon as cold and hunger drove them back. And if they didn't, his attitude seemed to say, so what? It was two fewer problems for him to deal with.

By the time they left the police station darkness had fallen. 'I can't bear to think of them out there in the cold,' Bet wailed.

'I've told you,' Rose repeated, 'they're probably home by

now. We'd best get back and see.' It was the only course of action she could think of.

They were halfway up Wrotham Hill when the dimmed headlights picked out two diminutive figures trudging along the side of the road.

'That's them!' Bet cried. 'It is! It's them!'

Monty brought the car to a standstill a few yards beyond the boys and Bet scrambled out.

'Billy! Sam! Oh, thank God you're safe!'

Rose, following her, was horrified to see the two boys draw back, as if frightened. Bet stood still, her arms outstretched. 'What's wrong? Don't you know me? You haven't forgotten your mum, have you?'

Billy edged away, gripping his little brother by the hand. 'Have you come to take us back?'

'Yes, darling, of course I have. Come along.' Bet moved towards them but they backed farther towards the verge, and Rose saw Billy looking around him as if seeking a way of escape.

'We're not going back there!' he said fiercely. 'We hate that woman. She hits us. She made Sam sleep in the dog's kennel.'

'She what?' Bet seemed to choke on the words.

Rose stepped in quickly. 'Your mum means take you home, Billy. We're not going to take you back to Mrs Marshall.'

Bet's voice was shaking, but it was not with fear now. 'Did you say that woman hit you?'

'Look!' Billy extended his hand. Monty had joined them, carrying a torch, and by its light they all saw the three red weals that crossed the little boy's palm.

'The cow! The cruel bitch! I'll have the law on her!' Bet stammered. 'What was that about sleeping in the dog kennel?'

'When Sam wet the bed she put him in the kennel and put the dog in his bed.'

'Oh my God!' Bet stretched out her arms again. 'I'm so

sorry! My darlings, I'm so sorry. If I'd known what she was like I'd never have let you go.'

Billy was still gazing at her, his small face pinched and pale in the torchlight. 'She said you didn't want us. She said you'd sent us away because we were too much trouble.'

'Oh, the wicked, wicked woman!' Bet sobbed. 'It's not true, Billy. I sent you because I thought you'd be safe from the bombs.'

'There aren't any bombs,' he said woodenly.

'No, but there might have been. Truly, Billy, I only wanted to do the best for you. Your dad said you'd be better off in the country.'

For a moment they all stared at each other in silence, then Sam broke the tension by throwing himself against his mother's legs. 'I want to go home,' he sobbed. 'I want to go home.'

'That's where we're going, all of us,' Rose said. 'Come on, Billy. Gran will be wondering where we've all got to.'

She held out her hand and after a moment the boy took it. Bet reached out an arm to him and a second later he, too, was sobbing against her breast.

In the car, Monty produced a bag of humbugs and soon the boys' cheeks were bulging. He offered the flask of brandy again and Bet took a large swallow, spluttered and began to giggle hysterically. Rose did not care for spirits, but she took a sip and was grateful for the sense of warmth. She realised for the first time that, like the others, she was shivering with cold.

'Here, Bet.' Monty pulled a rug from the boot. 'You and the kids snuggle up under this.'

Bet settled in the back seat with a boy on either side of her and Monty tucked the rug round the three of them. Rose got into the front seat beside him and pulled her coat closer round her. As they drove towards London she could hear Bet and the boys murmuring together, then the sounds ceased and, looking round, she saw that the children were fast asleep and Bet, too, had her eyes closed.

In the comfortable silence her thoughts turned towards the future, and immediately she felt a pang of guilt. She ought to be thankful that the boys were safe and that Bet had her children back – and she was – but the thought that came immediately into her mind was that now they would all move back to their own home. There was no room for all of them in the flat. That meant that her mother would be left alone, unless she stayed. Now she really was trapped.

As if he had read her mind Monty said, 'This ENSA group's coming together nicely. I've got Frank and Isabel signed up and I think Sally Castle's coming on board. It'll be nice to get the old Follies company together again – those of them that aren't in the forces, anyway.'

Rose took a deep breath. 'I'm sorry, Mr Prince. I don't like letting you down but I'm afraid I'll have to back out. I can't leave my mum to cope alone – not while there's a war on.'

HILARY GREEN

NOW IS THE HOUR

WAR TORE THEM APART, LOVE
HELD THE TOGETHER

In an empty theatre at the end of the pier the cast of the Fairbourne Follies gathers round the radio to hear Neville Chamberlain declare war on Germany. Four firm friends are forced to part. Rose, the beautiful dancer, must return to her family in London and the blitz, leaving singer Richard to enlist in the army with their relationship still unresolved. Gay, asthmatic Merry, the musical director, is destined for the army too, while the object of his unrequited love, charismatic magician, Felix, chooses the RAF.

Before long, Rose joins a group entertaining the troops in France. The Nazi war machine however is fast and merciless on the land and in the air and soon all of them find themselves in terrible danger. And as they are struck by the brutality of war they realise exactly who is most important to them and despite the odds, and in terrible circumstances, they determine to find each other again.

With the threat of capture, injury and death ever present, there is no certainty that they will make it through and the four of them will have to find reserves of courage, love and endurance that they did not know they possessed.

HODDER

HILARY GREEN

WE'LL MEET AGAIN

LOVE, DUTY AND DANGER

Liverpool 1942. Seventeen-year-old Frankie Franconi falls i
love with charismatic British officer Nick Harper as quickly
and certainly as the bomb that falls on their shelter.

He is impressed by her good looks and intelligence, and the
fact that, like him, she speaks fluent Italian. When she insists
on staying to help rescue others who have been trapped he
realises that she has courage, too. He gives her a business card
with a Baker Street address, and suggests she puts her skills to
good use.

Within a month Frankie has joined the FANYs and started
her training. Stationed first in England, then Africa and finally
Italy, Frankie and her fellow recruits work tirelessly decoding
messages from agents in the field by day, and enjoying the
wartime parties at night. But when she signs the Official
Secrets Act she has no idea of the danger, adventure and
terrible choices that are in store.

HODDER